THE BEST
AMERICAN CATHOLIC
SHORT STORIES

THE BEST AMERICAN CATHOLIC SHORT STORIES

A Sheed & Ward Collection

EDITED BY DANIEL MCVEIGH AND PATRICIA SCHNAPP

A SHEED & WARD BOOK

ROWMAN & LITTLEFIELD PUBLISHERS, INC.
Lanham • Boulder • New York • Toronto • Plymouth, UK

The acknowledgments section of this book constitutes an official extension of the copyright page.

A SHEED & WARD BOOK

ROWMAN & LITTLEFIELD PUBLISHERS, INC.

Published in the United States of America
by Rowman & Littlefield Publishers, Inc.
A wholly owned subsidiary of The Rowman & Littlefield Publishing Group, Inc.
4501 Forbes Boulevard, Suite 200, Lanham, Maryland 20706
www.rowmanlittlefield.com

Estover Road
Plymouth PL6 7PY
United Kingdom

British Library Cataloguing in Publication Information Available

Library of Congress Cataloging-in-Publication Data

The best American Catholic short stories : a Sheed & Ward collection / edited by Daniel McVeigh and Patricia Schnapp.
  p. cm.
"A Sheed & Ward book."
Includes bibliographical references and index.
ISBN-13: 978-1-58051-210-7 (pbk. : alk. paper)
ISBN-10: 1-58051-210-0 (pbk. : alk. paper)
1. American fiction—Catholic authors. 2. Short stories, American. 3. Catholics—Fiction. I. McVeigh, Daniel, 1948– II. Schnapp, Patricia, 1936–
PS647.C4B47 2007
813'.0108921282—dc22   2006024056

Printed in the United States of America

♾ ™ The paper used in this publication meets the minimum requirements of American National Standard for Information Sciences—Permanence of Paper for Printed Library Materials, ANSI/NISO Z39.48-1992.

TO OUR PARENTS:

James Edward and Sarah Reynolds McVeigh

Cletus Michael and Lorine Snyder Schnapp

THINGS SEEN AND UNSEEN

Blessed are the eyes that see what you see.

LUKE 10: 23

I've had visions.
Walking to school
I've been arrested by a vacant lot
heavily sprinkled with chicory.
Attempting to define
its precise shade
I've fallen into skies and deep lakes,
elbows of morning glories,
punctures in plums;
traveled to indigo rhythms
bluer than the blues;
dipped into inkwells;
swallowed boysenberries till their dye
leaked through my skin;
put feathers of a jay
in my hair
and might have knelt in adoration
and built a church there
if I'd had the time.

PATRICIA SCHNAPP, R.S.M.

I believe in God, the Father Almighty,
Who made heaven and earth,
and all that is seen and unseen. . . .

CONTENTS

ACKNOWLEDGMENTS

Much work went into the preparation of our typescript; thanks in particular go to Cindy Anderson and her Humanities work studies.

The costs of permission to reprint the stories in a collection such as this are considerable. The editors wish to thank in a heartfelt way donors Nancy Erhardt, Margaret Keller, Cynthia Theisen, Ann Tompert, James Keller, and Paul Keller. Siena Heights University President Rick Artman worked hard to secure alumni donations.

A special thank you goes to Jennifer Hamlin Church, without whose generous and energetic support on behalf of her late husband and lover of literature Tracy Church, this book would never have been published.

Finally, Br. Frank Rotsaert, C.S.C., worked on this project in its initial stages, until he suffered a debilitating stroke in October 2002. Br. Frank's enthusiasm about publishing this first anthology of American Catholic short fiction was indispensable in making the present volume a reality.

We gratefully acknowledge permission to reprint the following chapters.

1947, 1948, 1950, 1954 by Caroline Gordon; renewal copyright © 1959, 1961, 1973 by Caroline Gordon Tate; copyright © 1961, 1963, 1977, 1981 by Caroline Gordon. By permission of Ivan R. Dee, Publisher.

"The Peach Stone" from *The Peach Stone* by Paul Horgan. Copyright © 1967 by Paul Horgan. Copyright renewed 1995 by Thomas B. Catron, III. Reprinted by permission of Farrar, Straus and Giroux, LLC.

"Lions, Harts, Leaping Does" reprinted by permission of Powers Family Literary Trust, Katherine A. Powers, Trustee.

"The Devil in the Desert" from *The Peach Stone* by Paul Horgan. Copyright © 1967 by Paul Horgan. Copyright renewed 1995 by Thomas B. Catron, III. Reprinted by permission of Farrar, Straus and Giroux, LLC.

"Emmanuele! Emmanuele!" from *The Collected Stories of Caroline Gordon*, copyright © 1931, 1933, 1934, 1935 by Charles Scribner's Sons; copyright © 1944, 1945, 1947, 1948, 1950, 1954 by Caroline Gordon; renewal copyright © 1959, 1961, 1973 by Caroline Gordon Tate; copyright © 1961, 1963, 1977, 1981 by Caroline Gordon. By permission of Ivan R. Dee, Publisher.

"The Displaced Person" from *A Good Man Is Hard to Find and Other Stories*, copyright 1954 by Flannery O'Connor and renewed 1982 by Regina O'Connor. Reprinted by permission of Harcourt, Inc.

"Dawn" reprinted by permission of Powers Family Literary Trust, Katherine A. Powers, Trustee.

"Silent Retreats" from *Silent Retreats* by Philip F. Deaver, The University of Georgia Press, 1988. By permission of The University of Georgia Press.

"Keepsakes" from *Keepsakes and Other Stories*, copyright 1999, reprinted by permission of Afton Historical Society Press.

"Resident Priest" from *Keepsakes and Other Stories*, copyright 1999, reprinted by permission of Afton Historical Society Press.

"Geneseo" from *Silent Retreats* by Philip F. Deaver, The University of Georgia Press, 1988. By permission of The University of Georgia Press.

"Playland" from *Nebraska* by Ron Hansen, copyright © 1989 Ron Hansen. Used by permission of Grove/Atlantic, Inc.

"The Devil and Irv Cherniske" from *T. C. Boyle Stories: The Collected Stories of T. Coraghessan Boyle* by T. Coraghessan Boyle, copyright © 1998 by T. Coraghessan Boyle. Used by permission of Viking Penguin, a division of Penguin Group (USA) Inc.

"The Rich Brother" from *Back in the World: Stories* by Tobias Wolff, copyright © 1985 by Tobias Wolff. Reprinted by permission of International Creative Management, Inc.

"Mrs. Cassidy's Last Year" from *Temporary Shelter* by Mary Gordon, copyright © 1987 by Mary Gordon. Used by permission of Random House, Inc.

"The Whore's Child" copyright © 2002 by Richard Russo, from *The Whore's Child* by Richard Russo. Used by permission of Alfred A. Knopf, a division of Random House, Inc.

"Died and Gone to Vegas" from *Same Place, Same Things* by Tim Gautreaux, copyright © 1996 by the author. Reprinted by permission of St. Martin's Press, LLC.

"Good For the Soul" from *Welding with Children* by Tim Gautreaux, copyright © 1999 by the author. Reprinted by permission of St. Martin's Press, LLC.

"A Father's Story" from *The Times Are Never So Bad* by Andre Dubus, copyright © 1983 by Andre Dubus. Reprinted by permission of David R. Godine, Publisher, Inc.

INTRODUCTION

For Father Louis knew in a simple flatness of fact—fact as hard as
rock, as mysterious as water, as unrelenting as light—that without
God the richest life in the world was more arid than the desert; and
with Him the poorest life was after all complete in a harmony that
composed all things.

PAUL HORGAN, "The Devil in the Desert" (1950)

Toward the end of Flannery O'Connor's "The Displaced Person," a peacock curves his neck and "tiers of pregnant suns" rise on his magnificent tail. Open-mouthed, eccentric Fr. Flynn exclaims gaily, "Christ will
come like that!"

The farm's owner, Mrs. McIntyre, "practical" rather than "theological,"
wonders if she has ever seen such an old fool. A few pea chickens left by the
Judge, her dead reprobate husband, still clutter the premises. Dying one by
one—once there were twenty—they will not be replaced. As Blake's devils
know, the fool sees not the same tree that the wise man sees.

This anthology brings together some of the best short fiction written
by Roman Catholic writers in the United States during the last seventy-five
years. Prior to the Great Depression and World War II, many Americans
felt about Catholic immigrants the way O'Connor's Mr. Shortley does: "I
ain't going to have the Pope of Rome tell me how to run no dairy!" The word
"nasty," after all, comes from the name of the celebrated nineteenth-century
cartoonist who portrayed the Irish as lantern-jawed apes and bishops as alli-
gators about to seize American children. About the Irish in Liverpool fleeing the famine, most to the United States, Nathaniel Hawthorne commented
that they reminded him of "maggots in cheese."

On the other hand, Hawthorne's own daughter Rose became a nun. For such as her, the Church's tradition, universality, and community offer not an enemy but a healthy corrective to American youth, revolution, and individualism. Though Harold Bloom's 1996 *The American Religion* pays tribute to the vigor of American Catholicism by ignoring it completely, Catholics currently constitute more than a quarter of the nation's population, and the percentage is growing. To be sure, this huge group is not culturally or politically homogeneous, and a Richard Neuhaus sees the Church as moving in a different direction than a Garry Wills does.

The fiction is arranged in rough but not exact chronological order. We hope that readers will explore the entire anthology, which has been selected and ordered with an eye on not only inherent quality but also variety and color in religious themes: the hunger for transcendence; the trap of narcissism; the conflict of moral roles; contradictions involved in the impulse toward individualism; and the spiritual inadequacy of much of what passes for the "American dream." The writers, though all Roman Catholic in commitment to one degree or another, are men and women, converts and cradle Catholics, urban and rural, deceased and living. In many ways, the stories may be read as sometimes reinforcing but also as challenging each other. This anthology offers not ideology but *vision*, experienced as literature provides it, in paradox as much as idea, through question as much as answer.

So what *is* "Catholic fiction"? Ross Labrie lists a number of its characteristics in *The Catholic Imagination in American Literature* (1997): in a sacramental universe, the world retains some of its "inherent goodness"; *hope* as much as any virtue informs a Roman Catholic life; hierarchical and institutional allegiances often yield to an individualistic American impulse; still, even a secular world needs "vertical" reminders of transcendence through art, as well as Mass and the Church's own sacraments.

This volume's reader may descry all these markers. "Catholic fiction" may contain direct allusions to rituals, devotions, or religious symbols; it may highlight the rhythms of the liturgical seasons or the importance of the communion of saints. A number of our stories, including ones by J. F. Powers, Paul Horgan, and Jon Hassler, focus on Church matters. But in fiction, at least, the term "Catholic" may be viewed more usefully as a perspective than as subject matter. In this sense, Catholic stories can be about anything touched by literature itself, but they spring from a mind familiar with the creed, with the paradox of the Trinity, with belief in the Eucharistic presence, and, perhaps especially, with the crucial tenets of the "forgiveness of sins" and "life everlasting." For believing Catholics, death should be like that of Horgan's Father Louis Bellefontaine: the freest act of one's life, the moment of handing oneself over to Mystery.

In all of these stories there breathes, though sometimes in labored fashion, a rhythm of fall and redemption. What Labrie and such theologians as David Tracy mean by the "sacramental" imagination is the instinct that all reality leads us toward the Holy. Because God took flesh, materiality cannot be evil. The Catholic imagination perceives all that is sensual as inherently good, and the Eucharist concretizes this belief. So ancient ritual and devotions rich with incense, candles, music, stained glass, and statues have created that "enchanted world" Andrew Greeley describes as "haunted by a sense that the objects, events, and persons of daily life are revelations of grace." In the contemporary American Church, we find less incense and stained glass. But there continues the conviction that all events in life are meaningful and all lives worth living, that the most humdrum object can be for us a burning bush, our latest moral dilemma an angel to wrestle.

Unquestionably, the key event in Catholic life since the Depression was the Vatican II Council of forty years ago. The Council's deepest meaning is still debated, though only a tiny minority have ever rejected its essential reforms. Along with Flannery O'Connor's finest story (infrequently anthologized, because of its length), the collection includes three other major pre-Vatican II writers—Caroline Gordon, Paul Horgan, and J. F. Powers—less read today than they deserve to be.

These earlier writers assume some tension between being a "Catholic" and being an "American." Religious vision can be, as in O'Connor's familiar stories, countercultural, even shocking. Our earliest selection is the 1933 "Old Red," written fourteen years before **Caroline Gordon**'s conversion. Born in Kentucky in 1895, Gordon proved the younger O'Connor's most important mentor. A convert to Catholicism in 1947 and later a protester against some Vatican II changes, she died in 1981.

Robert Penn Warren considers "Old Red" her best story. Professor Aleck Maury, the central character in six Gordon stories (and the 1934 novel *Aleck Maury, Sportsman*) is a thoroughly Southern pantheist. In the family home "Merry Point," others cling to Time as if it were a child's security blanket:

> But time [to Maury] was a banner that whipped before him always in the wind! He stood on tiptoe to catch at the bright folds, to strain them to his bosom. They were bright and glittering. But they whipped by so fast and were whipping ever faster. The tears came into his eyes. Where, for instance, had this year gone? He could swear he had not wasted a minute of it, for no man living, he thought, knew better how to make each day a pleasure to him. Not a minute wasted and yet here it was already May.

Appealingly, even enviably, immersed in Nature's flow, Maury is haunted by the elusiveness of something meaningful and stable. "Old Red," the fox, is the never-caught American dream, like William Faulkner's bear or Herman Melville's whale. At one instant in the story, Maury's wife Mary is Old Red, glimpsed momentarily but always escaping afterward. At others, Old Red is Maury himself, escaping daily to the woods or river away from the rest of the race, which pursues him. His life in Nature comes with a price: isolation.

Modeled on Gordon's own father, Aleck Maury is a vigorous if fragile sixty-one. In "The Presence" (1948), published a year after Gordon's conversion, he is seventy-five. Now age has left him unable to indulge his passion for the hound and the hunt, fishing and paddling. No more can Maury "*know where he is*"—this apparently simple boarding house is not a pond where you can catch evening bream if you cast, like Ernest Hemingway's Nick Adams, there rather than here. The most intelligent of the characters, Maury is also the least aware of what goes on beneath the surface of human interaction.

In fact, though Warren calls him heroic, Maury's vision is finally vanity: immersion in the moment will never let him "know how his story turns out" (Pleyol's criticism of his friend Fäy's poetry in "Emmanuele! Emmanuele!"). For all Maury's charm and vitality, he has never understood women, and the boarding house's fallen world—even after such a long life!—startles him. In a touching exchange, Maury gently puts off fellow boarder Riva's small boy's plea for a bedtime story. But facing death, a lonely one by the story's tragic end, Maury himself badly needs a *story*, a "presence" of which Old Red was but the enticing specter. Is the Mary that Maury prays to afterward the mother of Jesus, but also his own wife, who over the years could never convert him?

In William Butler Yeats's poem, " 'The work is done,' grown old he thought, / 'According to my boyish plan.' " But " '*What then?' sang Plato's ghost. 'What then?*' " "The Presence" dramatizes the final inadequacy of pantheism and American optimism, the terrain of Walt Whitman and Hemingway, "Self Reliance" and *Cold Mountain*.

As "one, holy, catholic, and apostolic," then, the Church is an ancient foe of Gnosticism and its cult of the individual. Our proudly independent United States has always distrusted this claim to universality. Indeed, though since the Kennedy presidency Catholics have only occasionally needed to defend their patriotism, Catholic vision may on some uncomfortable level challenge America's Protestant sense of itself as a unique and sacred nation, in which the values of freedom and personal fulfillment offer an ultimate horizon by which all other aspects of life must be judged.

On the other hand, as much as Puritans Catholics *do* believe in the Fall, and this instinct that we live in not just an imperfect but an inescapably sinful world is equally at odds with the Transcendentalist streak so powerful throughout American literature. We see this theme in **Paul Horgan**, who before his death in 1995 at age ninety-two had published more than fifty books of fiction and history. In his 1942 "The Peach Stone" (which John Updike included among the century's best one hundred American short stories), the horrible burning on their small New Mexico ranch of their little girl has jolted Jodey Powers out of his thoroughly American assumption that he is just as good as any man, and forces his wife Cleotha to see life from a sharply altered perspective. On the grim drive back to her hometown of Weed to bury their child, the sight of old man Melendez (one might think here of William Wordsworth's enduring Leech Gatherer), which used to disgust and alarm Cleotha, suddenly fills her with joy. The peach stone, explicitly a parable, represents the theological virtues of faith, hope, and love—the virtues revealed to a Beatrice, not a Virgil. Were Jodey alone in his grief, "he could have solaced himself with heroic stupidities." But the fact that he, Cleotha, and their son Buddy confront death together makes their suffering sacramental and transformative. Horgan shares Dante's Trinitarian vision.

In contrast, Buddy's teacher Arleen Latcher—a victim of that nagging vanity that Gordon's husband Allen Tate, for some years a Catholic convert himself, called "the angelic imagination"—deeply envies those connections. A self-chooser, trapped in her mind, she cannot *feel* with this grieving family. What Arleen "had known as a child had been displaced by what she had heard in classrooms." A deracinated intellectual, she is one more of this anthology's many displaced persons.

Another prominent pre-Vatican II writer, **J. F. Powers**, tends to emphasize less the Church's windows on eternity than its immersion in the world. Powers' institutional Church seems all too human. He was born in Jacksonville, Illinois, in 1917 and died in 1999. In "Lions, Harts, Leaping Does" (1942), a priest, dying, faces his life's failures. Horgan's and O'Connor's clergy may understand better than lay characters the passing illusions of the World. But in many darkly comic Powers stories, clergy are caught up in its temptations.

Fr. Didymus' name is that of Doubting Thomas, the disciple who without proof could not quite bring himself to believe the Resurrection. Despite Didymus' desire, he cannot be among those who are blessed because they believe though they have not seen. His faith, unlike that of his fellow priests Seraphin or Titus, has "never been quite sure." Even after he becomes wheelchair bound, Didymus' imagination remains angelic, with vanity at constant war with a nagging Pharisaical scrupulosity. Didymus understands quite well that the canary that the kindly Titus gives him, "one of the Saint's own good birds," mirrors Didymus' own trapped soul. When he opens its cage, the canary escapes. But nevertheless, it will die in the snow.

In this dry land, Didymus' confused moral sense could not motivate him even to visit his own dying brother Seraphin, who was highly honored in their order. If resurrection lies ahead, this protagonist has no more prophetic vision of it than any other character does. At the moment of his stroke, "The floor, with fingers smelling of dust and genesis, reached up and held him. . . . For a radiant instant, which had something of eternity about it, he saw the justice of his position. Then there was nothing." The droll ambiguity of the term "justice" is pure Powers! Ever lukewarm, Didymus will soon get all doubt can aspire to: "a normal, uninspired death."

The Southwest landscape of most of Horgan's stories becomes programmatically Biblical in his "The Devil in the Desert" (1950). Against Powers' satiric realism, we may set Horgan's idealism. For all his faults, the old French priest Louis Bellefontaine is a "beautiful fountain" in this harsh land. This story traces Louis's "hard journey," his way of the cross. Dying, the priest's words echo those of Jesus and Mary, and his rosary and sunglasses become relics that can strengthen the more conventional Church represented by Pierre on his way back to France.

Modern readers may find Fr. Louis's epiphany in his last hours striking. When O'Connor's Mrs. Shortley dies grasping convulsively at shoulders, arms, and knees, like the human "parts" piled in concentration camp films, do her true country's tremendous frontiers look like those of Fr. Louis's?

> Presently Father Louis believed that he awoke.
>
> His mind was working sharply and with what seemed to him exquisite new ease and clarity. He saw all his thoughts as in crystal depths of cold fresh water. He knew he was in the mesquite thicket, and what had happened to him, and he possessed this knowledge with an elated purity such as he had always known in the state of grace, after receiving or administering the sacraments. . . . It was the real meaning of communion with all that lay beyond himself. In such a state truth needed no seeking, and no definition. It was here, within, and it was there, without.
>
> It was everywhere. When all was known there could be no astonishment.

At such vivid moments Horgan shares with O'Connor a frank, almost medieval vision, more "Catholic" than "American," that our familiar material world is not our true homeland. The "displaced person" (D.P.) is not foreign to us: he is us. Christ became a D.P., to call us home.

Readers should see links, thematic and symbolic, between "The Devil in the Desert" and the next two remarkable stories, written a few years after it. Caroline Gordon's "Emmanuele! Emmanuele!" was published in the same year, 1954, and journal, *The Sewanee Review*, as her young protegée's "The Displaced Person." It is our only story set outside the United States, on the North African coast and then in Normandy, France. Since age twelve, Guillaume Fäy has written poetry while gazing in a mirror. The snake not in a desert but in a disturbingly sensual African Eden, he is a potential "poisoner" of the young American idealist Heyward, in front of whom he dangles fruit (the second time, "a slightly misshapen apple"). A good Gnostic, Fäy suspects that he may create Nature himself! "Emmanuele," his nickname for his wife, means "God with us." But we do not find God in a mirror. No wonder Fäy wishes at times that he had never met his old rival Raoul Pleyol, who knows that "An artist's first duty is the same as any other man's—to serve, praise and worship God."

But then, Pleyol is an integral man, of one piece, while the equally gifted Fäy is a house divided against itself. Even as a boy, he had left the other children playing Indians to return to his mirror. Mrs. Rensslaer broke off her year-long engagement to him once she realized that Fäy would always be "married" to his own reflection. Heyward does not perceive that Fäy's secret letters are really addressed to Fäy himself. As Pleyol understands, "Do you think that a man sees himself when he looks into a mirror? He sees only the pose he has assumed. If you want to see yourself look into the eyes of your friends—or your enemies—who are made in the image of God."

At the bottom of Fäy's romantic abyss lies—nothing. Whether Louis Bellefontaine's or the catechism's, the devil is "a created being who chose to be nothing rather than something." Once again in this story, vision or its absence tells us all we need to know. Separated by an ocean, the young Heyward can still *see* his young wife more than Fäy and Emmanuele see each other across a table. But by the story's end it is uncertain what he will continue to see. Will the young American fall poisoned, following the Romantic ideology of art to its modern conclusion: the dissolution of personhood?

Bloom considers his own Gnosticism *the* American Religion. In this, Gordon's last short story, the worship of oneself amounts to a seductive nihilism, and Guillaume Fäy's is one of those rich but narcissistic lives that without God ends up desert-dry.

At the heart of **Flannery O'Connor**'s great stories lies the acute consciousness that all of life involves coping, usually ineptly, with the Fall. O'Connor spent most of her brief life in Milledgeville, Georgia; born in 1925, she died of lupus in 1964, many years after having been diagnosed with it. In "The Displaced Person," Mrs. McIntyre's farm in virtually every detail—Mrs. Shortley's lecture on race next to a manure spreader, Astor's spatial disorientation at his employer's rants about overpopulation, the cherub missing over the grinning skeleton of the Judge at the farm's center—is a comic arena of displacement. In terms of biography, of course, it must be hard to feel at home in a body racked by lupus.

But a vision of life that includes fundamental submission to mystery can also be richly and comically humane. In the 1950s daily missal used by both O'Connor and her mentor Gordon, the first Station of the Cross reads:

> Pilate dares to condemn the all-holy Savior to death. No, not Pilate; but my sins have condemned Jesus to be crucified. O Jesus, have mercy on me and remember Thou didst choose to die that I may have eternal life.

Suffering is universal. But so is sinfulness, and O'Connor's understanding of this truth allows a warm mercy toward even her villains. In "The Displaced Person," the worst of them are in truth very like us: our laughter betrays it. Chancey Shortley's name suggests his small vision, and by the end of the story only God can forgive his actions. But even we sinners may find it hard to condemn root and branch a man who makes love to his wife by pretending to swallow cigarette butts! And what reader's own heart has never descended into a dry well?

Displaced Persons, Mrs. Shortley explains, "Ain't where they were born at and there's nowhere for them to go." Perhaps Raoul Pleyol has explained the paradox on these paradigmatic fifty acres: to see our real selves, we have to look at others. But Mrs. McIntyre and the Shortleys cannot see what is right in front of them: the peacock tail full of Christ's promise, the Other's humanity. Guizac and Father Flynn are flawed, of course. O'Connor never entrusts the essence of human dignity to mere men. But unlike most of her characters they *can* see what is in front of them. Knowing he is a D.P., the Pole can shake a Negro's hand as though he were black himself, or even marry a blonde cousin to one. He can see the Other as a full man, and not just parts of one.

False religion, then, looks into the distance; true religion looks at one's neighbor. In the vision of a Shortley or McIntyre, the Thou is a grasshopper, a locust. In her prophesying, Mrs. Shortley blindly predicts her own death. But who knows? Perhaps if only in desire, she's touched Christ's garment. Mrs. McIntyre's will prove the longer purgatory.

Our last pre-Vatican II story, J. F. Power's "Dawn" (1956), lightly depicts a diocese's clerical anxieties, lay frustrations, and bureaucratic maneuvering. The Bishop's chancellor, Father Udovic, must cope with rumors that he holds this eminent position because he can touch type! "Dawn" both illustrates Powers' sardonic voice and reminds us of the need for Pope John XXIII's *aggiornamento* shortly afterward.

The Vatican II Council (1962–1965) urged laity to assume their responsibility for transforming the world. Many nuns left schools to work in social services and other ministries. English replaced Latin in the liturgy, and contemporary music Gregorian chant; vocations to the priesthood and Mass attendance diminished throughout the 1970s, while lay involvement in decision making and questioning of traditional authority grew.

In all this turmoil came much to fret about—and to celebrate. Our post-Council stories depict both losses and gains. Because of social changes, none of the later stories, however devout the writer, can exhibit the same confidence as Horgan, Caroline Gordon, and O'Connor in the reader's acceptance of the "objective" truth of Roman Catholicism. When priests appear, they no longer have such a center stage to act on.

Philip F. Deaver, winner of a literary award named after O'Connor, writes of Midwestern baby boomers suffering postmodern blues. In "Silent Retreats" (1988), a well-meaning modern priest cannot satisfy the main character's desire for an inward peace, one in which, as in Father Louis' desert epiphany, "truth needed no seeking, and no definition." In contrast, the voice of virtually everyone in this half-sophisticated suburban world is laden with a caustic irony. Martin Wolf's language is so drenched in cynicism that he can speak only fumblingly to his own young son Jeff. His culture apparently offers Martin no avenue to become a child again. To escape at least temporarily this jaundiced fall from idealism, the Church cannot now offer even a dignified silence. A prosperous and educated American Catholicism is now of the World, and Deaver's stories suggest the pains involved in its loss of transcendence.

The narrator of Andre Dubus's "A Father's Story" will comment sadly that more *ritual* might have saved his marriage where a lot of repetitious talking could not. By the end of Deaver's story Martin is still married. But his exasperated, worldly wife ("What's wrong with self-indulgence, or did he [the priest] say?") is ready to make other plans.

Jon Hassler has similarly described the descent of contemporary American culture into what one of his novels' characters, Agatha McGee, calls "the new Dark Ages." "Keepsakes," written in the 1970s, gently depicts seventy-four-year-old Fr. Fogarty, misunderstood in his parish and trying to hold on to that which has given his life meaning for decades, coping with this new world. The Bishop has even told him to give up his Douay translation for the New American Bible. There is more of sadness than of sentimentality about his retirement. Fogarty gives up his decades-old "keepsakes" simply because in this youthful world no one would have an interest in them. He leaves one boy, Roger, understanding more about him and perhaps the Church itself. But unlike Fr. Louis Bellefontaine, Fr. Fogarty cannot bequeath relics.

In the companion "Resident Priest," Fogarty's last vocation as chaplain to an isolated convent of nuns, charmingly drawn, proves short.

So one concern reflected in our later stories is the lessening, potentially to the point of disappearance, of Roman Catholic separateness from the rest of America: its medieval resonances, distinctive habits, parochial school mystique. Modern illusion often tries to fill in for the loss of sacrament and family. Deaver's collection *Silent Retreats* is filled with disappointed male protagonists in the 1970s and 1980s searching for replacements for their youthful faith—sexual affairs, political activism, pursuit of money. Many stories by Tobias Wolff, Andre Dubus, and T. C. Boyle echo these themes.

For all the changes from the 1940s to our new millenium, Catholic belief in both sin *and* redemption has, of course, survived Vatican II reforms. It continues to resist Utopian desire, either for Transcendentalist commune or Puritan "City on a Hill." Deaver's "Geneseo" (1988) depicts a New Age drive for both family attachment and radical personal freedom. But these values invariably conflict. Though it is sympathetically drawn, the "anarchist community" Geneseo is failing, with its customs and rhetoric having become increasingly nostalgic. The young mother Janet, alcoholic and poignantly countercultural, must head back with her daughter to a broken larger world. One might call Geneseo a religious community, even to the renaming of postulants, but without the Christianity. A spiritual mirage, this commune offers no preservative against the "raggedy ways people relate" lamented by Janet's friend Clay City (her name reeks of mortality). Will Janet's affair with the narrator Jerome last? Rootless and jaundiced, like many Deaver characters, even before their visit Jerome plans someday to paint Janet once before saying good-bye.

Ron Hansen's "Playland" (1989), the only story in this collection that might be called surrealistic, casts another contemporary writer's critical eye on our modern need for ultimately shallow religion substitutes. Playland is a 1940s park in Nebraska, a combination of Disneyland, beach, and Hollywood stereotype. Its characters step out of World War II–era films— the farm boy, soldier on leave, bored femme fatale, jaundiced man about town. This is a kind of "heaven" as Midwestern materialism imagines it, opposed to the harsh world of farming, winter, and drought. But Playland's separation from natural laws (or perhaps our knowledge of Original Sin?) leaves the park vulnerable to being exposed, like the commune Geneseo, as a bubble. To exist at all, Playland has to *pretend*, to insist too much on itself. Hansen's last lines dangle a key: this fantasy conceals rather than removes life's dangers: the piranhas, the snapping turtle, the smug Hollywood sexual predator. Along with the pleasures of jazz age culture, we find in Playland a diminution of ties that make us human, which after all (as with Horgan's grieving family in "The Peach Stone") involve shared pains as well as joys.

Noting that in Latin "re-ligare" means "to bind again," S. T. Coleridge claimed that a man's religion, both socially and within his own psyche, is the most important thing about him. But being Catholic may be just one thing about many post-Vatican II characters. In turn, as Americans they tend to be less eccentric or exceptional than the characters of a Horgan or Powers, and we see increasing emphasis on moral *dilemma*, the conflict between values in a confusing universe, rather than on the radical importance of right moral choice or "fundamental option" as such. For instance, **Tobias Wolff**'s "The Rich Brother" (1985), though it contains few direct references to Christianity, is filled with indirect allusions, to the Cain-Abel murder and the Prodigal Son, but also Jairus's sick daughter and the workers in the vineyard. In style and message "The Rich Brother" is, like Horgan's peach stone, a parable. Peter, a "Century 21" egocentric materialist, faces a crisis he would prefer to avoid. His younger brother Donald's spirituality is naïve: he proves too incompetent even for the simple life of a Christian commune. Donald's impracticality has a self-destructive as well as self-sacrificing quality. Even the "Try God" emblazoned on his sweatshirt is backward. Ironically, however, the "rich" brother needs the "poor" one more than vice versa. Donald proves dismayingly easy prey for a con game. Yet Peter senses that on some deep level his own sophistication has already cheated him out of some outrageous reward.

At the end we may infer that against Peter's desires he will go back to being his brother's keeper. But we must speculate. These more recent stories, typically, raise more questions than they provide answers. In literary terms, they resist closure.

Catholicism has often found itself at odds with the cruder forms of American materialism. Against the serious if ineffectual temptation of Horgan's devil, we may set **T. Coraghessan Boyle**'s satiric "The Devil and Irv Cherniske" (1985), in which sin in Reagan-era America turns out to be political and economic as well as personal. Boyle's comic retelling of a familiar folk tale argues the folly of exchanging the worship of God for that of

Mammon. In baptism, have we truly renounced Satan's works and pomps? In any event, Irv can find no more redemption in the Church of the Open Palm than O'Connor's Mrs. McIntyre could in the Judge's deserted sanctuary of an office: "When she sat with her intense constricted face turned toward the empty safe, she knew that there was nobody poorer in the world than she was." To McIntyre's purgatory in the rural South, we may add Irv's "prosperous" suburban Beechwood hell.

Mary Gordon's first three novels depicted women inhibited by their gender and struggling with guilt and a sense of duty. In "Mrs. Cassidy's Last Year" (1987), Gordon's protagonist is male. Idealistically, Joseph is determined to honor, despite his wife Rose's Alzheimers, an early vow he made to her that she would die in her own bed. The dilemma tests his integrity and values. In behavior, his wife is hardly the same person he married. Certainly, in an age given over increasingly to the needs and desires of the young, we have to admire Joseph's traditionalist commitment to honor Rose, despite her decay, to the end of her days. But care for the aged is agonizing, and perhaps his choices are ruled too much by the past. His angry son, at least, claims that Joseph's flaw is that he thinks that he, Joseph, is God.

Richard Russo's "The Whore's Child" (1998) offers not just a moral but an interpretative knot. It is this anthology's most obviously poststructuralist story. In "The Whore's Child," where is the line to be drawn, if it can be confidently drawn at all, between Sister Ursula's fictional efforts and a true "autobiography"? The narrator may be correct in taking her story to be essentially a personal memoir. But enough satire is directed at his Creative Writing pomposity that we might take such assumptions with more than one grain of salt. After all, Russo writes about a writer who writes about a writer who. . . .

In any event, this postmodern problem itself is an old one; Jesus, after all, lived a life whose outline had been hinted at centuries before in Israel's scriptures. In the roles of Caroline Gordon's Aleck Maury and Guillaume Fäy, we have already seen how much our personal decisions may depend on the story lines within which imagination sets our lives.

In his two novels and two collections of short fiction, **Tim Gautreaux**'s comic south Louisiana stories often portray a world of crushed hopes and broken ties to young children and aging parents. In "Died and Gone to Vegas" (1995), his affectionately drawn roughnecks create alternative worlds through the conventions of tall-tale telling—comic escapes from the gritty and far less malleable "real" life of work and disappointment. Raynelle's Vegas, one may be sure, is merely another Playland.

Gautreaux's "Good for the Soul" (1999) portrays the faintly squalid world of brandy and parish comforts that traps Father Ledet. Despite these sins of the flesh, however, Ledet's heart remains sound, and in comic fash-ion this Cajun whiskey priest ends up being a "beautiful fountain" himself for at least one lost parishioner.

The collection ends with **Andre Dubus**' "A Father's Story" (1984). Dubus, the son of Cajun and Irish parents, in 1986 lost the use of both legs when hit by a car; he died in 1999. In "A Father's Story," the narra-tor's faith is deep, though not uncomplicated by stresses in family life and strain with an institutional Church he considers too worldly. Though the prohibition against birth control hurt his marriage, and the law against remarriage leaves him alone, his days are still fundamentally sacramen-tal: a real life, and not a "lifestyle." Despite ties to the old teachings, how-ever, he is a decidedly post-Vatican II Catholic. His Catholicism is not at odds with pantheism, but includes it, in his own words, "like onions in a stew."

Yet this cultural openness leaves boundary lines vague. In terms of moral "absolutes," the narrator's decision to protect his modern daughter is sinful. We can hardly imagine Caroline Gordon or Flannery O'Connor applaud-ing! Yet Dubus's portrayal is sympathetic enough to invite a defense of what the father does. Perhaps his deception is forgivable on a concrete, culturally embedded plane. Still, the reader needs to be careful here. Moral relativism leads down many woodland paths, some of them dangerous. Among other documents decrying modern moral relativism we would have to count the late Pope John Paul II's 1993 encyclical *Veritatis Splendor*, as well, of course, as many of the writings of Pope Benedict XVI. One need not be an archaic conservative to acknowledge that there is a powerful case, increasingly made early in the twenty-first century, for the centrality of objective truth in Catholic vision.

But Dubus's narrator, while fond of the Church's ritual and cultural richness, voices a democratic suspicion of its pride and claims to moral authority. Not confession, but his daughter's simple going on with life helps to heal her. However individual readers judge this compelling psychologi-cal portrait, most significantly they are invited not to "learn" but to make their own judgments. In this modern Catholicism, the narrator can com-pare his tragedy to that of God, Who sacrificed His son. Nonetheless, he takes his own path, not the straight and narrow.

For demographic reasons the size and importance of Catholic America is likely to grow considerably in the next century. In seeing Irish farm workers, fled from the famine, around his beloved Walden, Henry David Thoreau found it hard to imagine these muddy wretches with *talaria*, the wings of Mercury, on their heels. The time of such condescension is largely past, though not entirely. This collection has mapped out some of the broad territory claimed by the American Catholic literary imagination up to this point. Only time will tell how this larger historical story continues. We hope readers will explore other works by all of these authors, including the older ones, Caroline Gordon, Horgan, and Powers, less famous today than Flannery O'Connor, but whose important body of fiction invites rediscovery.

Dan McVeigh
Pat Schnapp, R.S.M.
February 2006

1

OLD RED

Caroline Gordon

I

When the door had closed behind his daughter, Mr. Maury went to the window and stood a few moments looking out. The roses that had grown in a riot all along that side of the fence had died or been cleared away, but the sun lay across the garden in the same level lances of light that he remembered. He turned back into the room. The shadows had gathered until it was nearly all in gloom. The top of his minnow bucket just emerging from his duffel bag glinted in the last rays of the sun. He stood looking down at his traps all gathered neatly in a heap at the foot of the bed. He would leave them like that. Even if they came in here sweeping and cleaning up—it was only in hotels that a man was master of his own room—even if they came in here cleaning up he would tell them to leave all his things exactly as they were. It was reassuring to see them all there together, ready to be taken up in the hand, to be carried down and put into a car, to be driven off to some railroad station at a moment's notice.

As he moved toward the door he spoke aloud, a habit that was growing on him:

"Anyhow I won't stay but a week. . . . I ain't going to stay but a week, no matter what they say. . . ."

Downstairs in the dining room they were already gathered at the supper table: his white-haired, shrunken mother-in-law; his tall sister-in-law who had the proud carriage of the head, the aquiline nose, but not the spirit of his dead wife; his lean, blond, new son-in-law; his black-eyed daughter who,

1

but that she was thin, looked so much like him, all of them gathered there waiting for him, Alexander Maury. It occurred to him that this was the first time he had sat down in the bosom of the family for some years. They were always writing saying that he must make a visit this summer or certainly next summer—". . . all had a happy Christmas together, but missed you. . . ." They had even made the pretext that he ought to come up to inspect his new son-in-law. As if he hadn't always known exactly the kind of young man Sarah would marry! What was the boy's name? Stephen, yes, Stephen. He must be sure and remember that.

He sat down and, shaking out his napkin, spread it over his capacious paunch and tucked it well up under his chin in the way his wife had never allowed him to do. He let his eyes rove over the table and released a long sigh.

"Hot batter bread," he said, "and ham. Merry Point ham. I sure am glad to taste them one more time before I die."

The old lady was sending the little Negro girl scurrying back to the kitchen for a hot plate of batter bread. He pushed aside the cold plate and waited. She had bridled when he spoke of the batter bread and a faint flush had dawned on her withered cheeks. Vain she had always been as a peacock, of her housekeeping, her children, anything that belonged to her. She went on now, even at her advanced age, making her batter bread, smoking her hams according to the old recipe she was so proud of, but who came here now to this old house to eat or to praise?

He helped himself to a generous slice of batter bread, buttered it, took the first mouthful and chewed it slowly. He shook his head.

"There ain't anything like it," he said. "There ain't anything else like it in the world."

His dark eye roving over the table fell on his son-in-law. "You like batter bread?" he inquired.

Stephen nodded, smiling. Mr. Maury, still masticating slowly, regarded his face, measured the space between the eyes—his favorite test for man, horse, or dog. Yes, there was room enough for sense between the eyes. How young the boy looked! And infected already with the fatal germ, the *cacoëthes scribendi*. Well, their children—if he and Sarah ever had any children—would probably escape. It was like certain diseases of the eye, skipped every other generation. His own father had had it badly all his life. He could see him now sitting at the head of the table spouting his own poetry—or Shakespeare's—while the children watched the preserve dish to see if it was going around. He, Aleck Maury, had been lucky to have been born in the generation he had. He had escaped that at least. A few translations from Heine in his courting days, a few fragments from the Greek; but no, he had kept clear of that on the whole. . . .

His sister-in-law's eyes were fixed on him. She was smiling faintly. "You don't look much like dying, Aleck. Florida must agree with you."

The old lady spoke from the head of the table. "I can't see what you do with yourself all winter long. Doesn't time hang heavy on your hands?"

Time, he thought, *time!* They were always mouthing the word, and what did they know about it? Nothing in God's world! He saw time suddenly, a dull, leaden-colored fabric depending from the old lady's hands, from the hands of all of them, a blanket that they pulled about between them, now here, now there, trying to cover up their nakedness. Or they would cast it on the ground and creep in among the folds, finding one day a little more tightly rolled than another, but all of it everywhere the same dull gray substance. But time was a banner that whipped before him always in the wind! He stood on tiptoe to catch at the bright folds, to strain them to his bosom. They were bright and glittering. But they whipped by so fast and were whipping always ever faster. The tears came into his eyes. Where, for instance, had this year gone? He could swear he had not wasted a minute of it, for no man living, he thought, knew better how to make each day a pleasure to him. Not a minute wasted and yet here it was already May. If he lived to the biblical threescore-and-ten, which was all he ever allowed himself in his calculations, he had before him only nine more Mays. Only nine more Mays out of all eternity and they wanted him to waste one of them sitting on the front porch at Merry Point!

The butter plate that had seemed to swim before him in a glittering mist was coming solidly to rest upon the white tablecloth. He winked his eyes rapidly and, laying down his knife and fork, squared himself about in his chair to address his mother-in-law:

"Well, ma'am, you know I'm a man that always likes to be learning something. Now this year I learned how to smell out fish." He glanced around table, holding his head high and allowing his well-cut nostrils to flutter slightly with his indrawn breaths. "Yes, sir," he said, "I'm probably the only white man in this country knows how to smell out feesh."

There was a discreet smile on the faces of the others. Sarah was laughing outright. "Did you have to learn how or did it just come to you?"

"I learned it from an old nigger woman," her father said. He shook his head reminiscently. "It's wonderful how much you can learn from niggers. But you have to know how to handle them. I was half the winter wooing that old Fanny. . . ."

He waited until their laughter had died down. "We used to start off every morning from the same little cove and we'd drift in there together at night. I noticed how she always brought in a good string, so I says to her: 'Fanny, you just lemme go 'long with you.' But she wouldn't have nothing

3

to do with me. I saw she was going to be a hard nut to crack, but I kept right on. Finally I began giving her presents. . . ."

Laura was regarding him fixedly, a queer glint in her eyes. Seeing outrageous pictures in her mind's eye, doubtless. Poor Laura. Fifty years old if she was a day. More than half her lifetime gone and all of it spent drying up here in the old lady's shadow. She was speaking with a gasping little titter:

"What sort of presents did you give her, Aleck?"

He made his tones hearty in answer. "I give her a fine string of fish one day, and I give her fifty cents. And finally I made her a present of a Barlow knife. That was when she broke down. She took me with her that morning. . . ."

"Could she really *smell* fish?" the old lady asked curiously.

"You ought to a seen her," Mr. Maury said. "She'd sail over that lake like a hound on the scent. She'd row right along and then all of a sudden she'd stop rowing." He bent over and peered into the depths of imaginary water. "'Thar they are, White Folks, thar they are. Cain't you smell 'em?'"

Stephen was leaning forward, eying his father-in-law intently. "Could you?" he asked.

"I got so I could smell feesh," Mr. Maury told him. "I could smell out the feesh but I couldn't tell which kind they were. Now Fanny could row over a bed and tell just by the smell whether it was bass or bream. But she'd been at it all her life." He paused, sighing. "You can't just pick these things up. . . . Who was it said, 'Genius is an infinite capacity for taking pains?'"

Sarah was rising briskly. Her eyes sought her husband's across the table. She was laughing. "Sir Isaak Walton," she said. "We'd better go in the other room. Mandy wants to clear the table."

The two older ladies remained in the dining room. Mr. Maury walked across the hall to the sitting room, accompanied by Steve and Sarah. He lowered himself cautiously into the most solid-looking of the rocking chairs that were drawn up around the fire. Steve stood on the hearthrug, his back to the fire.

Mr. Maury glanced up at him curiously. "What you thinking about, feller?" he asked.

Steve looked down. He smiled but his gaze was still contemplative. "I was thinking about the sonnet," he said, "in the form in which it first came to England."

Mr. Maury shook his head. "Wyatt and Surrey," he said. "Hey, nonny, nonny. . . . You'll have hardening of the liver long before you're my age." He looked past Steve's shoulder at the picture that hung over the mantelshelf: Cupid and Psyche holding between them a fluttering veil and running along a rocky path toward the beholder. It had been hanging there ever since he could remember, would hang there, he thought, till the house fell down or

4

burned down, as it was more likely to do with the old lady wandering around at night carrying lighted lamps the way she did. "Old Merry Point," he said. "It don't change much, does it?"

He settled himself more solidly in his chair. His mind veered from the old house to his own wanderings in brighter places. He regarded his daughter and son-in-law affably.

"Yes, sir," he said, "this winter in Florida was valuable to me just for the acquaintances I made. Take my friend Jim Yost. Just to live in the same hotel with that man is an education." He paused, smiling reminiscently into the fire. "I'll never forget the first time I saw him. He came up to me there in the lobby of the hotel. 'Professor Maury,' he says, 'you been hearin' about me for twenty years and I been hearin' about you for twenty years. And now we've done met.'"

Sarah had sat down in the little rocking chair by the fire. She leaned toward him now, laughing. "They ought to have put down a cloth of gold for the meeting," she said.

Mr. Maury regarded her critically. It occurred to him that she was, after all, not so much like himself as the sister whom, as a child, he had particularly disliked. A smart girl, Sarah, but too quick always on the uptake. For his own part he preferred a softer-natured woman.

He shook his head. "Nature does that in Florida," he said. "I knew right off the reel it was him. There were half a dozen men standing around. I made 'em witness. 'Jim Yost,' I says, 'Jim Yost of Maysville or I'll eat my hat.'"

"Why is he so famous?" Sarah asked.

Mr. Maury took out his knife and cut off a plug of tobacco. When he had offered a plug to his son-in-law and it had been refused, he put the tobacco back in his pocket. "He's a man of imagination," he said slowly. "There ain't many in this world."

He took a small tin box out of his pocket and set it on the little table that held the lamp. Removing the top, he tilted the box so that they could see its contents: an artificial lure, a bug with a dark body and a red, bulbous head, a hook protruding from what might be considered its vitals.

"Look at her," he said. "Ain't she a killer?"

Sarah leaned forward to look and Steve, still standing on the hearthrug, bent above them. The three heads ringed the light. Mr. Maury disregarded Sarah and addressed himself to Steve. "She takes nine strips of pork rind," he said, "nine strips cut just thick enough." He marked off the width of the strips with his two fingers on the table, then, picking up the lure and cupping it in his palm, he moved it back and forth quickly so that the painted eyes caught the light.

"Look at her," he said, "look at the wicked way she sets forward."

Sarah was poking at the lure with the tip of her finger. "Wanton," she said, "simply wanton. What does he call her?"

"This is his Devil Bug," Mr. Maury said. "He's the only man in this country makes it. I myself had the idea thirty years ago and let it slip by me the way I do with so many of my ideas." He sighed, then, elevating his tremendous bulk slightly above the table level and continuing to hold Steve with his gaze, he produced from his coat pocket the oilskin book that held his flies. He spread it open on the table and began to turn the pages. His eyes sought his son-in-law's as his hand paused before a gray, rather draggled-looking lure.

"Old Speck," he said. "I've had that fly for twenty years. I reckon she's taken five hundred pounds of fish in her day. . . ."

The fire burned lower. A fiery coal rolled from the grate and fell onto the hearthrug. Sarah scooped it up with a shovel and threw it among the ashes. In the circle of the lamplight the two men still bent over the table looking at the flies. Steve was absorbed in them, but he spoke seldom. It was her father's voice that, rising and falling, filled the room. He talked a great deal but he had a beautiful speaking voice. He was telling Steve now about Little West Fork, the first stream ever he put a fly in. "My first love," he kept calling it. It sounded rather pretty, she thought, in his mellow voice. "My first love. . . ."

II

When Mr. Maury came downstairs the next morning the dining room was empty except for his daughter, Sarah, who sat dawdling over a cup of coffee and a cigarette. Mr. Maury sat down opposite her. To the little Negro girl who presented herself at his elbow he outlined his wants briefly. "A cup of coffee and some hot batter bread, just like we had last night." He turned to his daughter. "Where's Steve?"

"He's working," she said. "He was up at eight and he's been working ever since."

Mr. Maury accepted the cup of coffee from the little girl, poured half of it into his saucer, set it aside to cool. "Ain't it wonderful," he said, "the way a man can sit down and work day after day? When I think of all the work I've done in my time. . . . Can he work *every* morning?"

"He sits down at his desk every morning," she said, "but of course he gets more done some mornings than others."

Mr. Maury picked up his saucer, found the coffee cool enough for his taste. He sipped it slowly, looking out of the window. His mind was already busy with his day's program. No water—no running water—nearer than West Fork, three miles away. He couldn't drive a car and Steve was going to

6

be busy writing all morning. There was nothing for it but a pond. The Willow Sink. It was not much, but it was better than nothing. He pushed his chair back and rose.

"Well," he said, "I'd better be starting."

When he came downstairs with his rod a few minutes later the hall was still full of the sound of measured typing. Sarah sat in the dining room in the same position in which he had left her, smoking. Mr. Maury paused in the doorway while he slung his canvas bag over his shoulders. "How you ever going to get anything done if you don't take advantage of the morning hours?" he asked. He glanced at the door opposite as if it had been the entrance to a sick chamber. "What's he writing about?" he inquired in a whisper.

"It's an essay on John Skelton."

Mr. Maury looked at the new green leaves framed in the doorway. "John Skelton," he said. "God Almighty!"

He went through the hall and stepped down off the porch onto the ground that was still moist with spring rains. As he crossed the lower yard he looked up into the branches of the maples. Yes, the leaves were full-grown already even on the late trees. The year, how swiftly, how steadily it advanced! He had come to the far corner of the yard. Grown up it was in pokeberry shoots and honeysuckle, but there was a place to get through. The top strand of wire had been pulled down and fastened to the others with a ragged piece of rope. He rested his weight on his good leg and swung himself over onto the game one. It gave him a good, sharp twinge when he came down on it. It was getting worse all the time, that leg, but on the other hand he was learning better all the time how to handle it. His mind flew back to a dark, startled moment, that day when the cramp first came on him. He had been sitting still in the boat all day long and that evening when he stood up to get out his leg had failed him utterly. He had pitched forward among the reeds, had lain there a second, face downward, before it came to him what had happened. With the realization came a sharp picture out of his faraway youth. Uncle James, lowering himself ponderously out of the saddle after a hard day's hunting, had fallen forward in exactly the same way, into a knot of yowling little Negroes. He had got up and cursed them all out of the lot. It had scared the old boy to death, coming down like that. The black dog he had had on his shoulder all that fall. But he himself had never lost one day's fishing on account of his leg. He had known from the start how to handle it. It meant simply that he was slowed down that much. It hadn't really made much difference in fishing. He didn't do as much wading but he got around just about as well on the whole. Hunting, of course, had had to go. You couldn't walk all day shooting birds, dragging a game leg. He had just given it up right off the reel, though it was a shame when a man was as good a shot as he was. That day he was out with Tom Kensington, last November, the only day he got out during the bird season. Nine shots he'd had and he'd bagged nine birds. Yes, it was a shame. But a man couldn't do everything. He had to limit himself. . . .

He was up over the little rise now. The field slanted straight down before him to where the pond lay, silver in the morning sun. A Negro cabin was perched halfway up the opposite slope. A woman was hanging out washing on a line stretched between two trees. From the open door little Negroes spilled down the path toward the pond. Mr. Maury surveyed the scene, spoke aloud:

"Ain't it funny now? Niggers always live in the good places."

He stopped under a wild cherry tree to light his pipe. It had been hot crossing the field, but the sunlight here was agreeably tempered by the branches. And that pond down there was fringed with willows. His eyes sought the bright disc of the water, then rose to where the smoke from the cabin chimney lay in a soft plume along the crest of the hill.

When he stooped to pick up his rod again it was with a feeling of sudden keen elation. An image had risen in his memory, an image that was familiar but came to him infrequently of late and that only in moments of elation: the wide field in front of his uncle's house in Albemarle, on one side the dark line of undergrowth that marked the Rivanna River, on the other the blue of Peters' Mountain. They would be waiting there in that broad plain when they had the first sight of the fox. On that little rise by the river, loping steadily, not yet alarmed. The sun would glint on his bright coat, on his quick turning head as he dove into the dark of the woods. There would be a hullabaloo after that and shouting and riding. Sometimes there was the tailing of the fox—that time Old Whiskey was brought home on a mattress! All of that to come afterward, but none of it ever like that first sight of the fox there on the broad plain between the river and the mountain.

There was one fox, they grew to know him in time, to call him affectionately by name. Old Red it was who showed himself always like that there on the crest of the hill. "There he goes, the damn, impudent scoundrel. . . ." Uncle James would shout and slap his thigh and yell himself hoarse at Whiskey and Mag and the pups, but they would already have settled to their work. They knew his course, every turn of it, by heart. Through the woods and then down again to the river. Their hope was always to cut him off before he could circle back to the mountain. If he got in there among those old field pines it was all up. But he always made it. Lost 'em every time and dodged through to his hole in Pinnacle Rock. A smart fox, Old Red. . . .

He descended the slope and paused in the shade of a clump of willows. The little Negroes who squatted, dabbling in the water, watched him out of round eyes as he unslung his canvas bag and laid it on a stump. He looked down at them gravely.

"D'you ever see a white man that could conjure?" he asked.

The oldest boy laid the brick he was fashioning out of mud down on a plank. He ran the tip of his tongue over his lower lip to moisten it before he spoke. "Naw, suh."

"I'm the man," Mr. Maury told him. "You chillun better quit that playin' and dig me some worms."

He drew his rod out of the case, jointed it up, and laid it down on a stump. Taking out his book of flies, he turned the pages, considering. "Silver Spinner," he said aloud. "They ought to take that . . . in May. Naw, I'll just give Old Speck a chance. It's a long time now since we had her out."

The little Negroes had risen and were stepping quietly off along the path toward the cabin, the two little boys hand in hand, the little girl following, the baby astride her hip. They were pausing now before a dilapidated building that might long ago have been a hen house. Mr. Maury shouted at them: "Look under them old boards. That's the place for worms." The biggest boy was turning around. His treble "Yassuh" quivered over the water. Then their voices died away. There was no sound except the light turning of the willow boughs in the wind.

Mr. Maury walked along the bank, rod in hand, humming: "Bangum's gone to the wild boar's den. . . . *Bangum's* gone to the wild boar's den. . . ." He stopped where a white, peeled log protruded six or seven feet into the water. The pond made a little turn here. He stepped out squarely upon the log, still humming. The line rose smoothly, soared against the blue, and curved sweetly back upon the still water. His quick ear caught the little whish that the fly made when it clove the surface, his eye followed the tiny ripples made by its flight. He cast again, leaning a little backwards as he did sometimes when the mood was on him. Again and again his line soared out over the water. His eye rested now and then on his wrist. He noted with detachment the expert play of the muscles, admired each time the accuracy of his aim. It occurred to him that it was four days now since he had wet a line. Four days. One whole day packing up, parts of two days on the train, and yesterday wasted sitting there on that front porch with the family. But the abstinence had done him good. He had never cast better than he was casting this morning.

There was a rustling along the bank, a glimpse of blue through the trees. Mr. Maury leaned forward and peered around the clump of willows. A hundred yards away Steve, hatless, in an old blue shirt and khaki pants, stood jointing up a rod.

Mr. Maury backed off his log and advanced along the path. He called out cheerfully: "Well, feller, do any good?"

Steve looked up. His face had lightened for a moment but the abstracted expression stole over it again when he spoke. "Oh, I fiddled with it all morning," he said, "but I didn't do much good."

Mr. Maury nodded sympathetically. "*Minerva invita erat*," he said. "You can do nothing unless Minerva perches on the roof tree. Why, I been castin' here all morning and not a strike. But there's a boat tied up over on the other side. What say we get in it and just drift around?" He paused, looked at the rod Steve had finished jointing up. "I brought another rod along," he said. "You want to use it?"

Steve shook his head. "I'm used to this one," he said.

An expression of relief came over Mr. Maury's face. "That's right," he said, "a man always does better with his own rod."

The boat was only a quarter full of water. They heaved her over and dumped it out, then dragged her down to the bank. The little Negroes had come up, bringing a can of worms. Mr. Maury threw them each a nickel and set the can in the bottom of the boat. "I always like to have a few worms handy," he told Steve, "ever since I was a boy." He lowered himself ponderously into the bow and Steve pushed off and dropped down behind him.

The little Negroes still stood on the bank staring. When the boat was a little distance out on the water the boldest of them spoke:

"You reckon 'at ole jawnboat going to hold you up, Cap'm?"

Mr. Maury turned his head to call over his shoulder. "Go 'way, boy. Ain't I done tole you I's a conjure?"

The boat dipped ominously. Steve changed his position a little and she settled to the water. Sitting well forward, Mr. Maury made graceful casts, now to this side, now to that. Steve, in the stern, made occasional casts but he laid his rod down every now and then to paddle though there really was no use in it. The boat drifted well enough with the wind. At the end of half an hour seven sizable bass lay on the bottom of the boat. Mr. Maury had caught five of them. He reflected that perhaps he really ought to change places with Steve. The man in the bow certainly had the best chance at the fish. "But no," he thought, "it don't make no difference. He don't hardly know where he is now."

He stole a glance over his shoulder at the young man's serious, abstracted face. It was like that of a person submerged. Steve seemed to float up to the surface every now and then, his expression would lighten, he would make some observation that showed he knew where he was, then he would sink again. If you asked him a question he answered punctiliously, two minutes later. Poor boy, dead to the world and would probably be that way the rest of his life. A pang of pity shot through Mr. Maury and on the heels of it a gust of that black fear that occasionally shook him. It was he, not Steve, that was

10

the queer one. The world was full of people like this boy, all of them going around with their heads so full of this and that they hardly knew what they were doing. They were all like that. There was hardly anybody—there was *nobody* really in the whole world like him.

Steve, coming out of his abstraction, spoke politely. He had heard that Mr. Maury was a fine shot. Did he like to fish better than hunt?

Mr. Maury reflected. "Well," he said, "they's something about a covey of birds rising up in front of you . . . they's something . . . and a good dog. Now they ain't anything in this world that I like better than a good bird dog." He stopped and sighed. "A man has got to come to himself early in life if he's going to amount to anything. Now I was smart, even as a boy. I could look around me and see all the men of my family, Uncle Jeems, Uncle Quent, my father, every one of 'em weighed two hundred by the time he was fifty. You get as heavy on your feet as all that and you can't do any good shooting. But a man can fish as long as he lives. . . . Why, one place I stayed last summer there was an old man ninety years old had himself carried down to the river every morning. Yes, sir, a man can fish as long as he can get down to the water's edge."

There was a little plop to the right. He turned just in time to see the fish flash out of the water. He watched Steve take it off the hook and drop it on top of the pile in the bottom of the boat. Seven bass that made and one bream. The old lady would be pleased. "Aleck always catches me fish," she'd say.

The boat glided over the still water. There was no wind at all now. The willows that fringed the bank might have been cut out of paper. The plume of smoke hung perfectly horizontal over the roof of the Negro cabin. Mr. Maury watched it stream out in little eddies and disappear into the bright blue.

He spoke softly. "Ain't it wonderful . . . ain't it wonderful now that a man of my gifts can content himself a whole morning on this here little old pond?"

III

Mr. Maury woke with a start. He realized that he had been sleeping on his left side again. A bad idea. It always gave him palpitations of the heart. It must be that that had waked him up. He had gone to sleep almost immediately after his head hit the pillow. He rolled over, cautiously, as he always did since that bed in Leesburg had given down with him and, lying flat on his back, stared at the opposite wall.

The moon rose late. It must be at its height now. That patch of light was so brilliant he could almost discern the pattern of the wallpaper. It hung there, wavering, bitten by the shadows into a semblance of a human figure, a man striding with bent head and swinging arms. All the shadows in the room seemed to be moving toward him. The protruding corner of the washstand was an arrow aimed at his heart, the clumsy old-fashioned dresser was a giant towering above him.

They had put him to sleep in this same room after his wife died. In the summer it had been, too, in June; and there must have been a full moon, for the same giant shadows had struggled there with the same towering monsters. It would be like that here on this wall every full moon, for the pieces of furniture would never change their position, had never been changed, probably, since the house was built.

He turned back on his side. The wall before him was dark but he knew every flower in the pattern of the wallpaper, interlacing pink roses with, thrusting up between every third cluster, the enormous, spreading fronds of ferns. The wallpaper in the room across the hall was like it too. The old lady slept there, and in the room next to his own, Laura, his sister-in-law, and in the east bedroom downstairs, the young couple. He and Mary had slept there when they were first married, when they were the young couple in the house.

He tried to remember Mary as she must have looked that day he first saw her, the day he arrived from Virginia to open his school in the old office that used to stand there in the corner of the yard. He could see Mr. Allard plainly, sitting there under the sugar tree with his chair tilted back, could discern the old lady—young she had been then!—hospitably poised in the doorway, hand extended, could hear her voice: "Well, here are two of your pupils to start with." He remembered Laura, a shy child of nine hiding her face in her mother's skirts, but Mary that day was only a shadow in the dark hall. He could not even remember how her voice had sounded. "Professor Maury," she would have said, and her mother would have corrected her with "Cousin Aleck...."

That day she got off her horse at the stile blocks she had turned as she walked across the lawn to look back at him. Her white sunbonnet had fallen on her shoulders. Her eyes, meeting his, had been dark and startled. He had gone on and had hitched both the horses before he leaped over the stile to join her. But he had known in that moment that she was the woman he was going to have. He could not remember all the rest of it, only that moment stood out. He had won her, she had become his wife, but the woman he had won was not the woman he had sought. It was as if he had had her only in that moment there on the lawn. As if she had paused there only for that one moment and was ever after retreating before him down a devious, a dark way that he would never have chosen.

The death of the first baby had been the start of it, of course. It had been a relief when she took so definitely to religion. Before that there had been those sudden, unaccountable forays out of some dark lurking place that she had. Guerrilla warfare and trying to the nerves, but that had been only at first. For many years they had been two enemies contending in the open.

Toward the last she had taken mightily to prayer. He would wake often to find her kneeling by the side of the bed in the dark. It had gone on for years. She had never given up hope.

Ah, a stouthearted one, Mary! She had never given up hope of changing him, of making him over into the man she thought he ought to be. Time and again she almost had him. And there were long periods, of course, during which he had been worn down by the conflict, one spring when he himself said, when she had told all the neighbors, that he was too old now to go fishing anymore. . . . But he had made a comeback. She had had to resort to stratagem. His lips curved in a smile, remembering the trick.

It had come over him suddenly, a general lassitude, an odd faintness in the mornings, the time when his spirits ordinarily were at their highest. He had sat there by the window, almost wishing to have some ache or pain, something definite to account for his condition. But he did not feel sick in his body. It was rather a dulling of all his senses. There were no longer the reactions to the visible world that made his days a series of adventures. He had looked out of the window at the woods glistening with spring rain; he had not even taken down his gun to shoot a squirrel.

Remembering Uncle Quent's last days he had been alarmed, had decided finally that he must tell her so that they might begin preparations for the future—he had shuddered at the thought of eventual confinement, perhaps in some institution. She had looked up from her sewing, unable to repress a smile.

"You think it's your mind, Aleck. . . . It's coffee. . . . I've been giving you a coffee substitute every morning. . . ."

They had laughed together over her cleverness. He had not gone back to coffee but the lassitude had worn off. She had gone back to the attack with redoubled vigor. In the afternoons she would stand on the porch calling after him as he slipped down to the creek. "Now, don't stay long enough to get that cramp. You remember how you suffered last time. . . ." He would have forgotten all about the cramp until that moment but it would hang over him then through the whole afternoon's sport and it would descend upon him inevitably when he left the river and started for the house.

Yes, he thought with pride. She was wearing him down—he did not believe there was a man living who could withstand her a lifetime—she was wearing him down and would have had him in another few months, another year certainly. But she had been struck down just as victory was in her grasp. The paralysis had come on her in the night. It was as if a curtain had descended, dividing their life sharply into two parts. In the bewildered year and a half that followed he had found himself forlornly trying to reconstruct the Mary he had known. The pressure she had so constantly exerted upon him had become for him a part of her personality. This new, calm Mary was

not the woman he had lived with all these years. She had lain there—hero-
ically they all said—waiting for death. And lying there, waiting, all her faculties engaged now in defensive warfare, she had raised, as it were, her
lifelong siege; she had lost interest in his comings and goings, had once even
encouraged him to go for an afternoon's sport! He felt a rush of warm pity.
Poor Mary! She must have realized toward the last that she had wasted herself in conflict. She had spent her arms and her strength against an inglori-
ous foe when all the time the real, the invincible adversary waited. . . .

He turned over on his back again. The moonlight was waning, the contending shadows paler now and retreating toward the door. From across the
hall came the sound of long, sibilant breaths, ending each one on a little
upward groan. The old lady. . . . She would maintain till her dying day that
she did not snore. He fancied now that he could hear from the next room
Laura's light, regular breathing and downstairs were the young couple asleep
in each other's arms. . . .

All of them were quiet and relaxed now, but they had been lively enough
at dinnertime. It had started with the talk about Aunt Sally Crenfew's
funeral tomorrow. Living now, as he had for some years, away from women
of his family, he had forgotten the need to be cautious. He had spoken up
before he thought:

"But that's the day Steve and I were going to Barker's Mill. . . ."

Sarah had cried out at the idea. "Barker's Mill!" she had said. "Right on
the Crenfew land . . . well, if not on the very farm, in the very next field. It
would be a scandal if he, Professor Maury, known by everybody to be in the
neighborhood, could not spare one afternoon, one insignificant summer
afternoon, from his fishing long enough to attend the funeral of his cousin,
the cousin of all of them, the oldest lady in the whole family connection. . . ."

Looking around the table he had caught the same look in every eye; he
had felt a gust of that same fright that had shaken him there on the pond.
That look! Sooner or later you met it in every human eye. The thing was to
be up and ready, ready to run for your life at a moment's notice. Yes, it had
always been like that. It always would be. His fear of them was shot through
suddenly with contempt. It was as if Mary were there laughing with him.
She knew that there was not one of them who could have survived as he had
survived, could have paid the price for freedom that he had paid. . . .

Sarah had come to a stop. He had to say something. He shook his head.

"You think we just go fishing to have a good time. The boy and I hold
high converse on that pond. I'm starved for intellectual companionship, I
tell you. . . . In Florida I never see anybody but niggers."

They had all laughed out at that. "As if you didn't *prefer* the society of
niggers!" Sarah said scornfully.

The old lady had been moved to anecdote:

"I remember when Aleck first came out here from Virginia, Cousin Sophy said: 'Professor Maury is so well educated. Now Cousin Cave Maynor is dead who is there in the neighborhood for him to associate with?' 'Well,' I said, 'I don't know about that. He seems perfectly satisfied with Ben Hooser. They're off to the creek together every evening soon as school is out.'"

Ben Hooser. . . . He could see now the wrinkled face, overlaid with that ashy pallor of the aged Negro, smiling eyes, the pendulous lower lip that, drooping away, showed always some of the rotten teeth. A fine nigger, Ben, and on to a lot of tricks, the only man really that he'd ever cared to take fishing with him.

But the first real friend of his bosom had been old Uncle Teague, the factotum at Hawkwood. Once a week or, more likely, every ten days, he fed the hounds on the carcass of a calf that had had time to get pretty high. They would drive the spring wagon out into the lot; he, a boy of ten, beside Uncle Teague on the driver's seat. The hounds would come in a great rush and rear their slobbering jowls against the wagon wheels. Uncle Teague would wield his whip chuckling while he threw the first hunk of meat to Old Mag, his favorite.

"Dey goin' run on dis," he'd say. "Dey goin' run like a shadow. . . ."

He shifted his position again, cautiously. People, he thought . . . people . . . so bone ignorant, all of them. Not one person in a thousand realized that a foxhound remains at heart a wild beast and must kill and gorge and then, when he is ravenous, kill and gorge again. . . . Or that the channel cat is a night feeder. . . . Or . . . his daughter had told him once that he ought to set all his knowledge down in a book. "Why?" he had asked. "So everybody else can know as much as I do?"

If he allowed his mind to get active, really active, he would never get any sleep. He was fighting an inclination now to get up and find a cigarette. He relaxed again upon his pillows, deliberately summoned pictures before his mind's eye. Landscapes—and streams. He observed their outlines, watched one flow into another. The Black River into West Fork, that in turn into Spring Creek and Spring Creek into the Withlicoochee. Then they were all flowing together, merging into one broad plain. He watched it take form slowly: the wide field in front of Hawkwood, the Rivanna River on one side, on the other Peters' Mountain. They would be waiting there till the fox showed himself on that little rise by the river. The young men would hold back till Uncle James had wheeled Old Filly, then they would all be off pellmell across the plain. He himself would be mounted on Jonesboro. Almost blind, but she would take anything you put her at. That first thicket on the edge of the woods. They would break there, one half of them going around, the other half streaking it through the woods. He was always of those going around to try to cut the fox off on the other side. No, he was down off his horse. He was coursing with the fox through the trees. He could hear the sharp, pointed feet padding on the dead leaves, see the quick head turned now and then over the shoulder. The trees kept flashing by, one black trunk after another. And now it was a ragged mountain field and the sage grass running before them in waves to where a narrow stream curved in between the ridges. The fox's feet were light in the water. He moved forward steadily, head down. The hounds' baying grew louder. Old Mag knew the trick. She had stopped to give tongue by that big rock and now they had all leaped the gulch and were scrambling up through the pines. But the fox's feet were already hard on the mountain path. He ran slowly, past the big boulder, past the blasted pine to where the shadow of the Pinnacle Rock was black across the path. He ran on and the shadow swayed and rose to meet him. Its cool touch was on his hot tongue, his heaving flanks. He had slipped in under it. He was sinking down, panting, in black dark, on moist earth while the hounds' baying filled the valley and reverberated from the mountainside.

Mr. Maury got up and lit a cigarette. He smoked it quietly, lying back upon his pillows. When he had finished smoking he rolled over on his side and closed his eyes. It was still a good while till morning, but perhaps he could get some sleep. His mind played quietly over the scene that would be enacted in the morning. He would be sitting on the porch after breakfast, smoking, when Sarah came out. She would ask him how he felt, how he had slept.

He would heave a groan, not looking at her for fear of catching that smile on her face—the girl had little sense of decency. He would heave a groan, not too loud or overdone. "My kidney trouble," he would say, shaking his head. "It's come back on me, daughter, in the night."

She would express sympathy and go on to talk of something else. She never took any stock in his kidney trouble. He would ask her finally if she reckoned Steve had time to drive him to the train that morning. He'd been thinking about how much good the chalybeate water of Estill Springs had done him last year. He might heave another groan here to drown her protests. "No. . . . I better be getting on to the Springs. . . . I need the water. . . ."

She would talk on a lot after that. He would not need to listen. He would be sitting there thinking about Elk River, where it runs through the village of Estill Springs. He could see that place by the bridge now: a wide, deep pool with plenty of lay-bys under the willows.

The train would get in around one o'clock. That nigger, Ed, would hustle his bags up to the boardinghouse for him. He would tell Mrs. Rogers he must have the same room. He would have his bags packed so he could get at everything quick. He would be into his black shirt and fishing pants before you could say Jack Robinson. . . . Thirty minutes after he got off the train he would have a fly in that water.

2

THE PRESENCE

Caroline Gordon

Mr. Maury woke from his nap late. When he came downstairs Miss Gilbert was already settled in his big wicker chair at the north end of the porch. Mr. Maury stood in the doorway and waved the palm-leaf fan. The leaves of the hibiscus vine fluttered. Miss Gilbert inclined her aquiline nose. Mr. Maury waited. The nose disappeared into a great scarlet cup, then tilted upward again, unpolluted by any golden grain.

"Damned hummingbird!" Mr. Maury said under his breath as he took his seat in the chair next to hers, sighing to feel the wooden slats pressing into the fleshy part of his back. Some lines from an old song came into his head:

"All dressed in white linen,
As cold as the clay. . . ."

She dressed in white, winter and summer, to set off her white hair and blue eyes; she would ask to be dressed in white when it came time to lay her out. But that was a long way off. Take her all in all, liver, lights, kidneys— he winced—she was sounder than he was.

Miss Gilbert looked up from her book. "Jenny's train was two hours late," she said.

"Well, she got here," Mr. Maury said. "It was time. Life's not worth living without her. At least my life isn't. . . . But my life's hardly worth living, anyhow." He sighed again.

Miss Gilbert's pince-nez glittered as she turned toward him. "Oh, how I wish I could persuade you to read this book!" she said earnestly. She held it up. Gold letters were incised on its limp white leather cover: *In Tune with the Infinite*, by Ralph Waldo Trine.

Mr. Maury shook his head. "I can't hardly stand Ralph Waldo Emerson." He leaned forward suddenly. "You rascal!" he shouted. "You come out of those bushes."

A blue-ticked setter burst through the shrubbery and, rushing up to him, stood, panting, saliva drooling from her open jaws onto his knee. Mr. Maury held her in the crook of his arm and pulled the cockleburs from her ears.

A big, sunburned man in hunting clothes came up on the porch. He slid a game bag from his shoulder. Mr. Maury released the dog and, bending over, his legs spread wide apart, emptied the bag of birds. "Nine," he said, and, bending farther forward, touched a warm, speckled feather with the tip of his finger. "Nine, not counting what you got in your pockets, you scoundrel! . . . Well, which way'd you go?"

The hunter sat down at the foot of one of the big columns that supported the gallery. "You know that biggest stand of pine out at Tom Sullivan's?"

Mr. Maury nodded eagerly. "There's a branch runs through it, southeast. Grapevines thick as fleas on a dog's back. . . . But you didn't find anything there?"

"That big dog of Joe's found our first covey in the next field."

"She back him?"

"I'll say. I brought down two birds."

Mr. Maury pulled the dog's ear ecstatically. "That old big dog, how'd he work?"

"He sure gets over the ground, but he ain't got the nose she's got."

"How was she on the singles?"

"Man, you ought to seen her!"

Mr. Maury let out a whistle. "You got something, Jim!"

Jim Mowbray leaned back against the column. His brown eyes, mottled, Mr. Maury had always thought, like the sides of a trout, met Mr. Maury's in a long, companionable look. "Just give me another season on her!"

"You're tired, man," Mr. Maury said solicitously. "You go and take a hot bath. I'll feed her."

Jim Mowbray was stuffing the birds back into the bag. Mr. Maury took it from him and went down the steps and along the path, edged with night-blooming jasmine, to the kitchen quarters. In the twilight the blossoms were already giving off a faint fragrance. But there was a sharper smell in the air. He came to the old pine tree, where the paths forked, one path going on to the little back court, the other leading into the grove. Mingled with the mimosas and cork bark trees were clusters of bamboo shoots which Mrs. Mowbray had allowed Mr. Maury to root there when he had first come to board with her ten years ago. Mr. Maury paused beside the pine tree and let the game bag trail on the ground. The bruised, brown needles gave off a smell of resin. A mimosa bough ahead of him was suddenly feathered with light; the new moon was rising behind the grove. He slung the game bag up over his shoulder by its canvas strap. His nostrils widened. The grove ended, he knew, at the fence that divided the Mowbray lot from the Hamlins', yet as he stood there, the pine needles crisp under his feet, their smell sharp in his nostrils, the grove seemed larger. That dark round at his right was not the ridged column of a bamboo shoot but the smooth bole of a beech. There were elms and oaks and hickories ahead. He might have been making his way home, at day's end, by the slanting rays of the sun, his game bag heavy on his shoulder. . . .

The setter whined and pressed against his leg. "Come on," he said, and turned back toward the kitchen.

The cook looked up from the electric mixer she was operating. "Doctor, git that dog off my clean floor," she said plaintively.

Mr. Maury took a quarter from his pocket and tossed it on the table. "Go on, get me that ham bone you got in the refrigerator. This is a big day in this dog's life."

"Big day in *my* life," she said. "Be picking birds off here till midnight." She stilled her machine and, opening the refrigerator, drew the remains of a ham out of a cellophane wrapper. The dog leaped up, whining. She kicked her aside. "You better cut it off," she said, "I got my mayonnaise to make."

Mr. Maury swiftly stripped the bone of meat and threw it through the open doorway. The dog whirled after it. "Now give me some more scraps," he said. She pointed to a garbage can. He bent and patiently disentangled some scraps of meat from the vegetable refuse, heaped them on a plate, and, going to the door, called the setter. A growl came from the shrubbery. Mr. Maury laughed as he set the plate on the ground. He glanced overhead. The moon had climbed over the mimosas and was riding into the branches of the pine. They said it was bad luck to look at the new moon through the leaves, but he was not engaged now—had not been engaged since those wharf rats had reported to Miss Jenny that he had almost drowned getting in and out of his boat, and she had made him stop fishing—in any enterprise that called for the favor of the gods. . . . But what a night for high emprise! The dog growled again from her cover. He stood and gazed into the grove. A cloud was sailing toward the moon. They met in the branches of the pine. The cloud passed. Light welled from the moon, ran quicksilver down a bamboo shoot, splashed onto the brown earth. What he had thought was the trunk of a tree stirred. Another shape was moving toward it. They merged into one. The dark mass remained motionless for several seconds, then resolved into two blunt columns that passed slowly between the trunks of the trees. One was shorter than the other.

"Jim?" he shouted.

There was no answer. In the kitchen Daisy was singing, loud enough to drown the whir of the mixer. The bushes rustled. The setter had finished burying her bone and, wagging her tail, now approached her plate. He patted her on the head and turned back into the house.

There was no one in the living room. He went out on the porch. Miss Gilbert still had his chair. The streetlight at the corner had come on. He dragged the clumsy wooden chair back into the shadow of the vines. "That Jim Mowbray is a remarkable fellow," he said meditatively.

A sound came from Miss Gilbert. A sniff? Or was she merely clearing her throat? "I have no doubt that he's a competent game warden," she said.

"*Game warden?*" Mr. Maury repeated. "Any fool can be a game warden. This fellow's one of the greatest trainers ever lived. Good as Uncle Jim Avent, if you ask me. And he was the greatest trainer and handler this country ever produced, till he got mixed up with those rich Yankee women."

"What happened to him?" Miss Gilbert asked.

"Oh, he didn't lose his virtue," Mr. Maury said coarsely, "they just took him to the cleaner's. . . . But this Mowbray now, he's got as much natural talent as Uncle Jim and I be dog if I don't find him more inventive. He's worked out some shortcuts that'd astonish you. At least they astonish *me*. . . . Take this little bitch. He got her only last September, and look at her . . . just look at her!"

Miss Gilbert made the same sound. A sniff, or he was a Dutchman. "I am no judge of his sportsmanship," she said. "I could never bear to take the life of any fellow creature." And she got up and went into the house.

"No," Mr. Maury said aloud to the semitropical night. "No, but Nature is sure red in your tooth and claw. Nose, too, if you ask me."

The supper bell rang. He entered the dining room before its last peal had died away. Jenny Mowbray, who had been away in Kentucky visiting her father for the last three weeks, was already in her place at the head of the table. She wore a camellia in her brown hair; her face, flushed from the ardors of the kitchen, was almost as pink as the petals of the flower. She made a face at him as he sat down beside her. "You haven't said a word about being glad to see me," she told him, and took his fan from him and fanned herself so vigorously that the damp tendrils of hair curling about her forehead quivered.

"My heart is too full for words," Mr. Maury said.

She gave a childlike giggle and looked about the table with bright eyes; a bantam hen, counting her chickens. She took a fierce, motherly interest in all her boarders. But there was malice in her too. She had him and the cook in stitches sometimes at her imitation of the way old Mr. Sloane walked, one hand curved over the small of his back, protecting his kidneys, Jenny said. She kept a straight face whenever Miss Gilbert's name was mentioned—"She's really a very kind person, Doctor"—but you couldn't tell *him* that she didn't see through that old sack of acid.

The other boarders had assembled. Phyllis, the waitress, brought a great platter through the swinging door. "Chicken and dumplings," Mr. Maury said with satisfaction. He looked at Riva Gaines, the young divorcée who had kept the boardinghouse while Miss Jenny was away. One Sunday Riva had given them hash, baked, it is true, and crusted with cheese, but hash, for all that, from the remains of Friday's roast. Miss Jenny would never do a thing like that. He helped himself to a piece of breast and three tender dumplings and detained Phyllis until he had poured out four ladlefuls of the delicate golden gravy, but before he took a bite he turned to Jenny. "Those shots do your father's arthritis any good?" he asked.

She shook her head. Her soft, red mouth drooped. "Papa's hands are so crippled up he can't even hold the paper to read. But his mind's failed so now he can't remember what he reads. . . . It's a terrible thing to lose your faculties, Doctor."

A pang shot through the knucklebone of Mr. Maury's right index finger. Before him a vista seemed to open, a tunnel, whose low, arched side oozed dark mist. At the far end a stooping, shawled figure slowly raised a clumsy, bandaged hand. From the dank walls the moisture poured faster; the figure was dissolving in gray mist; he could no longer see even the feebly raised right hand. . . . A terrible thing to lose your faculties. . . . What a terrible thing it would be if he lost his mind that to him such a kingdom was! He turned to Jenny, his lip trembling. "I haven't been so well," he said. "My kidneys trouble me a great deal."

She gave his arm a quick pressure. "Dr. Weathers wrote me out a prescription for you."

"Now that was clever of him," he said. "I'll get it filled first thing in the morning."

Riva Gaines asked Mr. Maury to pass her the salt.

"You'd better not eat so much salt," Mr. Maury said. "Don't you know it's fattening?"

Riva shook her long bob back and sat up straighter. "You think I need to diet?" she asked.

Mr. Maury looked at the narrow gray belt that set off a waist that a man might almost have spanned with one hand. She had on her pearl necklace tonight and every blond, sinuously waved hair shone as if it had been polished. "You going juking tonight?" he inquired.

"You going to the movies?" she parried.

"It's Dorothy Lamour," Mr. Maury said. "I'm kind of tired of her."

"If you don't go, will you keep an eye on Benny?"

Mr. Maury allowed his dark, crafty eye to rest on the breasts showing under the gray sweater as firm and pointed as new hickory buds. "You ought to get married again," he said, "then you wouldn't run around so much, nights."

Her full mouth widened in its ready smile as her gray eyes engaged his, but her glance was abstracted; she was thinking about her unhappy marriage. Joe Gaines had had the best-equipped service station in town and the Cadillac agency to boot, but he had got to running with a tough gang and neglected his business and one day walked out, owing everybody in town. Riva had had to go to work at the packing plant, handling the payroll, working overtime two or three nights a week. Still, nobody ever heard her complain. Her eyes were brightening, her smile turned arch. "You didn't need to say that in front of everybody!" she said.

Jim Mowbray came in, greeted the guests, and took his place at the foot of the table.

"You heard that, Jim?" Mr. Maury called.

Jim looked up. "You want to watch her," he said. He had changed into a fresh white suit and wore a new tie in a striking pattern of brown and yellow, but an outdoor air still clung to him. His face was ordinarily the color of cured tobacco but tonight his nose and his forehead—he always pushed his cap to one side when he got excited—carried a fresh burn, and the handsome tie, knotted loosely across his unbuttoned shirt collar, did not conceal the raw, brick-red patch at the base of his powerful neck.

"She's trying to back me into a corner, Jim," Mr. Maury said, elaborating the agreeable fiction that the attractive twenty-eight-year-old woman was attempting to extract an offer of marriage from him in order that she might sue him for breach of promise. "Now what would *you* do in a case like that?"

Jim looked up again, briefly. Mr. Maury had never noticed before how long and thick his lashes were, long enough for a woman. "I wouldn't hardly know how to advise a fellow in a case like that," he said, and looked down at his plate and began to eat, steadily and silently.

The dessert came on: lemon pudding. Mr. Maury shook his head at Phyllis. "You know I can't eat anything with lemon in it."

Mrs. Mowbray started and spoke quietly. "Phyllis, bring Doctor some of that new quince preserves."

Phyllis took the pudding away and set a small glass preserve dish before Mr. Maury. He regarded it with delight and called for more hot biscuits and butter. Miss Gilbert was eyeing the golden crescents, which seemed, so delicate was Miss Jenny's art, to swim in their own honey. He pushed the dish a little to one side of his plate. "How much of these preserves have you got?" he inquired.

Jenny laughed. "A gallon. Enough to last you all winter." She looked at Miss Gilbert. "Miss Anna, I didn't stay on that diet but two days. My brother had a fresh Jersey cow. I declare, the cream was as thick as butter."

"I thought you'd taken on a little weight," Miss Gilbert said, stiffening her slender back.

Mr. Maury pulled the butter plate toward him. "Miss Jenny don't want to get long and stringy," he said. "She's the Junoesque type."

"Now you know I'd look better if I fell off about ten pounds," Jenny said.

"Fifteen," Miss Gilbert said.

Mr. Maury helped himself again to preserves. "A woman gets too thin, her better nature dries up," he said. He looked about the table. "'Who can find a virtuous woman,'" he asked, "'for her price is far above rubies. . . . She seeketh wool, and flax, and worketh willingly with her hands. . . .'"

"I do know how to knit. . ." Jenny said.

"'She looketh well to the ways of her household, and eateth not the bread of idleness,'" Mr. Maury said. He shook a fork, dripping with golden syrup, at Riva Gaines. "You'd better learn how to make preserves like this if you want me to marry you."

She rose from the table, laughing. The two drugstore clerks and old Mr. Sloane followed her out into the hall. Jim, Miss Gilbert, and the Jacksons went, too. There was no one left in the room except himself and Jenny. He pushed his chair back from the table but did not rise, the words he had just spoken still echoing in his mind: ". . .The heart of her husband doth safely trust in her . . . Her children arise up and call her blessed . . ." Jim and Jenny had no children, no young to cherish, unless you could count the bird dogs; there were always half a dozen back there in the yard. Jenny was as crazy about them as Jim was. And she did not spoil them, one of the few women he had ever known who knew how to treat a bird dog. Phyllis moved softly about, loading her tray with dishes. Jenny, who ordinarily, at this hour of the day, was all bustle and directions, sat, leaning her elbow on the table, her dark blue eyes fixed on his face. He met her gaze with surprise. She had never looked at him like that before, as if she had for a long time taken him on his own recommendation and was only now asking herself what manner of man he really was. "You tired?" he asked.

She arched her dark, silky brows. Her expression became lively, though still a little tinged with melancholy. "I've got to go out to see Betty Slocomb with Miss Anna. . . . She can't even sit up in bed now. It's a sad world, Doctor."

"It is, for a fact," Mr. Maury said. "I'm glad I'm not long for it."

"Oh, *you!*" she said. "All the friends you've got!"

"What's friends?" Mr. Maury inquired gloomily. "You say I'm too old to go hunting or fishing. What am I going to do? I'm like Milton in his blindness. 'That one talent it were death to hide, lodged in me useless.' . . . Miss Jenny, you don't know what it is to sit around all day, doing nothing. . . ."

She patted him on the shoulder. "You know I couldn't run this boardinghouse without you. All these people, with all their temperaments. . . ."

"They are a set of catamounts," Mr. Maury said. "Takes somebody to keep 'em in order." He cut himself a plug of tobacco and went out on the porch.

There was no one there except old Mr. Sloane. He asked Mr. Maury if he would like a game of checkers. "I'm not in the mood for it," Mr. Maury said. Mr. Sloane said that he himself didn't care whether he played or not. The two old men sat and silently gazed out on the street where the young people passed, on their way to the movies or the juke joints.

After a little, Riva Gaines came down. Mr. Maury told her that he had decided not to go to the movies and would take care of Benny if he woke. "But he ought not to go waking up so much at night," he added irritably. Riva thanked him in what was for her an unusually subdued tone and went on through the gate, to the house of her intimate friend, Mabel Turner, he supposed. A few minutes later Jim Mowbray came out, with his wife and Miss Gilbert.

"Well, Jim, we got her back," Mr. Maury said.

Jenny settled herself with a hand on her husband's arm while she pinned a fresh camellia in her hair. "Doctor, he didn't write to me but once while I was in Kentucky. Does that look like he wanted me back?"

"He was afraid you would find out how things were going here," Mr. Maury said.

She laughed. "Was it all that bad?"

"Scandalous," Mr. Maury said. "I was about to move over to Wares'," naming the rival boardinghouse of the town.

Jim took a step forward. "Jim," Mr. Maury said, "where'd you go from Tom's place?"

"Over to Tillot's. Started two coveys there."

"That big live oak still standing in his east field?"

"Hurricane seems to have got it." He was turning off on the path to the garage.

"Where you going?" Mr. Maury asked.

"Thought I'd shoot a little pool."

The two women went down the front walk. "Where *you* going?" Mr. Maury called.

Jenny turned around. "Out to Betty Slocomb's. If anybody calls, will you answer the phone, Doctor?"

Mr. Maury assured her that he would. Jim Mowbray brought the car around from the garage and halted it at the gate. He climbed out and held the door open while the women got in. The car moved off down the quiet street.

Mr. Sloane yawned and said he thought he would go up to bed. Mr. Maury rose and dragged his chair over to where a gap in the vines gave a better view of the street. While they had been indoors the night had come closer. The sky was a deep gentian blue. His eyes, as always—for he could not believe that he would rise to a dawn whose doings took no account of fair or foul weather—roamed the heavens until they found the elongated diamond shape, rough with small stars: Cygnus, the Swan, who always flies west in fair weather. He had first seen it when he was ten or eleven years old, coming home from duck hunting with Uncle James. They had been wondering whether it would rain tomorrow, when Uncle James looked up and saw the Bird flying west. He had stopped and made him crane his neck and stare until he saw it, too: "Cygnus, the Swan, Aleck, the shape Zeus took when he wooed Leda. . . ." But Zeus had wooed Io, too, and many another mortal. His wife, Juno, who suffered from jealousy, for all that she was Queen of Heaven, had set her servant, Argus, to spy on them. When Argus fell asleep Juno was so enraged that she tore out his hundred eyes and cast them, not into the heavens, but onto the peacock's tail. . . . Was it in the *Iliad* or the *Odysssey* that Zeus had hung her up for three days in a golden net of old Vulcan's contriving and called on all the gods to come and taunt her? As a boy he had been distressed by the figure she cut. In his childish mind pagan and Christian symbols had mingled. He had always thought of Uncle James's wife, Aunt Victoria, the tall, statuesque, blue-eyed woman who had brought him up, as a sort of queen of heaven. Was that because she was noted for her piety and her good works or because Uncle James sometimes referred to her as "Junoesque"?

Soft, bare feet brushed the hall carpet. Mr. Maury did not turn around.

"Where's my mother?" the little boy asked.

"Said she's going over to Mabel Turner's. . . . What you want?"

"I want a drink of water."

25

Mr. Maury turned around. "When a big man like you wants a drink of water, what's to keep him from getting it out of the cooler himself?"

A thin, towheaded child came slowly through the doorway and fixed Mr. Maury's face with glittering, accusing eyes. "You tell me about Br'er Rabbit," he said.

"I ain't going to do anything of the kind," Mr. Maury said.

The child pressed up against his knee, shaking it a little. "Why?"

Mr. Maury set his hand on the fragile shoulder and held the child's body still. "What you reckon Br'er Rabbit's got them long ears for? He can hear every word we say."

The child tossed his head. In his faded, shrunken pajamas, his shock of almost white hair shining faintly in the moonlight, he looked like some albino woods creature, strayed from its burrow. "We ain't saying anything," he said defiantly.

"He don't like to hear *no* kind of talking at night," Mr. Maury said. He got up. The child caught at his hand. "Where you going?"

Mr. Maury went through the hall and started up the stairs. "I'm going to leave my door open a crack," he said, "and if I hear one peep out of you I ain't going to tell you another story as long as I live."

They were at the head of the stairs. The boy halted at the door of the bedroom he shared with his mother. "Which one you going to tell me in the morning?"

Mr. Maury, in his room, sat down heavily in a chair. "Might be about the time Br'er Fox lost his tail. But it ain't no use talking about it. You ain't going to be quiet." He bent and began unlacing his shoes. The child slipped away. Mr. Maury could hear the door to his bedroom creaking as he stood and swung it to and fro. Mr. Maury went to the closet and got out his bedroom slippers. "Good night," he said. There was a subdued "Good night" and then light, skittering sounds; the little creature was hurling himself into bed. Mr. Maury finished undressing, put on his nightshirt, got into bed, and, propping himself up on two pillows, took up his book, *The Light of Western Stars*, and began to read.

But he had read the book three times before. And Zane Gray, he reflected, was poor pabulum for a man who had known the real thing. Why, he himself, in his faraway youth, had roved all over the West, had seen all that Zane Gray had seen, and more, and could tell about it better. But that was long ago. Now he could only lie in bed and read about what other men did . . . or sit on the porch till they came home and told you what kind of day they had had in the field. . . . Jim Mowbray, out hunting since sunup and going off, after supper, as fresh as a daisy, to shoot pool! A good fellow, Jim, a real Florida cracker, to hear him talk, but he came, like his wife, of good

Kentucky stock. It showed, in unexpected reticences, in little deferential ways toward women. . . . He was blessed with a good wife, the daughter of old Judge Beckitt, who had emigrated here in '98 and then, when he went broke in '32, had gone back to Kentucky to die. She was forty-five to Jim's forty-seven, but she looked older, because she was plump. Miss Gilbert was always at her to reduce, but there was no need for a settled woman to starve herself and get as lean and nervous as a cat, like Riva Gaines, for instance. Jenny Mowbray relished her own food—you could tell that from her rosy complexion—and why shouldn't she, for where could you find a better cook?

The front door opened. There was the sound of voices and steps on the stairs. Two women were ascending. One of them seemed to have to be urged to mount, for he heard a whisper, "Come on. Come *on*, now!"

He leaned forward but could see nothing except the sliver of light from the hall shining through the crack in his door. The steps passed his door, stopped. At the Mowbrays' bedroom or Miss Gilbert's? A door closed. A murmuring, low but ominous, like the gathering hum of bees, was interrupted by a moan. It lasted only a second but it rang on in his head after it had died away.

He got out of bed and took a bottle down from the glass shelf over his washbowl. He had forgotten to take his medicine before he went to bed. This was as good a time as any to take it, now that they had roused him. That was the trouble with a boardinghouse. People came in at all hours of the night. Riva Gaines had probably had too much to drink and some of her gang were seeing her home.

There was a tap on his door. "Well, what is it?" he called, and moved forward, glass in hand.

Miss Gilbert put her head in. "Have you got any spirits of ammonia?"

He shook his head. "Ring up the drugstore."

She seemed not to realize that he was in his nightshirt. She advanced into the room. Her eyes stared palely into his. She wrung her long bird's claws and then with one of them caught at the back of a chair. "I'm afraid to leave her," she said.

Mr. Maury hastily slipped on his trousers. "Who's sick?" he asked when he had finished buttoning the last button.

She raised her head. The cry had come again, a faint, sharp, anguished question. . . . Where had he heard that cry before?

He went with her into the hall. She paused before the door of Mrs. Mowbray's bedroom, opened the door a little, paused again. "Jenny," she said in a low voice, "Doctor Maury wants to see you."

Mr. Maury pushed her aside and entered the room. The ceiling light was on. Jenny lay on the bed, on her back, her arms flung out on each side of her.

Her jaw was slack, her mouth a little open. Her eyes fixed the ceiling widely. He had the feeling that she was trying to stare it down on top of them.

He went nearer the bed. "Miss Jenny. . ." he said gently.

Miss Gilbert was at his side. "*Pool!*" she whispered. "Shooting a little pool!"

Mr. Maury drew back. "There isn't any law against that."

She came closer. "Jenny wanted to get some raspberry ice, to take home, so we stopped at the Mayfair and there they were, out on the floor, *dancing*."

"Dancing," Mr. Maury said slowly. "Jim and that Gaines woman. . . ."

Her eyes shone tigerishly into his. "I wondered how long it would take you to see it. All the time Jenny was in Kentucky. I started to write her. Oh, I was never so torn! There's no faith in men."

Jenny sat up. She passed her hands over her face, hiding her eyes for a second behind her cupped palms, then her hands went to her disordered hair. "You all will have to excuse me," she said, "you'll just have to excuse me." Her voice broke. She shuddered and flung herself downward on the bed.

"Miss Gilbert," Mr. Maury said, "you go downstairs and fix Miss Jenny a hot toddy."

She hesitated, looking from him to the prone figure. "Make it plenty hot," he said calmly, as if he were speaking to a recalcitrant boy in the schoolroom. "It'll cool off some before you get it upstairs."

She was gone. He crossed the room and sat down in a chair beside the open window. The heap on the bed stirred.

"Doctor, you go on to bed," Jenny said weakly.

He shook his head. "You sat up with me when I was sick."

He had been ill with influenza for two weeks. She had nursed him well and he had recovered. . . . But here was a kind of death. She lay there like a shot bird.

"Did you have any talk with him?" he asked.

She sat up on the side of the bed. "He came out to the car. . . . Doctor, he wants to marry that woman."

"He don't want to do anything of the kind," he said.

"Oh, yes," she said, and twisted her delicate mouth that he had always thought so pretty. "I hope they'll be happy. She must want him mighty bad." Her low, hoarse voice broke into a sob. She crossed the room heavily, went behind a screen. He could hear her washing her face and hands. She came out from behind the screen. The pale yellow towel was still crumpled in her hands. She looked at it in a kind of surprise and flung it from her onto the floor. "It doesn't take too long in Florida," she said.

"I wouldn't do anything in a hurry," he said.

She began to cry again. She put her empty hands down at her sides and walked to the window. "To think of her staying here . . . letting me keep her child, nights. . . ."

"Women'll do anything these days," Mr. Maury said.

She turned toward him a face stonier for having been bathed in fresh tears. "I'm going to call Mr. Murphy in the morning."

Sanders Murphy had been her father's law partner. He had influence with the circuit judge. Jim Mowbray would be divorced and married again before he knew what had happened to him.

"You don't need to go so fast," he said. "Listen . . . Miss Jenny. . . ."

She left the window. Her head cocked on one side, her eyes bright with tears, she spoke musingly: "I think I'll sell this place and go to Kentucky. . . ."

"What about me?" his heart cried out. "You'll run off to Kentucky. I'll have to find some other place to live." And he could not live just anywhere. She knew that.

"Yes," she said. "I'll list it—tomorrow."

"You could get your money out, all right," he said drearily.

Miss Gilbert came back with the toddy. He said good night and went to his room, put his coat on over his nightshirt, and went down the stairs, stumbling on the last step, and out onto the porch.

There was no sound anywhere on the street. The town slept. He wondered where Jim and that girl were. They would not dare to come back to the house tonight. In some tourist cabin, probably, some place that took fly-by-nighters. Well, they might as well get used to being on the bum. Jim Mowbray was not a man to stand up to women . . . as fine a wing shot as ever lived, as gifted a handler! His heavy hand fell slack on his knee. There were places on this earth's surface that he would never revisit. . . . Oh, the light on the long grass, on the green, willowy pool! They did not know why you went or where, but let a man break a lockstep and go over the hill and they grew frightened and watched his return with implacable eyes; sometimes they denied him the privilege of resuming his chains. . . .

Miss Gilbert came out on the porch and sat down in the chair next to his. She had on a white, wooly wrap and held a glass full of some milky fluid in her hand. "Will you have a glass of Theno-Malt?" she asked.

"No," Mr. Maury said. *Sthenos, the Greek word for strength. As a man's days, so is his strength . . . Seventy-five years old and no place to lay his head.*

"She got quieter before I left. I read to her a little."

"And what, pray, did you select to read to her?"

She turned a cold, bird's eye on him as she held up her book—she had as many litanies as an orthodox Catholic. She said: "It is at a time like this, when the hard core of the personality is shattered, that the real self has a chance to emerge. . . ."

"*Women!*" Mr. Maury cried passionately. "I've been watching them. They'll rock the world if they don't look out!"

Her white-shod feet rustled on the worn boards. Her shawl fluttered as she passed, bearing the empty glass before her like a chalice. He turned his face up to the night. The heavens were dark, for all their gold stars. It would be a long time till morning. When it came they would shut their eyes against the light and lie quiet until the brain, rattling inside the cold skull, set them moving about the hateful business of the day. . . . There were no women in his life now, and yet he seemed to have been in servitude to them all his life. He had loved his wife. Until the day of her death the mere touch of her hand could stir him. But she had been dead for fifteen years. He seldom saw his daughter, a dark, flighty girl, bound for an unhappy life. He had never known his mother. Orphaned at four and raised by Uncle James and Aunt Vic. . . . Aunt Vic had pretended that she was taking him to Grassdale to live to teach him Latin and mathematics, but it was really to save his immortal soul. The prayers, morning and evening! Uncle James said that she trained him and Julian, her son, like bird dogs, to charge, that is, to kneel, at one word of command, to point in prayer at another. And it was a fact that they used to kneel at one wave of her fine, long-fingered hand and start praying at the next. He had been kneeling at her bedside, praying, when she died. She had been ill so long that the family was worn out. He had been called in to sit with her while old Aunt Beck got some sleep. She had seemed better that evening and had talked to him for a while about his soul. It grew dark. Her voice trailed off. Her hand moved restlessly on the counterpane. He slid to his knees and began mumbling the Angelic Salutation:

Hail, Mary, full of grace! The Lord is with thee: blessed art thou among women . . .

She uttered a cry and raised her head from the pillow. Her eyes fixed a point beyond his shoulder. He turned and saw nothing. Another, softer sound broke from her and her head fell back on the pillow and she was still. As he ran, weeping, to tell the others that she was gone, he had wondered what it was that he could not see. But that had been a long time ago, when he was a boy of thirteen. He had not thought about such things often since that time. . . . Holy Mary, Mother of God, pray for us sinners, now and at the *hour* . . . of our death.

3

THE PEACH STONE

Paul Horgan

As they all knew, the drive would take them about four hours, all the way to Weed, where *she* came from. They knew the way from traveling it so often, first in the old car, and now in the new one; new to them, that is, for they'd bought it secondhand, last year, when they were down in Roswell to celebrate their tenth wedding anniversary. They still thought of themselves as a young couple, and *he* certainly did crazy things now and then, and always laughed her out of it when she was cross at the money going where it did, instead of where it ought to go. But there was so much droll orneriness in him when he did things like that that she couldn't stay mad, hadn't the heart, and the harder up they got, the more she loved him, and the little ranch he'd taken her to in the rolling plains just below the mountains.

This was a day in spring, rather hot, and the mountain was that melting blue that reminded you of something you could touch, like a china bowl. Over the sandy brown of the earth there was coming a green shadow. The air struck cool and deep in their breasts. *He* came from Texas, as a boy, and had lived here in New Mexico ever since. The word *home* always gave *her* a picture of unpainted, mouse-brown wooden houses in a little cluster by the rocky edge of the last mountain-step—the town of Weed, where Jodey Powers met and married her ten years ago.

They were heading back that way today.

Jodey was driving, squinting at the light. It never seemed so bright as now, before noon, as they went up the valley. He had a rangy look at the wheel of the light blue Chevvie—a bony man, but still fuzzed over with some look of a cub about him, perhaps the way he moved his limbs, a slight appealing clumsiness, that drew on thoughtless strength. On a rough road, he flopped and swayed at the wheel as if he were on a bony horse that galloped a little sidewise. His skin was red-brown from the sun. He had pale blue eyes, edged with dark lashes. *She* used to say he "turned them on" her, as if they were lights. He was wearing his suit, brown-striped, and a fresh blue shirt, too big at the neck. But he looked well dressed. But he would have looked that way naked, too, for he communicated his physical essence through any covering. It was what spoke out from him to anyone who encountered him. Until Cleotha married him, it had given him a time, all right, he used to reflect.

Next to him in the front seat of the sedan was Buddy, their nine-year-old boy, who turned his head to stare at them both, his father and mother.

She was in back.

On the seat beside her was a wooden box, sandpapered, but not painted. Over it lay a baby's coverlet of pale yellow flannel with cross-stitched flowers down the middle in a band of bright colors. The mother didn't touch the box except when the car lurched or the tires danced over corrugated places in the gravel highway. Then she steadied it, and kept it from creeping on the seat cushions. In the box was coffined the body of their dead child, a two-year-old girl. They were on their way to Weed to bury it there.

In the other corner of the back seat sat Miss Latcher, the teacher. They rode in silence, and Miss Latcher breathed deeply of the spring day, as they all did, and she kept summoning to her aid the fruits of her learning. She felt this was a time to be intelligent, and not to give way to feelings.

The child was burned to death yesterday, playing behind the adobe chickenhouse at the edge of the arroyo out back, where the fence always caught the tumbleweeds. Yesterday, in a twist of wind, a few sparks from the kitchen chimney fell in the dry tumbleweeds and set them ablaze. Jodey had always meant to clear the weeds out: never seemed to get to it: told Cleotha he'd get to it next Saturday morning, before going down to Roswell: but Saturdays went by, and the wind and the sand drove the weeds into a barrier at the fence, and they would look at it every day without noticing, so habitual had the sight become. And so for many a spring morning, the little girl had played out there, behind the gray stucco house, whose adobe bricks showed through in one or two places.

The car had something loose; they believed it was the left rear fender: it chattered and wrangled over the gravel road.

Last night Cleotha stopped her weeping.

Today something happened; it came over her as they started out of the ranch lane, which curved up toward the highway. She looked as if she were trying to see something beyond the edge of Jodey's head and past the windshield.

Of course, she had sight in her eyes; she could not refuse to look at the world. As the car drove up the valley that morning, she saw in two ways—one, as she remembered the familiar sights of this region where she lived; the other, as if for the first time she were really seeing, and not simply looking. Her heart began to beat faster as they drove. It seemed to knock at her breast as if to come forth and hurry ahead of her along the sunlighted lanes of the life after today. She remembered thinking that her head might be a little giddy, what with the sorrow in her eyes so bright and slowly shining. But it didn't matter what did it. Ready never to look at anyone or anything again, she kept still; and through the window, which had a meandering crack in it like a river on a map, all that she looked upon seemed dear to her. . . .

Jodey could only drive. He watched the road as if he expected it to rise up and smite them all over into the canyon, where the trees twinkled and flashed with bright drops of light on their new-varnished leaves. Jodey watched the road and said to himself that if it thought it could turn him over or make him scrape the rocks along the near side of the hill they were going around, if it thought for one minute that he was not master of this car, this road, this journey, why, it was just crazy. The wheels spraying the gravel across the surface of the road traveled on outward from his legs; his muscles were tight and felt tired as if he were running instead of riding. He tried to *think*, but he could not; that is, nothing came about that he would speak to her of, and he believed that she sat there, leaning forward, waiting for him to say something to her.

But this he could not do, and he speeded up a little, and his jaw made hard knots where he bit on his own rage; and he saw a lump of something coming in the road, and it aroused a positive passion in him. He aimed directly for it, and charged it fast, and hit it. The car shuddered and skidded, jolting them. Miss Latcher took a sharp breath inward, and put out her hand to touch someone, but did not reach anyone. Jodey looked for a second into the rear-view mirror above him, expecting something; but his wife was looking out of the window beside her, and if he could believe his eyes, she was smiling, holding her mouth with her fingers pinched up in a little claw.

The blood came up from under his shirt, he turned dark, and a sting came across his eyes.

He couldn't explain why he had done a thing like that to her, as if it were she he was enraged with, instead of himself.

He wanted to stop the car and get out and go around to the back door on the other side, and open it, and take her hands, bring her out to stand before him in the road, and hang his arms around her until she would be locked upon him. This made a picture that he indulged like a dream, while the car ran on, and he made no change, but drove as before. . . .

The little boy, Buddy, regarded their faces, again, and again, as if to see in their eyes what had happened to them.

He felt the separateness of the three.

He was frightened by their appearance of indifference to each other. His father had a hot and drowsy look, as if he had just come out of bed. There was something in his father's face that made it impossible for Buddy to say anything. He turned around and looked at his mother, but she was gazing out the window, and did not see him; and until she should see him, he had no way of speaking to her, if not with his words, then with his eyes, but if she should happen to look at him, why, he would wait to see what she looked *like*, and if she *did*, why, then he would smile at her, because he loved her, but he would have to know first if she was still his mother, and if every-thing was all right, and things weren't blown to smithereens—bla-a-ash! wh-o-o-m!—the way the dynamite did when the highway came past their ranch house, and the men worked out there for months, and whole hillsides came down at a time. All summer long, that was, always something to see. The world, the family, he, between his father and mother, had been safe.

He silently begged her to face toward him. There was no security until she should do so.

"Mumma?"

But he said it to himself, and she did not hear him this time, and it seemed intelligent to him to turn around, make a game of it (the way things often were worked out), and face the front, watch the road, delay as long as he possibly could bear to, and *then* turn around again, and *this* time, why, she would probably be looking at him all the time, and it would *be*: it would simply *be*.

So he obediently watched the road, the white gravel ribbon passing under their wheels as steadily as time.

He was a sturdy little boy, and there was a silver nap of child's dust on his face, over his plum-red cheeks. He smelled rather like a raw potato that has just been pared. The sun crowned him with a ring of light on his dark hair.

What Cleotha was afraid to do was break the spell by saying anything or looking at any of them. This was *vision*, it was all she could think; never had anything looked so in all her life; everything made her heart lift, when she had believed this morning, after the night, that it would never lift again. There wasn't anything to compare her grief to. She couldn't think of any-thing to answer the death of her tiny child with. In her first hours of hardly believing what had happened, she had felt her own flesh and tried to imagine how it would have been if she could have borne the fire instead of the child. But all she got out of that was a longing avowal to herself of how gladly she would have borne it. Jodey had lain beside her, and she clung to his hand until she heard how he breathed off to sleep. Then she had let him go, and had wept at what seemed faithless in him. She had wanted his mind beside her then. It seemed to her that the last degree of her grief was the compassion she had to bestow upon him while he slept.

But she had found this resource within her, and from that time on, her weeping stopped.

It was like a wedding of pride and duty within her. There was nothing she could not find within herself, if she had to, now, she believed.

And so this morning, getting on toward noon, as they rode up the valley, climbing all the way, until they would find the road to turn off on, which would take them higher and higher before they dropped down toward Weed on the other side, she welcomed the sights of that dusty trip. Even if she had spoken her vision aloud, it would not have made sense to the others.

Look at that orchard of peach trees, she thought. I never saw such color as this year; the trees are like lamps, with the light coming from within. It must be the sunlight shining from the other side, and of course, the petals are very thin, like the loveliest silk; so any light that shines upon them will pierce right through them and glow on this side. But they are so bright! When I was a girl at home, up to Weed, I remember we had an orchard of peach trees, but the blossoms were always a deeper pink than down here in the valley.

My! I used to catch them up by the handful, and I believed when I was a girl that if I crushed them and tied them in a handkerchief and carried the handkerchief in my bosom, I would come to smell like peach blossoms and have the same high pink in my face, and the girls I knew said that if I took a peach *stone* and held it *long enough* in my hand, it would *sprout*; and I dreamed of this one time, though, of course I knew it was nonsense; but that was how children thought and talked in those days—we all used to pretend that *nothing* was impossible, if you simply did it hard enough and long enough.

But nobody wanted to hold a peach stone in their hand until it *sprouted*, to find out, and we used to laugh about it, but I think we believed it. I think I believed it.

It seemed to me, in between my *sensible* thoughts, a thing that any woman could probably do. It seemed to me like a parable in the Bible. I could preach you a sermon about it this day.

I believe I see a tree down there in that next orchard which is dead; it has old black sprigs, and it looks twisted by rheumatism. There is one little shoot of leaves up on the top branch, and that is all. No, it is not dead, it is aged, it can no longer put forth blossoms in a swarm like pink butterflies; but there is that one little swarm of green leaves—it is just about the prettiest thing I've seen all day, and I thank God for it, for if there's anything I love, it is to see something growing. . . .

Miss Latcher had on her cloth gloves now, which she had taken from her blue cloth bag a little while back. The little winds that tracked through the moving car sought her out and chilled her nose, and the tips of her ears, and her long fingers, about which she had several times gone to visit various doctors. They had always told her not to worry, if her fingers seemed cold, and her hands moist. It was just a nervous condition, nothing to take very seriously; a good hand lotion might help the sensation, and in any case, some kind of digital exercise was a good thing—did she perhaps play the piano. It always seemed to her that doctors never *paid any attention* to her.

Her first name was Arleen, and she always considered this a very pretty name, prettier than Cleotha; and she believed that there was such a thing as an *Arleen look*, and if you wanted to know what it was, simply look at her. She had a long face, and pale hair; her skin was white, and her eyes were light blue. She was wonderfully clean, and used no cosmetics. She was a girl from "around here," but she had gone away to college, to study for her career, and what she had known as a child was displaced by what she had heard in classrooms. And she had to admit it: people *here* and *away* were not much alike. The men were different. She couldn't imagine marrying a rancher and "sacrificing" everything she had learned in college.

This poor little thing in the other corner of the car, for instance: she seemed dazed by what had happened to her—all she could do evidently was sit and stare out the window. And that man in front, simply driving, without a word. What did they have? What was their life like? They hardly had good clothes to drive to Roswell in, when they had to go to the doctor, or on some social errand.

But I must not think uncharitably, she reflected, and sat in an attitude of sustained sympathy, with her face composed in Arleenish interest and tact. The assumption of a proper aspect of grief and feeling produced the most curious effect within her, and by her attitude of concern she was suddenly reminded of the thing that always made her feel like weeping, though of course, she never did, but when she stopped and *thought—*

Like that painting at college, in the long hallway leading from the Physical Education lecture hall to the stairway down to the girls' gym: an enormous picture depicting the Agony of the Christian Martyrs, in ancient Rome. There were some days when she simply couldn't look at it; and there were others when she would pause and see those maidens with their tear-ful faces raised in calm prowess, and in them, she would find herself—they were all Arleens; and after she would leave the picture she would proceed in her imagination to the arena, and there she would know with exquisite sorrow and pain the ordeals of two thousand years ago, instead of those in her own lifetime. She thought of the picture now, and traded its remote sorrows for those of today until she had sincerely forgotten the mother and the father and the little brother of the dead child with whom she was riding up the spring-turning valley, where noon was warming the dust that arose from the graveled highway. It was white dust, and it settled over them in an enriching film, ever so finely. . . .

Jody Powers had a fantastic scheme that he used to think about for taking and baling tumbleweed and make a salable fuel out of it. First, you'd compress it—probably down at the cotton compress in Roswell—where a loose bale was wheeled in under the great power-drop, and when the Negro at the handle gave her a yank, down came the weight, and packed the bale into a little thing, and then they let the steam exhaust go, and the press sighed once or twice, and just seemed to *lie* there, while the men ran wires through the gratings of the press and tied them tight. Then up came the weight, and out came the bale.

If he did that to enough bales of tumbleweed, he believed he'd get rich. Burn? It burned like a house afire. It had oil in it, somehow, and the thing to do was to get it in shape for use as a fuel. Imagine all the tumbleweed that blew around the state of New Mexico in the fall, and sometimes all winter. In the winter, the weeds were black and brittle. They cracked when they blew against fence posts, and if one lodged there, then another one caught at its thorny lace; and next time it blew, and the sand came trailing, and the tumbleweeds rolled, they'd pile up at the same fence and built out, locked together against the wires. The wind drew through them, and the sand dropped around them. Soon there was a solid-looking but airy bank of tumbleweeds built right to the top of the fence, in a long windward slope; and the next time the wind blew, and the weeds came, they would roll up the little hill of brittle twigs and leap off the other side of the fence, for all the world like horses taking a jump, and go galloping ahead of the wind across the next pasture on the plains, a black and witchy procession.

If there was an arroyo, they gathered there. They backed up in the miniature canyons of dirt-walled watercourses, which were dry except when it rained hard up in the hills. Out behind the house, the arroyo had filled up with tumbleweeds; and in November, when it blew so hard and so cold, but without bringing any snow, some of the tumbleweeds had climbed out and scattered, and a few had tangled at the back fence, looking like rusted barbed wire. Then there came a few more; all winter the bank grew. Many times he'd planned to get out back there and clear them away, just e-e-ease them off away from the fence posts, so's not to catch the wood up, and then set a match to the whole thing, and in five minutes, have it all cleared off. If he did like one thing, it was a neat place.

How Cleotha laughed at him sometimes when he said that, because she knew that as likely as not he would forget to clear the weeds away. And if he'd said it once he'd said it a thousand times, that he was going to gather up that pile of scrap iron from the front yard, and haul it to Roswell, and sell it—old car parts, and the fenders off a truck that had turned over up on the highway, which he'd salvaged with the aid of the driver.

But the rusting iron was still there, and he had actually come to have a feeling of fondness for it. If someone were to appear one night and silently make off with it, he'd be aroused the next day, and demand to know who had robbed him: for it was dear junk, just through lying around and belonging to him. What was his was part of him, even that heap of fenders that rubbed off on your clothes with a rusty powder, like a caterpillar fur.

But even by thinking hard about all such matters, treading upon the fringe of what had happened yesterday, he was unable to make it all seem long ago, and a matter of custom, and even of indifference. There was no getting away from it—if anybody was to blame for the terrible moments of yesterday afternoon, when the wind scattered a few sparks from the chimney of the kitchen stove, why, he was.

Jodey Powers never claimed to himself or anybody else that he was any *better* man than another. But everything he knew and hoped for, every reassurance his body had had from other people, and the children he had begotten, had made him know that he was *as good* a man as any.

And of this knowledge he was now bereft.

If he had been alone in his barrenness, he could have solaced himself with heroic stupidities. He could have produced out of himself abominations, with the amplitude of biblical despair. But he wasn't alone; there they sat, there was Buddy beside him, and Clee in back, even the teacher, Arleen—even to her he owed some return of courage.

All he could do was drive the damned car, and keep *thinking* about it.

He wished he could think of something to say, or else that Clee would.

But they continued in silence, and he believed that it was one of his making. . . .

The reverie of Arleen Latcher made her almost ill, from the sad, sweet experiences she had entered into with those people so long ago. How wonderful it was to have such a rich life, just looking up things!—And the most wonderful thing of all was that even if they were beautiful, and wore semi-transparent garments that fell to the ground in graceful folds, the maidens were all pure. It made her eyes swim to think how innocent they went to their death. Could anything be more beautiful, and reassuring, than this? Far, far better. Far better those hungry lions, than the touch of lustful men. Her breath left her for a moment, and she closed her eyes, and what threatened her with real feeling—the presence of the Powers family in the faded blue sedan climbing through the valley sunlight toward the turnoff that led to the mountain road—was gone. Life's breath on her cheek was not so close. Oh, others had suffered. She could suffer.

"All that pass by clap their hands at thee: they hiss and wag their heads at the daughter of Jerusalem—"

This image made her wince, as if she herself had been hissed and wagged at. Everything she knew made it possible for her to see herself as a proud and threatened virgin of Bible times, which were more real to her than many of the years she had lived through. Yet must not Jerusalem have sat in country like this with its sandy hills, the frosty stars that were so bright at night, the simple Mexicans riding their burros as if to the Holy Gates? We often do not see our very selves, she would reflect, gazing ardently at the unreal creature that the name Arleen brought to life in her mind.

On her cheeks there had appeared two islands of color, as if she had a fever. What she strove to save by her anguished retreats into the memories of the last days of the Roman Empire was surely crumbling away from her. She said to herself that she must not give way to it, and that she was just wrought up; the fact that she really *didn't* feel anything—in fact, it was a pity that she *couldn't* take that little Mrs. Powers in her arms, and comfort her, just *let* her go ahead and cry, and see if it wouldn't probably help some. But Miss Latcher was aware that she felt nothing that related to the Powers family and their trouble.

Anxiously she searched her heart again, and wooed back the sacrifice of the tribe of heavenly Arleens marching so certainly toward the lions. But they did not answer her call to mind, and she folded her cloth-gloved hands and pressed them together, and begged of herself that she might think of some way to comfort Mrs. Powers; for if she could do that, it might fill her own empty heart until it became a cup that would run over. . . .

Cleotha knew Buddy wanted her to see him; but though her heart turned toward him, as it always must, no matter what he asked of her, she was this time afraid to do it because if she ever lost the serenity of her sight now she might never recover it this day; and the heaviest trouble was still before her.

So she contented herself with Buddy's look as it reached her from the side of her eye. She glimpsed his head and neck, like a young cat's, the wide bones behind the ears, and the smooth but visible cords of his nape, a sight of him that always made her want to laugh because it was so pathetic. When she caressed him she often fondled those strenuous hollows behind his ears. Heaven only knew, she would think, what went on within the shell of that topknot! She would pray between her words and feelings that those unseen thoughts in the boy's head were ones that would never trouble him. She was often amazed at things in him that she recognized as being like herself; and at those of Buddy's qualities which came from some alien source, she suffered pangs of doubt and fear. He was so young to be a stranger to her!

The car went around the curve that hugged the rocky fall of a hill; and on the other side of it, a green quilt of alfalfa lay sparkling darkly in the light. Beyond that, to the right of the road, the land leveled out, and on a sort of platform of swept earth stood a two-room hut of adobe. It had a few stones cemented against the near corner, to give it strength. Clee had seen it a hundred times—the place where that old man Melendez lived, and where his wife had died a few years ago. He was said to be simple-minded and claimed he was a hundred years old. In the past, riding by here, she had more or less delicately made a point of looking the other way. It often distressed her to think of such a helpless old man, too feeble to do anything but crawl out when the sun was bright and the wall was warm, and sit there, with his milky gaze resting on the hills he had known since he was born, and had never left. Somebody came to feed him once a day, and see if he was clean enough to keep his health. As long as she could remember, there'd been some kind of dog at the house. The old man had sons and grandsons and great-grandsons—you might say a whole orchard of them, sprung from this one tree that was dying, but that still held a handful of green days in its ancient veins.

Before the car had quite gone by, she had seen him. The sun was bright, and the wall must have been warm, warm enough to give his shoulders and back a reflection of the heat that was all he could feel. He sat there on his weathered board bench, his hands on his branch of apple tree that was smooth and shiny from use as a cane. His house door was open, and a deep tunnel of shade lay within the sagged box of the opening. Cleotha leaned forward to see him, as if to look at him were one of her duties today. She saw his jaw moving up and down, not chewing, but just opening and closing. In the wind and flash of the car going by, she could not hear him; but from his closed eyes, and his moving mouth, and the way his head was raised, she wouldn't have been surprised if she had heard him singing. He was singing some thread of song, and it made her smile to imagine what kind of noise it made, a wisp of voice.

She was perplexed by a feeling of joyful fullness in her breast, at the sight of the very same old witless sire from whom in the past she had turned away her eyes out of delicacy and disgust.

40

The last thing she saw as they went by was his dog, who came around the corner of the house with a caracole. He was a mongrel puppy, partly hound—a comedian by nature. He came prancing outrageously up to the old man's knees, and invited his response, which he did not get. But as if his master were as great a wag as he, he hurled himself backward, pretending to throw himself recklessly into pieces. Everything on him flopped and was flung by his idiotic energy. It was easy to imagine, watching the puppy-fool, that the sunlight had entered him as it had entered the old man. Cleotha was reached by the hilarity of the hound, and when he tripped over himself and plowed the ground with his flapping jowls, she wanted to laugh out loud.

But they were past the place, and she winked back the merriment in her eyes, and she knew that it was something she could never have told the others about. What it stood for, in her, they would come to know in other ways, as she loved them. . . .

Jodey was glad of one thing. He had telephoned from Hondo last night, and everything was to be ready at Weed. They would drive right up the hill to the family burial ground. They wouldn't have to wait for anything. He was glad, too, that the wind wasn't blowing. It always made his heart sink when the wind rose on the plains and began to change the sky with the color of dust.

Yesterday: it was all he could see, however hard he was *thinking* about everything else.

He'd been on his horse, coming back down the pasture that rose up behind the house across the arroyo, nothing particular in mind—except to make a joke with himself about how far along the peaches would get before the frost killed them all, *snap*, in a single night, like that—when he saw the column of smoke rising from the tumbleweeds by the fence. Now who could've lighted them, he reflected, following the black smoke up on its billows into the sky. There was just enough wind idling across the long front of the hill to bend the smoke and trail it away at an angle, toward the blue.

The hillside, the fire, the wind, the column of smoke.

Oh my God! And the next minute he was tearing down the hill as fast as his horse could take him, and the fire—he could see the flames now—the fire was like a bank of yellow rags blowing violently and torn in the air, rag after rag tearing up from the ground. Cleotha was there, and in a moment, so was he, but they were too late. The baby was unconscious. They took her up and hurried to the house, the back way where the screen door was standing open with its spring trailing on the ground. When they got inside where it seemed so dark and cool, they held the child between them, fearing to lay her down. They called for Buddy, but he was still at school up the road, and would not be home until the orange school bus stopped by their mailbox out front at the highway after four o'clock. The fire poured in cracking tumult through the weeds. In ten minutes they were only little airy lifts of ash off the ground. Everything was black. There were three fence posts still afire; the wires were hot. The child was dead. They let her down on their large bed.

He could remember every word Clee had said to him. They were not many, and they shamed, in his heart, because he couldn't say a thing. He comforted her, and held her while she wept. But if he had spoken then, or now, riding in the car, all he could have talked about was the image of the blowing rags of yellow fire, and blue, blue, plaster blue sky above and beyond the mountains. But he believed that she knew why he seemed so short with her. He hoped earnestly that she knew. He might just be wrong. She might be blaming him, and keeping so still because it was more proper, now, to *be* still than full of reproaches.

But of the future, he was entirely uncertain; and he drove, and came to the turnoff, and they started winding in back among the sand hills that lifted them toward the rocky slopes of the mountains. Up and up they went; the air was so clear and thin that they felt transported, and across the valleys that dropped between the grand shoulders of the pine-haired slopes, the air looked as if it were blue breath from the trees.

Cleotha was blinded by a dazzling light in the distance, ahead of them, on the road.

It was a ball of diamond-brilliant light.

It danced, and shook, and quivered above the road far, far ahead. It seemed to be traveling between the pine trees on either side of the road, and somewhat above the road, and it was like nothing she had ever seen before. It was the most magic and exquisite thing she had ever seen, and wildly, even hopefully as a child is hopeful when there is a chance and a need for something miraculous to happen, she tried to explain it to herself. It could be a star in the daytime, shaking and quivering and traveling ahead of them, as if to lead them. It was their guide. It was shaped like a small cloud, but it was made of shine, and dazzle, and quiver. She held her breath for fear it should vanish, but it did not, and she wondered if the others in the car were smitten with the glory of it as she was.

It was brighter than the sun, whiter; it challenged the daytime, and obscured everything near it by its blaze of flashing and dancing light.

It was almost as if she had approached perfect innocence through her misery, and were enabled to receive portents that might not be visible to anyone else. She closed her eyes for a moment.

But the road curved, and everything traveling on it took the curve too, and the trembling pool of diamond-light ahead lost its liquid splendor, and turned into the tin signs on the back of a huge oil truck which was toiling over the mountain, trailing its links of chain behind.

When Clee looked again, the star above the road was gone. The road and the angle of the sun to the mountaintop and the two cars climbing upward had lost their harmony to produce the miracle. She saw the red oil truck, and simply saw it, and said to herself that the sun might have reflected off the big tin signs on the back of it. But she didn't believe it, for she was not thinking, but rather dreaming; fearful of awakening. . . .

The high climb up this drive always made Miss Latcher's ears pop, and she had discovered once that to swallow often prevented the disagreeable sensation. So she swallowed. Nothing happened to her ears. But she continued to swallow, and feel her ears with her cloth-covered fingers, but what really troubled her now would not be downed, and it came into her mouth as a taste; she felt giddy—that was the altitude, of course—when they got down the other side, she would be all right.

What it was was perfectly clear to her, for that was part of having an education and a trained mind—the processes of thought often went right on once you started them going.

Below the facts of this small family, in the worst trouble it had ever known, lay the fact of envy in Arleen's breast.

It made her head swim to realize this. But she envied them their entanglement with one another, and the dues they paid each other in the humility of the duty they were performing on this ride, to the family burial ground at Weed. Here she sat riding with them, to come along and be of help to them, and she was no help. She was unable to swallow the lump of desire that rose in her throat, for life's uses, even such bitter ones as that of the Powers family today. It had been filling her gradually, all the way over on the trip, this feeling of jealousy and degradation.

Now it choked her and she knew she had tried too hard to put from her the thing that threatened her, which was the touch of life through anybody else. She said to herself that she must keep control of herself.

But Buddy turned around again, just then, slowly, as if he were a young male cat who just happened to be turning around to see what he could see, and he looked at his mother with his large eyes, so like his father's: pale petal-blue, with drops of light like the centers of cats' eyes, and dark lashes. He had a solemn look, when he saw his mother's face, and he prayed for her silently to acknowledge him. If she didn't, why, he was still alone. He would never again feel safe about running off to the highway to watch the scrapers work, or the huge Diesel oil tankers go by, or the cars with strange license plates—of which he had already counted thirty-two different kinds, his collection, as he called it. So if she didn't see him, why, what might he find when he came home at times like those, when he went off for a little while just to play?

They were climbing down the other side of the ridge now. In a few minutes they would be riding into Weed. The sights as they approached were like images of awakening to Cleotha. Her heart began to hurt when she saw them. She recognized the tall iron smokestack of the sawmill. It showed above the trees down on the slope ahead of them. There was a stone house that had been abandoned even when she was a girl at home here, and its windows and door standing open always seemed to her to depict a face with an expression of dismay. The car dropped farther down—they were making that last long curve of the road to the left—and now the town stood visible, with the sunlight resting on so many of the unpainted houses and turning their weathered gray to a dark silver. Surely they must be ready for them, these houses: all had been talked over by now. They could all mention that they knew Cleotha as a little girl.

She lifted her head.

There were claims upon her.

Buddy was looking at her soberly, trying to predict to himself how she would *be*. He was ready to echo with his own small face whatever her face would show him.

Miss Latcher was watching the two of them. Her heart was racing in her breast.

The car slowed up. Now Cleotha could not look out the windows at the wandering earthen street, and the places alongside it. They would have to drive right through town, to the gently rising hill on the other side.

"Mumma?" asked the boy softly.

Cleotha winked both eyes at him, and smiled, and leaned toward him a trifle.

And then he blushed, his eyes swam with happiness, and he smiled back at her, and his face poured forth such radiance that Miss Latcher took one look at him, and with a choke, burst into tears.

She wept into her hands, her gloves were moistened, her square shoulders rose to her ears, and she was overwhelmed by what the mother had been able to do for the boy. She shook her head and made long gasping sobs. Her sense of betrayal was not lessened by the awareness that she was weeping for herself.

Cleotha leaned across to her, and took her hand, and murmured to her. She comforted her, gently.

"Hush, honey, you'll be all right. Don't you cry, now. Don't you think about us. We're almost there, and it'll soon be over. God knows you were mighty sweet to come along and be with us. Hush, now, Arleen, you'll have Buddy crying too."

But the boy was simply watching the teacher, in whom the person he knew so well every day in school had broken up, leaving an unfamiliar likeness. It was like seeing a reflection in a pond, and then throwing a stone in. The reflection disappeared in ripples of something else.

Arleen could not stop.

The sound of her 'ooping made Jodey furious. He looked into the rearview mirror and saw his wife patting her and comforting her. Cleotha looked so white and strained that he was frightened, and he said out, without turning around: "Arleen, you cut that out, you shut up, now. I won't have you wearin' down Clee, God damn it, you quit it!"

But this rage, which arose from a sense of justice, made Arleen feel guiltier than ever; and she laid her head against the car window, and her sobs drummed her brow bitterly on the glass.

"Hush," whispered Cleotha, but she could do no more, for they were arriving at the hillside, and the car was coming to a stop. They must awaken from this journey, and come out onto the ground, and begin to toil their way up the yellow hill, where the people were waiting. Over the ground grew yellow grass that was turning to green. It was like velvet, showing dark or light, according to the breeze and the golden afternoon sunlight. It was a generous hill, curving easily and gradually as it rose. Beyond it was only the sky, for the mountains faced it from behind the road. It was called Schoolhouse Hill, and at one time, the whole thing had belonged to Cleotha's father; and even before there was any schoolhouse crowning its noble swell of earth, the departed members of his family had been buried halfway up the gentle climb.

Jodey helped her out of the car, and he tried to talk with her with his holding fingers. He felt her trembling, and she shook her head at him. Then she began to walk up there, slowly. He leaned into the car and took the covered box in his arms, and followed her. Miss Latcher was out of the car on her side, hiding from them, her back turned, while she used her handkerchief and positively clenched herself back into control of her thoughts and sobs. When she saw that they weren't waiting for her, she hurried, and in humility, reached for Buddy's hand to hold it for him as they walked. He let her have it, and he marched, watching his father, whose hair was blowing in the wind and sunshine. From behind, Jodey looked like just a kid. . . .

And now for Cleotha her visions on the journey appeared to have some value, and for a little while longer, when she needed it most, the sense of being in blind communion with life was granted her, at the little graveside where all those kind friends were gathered on the slow slope up the hill on the summit of which was the schoolhouse of her girlhood.

It was afternoon, and they were all kneeling toward the upward rise, and Judge Crittenden was reading the prayer book.

Everything left them but a sense of their worship, in the present.

And a boy, a late scholar, is coming down the hill from the school, the sunlight edging him; and his wonder at what the people kneeling there are doing, is, to Cleotha, the most memorable thing she is to look upon today; for she has resumed the life of her infant daughter, whom they are burying, and on whose behalf, something rejoices in life anyway, as if to ask the mother whether love itself is not ever-living. And she watches the boy come discreetly down the hill, trying to keep away from them, but large-eyed with a hunger *to know* which claims all acts of life, for him, and for those who will be with him later; and his respectful curiosity about those kneeling mourners, the edge of sunlight along him as he walks away from the sun and down the hill, is of all those things she saw and rejoiced in, the most beautiful; and at that, her breast is full, with the heaviness of a baby at it, and not for grief alone, but for praise.

"I believe, I believe!" her heart cries out in her, as if she were holding the peach stone of her eager girlhood in her woman's hand.

She puts her face into her hands, and weeps, and they all move closer to her. Familiar as it is, the spirit has had a new discovery. . . .

Jodey then felt that she had returned to them all; and he stopped seeing, and just remembered, what happened yesterday; and his love for his wife was confirmed as something he would never be able to measure for himself or prove it to her in words.

4

LIONS, HARTS,
LEAPING DOES

J. F. Powers

"‘THIRTY-NINTH POPE. Anastasius, a Roman, appointed that while the Gospel was reading they should stand and not sit. He exempted from the ministry those that were lame, impotent, or diseased persons, and slept with his forefathers in peace, being a confessor.’"

"Anno?"

"‘Anno 404.’"

They sat there in the late afternoon, the two old men grown gray in the brown robes of the Order. Angular winter daylight forsook the small room, almost a cell in the primitive sense, and passed through the window into the outside world. The distant horizon, which it sought to join, was still bright and strong against approaching night. The old Franciscans, one priest, one brother, were left among the shadows in the room.

"Can you see to read one more, Titus?" the priest Didymus asked. "Number fourteen." He did not cease staring out the window at day becoming night on the horizon. The thirty-ninth pope said Titus might not be a priest. Did Titus, reading, understand? He could never really tell about Titus, who said nothing now. There was only silence, then a dry whispering of pages turning. "Number fourteen," Didymus said. "That's Zephyrinus. I always like the old heretic on that one, Titus."

According to one bibliographer, Bishop Bale's *Pageant of Popes Contayninge the Lyves of all the Bishops of Rome, from the Beginning of them to the Year of Grace 1555* was a denunciation of every pope from Peter to Paul

IV. However inviting to readers that might sound, it was, in sober fact, a lie. The first popes, persecuted and mostly martyred, wholly escaped the author's remarkable spleen and even enjoyed his crusty approbation. Father Didymus, his aged appetite for biography jaded by the orthodox lives, found the work fascinating. He usually referred to it as "Bishop Bale's funny book" and to the Bishop as a heretic.

Titus squinted at the yellowed page. He snapped a glance at the light hovering at the window. Then he closed his eyes and with great feeling recited:

" 'O how joyous and how delectable is it to see religious men devout and fervent in the love of God, well-mannered—' "

"Titus," Didymus interrupted softly.

" '—and well taught in ghostly learning.' "

"Titus, read." Didymus placed the words in their context. The First Book of *The Imitation* and Chapter, if he was not mistaken, XXV. The trick was no longer in finding the source of Titus's quotations; it was putting them in their exact context. It had become an unconfessed contest between them, and it gratified Didymus to think he had been able to place the fragment. Titus knew two books by heart, *The Imitation* and *The Little Flowers of St. Francis*. Lately, unfortunately, he had begun to learn another. He was more and more quoting from Bishop Bale. Didymus reminded himself he must not let Titus read past the point where the martyred popes left off. What Bale had to say about Peter's later successors sounded incongruous— "unmete" in the old heretic's own phrase—coming from a Franciscan brother. Two fathers had already inquired of Didymus concerning Titus. One had noted the antique style of his words and had ventured to wonder if Brother Titus, Christ preserve us, might be slightly possessed. He cited the case of the illiterate Missouri farmer who cursed the Church in a forgotten Aramaic tongue.

"Read, Titus."

Titus squinted at the page once more and read in his fine dead voice.

" 'Fourteenth pope, Zephyrinus. Zephyrinus was a Roman born, a man as writers do testify, more addicted with all endeavor to the service of God than to the cure of any worldly affairs. Whereas before his time the wine in the celebrating the communion was ministered in a cup of wood, he first did alter that, and instead thereof brought in cups or chalices of glass. And yet he did not this upon any superstition, as thinking wood to be unlawful, or glass to be more holy for that use, but because the one is more comely and seemly, as by experience it appeareth than the other. And yet some wooden dolts do dream that the wooden cups were changed by him because that part of the wine, or as they thought, the royal blood of Christ, did soak into the wood, and so it cannot be in glass. Surely sooner may wine soak into any wood than any wit into those winey heads that thus both deceive themselves and slander this Godly martyr.'"

"Anno?"

Titus squinted at the page again. "'Anno 222,'" he read.

They were quiet for a moment that ended with the clock in the tower booming once for the half hour. Didymus got up and stood so close to the window his breath became visible. Noticing it, he inhaled deeply and then, exhaling, he sent a gust of smoke churning against the freezing pane, clouding it. Some old unmelted snow in tree crotches lay dirty and white in the gathering dark.

"It's cold out today," Didymus said.

He stepped away from the window and over to Titus, whose face was relaxed in open-eyed sleep. He took Bishop Bale's funny book unnoticed from Titus's hands.

"Thank you, Titus," he said.

Titus blinked his eyes slowly once, then several times quickly. His body gave a shudder, as if coming to life.

"Yes, Father?" he was asking.

"I said thanks for reading. You are a great friend to me."

"Yes, Father."

"I know you'd rather read other authors." Didymus moved to the window, stood there gazing through the tops of trees, their limbs black and bleak against the sky. He rubbed his hands. "I'm going for a walk before vespers. Is it too cold for you, Titus?"

"'A good religious man that is fervent in his religion taketh all things well, and doth gladly all that he is commanded to do.'"

Didymus, walking across the room, stopped and looked at Titus just in time to see him open his eyes. He was quoting again: *The Imitation* and still in Chapter XXV. Why had he said that? To himself Didymus repeated the words and decided Titus, his mind moving intelligently but so pathetically largo, was documenting the act of reading Bishop Bale when there were other books he preferred.

"I'm going out for a walk," Didymus said.

Titus rose and pulled down the full sleeves of his brown robe in anticipation of the cold.

"I think it is too cold for you, Titus," Didymus said.

Titus faced him undaunted, arms folded and hands muffled in his sleeves, eyes twinkling incredulously. He was ready to go. Didymus got the idea Titus knew himself to be the healthier of the two. Didymus was vaguely annoyed at this manifestation of the truth. *Vanitas.*

"Won't they need you in the kitchen now?" he inquired.

Immediately he regretted having said that. And the way he had said it, with some malice, as though labor *per se* was important and the intention not so. *Vanitas* in a friar, and at his age, too. Confronting Titus with a distinction his simple mind could never master and which, if it could, his great soul would never recognize. Titus only knew all that was necessary, that a friar did what he was best at in the community. And no matter the nature of his toil, the variety of the means at hand, the end was the same for all friars. Or indeed for all men, if they cared to know. Titus worked in the kitchen and garden. Was Didymus wrong in teaching geometry out of personal preference and perhaps—if this was so he was—out of pride? Had the spiritual worth of his labor been vitiated because of that? He did not think so, no. No, he taught geometry because it was useful and eternally true, like his theology, and though of a lower order of truth it escaped the common fate of theology and the humanities, perverted through the ages in the mouths of dunderheads and fools. From that point of view, his work came to the same thing as Titus's. The vineyard was everywhere; they were in it, and that was essential.

Didymus, consciously humble, held open the door for Titus. Sandals scraping familiarly, they passed through dark corridors until they came to the stairway. Lights from floors above and below spangled through the carven apertures of the winding stair and fell in confusion upon the worn oaken steps.

At the outside door they were ambushed. An old friar stepped out of the shadows to intercept them. Standing with Didymus and Titus, however, made him appear younger. Or possibly it was the tenseness of him.

"Good evening, Father," he said to Didymus. "And Titus."

Didymus nodded in salutation and Titus said deliberately, as though he were the first one ever to put words in such conjunction:

"Good evening, Father Rector."

The Rector watched Didymus expectantly. Didymus studied the man's face. It told him nothing but curiosity—a luxury that could verge on vice at the cloister. Didymus frowned his incomprehension. He was about to speak. He decided against it, turning to Titus:

"Come on, Titus, we've got a walk to take before vespers."

The Rector was left standing.

They began to circle the monastery grounds. Away from the buildings it was brighter. With a sudden shiver, Didymus felt the freezing air bite into his body all over. Instinctively he drew up his cowl. That was a little better. Not much. It was too cold for him to relax, breathe deeply, and stride freely. It had not looked this cold from his window. He fell into Titus's gait. The steps were longer, but there was an illusion of warmth about moving in unison. Bit by bit he found himself duplicating every aspect of Titus in motion. Heads down, eyes just ahead of the next step, undeviating, they seemed peripatetic figures in a Gothic frieze. The stones of the walk were trampled over with frozen footsteps. Titus's feet were gray and bare in their open sandals. Pieces of ice, the thin edges of ruts, cracked off under foot, skittering sharply away. A crystal fragment lit between Titus's toes and did not melt there. He did not seem to notice it. This made Didymus lift his eyes.

A fine Franciscan! Didymus snorted, causing a flurry of vapors. He had the despicable caution of the comfortable who move mountains, if need be, to stay that way. Here he was, cowl up and heavy woolen socks on, and regretting the weather because it exceeded his anticipations. Painfully he stubbed his toe on purpose and at once accused himself of exhibitionism. Then he damned the expression for its modernity. He asked himself wherein lay the renunciation of the world, the flesh, and the devil, the whole point of following after St. Francis today. Poverty, Chastity, Obedience—the three vows. There was nothing of suffering in the poverty of the friar nowadays: he was penniless, but materially rich compared to—what was the phrase he used to hear?—"one third of the nation." A beggar, a homeless mendicant by very definition, he knew nothing—except as it affected others "less fortunate"—of the miseries of begging in the street. Verily, it was no heavy cross, this vow of Poverty, so construed and practiced, in the modern world. Begging had become unfashionable. Somewhere along the line the meaning had been lost; they had become too "fortunate." Official agencies, to whom it was a nasty but necessary business, dispensed Charity without mercy or grace. He recalled with wry amusement Frederick Barbarossa's appeal to fellow princes when opposed by the might of the medieval Church: "We have a clean conscience, and it tells us that God is with us. Ever have we striven to bring back priests, and, in especial, those of the topmost rank, to the condition of the first Christian Church. In those days the clergy raised their eyes to the angels, shone through miracles, made whole the sick, raised the dead, made Kings and Princes subject to them, not with arms but with their holiness. But now they are smothered in delights. To withdraw from them the harmful riches which burden them to their own undoing is a labor of love in which all Princes should eagerly participate."

And Chastity, what of that? Well, that was all over for him—a battle he had fought and won many years ago. A sin whose temptations had prevailed undiminished through the centuries, but withal for him, an old man, a dead issue, a young man's trial. Only Obedience remained, and that, too, was no longer difficult for him. There was something—much as he disliked the term—to be said for "conditioning." He had to smile at himself: why should he bristle so at using the word? It was only contemporary slang for a theory the Church had always known. "Psychiatry," so called, and all the ghastly superstition that attended its practice, the deification of its high priests in the secular schools, made him ill. But it would pass. Just look how alchemy had flourished, and where was it today?

Clearly an abecedarian observance of the vows did not promise perfection. Stemmed in divine wisdom, they were branches meant to flower forth, but requiring of the friar the water and sunlight of sacrifice. The letter led nowhere. It was the spirit of the vows that opened the way and revealed to the soul, no matter the flux of circumstance, the means of salvation.

He had picked his way through the welter of familiar factors again— again to the same bitter conclusion. He had come to the key and core of his trouble anew. When he received the letter from Seraphin asking him to come to St. Louis, saying his years prohibited unnecessary travel and endowed his request with a certain prerogative—No, he had written back, it's simply impossible, not saying why. God help him, as a natural man, he had the desire, perhaps the inordinate desire, to see his brother again. He should not have to prove that. One of them must die soon. But as a friar, he remembered: "Unless a man be clearly delivered from the love of all creatures, he may not fully tend to his Creator." Therein, he thought, the keeping of the vows having become an easy habit for him, was his opportunity—he thought! It was plain and there was sacrifice and it would be hard. So he had not gone.

Now it was plain that he had been all wrong. Seraphin was an old man with little left to warm him in the world. Didymus asked himself—recoiling at the answer before the question was out—if his had been the only sacrifice. Rather, had he not been too intent on denying himself at the time to notice that he was denying Seraphin also? Harshly Didymus told himself that he had used his brother for a hair shirt. This must be the truth, he thought; it hurts so.

The flesh just above the knees felt frozen. They were drawing near the entrance again. His face, too, felt the same way, like a slab of pasteboard, stiffest at the tip of his nose. When he wrinkled his brow and puffed out his cheeks to blow hot air up to his nose, his skin seemed to crackle like old parchment. His eyes watered from the wind. He pressed a hand, warm from his sleeve, to his exposed neck. Frozen, like his face. It would be chapped tomorrow.

Titus, white hair awry in the wind, looked just the same.

They entered the monastery door. The Rector stopped them. It was almost as before, except that Didymus was occupied with feeling his face and patting it back to life.

"Ah, Didymus! It must be cold indeed!" The Rector smiled at Titus and returned his gaze to Didymus. He made it appear that they were allied in being amused at Didymus's face. Didymus touched his nose tenderly. Assured it would stand the operation, he blew it lustily. He stuffed the handkerchief up his sleeve. The Rector, misinterpreting all this ceremony, obviously was afraid of being ignored.

"The telegram, Didymus. I'm sorry; I thought it might have been important."

"I received no telegram."

They faced each other, waiting, experiencing a hanging moment of uneasiness.

Then, having employed the deductive method, they both looked at Titus. Although he had not been listening, rather had been studying the naked toes in his sandals, he sensed their eyes questioning him.

"Yes, Father Rector?" he answered.

"The telegram for Father Didymus, Titus?" the Rector demanded. "Where is it?" Titus started momentarily out of willingness to be of service, but ended, his mind refusing to click, impassive before them. The Rector shook his head in faint exasperation and reached his hand down into the folds of Titus's cowl. He brought forth two envelopes. One, the telegram, he gave to Didymus. The other, a letter, he handed back to Titus.

"I gave you this letter this morning, Titus. It's for Father Anthony." Intently Titus stared unremembering at the letter. "I wish you would see that Father Anthony gets it right away, Titus. I think it's a bill."

Titus held the envelope tightly to his breast and said, "Father Anthony."

Then his eyes were attracted by the sound of Didymus tearing open the telegram. While Didymus read the telegram, Titus's expression showed he at last understood his failure to deliver it. He was perturbed, mounting inner distress moving his lips silently.

Didymus looked up from the telegram. He saw the grief in Titus's face and said, astonished, "How did you know, Titus?"

Titus's eyes were both fixed and lowered in sorrow. It seemed to Didymus that Titus knew the meaning of the telegram. Didymus was suddenly weak, as before a miracle. His eyes went to the Rector to see how he was taking it. Then it occurred to him the Rector could not know what had happened.

As though nothing much had, the Rector laid an absolving hand lightly upon Titus's shoulder.

"Didymus, he can't forgive himself for not delivering the telegram now that he remembers it. That's all."

Didymus was relieved. Seeing the telegram in his hand, he folded it quickly and stuffed it back in the envelope. He handed it to the Rector.

53

Calmly, in a voice quite drained of feeling, he said, "My brother, Father Seraphin, died last night in St. Louis."

"Father Seraphin *from Rome?*"

"Yes," Didymus said, "in St. Louis. He was my brother. Appointed a confessor in Rome, a privilege for a foreigner. He was ninety-two."

"I know that, Didymus, an honor for the Order. I had no idea he was in this country. Ninety-two! God rest his soul!"

"I had a letter from him only recently."

"You did?"

"He wanted me to come to St. Louis. I hadn't seen him for twenty-five years at least."

"Twenty-five years?"

"It was impossible for me to visit him."

"But if he was in this country, Didymus . . ."

The Rector waited for Didymus to explain.

Didymus opened his mouth to speak, heard the clock in the tower sound the quarter hour, and said nothing, listening, lips parted, to the last of the strokes die away.

"Why, Didymus, it could easily have been arranged," the Rector persisted.

Didymus turned abruptly to Titus, who, standing in a dream, had been inattentive since the clock struck.

"Come, Titus, we'll be late."

He hastened down the corridor with Titus. "No," he said in agitation, causing Titus to look at him in surprise. "I told him no. It was simply impossible." He was conscious of Titus's attention. "To visit him, Seraphin, who is dead." That had come naturally enough, for being the first time in his thoughts that Seraphin was dead. Was there not some merit in his dispassionate acceptance of the fact?

They entered the chapel for vespers and knelt down.

The clock struck. One, two . . . two. Two? No, there must have been one or two strokes before. He had gone to sleep. It was three. At least three, probably four. Or five. He waited. It could not be two: he remembered the brothers filing darkly into the chapel at that hour. Disturbing the shadows for matins and lauds. If it was five—he listened for faint noises in the building— it would only be a few minutes. They would come in, the earliest birds, to say their Masses. There were no noises. He looked toward the windows on the St. Joseph side of the chapel. He might be able to see a light from a room across the court. That was not certain even if it was five. It would have to come through the stained glass. Was that possible? It was still night. Was there a moon? He looked round the chapel. If there was, it might still shine on a window. There was no moon. Or it was overhead. Or powerless against the glass. He yawned. It could not be five. His knees were numb from kneeling. He shifted on them. His back ached. Straightening it, he gasped for breath. He saw the sanctuary light. The only light, red. Then it came back to him. Seraphin was dead. He tried to pray. No words. Why words? Meditation in the Presence. The perfect prayer. He fell asleep . . .

. . . Spiraling brown coil on coil under the golden sun the river slithered across the blue and flower-flecked land. On an eminence they held identical hands over their eyes for visors and mistook it with pleasure for an endless murmuring serpent. They considered unafraid the prospect of its turning in its course and standing on tail to swallow them gurgling alive. They sensed it was in them to command this also by a wish. Their visor hands vanished before their eyes and became instead the symbol of brotherhood clasped between them. This they wished. Smiling the same smile back and forth they began laughing: "Jonah!" And were walking murkily up and down the brown belly of the river in mock distress. Above them, foolishly triumphant, rippling in contentment, mewed the waves. Below swam an occasional large fish, absorbed in ignoring them, and the mass of crustacea, eagerly seething, too numerous on the bottom to pretend exclusiveness. "Jonah indeed!" the brothers said, surprised to see the bubbles they birthed. They strolled then for hours this way. The novelty wearing off (without regret, else they would have wished themselves elsewhere), they began to talk and say ordinary things. Their mother had died, their father too, and how old did that make them? It was the afternoon of the funerals, which they had managed, transcending time, to have held jointly. She had seemed older and, for some reason, he otherwise. How, they wondered, should it be with them, *memento mori* clicking simultaneously within them, lackaday. The sound of dirt descending six feet to clatter on the coffins was memorable but unmentionable. Their own lives, well . . . only half curious (something to do) they halted to kick testingly a waterlogged rowboat resting on the bottom, the crustacea complaining and olive-green silt rising to speckle the surface with dark stars . . . well, what *had* they been doing? A crayfish pursued them, clad in sable armor, dearly desiring to do battle, brandishing hinged swords. Well, for one thing, working for the canonization of Fra Bartolomeo, had got two cardinals interested, was hot after those remaining who were at all possible, a slow business. Yes, one would judge so in the light of past canonizations, though being stationed in Rome had its advantages. Me, the same old grind, teaching, pounding away, giving Pythagoras no rest in his grave. . . . They made an irresolute pass at the crayfish, who had caught up with them. More about Fra Bartolomeo, what else is there?

Except, you will laugh or have me excommunicated for wanton presumption, though it's only faith in a faithless age, making a vow not to die until he's made a saint, recognized rather—he is one, convinced of it, Didymus (never can get used to calling you that), a saint sure as I'm alive, having known him, no doubt of it, something wrong with your knee? Knees then? The crayfish, he's got hold of you there, another at your back. If you like, we'll leave—only I do like it here. Well, go ahead then, you never did like St. Louis, isn't that what you used to say? Alone, in pain, he rose to the surface parting the silt stars. The sun like molten gold squirted him in the eye. Numb now, unable to remember, and too blind to refurnish his memory by observation, he waited for this limbo to clear away . . .

Awake now, he was face to face with a flame, blinding him. He avoided it. A dead weight bore him down, his aching back. Slowly, like ink in a blotter, his consciousness spread. The supports beneath him were kneeling limbs, his, the veined hands, bracing him, pressing flat, his own. His body, it seemed, left off there; the rest was something else, floor. He raised his head to the flame again and tried to determine what kept it suspended even with his face. He shook his head, blinking dumbly, a four-legged beast. He could see nothing, only his knees and hands, which he felt rather, and the flame floating unaccountably in the darkness. That part alone was a mystery. And then there came a pressure and pull on his shoulders, urging him up. Fingers, a hand, a rustling related to its action, then the rustling in rhythm with the folds of a brown curtain, a robe naturally, ergo a friar, holding a candle, trying to raise him up, Titus. The clock began striking.

"Put out the candle," Didymus said.

Titus closed his palm slowly around the flame, unflinching, snuffing it. The odor of burning string. Titus pinched the wick deliberately. He waited a moment, the clock falling silent, and said, "Father Rector expects you will say a Mass for the Dead at five o'clock."

"Yes, I know." He yawned deliciously. "I told him *that*." He bit his lips at the memory of the disgusting yawn. Titus had found him asleep. Shame overwhelmed him, and he searched his mind for justification. He found none.

"It is five now," Titus said.

It was maddening. "I don't see anyone else if it's five," he snapped. Immediately he was aware of a light burning in the sacristy. He blushed and grew pale. Had someone besides Titus seen him sleeping? But, listening, he heard nothing. No one else was up yet. He was no longer pale and was only blushing now. He saw it all hopefully. He was saved. Titus had gone to the sacristy to prepare for Mass. He must have come out to light the candles on the main altar. Then he had seen the bereaved keeping vigil on all fours, asleep, snoring even. What did Titus think of that? It withered him to remember, but he was comforted some that the only witness had been Titus. Had the sleeping apostles in Gethsemane been glad it was Christ?

Wrong! Hopelessly wrong! For there had come a noise after all. Someone else was in the sacristy. He stiffened and walked palely toward it. He must go there and get ready to say his Mass. A few steps he took only, his back buckling out, humping, his knees sinking to the floor, his hands last. The floor, with fingers smelling of dust and genesis, reached up and held him. The fingers were really spikes and they were dusty from holding him this way all his life. For a radiant instant, which had something of eternity about it, he saw the justice of his position. Then there was nothing.

A little snow had fallen in the night, enough to powder the dead grass and soften the impression the leafless trees etched in the sky. Grayly the sky promised more snow, but now, at the end of the day following his collapse in the chapel, it was melting. Didymus, bundled around by blankets, sat in a wheelchair at the window, unsleepy. Only the landscape wearied him. Dead and unmoving though it must be—of that he was sure—it conspired to make him see everything in it as living, moving, something to be watched, each visible tuft of grass, each cluster of snow. The influence of the snow, perhaps? For the ground, ordinarily uniform in texture and drabness, had split up into individual patches. They appeared to be involved in a struggle of some kind, possibly to overlap each other, constantly shifting. But whether it was equally one against one, or one against all, he could not make out. He reminded himself he did not believe it was actually happening. It was confusing and he closed his eyes. After a time this confused and tired him in the same way. The background of darkness became a field of varicolored factions, warring, and, worse than the landscape, things like worms and comets wriggled and exploded before his closed eyes. Finally, as though to orchestrate their motions, they carried with them a bewildering noise or music which grew louder and cacophonous. The effect was cumulative, inevitably unbearable, and Didymus would have to open his eyes again. The intervals of peace became gradually rarer on the landscape. Likewise when he shut his eyes to it the restful darkness dissolved sooner than before into riot.

The door of his room opened, mercifully dispelling his illusions, and that, because there had been no knock, could only be Titus. Unable to move in his chair, Didymus listened to Titus moving about the room at his back. The tinkle of a glass once, the squeak of the bookcase indicating a book taken out or replaced—they were sounds Didymus could recognize. But that first tap-tap and the consequent click of metal on metal, irregular and scarcely audible, was disconcertingly unfamiliar. His curiosity, centering on it, raised it to a delicious mystery. He kept down the urge to shout at Titus. But he attempted to fish from memory the precise character of the corner from which the sound came with harrowing repetition. The sound stopped then, as though to thwart him on the brink of revelation. Titus's footsteps scraped across the room. The door opened and closed. For a few steps, Didymus heard Titus going down the corridor. He asked himself not to be moved by idle curiosity, a thing of the senses. He would not be tempted now.

A moment later the keystone of his good intention crumbled, and the whole edifice of his detachment with it. More shakily than quickly, Didymus moved his hands to the wheels of the chair. He would roll over to the corner and investigate the sound . . . He would? His hands lay limply at the wheels, ready to propel him to his mind's destination, but, weak, white, powerless to grip the wheels or anything. He regarded them with contempt. He had known they would fail him; he had been foolish to give them another chance. Disdainful of his hands, he looked out the window. He could still do that, couldn't he? It was raining some now. The landscape started to move, rearing and reeling crazily, as though drunken with the rain. In horror, Didymus damned his eyes. He realized this trouble was probably going to be chronic. He turned his gaze in despair to the trees, to the branches level with his eyes and nearer than the insane ground. Hesitating warily, fearful the gentle boughs under scrutiny would turn into hideous waving tentacles, he looked. With a thrill, he knew he was seeing clearly.

Gauzily, rain descended in a fine spray, hanging in fat berries from the wet black branches where leaves had been and buds would be, cold crystal drops. They fell now and then ripely of their own weight, or shaken by the intermittent wind they spilled before their time. Promptly they appeared again, pendulous.

Watching the raindrops prove gravity, he was grateful for nature's, rather than his, return to reason. Still, though he professed faith in his faculties, he would not look away from the trees and down at the ground, nor close his eyes. Gratefully he savored the cosmic truth in the falling drops and the mildly trembling branches. There was order, he thought, which in justice and science ought to include the treacherous landscape. Risking all, he ventured a glance at the ground. All was still there. He smiled. He was going to close his eyes (to make it universal and conclusive), when the door opened again.

Didymus strained to catch the meaning of Titus's movements. Would the clicking sound begin? Titus did go to that corner of the room again. Then it came, louder than before, but only once this time.

Titus came behind his chair, turned it, and wheeled him over to the corner.

On a hook that Titus had screwed into the wall hung a birdcage covered with black cloth.

"What's all this?" Didymus asked.

Titus tapped the covered cage expectantly.

A bird chirped once.

"The bird," Titus explained in excitement, "is inside."

Didymus almost laughed. He sensed in time, however, the necessity of seeming befuddled and severe. Titus expected it.

"I don't believe it," Didymus snapped.

Titus smiled wisely and tapped the cage again.

"There!" he exclaimed when the bird chirped.

Didymus shook his head in mock anger. "You made that beastly noise, Titus, you mountebank!"

Titus, profoundly amused by such skepticism, removed the black cover.

The bird, a canary, flicked its head sidewise in interest, looking them up and down. Then it turned its darting attention to the room. It chirped once in curt acceptance of the new surroundings. Didymus and Titus came under its black dot of an eye once more, this time for closer analysis. The canary chirped twice, perhaps that they were welcome, even pleasing, and stood on one leg to show them what a gay bird it was. It then returned to the business of pecking a piece of apple.

"I see you've given him something to eat," Didymus said, and felt that Titus, though he seemed content to watch the canary, waited for him to say something more. "I am very happy, Titus, to have this canary," he went on. "I suppose he will come in handy now that I must spend my days in this infernal chair."

Titus did not look at him while he said, "He is a good bird, Father. He is one of the Saint's own good birds."

Through the window, Didymus watched the days and nights come and go. For the first time, though his life as a friar had been copiously annotated with significant references, he got a good idea of eternity. Monotony, of course, was one word for it, but like all the others, as well as the allegories worked up by imaginative retreat masters, it was empty beside the experience itself, untranslatable. He would doze and wonder if by some quirk he had been cast out of the world into eternity, but since it was neither heaven nor exactly purgatory or hell, as he understood them, he concluded it must be an uncharted isle subscribing to the mother forms only in the matter of time. And having thought this, he was faintly annoyed at his ponderous whimsy. Titus, like certain of the hours, came periodically. He would read or simply sit with him in silence. The canary was there always, but except as it showed signs of sleepiness at twilight and spirit at dawn, Didymus regarded it as a subtle device, like the days and nights and bells, to give the lie to the vulgar error that time flies. The cage was small and the canary would not sing. Time, hanging in the room like a jealous fog, possessed him and voided everything except it. It seemed impossible each time Titus came that he should be able to escape the room.

"'After him,'" Titus read from Bishop Bale one day, "'came Fabius, a Roman born, who (as Eusebius witnesseth) as he was returning home out of the field, and with his countrymen present to elect a new bishop, there was a pigeon seen standing on his head and suddenly he was created pastor of the Church, which he looked not for.'"

They smiled at having the same thought and both looked up at the canary. Since Didymus sat by the window most of the day now, he had asked Titus to put a hook there for the cage. He had to admit to himself he did this to let Titus know he appreciated the canary. Also, as a secondary motive, he reasoned, it enabled the canary to look out the window. What a little yellow bird could see to interest it in the frozen scene was a mystery, but that, Didymus sighed, was a two-edged sword. And he took to watching the canary more.

So far as he was able to detect the moods of the canary he participated in them. In the morning the canary, bright and clownish, flitted back and forth between the two perches in the cage, hanging from the sides and cocking its little tufted head at Didymus querulously. During these acrobatics Didymus would twitch his hands in quick imitation of the canary's stunts. He asked Titus to construct a tiny swing, such as he had seen, which the canary might learn to use, since it appeared to be an intelligent and daring sort. Titus got the swing, the canary did master it, but there seemed to be nothing Didymus could do with his hands that was like swinging. In fact, after he had been watching awhile, it was as though the canary were fixed to a pendulum, inanimate, a piece of machinery, a yellow blur—ticking, for the swing made a little sound, and Didymus went to sleep, and often when he woke the canary was still going, like a clock. Didymus had no idea how long he slept at these times, maybe a minute, maybe hours. Gradually the canary got bored with the swing and used it less and less. In the same way, Didymus suspected, he himself had wearied of looking out the window. The first meager satisfaction had worn off. The dead trees, the sleeping snow, like the swing for the canary, were sources of diversion that soon grew stale. They were captives, he and the canary, and the only thing they craved was escape. Didymus slowly considered the problem. There was nothing, obviously, for him to do. He could pray, which he did, but he was not sure the only thing wrong with him was the fact he could not walk and that to devote his prayer to that end was justifiable. Inevitably it occurred to him his plight might well be an act of God. Why this punishment, though, he asked himself, and immediately supplied the answer. He had, for one thing, gloried too much in having it in him to turn down Seraphin's request to come to St. Louis. The intention—that was all-important, and he, he feared, had done the right thing for the wrong reason. He had noticed something of the faker in himself before. But it was not clear if he had erred. There was a certain consolation, at bottom dismal, in this doubt. It was true there appeared to be a nice justice in being stricken a cripple if he had been wrong in refusing to travel to see Seraphin, if human love was all he was fitted for, if he was incapable of renunciation for the right reason, if the mystic counsels were too strong for him, if he was still too pedestrian after all these years of prayer and contemplation, if . . .

The canary was swinging, the first time in several days.

The reality of his position was insupportable. There were two ways of regarding it and he could not make up his mind. Humbly he wished to get well and to be able to walk. But if this was a punishment, was not prayer to lift it declining to see the divine point? He did wish to get well; that would settle it. Otherwise his predicament could only be resolved through means more serious than he dared cope with. It would be like refusing to see Seraphin all over again. By some mistake, he protested, he had at last been placed in a position vital with meaning and precedents inescapably Christian. But was he the man for it? Unsure of himself, he was afraid to go on trial. It would be no minor trial, so construed, but one in which the greatest values were involved—a human soul and the means of its salvation or damnation. Not watered down suburban precautions and routine pious exercises, but Faith such as saints and martyrs had, and Despair such as only they had been tempted by. No, he was not the man for it. He was unworthy. He simply desired to walk and in a few years to die a normal, uninspired death. He did not wish to see (what was apparent) the greatest significance in his affliction. He preferred to think in terms of physical betterment. He was so sure he was not a saint that he did not consider this easier road beneath him, though attracted by the higher one. That was the rub. Humbly, then, he wanted to be able to walk, but he wondered if there was not presumption in such humility.

Thus he decided to pray for health and count the divine hand not there. Decided. A clean decision—not distinction—no mean feat in the light of all the moral theology he had swallowed. The canary, all its rocking come to naught once more, slept motionless in the swing. Despite the manifest prudence of the course he had settled upon, Didymus dozed off ill at ease in his wheelchair by the window. Distastefully, the last thing he remembered was that "prudence" is a virtue more celebrated in the modern Church.

At his request in the days following a doctor visited him. The Rector came along, too. When Didymus tried to find out the nature of his illness, the doctor looked solemn and pronounced it to be one of those things. Didymus received this with a look of mystification. So the doctor went on to say there was no telling about it. Time alone would tell. Didymus asked the doctor to recommend some books dealing with cases like his. They might have one of them in the monastery library. Titus could read to him in the meantime. For, though he disliked being troublesome, "one of those things" as a diagnosis meant very little to an unscientific beggar like him. The phrase had a philosophic ring to it, but to his knowledge neither the Early Fathers nor the Scholastics seemed to have dealt with it. The Rector smiled. The doctor, annoyed, replied drily:

"Is that a fact?"

Impatiently, Didymus said, "I know how old I am, if that's it."

Nothing was lost of the communion he kept with the canary. He still watched its antics and his fingers in his lap followed them clumsily. He did not forget about himself, that he must pray for health, that it was best that way—"prudence" dictated it—but he did think more of the canary's share of their captivity. A canary in a cage, he reasoned, is like a bud that never blooms.

He asked Titus to get a book on canaries, but nothing came of it and he did not mention it again.

Some days later Titus read:

" 'Twenty-ninth pope, Marcellus, a Roman, was pastor of the Church, feeding it with wisdom and doctrine. And (as I may say with the Prophet) a man according to God's own heart and full of Christian works. This man admonished Maximianus the Emperor and endeavored to remove him from persecuting the saints—' "

"Stop a moment, Titus," Didymus interrupted.

Steadily, since Titus began to read, the canary had been jumping from the swing to the bottom of the cage and back again. Now it was quietly standing on one foot in the swing. Suddenly it flew at the side of the cage nearest them and hung there, its ugly little claws, like bent wire, hooked to the slender bars. It observed them intently, first Titus and then Didymus, at whom it continued to stare. Didymus's hands were tense in his lap.

"Go ahead, read," Didymus said, relaxing his hands.

" 'But the Emperor being more hardened, commanded Marcellus to be beaten with cudgels and to be driven out of the city, wherefore he entered into the house of one Lucina, a widow, and there kept the congregation secretly, which the tyrant hearing, made a stable for cattle of the same house and committed the keeping of it to the bishop Marcellus. After that he governed the Church by writing Epistles, without any other kind of teaching being condemned to such a vile service. And being thus daily tormented with strife and noisomeness, at length gave up the ghost. Anno 308.'"

"Very good, Titus. I wonder how we missed that one before."

The canary, still hanging on the side of the cage, had not moved, its head turned sidewise, its eye as before fixed on Didymus.

"Would you bring me a glass of water, Titus?"

Titus got up and looked in the cage. The canary hung there, as though waiting, not a feather stirring.

"The bird has water here," Titus said, pointing to the small cup fastened to the cage.

"For me, Titus, the water's for me. Don't you think I know you look after the canary? You don't forget us, though I don't see why you don't."

Titus left the room with a glass.

Didymus's hands were tense again. Eyes on the canary's eye, he got up from his wheelchair, his face strained and white with the impossible effort, and, his fingers somehow managing it, he opened the cage. The canary darted out and circled the room chirping. Before it lit, though it seemed about to make its perch triumphantly the top of the cage, Didymus fell over on his face and lay prone on the floor.

In bed that night, unsuffering and barely alive, he saw at will everything revealed in his past. Events long forgotten happened again before his eyes. Clearly, sensitively, he saw Seraphin and himself, just as they had always been—himself, never quite sure. He heard all that he had ever said, and that anyone had said to him. He had talked too much, too. The past mingled with the present. In the same moment and scene he made his first Communion, was ordained, and confessed his sins for the last time.

The canary perched in the dark atop the cage, head warm under wing, already, it seemed to Didymus, without memory of its captivity, dreaming of a former freedom, an ancestral summer day with flowers and trees. Outside it was snowing.

The Rector, followed by others, came into the room and administered the last sacrament. Didymus heard them all gathered prayerfully around his bed thinking (they thought) secretly: this sacrament often strengthens the dying, tip-of-the-tongue wisdom indigenous to the priesthood, Henry the Eighth had six wives. He saw the same hackneyed smile, designed to cheer, pass bravely among them, and marveled at the crudity of it. They went away then, all except Titus, their individual footsteps sounding (for him) the character of each friar. He might have been Francis himself for what he knew then of the little brothers and the cure of souls. He heard them thinking their expectation to be called from bed before daybreak to return to his room and say the office of the dead over his body, become the body, and whispering hopefully to the contrary. Death was now an unwelcome guest in the cloister.

He wanted nothing in the world for himself at last. This may have been the first time he found his will amenable to the Divine. He had never been less himself and more the saint. Yet now, so close to sublimity, or perhaps only tempted to believe so (the Devil is most wily at the deathbed), he was beset by the grossest distractions. They were to be expected, he knew, as indelible in the order of things: the bingo game going on under the Cross for the seamless garment of the Son of Man: everywhere the sign of the contradiction, and always. When would he cease to be surprised by it? Incidents repeated themselves, twined, parted, faded away, came back clear, and would not be prayed out of mind. He watched himself mounting the pulpit of a metropolitan church, heralded by the pastor as the renowned Franciscan father sent by God in His goodness to preach this novena—like to say a little prayer to test the microphone, Father?—and later reading through the petitions to Our Blessed Mother, cynically tabulating the pleas for a Catholic boyfriend, drunkenness banished, the sale of real estate and coming furiously upon one: "that I'm not pregnant." And at the same church on Good Friday carrying the crucifix along the communion rail for the people to kiss, giving them the indulgence, and afterwards in the sacristy wiping the lipstick of the faithful from the image of Christ crucified.

"Take down a book, any book, Titus, and read. Begin anywhere."

Roused by his voice, the canary fluttered, looked sharply about and buried its head once more in the warmth of its wing.

" 'By the lions,' " Titus read, " 'are understood the acrimonies and impetuosities of the irascible faculty, which faculty is as bold and daring in its acts as are the lions. By the harts and the leaping does is understood the other faculty of the soul, which is the concupiscible—that is—' "

"Skip the exegesis," Didymus broke in weakly. "I can do without that now. Read the verse."

Titus read: " 'Birds of swift wing, lions, harts, leaping does, mountains, valleys, banks, waters, breezes, heats and terrors that keep watch by night, by the pleasant lyres and by the siren's song, I conjure you, cease your wrath and touch not the wall . . .' "

"Turn off the light, Titus."

Titus went over to the switch. There was a brief period of darkness during which Didymus's eyes became accustomed to a different shade, a glow rather, which possessed the room slowly. Then he saw the full moon had let down a ladder of light through the window. He could see the snow, strangely blue, falling outside. So sensitive was his mind and eye (because his body, now faint, no longer blurred his vision?) he could count the snowflakes, all of them separately, before they drifted, winding, below the sill.

With the same wonderful clarity, he saw what he had made of his life. He saw himself tied down, caged, stunted in his apostolate, seeking the crumbs, the little pleasure, neglecting the source, always knowing death changes nothing, only immortalizes . . . and still ever lukewarm. In trivial attachments, in love of things, was death, no matter the appearance of life. In the highest attachment only, no matter the appearance of death, was life. He had always known this truth, but now he was feeling it. Unable to move his hand, only his lips, and hardly breathing, was it too late to act?

"Open the window, Titus," he whispered.

And suddenly he could pray. *Hail Mary . . . Holy Mary, Mother of God, pray for us sinners now and at the hour of our death . . .* finally the time to say, *pray for* me *now—the hour of* my *death, amen.* Lest he deceive himself at the very end that this was the answer to a lifetime of praying for a happy death, happy because painless, he tried to turn his thoughts from himself, to join them to God, thinking how at last he did—didn't he *now?*—prefer God above all else. But ashamedly not sure he did, perhaps only fearing hell, with an uneasy sense of justice he put himself foremost among the wise in their own generation, the perennials seeking after God when doctor, lawyer, and bank fails. If he wronged himself, he did so out of humility—a holy error. He ended, to make certain he had not fallen under the same old presumption disguised as the face of humility, by flooding his mind with maledictions. He suffered the piercing white voice of the Apocalypse to echo in his soul: *But because thou art lukewarm, and neither cold nor hot, I will begin to vomit thee out of my mouth.* And St. Bernard, fiery-eyed in a white habit, thundered at him from the twelfth century: "Hell is paved with the bald pates of priests!"

There was a soft flutter, the canary flew to the windowsill, paused, and tilted into the snow. Titus stepped too late to the window and stood gazing dumbly after it. He raised a trembling old hand, fingers bent in awe and sorrow, to his forehead, and turned stealthily to Didymus.

Didymus closed his eyes. He let a long moment pass before he opened them. Titus, seeing him awake then, fussed with the window latch and held a hand down to feel the draught, nodding anxiously as though it were the only evil abroad in the world, all the time straining his old eyes for a glimpse of the canary somewhere in the trees.

Didymus said nothing, letting Titus keep his secret. With his whole will he tried to lose himself in the sight of God, and failed. He was not in the least transported. Even now he could find no divine sign within himself. He knew he still had to look outside, to Titus. God still chose to manifest Himself most in sanctity.

Titus, nervous under his stare, and to account for staying at the window so long, felt for the draught again, frowned, and kept his eye hunting among the trees.

The thought of being the cause of such elaborate dissimulation in so simple a soul made Didymus want to smile—or cry, he did not know which . . . and could do neither. Titus persisted. How long would it be, Didymus wondered faintly, before Titus ungrievingly gave the canary up for lost in the snowy arms of God? The snowflakes whirled at the window, for a moment for all their bright blue beauty as though struck still by lightning, and Didymus closed his eyes, only to find them there also, but darkly falling.

5

THE DEVIL IN THE DESERT

Paul Horgan

to Virginia Rice

One summer morning almost a hundred years ago in the town of
Brownsville near the mouth of the Rio Grande on the Gulf of Mexico,
Father Pierre Arnoud awoke before dawn in great distress.

"Yesterday," he said to himself bitterly, "I should have told him yesterday."

He listened in the dark of his room whose little window was just showing the ghost of day over the Gulf. Yes, he could hear what he dreaded to
hear. Deep in the house were sounds of footsteps moving about. Father
Pierre could tell where those steps went, and what their maker was doing.
Now he was in the study taking up certain printed materials—a breviary, a
missal, a handful of ornately printed blanks for baptism, marriages, and first
communions, which could be filled in as occasion required. The footsteps
receded toward the refectory, and there a battered leather knapsack soon was
being filled with a cheese, two loaves of bread, a little sack of dried meal, a
flask of red wine, and a jug of water. Presently, a distant door opened and
closed and the footsteps went across the paved garden to the side door of
the sacristy in the church, where another leather case would be stocked with
sacred vessels, holy oils, communion wafers, and a set of vestments made in
France of thin silk from Lyon. The sacristy door sounded again, and Father
Pierre knew that the next stage of all these preparations for a journey would

move out beyond the rectory and the church to the ragged field where in a corral the two priests of the parish kept their horses. There, he knew, Pancho, the eight-year-old gelding who was the color of rusty weeds along the river, was going to be captured after an absurd moment of delicacy and apprehension, saddled, and brought back to the courtyard where the saddlebags and knapsacks were waiting. By then it would be light enough outdoors to see where you were going. It would be time to go.

From the sounds he could hear and the activities he could imagine, Father Pierre knew all over again something of the formidable man who was getting ready to depart. If those footsteps sounded like those of an old man, trotting and tentative, yet there was in them a stubborn force. There was plain contempt for human comfort in the noise he made before dawn when others might be sleeping; he seemed to say that if one man could get up to make all that noise in the name of God then any other should be glad to awaken to it.

Father Pierre knew there was grim joy in the world that morning for his friend and colleague Father Louis Bellefontaine. He knew also that Father Louis tried to control a capacity for anger that could flare as quickly and as madly as a cat's. In the new stone rectory the two men lived harmoniously for the most part. It took much government of their natural temperaments to make this possible, for over everything lay the difficulty that Father Pierre, who was many years the younger, was the pastor; while Father Louis, who had come from France a generation before Father Pierre, was the assistant, and so subject to the orders of his junior. But they made jokes about this, as they did about Father Pierre's education. Father Louis knew only his God, his duties, and what he had learned from hard contests with nature. He knew it was proper for a fine gentleman like Father Pierre to be his superior; and he would wrinkle his old face with shrewd estimate and relish of silken details when Father Pierre was busy with narratives about life at home—which meant France, where one day without doubt the younger priest would be consecrated a bishop. But Father Louis never envied his superior anything, for he knew that in his own work he was a great master—a master of the distance, the heat, the fatigue, the menace of time in slow travel, the harsh vegetation of the brush desert, the ungoverned Indian whose soul was within him but not yet claimed, the fears, hopes, and needs of the Mexican families who lived so widely separated, along the inland course of the Rio Grande. For thirty years Father Louis had ridden, mostly alone, and twice a year, on his journeys up the river.

He always undertook them with a sense not only of duty but of escape. Nowhere else did he feel so close to God as alone in the hard brush country riding to bring comfort, news, and the sacraments to some family in a *jacal* hidden by solitude open to the hot sky. The older he grew, the more Father Louis longed for his escapes from parish authority. The more infirm he became with the years, the stronger was his sense of mission. Father Pierre would see a glow of youth come back over that sun-stung, seamed old face as time drew near for Father Louis to make his plans to go on his ride into the upriver country, which would take him from two to three months. If his eyes were dim with age, not so the vision in his mind, which showed him so much of what people wanted of him, and of what he could bring to them. If his hand now trembled so that he could hardly write down the names and dates on one of his sacramental certificates, he could always joke about it, and assure his families that the deed was recorded in heaven, anyway. If sometimes his heart fluttered like a dusty bird in the cage of his ribs, and made him wonder what was ready to take flight, he could lie down for a few minutes and feel the thing calm itself; and however unworldly he may have been, he always clamped his jaws together with sardonic satisfaction that his time had not yet quite come. He had things to do, and would do them.

Much of this was known to Father Pierre by intuition, and he recalled it as he arose this morning. He hastened, for if he was going to catch Father Louis and say to him what should have been said yesterday, and even long before that, he would have to hurry. Do you suppose it could be, thought Father Pierre, that I am afraid of him? Or am I afraid for my dignity? What if he simply will not listen to me? He has pretended before this to be deaf when he has preferred not to hear me. Or do I not want to see a look of pain in his small, old, blue eyes? Actually, is there not a possibility that what I must tell him will shock him so that it might make him ill?

Father Pierre shrugged angrily at his doubts and tried to answer them reasonably.

Nonsense. After all, a letter from the bishop has approved my decision and given me authority for what is wise. Why must I heed for a second the individual feelings of anyone, myself included, when a duty is to be done? If I have been a coward for days, in spite of all my prayers for strength and enlightenment on how best to do what needs doing, must I not be doubly strong today?

And yet, as he went downstairs and out to the courtyard where a rosy daylight seemed to emerge from the ochre limestone of the church wall and glow in the very air, Father Pierre was as never before conscious of the difference in years between him and the old man who was at this moment hauling at straps and buckles, with one knee raised against Pancho's belly to brace himself.

It was a picture, as Father Pierre could not help pausing to notice.

The horse was laden, ready and patient. His summer coat was nicely brushed. His bridle was of woven horsehair. His saddle was bulky and tall, with some of the leather worn away so that the wooden forms of horn and cantle showed through. That saddle was chair and pillow, living room and store to Father Louis. To it he had attached many ingenious and cranky accessories, among which there was nowhere any provision for carrying a weapon. Father Louis went unarmed.

The old priest was dressed in a long homespun coat and heavy trousers. On his head was a woven cane hat with a wide brim under which his face, peering around at Father Pierre, looked like a crab apple underneath a shelf. His boots were high, the color of dried clay. Now, in the presence of the younger man, he redoubled his efforts at finishing his preparations. He made extra movements to show how difficult the job was, and he completed them with a little flourish to show how easily he overcame all. His breath went fast, making his voice dry and thin when he spoke.

"Well, Pierre, I am just about off. I hoped I'd see you before I went."

Father Pierre laughed. His heart beat. He said to himself, Now, now, I must tell him now. But he heard himself reply only,

"How did you think anybody could sleep with all your racket?"

"Ha."

It was a dry, indifferent comment. And then Father Louis looked sharply into his superior's eyes. What he saw there made him hurry.

"Well, I have everything. I'll send word back to you, if I meet anybody coming this way."

"Yes. Do. But before you go—"

Father Louis began to slap at his breast pockets with sudden dismay.

"Oh, Pierre, think of it. I nearly forgot my sunglasses, the new ones, you know the pair, which my niece sent to me from Vitry-le-François?"

"I have seen them, yes. They have green glass and metal rims, I believe?"

"The ones! Would you be a good angel and just get them for me? They must be in my room."

"You'll wait for me?"

"But of course."

"I'll be right back."

How could it be; and yet it was. Father Pierre, at the very point of discharging his sorry duty, was sent off on an errand by his victim. He shook his head. What did he fear so? The acid rage of Father Louis? The years of unspoken submission of the older man to the younger? The human aches that can invade the hearts even of those promised to God? He didn't know. All he could believe was that the unshaven knobbled old man waiting down there by his packed horse, with his hands that trembled on a regular slow beat, and his old blue eyes, was stronger than he. Father Pierre was tall and slender and chiseled in man's noble likeness. His soutane was always clean. His white face and dark eyes could blaze with the Holy Ghost. He had proper respect for authority, but could not now use his own.

Lifting piles of papers, and putting aside apples that had dried up, and mineral specimens blanched by dust, he searched Father Louis's room for the green sunglasses with their oval lenses and tin rims. He smiled at the condition of the room. He did not find the glasses. He returned to the courtyard.

Father Louis was already in his saddle. In his hand he held the sunglasses.

"I found them," he said. "I am sorry you had to go for them. Goodbye, Pierre. Give me your blessing. I must be getting along now."

Through his thin old voice, and his clouded eyes, there spoke a boy who was off to a picnic. Father Pierre's heart sank as he looked at him. He knew now that he was not going to tell what it was his duty to tell. Chagrined at his own weakness, and touched by the joy in the face of the impatient old man, he lifted his hand and blessed him with the sign of the cross, to which Father Louis bent his body, leaning forward with the elegance which, no matter what they may be on the ground, men used to the saddle assume the minute they are mounted. Then with a tart smile on his face under the woven cane hat, Father Louis waved grandly to his superior, turned his reins, and at a rapid hilarious walk was taken by his willing horse out of the courtyard and down the road toward the river, where the first light of the sun lapped at the brown ruffled water which came from so far beyond even the country where he was going.

After all these years he had a map in his head. The river came on a long diagonal, so. An old Indian trail went off northwestward at another angle, so. The farther inland, the farther apart they were from one another. There was one kind of country here by the seacoast. Presently it changed to another kind. Finally, in the distance of weeks, where the map would have only faltering scratches of the pen, based on rumor and legend, lay the farthest wilderness of Father Louis's journeys. The natural limits of his endurance were determined by water. His private map had an X for the end of each stage of travel—a settlement, a farm, a creek, a spring, a water hole (and pray it was not dry).

For the first several days, on these journeys, he hardly seemed to have left home. The earth was still low and sandy, and he could read in it how epochs ago the sea itself was here, hauling and grinding the stuff of ocean bottoms where now he rode. The air was moist and little clouds came to be and to vanish almost before his gaze. He could not closely follow the river for it wandered and turned, in some places doubling back upon itself in its last exhausted efforts to reach the sea. And so he followed the Indian trail, leaving it only to go to the isolated river farms in turn.

At such a one he might spend the night, or longer, depending on what he found. Sometimes death approached in the family, and he gave the last sacraments. Sometimes there were infants to baptize. In the mornings under a tree at roughhewn planks set across a pair of hogsheads he would say Mass and give communion. He listened to the local news from Mexico across the Rio Grande—there was talk of another war between the ranchers of Coahuila and the Mexican troops; it had not rained for a hundred and seventy days; robbers came over the river a while back and killed four men here in Texas and stole some cattle and horses and went back across the river; a child was born in the Bolsón de Mapimí who spoke, quite clearly, at three days old, of a flood that would come but who when further questioned seemed to have lost the power of speech; and so on. Father Louis in his turn told how things were at Brownsville, and farther up the coast at Corpus Christi and Galveston, and across the sea in France, where under the new emperor business was booming, and trade with Mexico was growing, as you could tell by the many ships that came from Marseilles and Le Havre into the Gulf of Mexico. And then after receiving gifts of food from such a family, the rider would leave the river and return to the trail, going northwestward once more.

Days later, though the sky did not cool during the daytime, the quality of the heat changed, and was dry, as the old seacoast plain gave way to a wilderness of rolling country thickly covered with thorny brush. When he encountered it as it wandered, the riverbed was rocky, and rock showed through the hard, prickly ground. Everywhere he looked he saw only that endless roll of empty land. Here, near to him, it was speckled with the colors of the olive, both green and ripe, but not with any of the grace he remembered from long ago in Southern France, where the olive trees gave a silver sweetness to the landscape. Farther away in the distance, the land rolls swam in glassy heat. Way off at the horizon there was a stripe of hazy blue where the hot white sky met the earth. Nowhere could he see a mountain, either in Mexico or in Texas.

As he rode, the country tried to hold him back. The thorns of the mesquite dragged at his boots and tore his clothes. Pancho was clever at avoiding most of the hazards, but in places these were so thick that all they could do, man and horse, was to go slowly and stoutly through them. But this was nothing new. Father Louis had persisted before against the thorns and had prevailed.

As for water, there was always too much or too little. Too little when, after years of drought, certain springs he looked forward to would, as he came upon them, reveal only dried white stones. Too much when, in hot spells so violent that they could only be ended with violence, there would be a cloudburst and the heavens would fall almost solid and bring the first water which as it struck the baked earth actually hissed and made cracking sounds until the varnished desert was slaked enough to receive the water in its fissures and let it run. When it ran in such quantity, every finger-like draw became a torrent in which a man and a horse could easily be drowned. If he crossed one in safety, another was waiting to engulf him beyond the next roll. There was no place for shelter. When the rain stopped, the sun came back and dried everything the same day except the running arroyos, which went dry the next day. All too soon there was bitter dust that sparkled in the light and rose with the hot wind. Against it Father Louis tied across his face his great bandanna that came from New Orleans.

And they went on, making a small shadow of horse and man moving slowly yet certainly across that huge empty map where days apart, each from the other, little clusters of human life and need clung to being and shone in Father Louis's mind and purpose like lanterns in the darkness—which usually was the first image he saw of his destination when by his reckoning it was time to reach another of his families.

Was this a hard journey?

Very well, then, it was a hard journey.

But so was the life hard that he found at the end of each stage of his travels. He had seen men grow old and die in his visits here, and their sons with their wives bring new souls to this wilderness in turn. They learned severe lessons in isolation, heat, and the hostility of the animal and vegetable world. Everyone, the child, the grandfather, the husband, the wife, the youth, the horse, the maiden, worked unceasingly against dust, thorn, ignorance, and scarcity from dawn to dark. The great world was but a rumor here, and by the time it came to the brush deserts, mostly wrong. But a world without limits of dimension dwelt behind the eyes of all those parched, brown people obedient to the natural terms of their lives. It was the world of the human soul, in which the betrayals of impersonal nature could be survived, if only someone came from time to time with the greatest news in all life.

For Father Louis knew in a simple flatness of fact—fact as hard as rock, as mysterious as water, as unrelenting as light—that without God the richest life in the world was more arid than the desert; and with Him the poorest life was after all complete in a harmony that composed all things.

To be the agent of such a composition put upon him a duty in the light of which all peril on his journeys became at worst mere inconvenience. Everyone he toiled overland to see needed and deserved that which he, at the moment, under existing circumstances, alone could bring. In a practical way he was still awed by the mystery of his office. And as a human being he could never deny himself the joy it gave him to see in their faces what his coming meant to his people in the harsh wilderness. They knew what he had come through. They were proud to be thought worth such labor and danger.

His mind was active in the solitude through which he crawled day after day mounted on Pancho. One of his favorite fancies was this: that a great triangle existed between God in heaven and any little ranch toward which he rode through the days and himself. It was an always-changing triangle, for one of its points was not fixed: his own. As he came nearer and nearer to his goal of the moment, the great hypotenuse between himself and God grew shorter and shorter, until at the last, when he arrived, there was a straight line with all in achieved communion. He smiled over this idea, but he respected it, too; and sometimes he would take a piece of charcoal from a fire and draw a series of pictures of what he meant, explaining it to the people he was visiting, and they would murmur, and nod, and consult each other, and enjoy the notion with him, marveling.

One day at noon on the present journey he knew he should soon see what would look like a long thin blade of cloud shadow far ahead on the earth that slowly quivered with wafts of light like those in wavering mirrors. But it was not a cloud shadow, as he had found out nearly thirty years ago. It was the distant gash of a long canyon whose yellow rock walls were stained with great stripes of slate blue. It came from the north and far away to the south opened into the rocky trough of the Rio Grande. In its bottom were all the signs of a river but running water. Here and there were shallow pools fed by the underground flow that needed storm water to call it flowingly to the surface. Father Louis always paused at such a pool for a bath. There were sores on his body from the catch of thorns through which he rode. Sometimes a needle of the brush would break in his flesh and burrow its way under his skin. For the most part he was unaware of such an affliction, but by its comfort the warm alkaline water of the pool reminded him of the misery he had forgotten to notice. It was usually midafternoon by the time he reached the canyon wall as the sun went lower. The place was like a palace to him, open to the brassy sky. Wrens and hawks came to look at him in their wary turns. To be below the surface of the rolling plain in the canyon was to have for a little while the luxury of privacy, somehow. He bathed, and dozed as he dried, and sat in the shade reading his breviary.

He knew when it was just time to gather himself together and resume his ride in order to come by nightfall to the house and the spring of Encarnadino Guerra, where he would spend the night.

This friend was a boy of ten when Father Louis first met him. He was now the father of six children, the husband of a silent, smiling woman named Cipriana, the son of a widowed mother called Doña Luz who on his last visit told Father Louis she would not live to enjoy his next one. He remembered how she sat blinking in the brilliant shade of the desert bowing to him over and over, while a triumph of patience went over her face eroded by time and trouble and work and pain, as she said,

"At night, when everything is quiet, and I am awake and alone, for I cannot sleep much any more, something speaks to me, and tells me to be ready, and not to make any other plans."

She looked at him with hardly any light in her small eyes, and he knew she was right. When he said Mass for them that time, he thought he saw in her face some powerful, direct understanding of the holy sacrifice which during all her pious life had slumbered within her but which at last came clear in her whole, small, withered being.

He wondered whether through any dry, desert-like tenacity she might still be living.

But when he rode up in the arching twilight to the dwelling of the Guerras, almost the first thing they told him after their excited greeting was that Doña Luz had died early in the summer while sitting in the shade on her bench holding her stick of ocotillo wood which her hands had shined so smooth.

In the light of the candle lantern the family looked at him and then at each other. They were shocked by how he had changed since last year. He was stooped and he slowly trembled all the time. He had to peer at them to see them, even though he preserved a smile to make nothing of this. Burned by the wind and sun, his face looked smaller. He breathed shallowly, with his mouth a little open. He seemed to them a very old man, all of a sudden.

It was like a secret they must keep from him.

After their first start, they got busy making his supper. The younger children lost their shyness and came from behind chairs and the edges of the table to see him, and at last to climb upon him. He smelled dry and dusty to them, like the earth.

After supper he held lessons in catechism for the younger children, who tomorrow would receive their first communions. The parents and the two older sons listened also.

After that, there was a little time left for gossip. The family's news was all of the seasons. The priest's was boiled down out of letters and newspapers from France. The Guerras already knew that the earthly love of his life was in his native country, which he had not seen for over thirty years, but which still spoke in his darting eyes, his cleverness at description, and in the accent with which he spoke Spanish. They listened respectfully while he made picture after picture in his talk of what he loved and missed; but they could not really see with him either the cool green fields, the ancient stone farmhouses, the lanes of poplar trees, the clear rivers, or the proud old towns, or the towering cathedrals, or the silvery web of his city of Paris sparkling delicately in daytime, glowing in the long dusk with golden lamps and violet distance.

But they were honored simply to have him here, and stared before his marvels, and held their breath for tomorrow, when he would give them sacraments.

In the morning he visited the grave of Doña Luz. Everybody went with him. She was buried a little way off from the adobe house. When he saw how little earth she displaced, he nodded and smiled, as though meeting all over again her modest character which he knew so well. Guerra brought some water in an earthen vessel, not much, but enough. Father Louis took the jug and held it in both hands a moment, and gazed into it. They were all reminded of how precious water was on the earth, how it determined by its presence the very presence of life. Then he blessed it, and they all knew what this meant in terms of their daily struggle. Then, reciting prayers for the dead, he walked around the small mound of the grandmother and sprinkled the holy water upon it, and they knew he was affirming once again a promise made between heaven and earth a long time ago.

After that they returned to the house and he took them one by one and heard them confess their sins, of which, as they were contrite, he relieved them. Then, at an altar improvised against the wall where the old woman used to sit for so many hours, he said Mass, wearing his embroidered French silks, and using the pewter chalice that came out of his saddlebag. The family knelt on the ground in a straight line facing the altar. The famous triangle of Father Louis was brought into a straight line also. God and mankind were made one. As he recited the words during the offertory, "Oh, God, Who hast established the nature of man in wondrous dignity, and even more wondrously hast renewed it . . ." Father Louis felt behind him the bodily presences of that isolated family, and an almost bitter sense of the dearness of each of their souls humbled him at his altar.

When Mass was over, they returned within the house, where, at the raw table polished by countless unnoticed contacts of all the family, Father Louis sat down to fill in certificates of first communion for the younger children.

He had a flask of guizache ink and a German steel pen. Sitting as far back from the documents as he could the better to read, he began to write. A look of disgust came over his face as his trembling hand gave him trouble. Exclaiming impatiently, he put his left hand on his right wrist to add strength and steadiness where they were needed; but this did not help much, and when he was done, he pushed the papers toward the head of the family saying,

"Nobody ever can read my writing except God."

They all took him seriously, prouder than before of their papers.

"But that is enough, isn't it?" he demanded in comic ferocity.

They had a merry breakfast when all talked as though they would not soon again have a chance to talk, which was true; all except Guerra, who was going to speak of something as soon as he had built up enough of his own silence. Finally he was ready.

"Father," he said, leaning back a trifle in his chair, and half closing his eyes to disguise deep feelings, "you won't be going on anywhere else, after us, will you?"

"Oh, yes."

"Where will you go, Father?"

"Why, I plan to ride from here over toward the river—I have a couple of families over there—and I may go as far as the town of San Ygnacio, to see if the priests from Mier are making visits there, as they ought to. Why?"

Guerra put his head on one side and shrugged.

He did not want to say that the old man was exhausted and ought not to go so far in the pitiless country under the searing sun. It would not be polite to say the old man was older than his years, and he must be seventy anyway. He might be misunderstood if he said that everybody reached a time after a life of hard work when he must pause and rest and let stronger people do what needed doing. It would hardly do to show outright that he thought Father Louis should give up, and stay here, and rest a few weeks, and then perhaps Encarnacion Guerra might leave everything here in the hands of his two strong, quiet boys, and just ride with Father Louis until he saw him safely back in Brownsville.

Father Louis peered close to his younger friend and saw enough of these thoughts to stir him up.

"Eh?" he cried, rapping hard with his knuckles on Guerra's skull, "What goes on in there?" He was sharp and angry. What were they all thinking? That he was a feeble old man? He knew all there was to know about that; but if anything was to be said about it, he, not they, or anyone else, was the one to say it. "Mind your manners, you, boy," he said to Guerra, screwing up his small eyes until all that showed of them were two sharp blue points of light. "Eh?

You have opinions, have you? Who told you to think anything! Eh? When I want you to think anything about anybody, I'll tell you. Eh? I got here, didn't I? How many times have I managed to come? And what for! Does anybody tell me to come? Or where to go? Or when? Or why? Then you keep your place, and thank God for your blessings, and for your friends, and understand that it is just as bad to hold an impolite thought as it is to say an impolite thing. Eh?" His whole body shook with the passion he failed to control. "Bad. You'd better just be careful, that's all I have to say, do you hear?"

The family was appalled at this burst of feeling. They sat with downcast eyes, fearing that it would be disrespectful to look upon Father Louis in his rage. But they had little glimpses of his unshaven face whitened with anger, and they could hear how pulse-shaken his voice was. Guerra was more Indian than anything else, and his countenance became fixed. He leaned back, let his eyelids cut his gaze in half, and took his dressing-down without response. He was not even hurt by it. He knew why it came to him. He knew how much it proved him right in his concern. He admired the flare of spirit in the old man. He was at peace with himself for trying what he had tried.

The youngest child, not understanding what had taken place, now, belatedly, felt the emotion among all the older ones, and turning up her little clay-doll face she burst into wails of misery and fear, bringing her tiny creature-paws to her howling mouth until she resembled the small sculptured masks of earth buried with the dead centuries ago deep in Mexico.

Father Louis roughly took her upon his lap. He bent his bristly face close to hers, cactus and blossom together, and in barely audible murmurs quieted the child, and himself, which took about five minutes.

This act reclaimed them all for each other. Once again the visitor was kind and smiling, and the family without fear.

"And so, goodbye for this time," said Father Louis, putting the child down and standing up. "If you will get my horse for me?"

Guerra spoke to one of the boys, who went to fetch Pancho. They all met him outside. Cipriana brought some tortillas for the saddlebag. Everyone knelt down to be blessed. The hot sunlight smote them. They had lingered over their breakfast. It was late. Father Louis, mounted and ready, blessed them three times, and then turned and rode off to the south. After a while he looked back. They were still kneeling. The next time he looked back it was hard to see them, for at even a little distance they made the same shadows as the scrubby bushes that grew on the caked earth, and seemed just as eternally rooted there.

He had a bad morning.

The sun seemed hotter to him than before. The savage brush seemed animated with spite as it clawed at his legs going by. Pancho, after a lifetime in the brush country, took it into his head to be terrified of familiar things, and from time to time, without warning, executed a rapid dance step to one side while throwing his head back and rolling his eyes at his rider.

"Hush, you fool!" Father Louis exclaimed at such times. "You fool!"

But he addressed himself as much as he did the horse. For the first few hours of that day's ride, he reviewed many times the loss of his temper at Guerra, and developed a masterly case, closely reasoned, lucid as only a French argument could be, compassionate with a largeness of heart, yet as logical as music in its progression, about why it had been not only natural, but actually necessary to reprove Guerra for having presumed to hold views about him. Reprove? Perhaps actually more of a scolding. Scolding? Thinking it over, possibly even a tongue-lashing. And the knuckles? The furious raps on the head? Still, how else could he be made to understand? But understand what?

It was no good.

As he always did, in the end, he lost the argument with himself. He knew that after hours of exhausting search for conclusions that would excuse him for what he had done, he would at last come to the truth, which was that he had offended God and man through his lifelong besetting sins of pride, self-esteem, and attempted condonement of his own shortcomings; and that there would be nothing left to do but go down upon his knees and admit how wrong he had been and pray to be forgiven and to be granted strength once more to conquer himself.

He began his penance with a resolve not to eat or drink until nightfall.

By midafternoon, the brush grew thicker. Only occasionally did he come to a little clearing between the mesquite bushes, which rose higher than himself mounted on Pancho. In spite of his green sunglasses, the ground sparkled and glared enough to hurt his eyes. He watched for but he could not see the long pale blur which would tell him that another canyon lay ahead which he would follow until it took him finally to the Rio Grande. He kept the sun on his right, for it was declining in the west in the white sky and he was going south. The day was still.

But how was this?

He thought that he heard a singing wind, but when he tried to notice whether he could feel the air stirring, or see dust rising ahead of him, there was no sign of wind. He halted Pancho. What did he hear, then? He turned his head. Yes, he could hear something, now far ahead, now here in his very ear. He searched the undulating horizon but he saw nothing except the wavering image of heat where the white sky met the dusty earth.

As he rode on, the singing in the air became louder. It sounded like the voice of the desert heat. He shook his head, resentful of natural conditions that hid behind mystery. And then suddenly he knew, and scornfully he rebuked himself for taking so long about it.

He was riding into a swarm of cicadas, and now he could see the first ones, clinging to the mesquite as they raised their shrieking song of the heat. The farther he rode the louder they became. He bent his head under their stinging assault upon his hearing. There were thousands and millions of them. Blindly they fulfilled their natures in their collective scream of response to the sun and the desert. The very atmosphere seemed to be in flames, and the sound of the stridulating insects added to the illusion.

Father Louis had touched the desert often enough. He had smelled it. He had tasted it when its dust rose on the wind. He had seen it in every state. But never before in so real a sense had he heard it.

He was suddenly exhausted.

In a clearing, a little lake of baked dust a few yards in diameter, he halted and dismounted, tying Pancho to a stout mesquite branch. Disturbed, a cloud of cicadas rose on crackling threads of flight and found another bush. The ringing song rose all about him. He could not even hear the sound of Pancho stamping his foot to shake off flies. He clapped his hands, but made barely a sound against the strident song in the air. He felt removed from himself. All desert natures combined to render him impersonal. Here, humbled not only from within but from without, he could find real contrition. He knelt down to pray.

Sunlight was brilliant in the center of the clearing, a little open room hidden by time, distance, and mesquite clumps. At the west side of it there was lacy shade, cast by tall bushes. But Father Louis rejected it and knelt in the plain sunlight. He bent his head under the beat of his spirit and of the insect scream that seemed to invoke the zenith. He prayed to be forgiven for his miserable anger.

His thoughts came alive in French, the language through which he had first met God.

He was not long now at his contrition, for he knew that prayer was not so often a matter of length as of depth. Much sobered, even saddened, by his intense self-discovery, he arose wearily from his knees and went over to the shade to lie down. He went as deeply as he could into the underboughs of the thorny mesquite. He closed his eyes. At once he felt cooler, just to have the hot light shaded from his sight. Ah, this was delicious, just to lie for a few moments and gather strength to go on for the remaining hours of daylight. He felt how his limbs all went heavy on the earth as he let himself drift off to sleep.

Little coins of light fell over him through the intricate branches. Where he lay, he made solid shadow himself under the mesquite tree. He was as quiet and substantial as a rock. And if he used nature, it in turn used him, without his knowing, for he was asleep.

He did not see, or smell, or feel what came in slow inquiry along the trackless ground, striving forward in orderly, powerful progress, flowing in a dry glitter and advancing through always new and always repeated thrust of form from side to side and yet ahead. It was a diamondback rattlesnake in search of shade and cool. It came from deep in the scattered brush, and it found the heavy sleeping man under the bushy tree. With what seemed almost conscious caution against awakening the sleeper, the snake drew closer and closer in infinite delicacy, until in the shade of Father Louis's right shoulder it lay heavily at rest, its length doubled back and forth in inert splendor.

The sleepers did not stir for a while; and then Father Louis grew tense in dream, his mouth fell open, and awakening with a jerk he sat up, lost in forgetfulness of where he was or how he came there. He stared at the white sky.

The thick snake at the first quiver of motion beside itself drew instantly into its coil and shook its dozen rattles.

Their dry buzz could not be heard over the general din of the cicadas.

"Ah, yes," sighed Father Louis, as he discovered where he was, and why, and whither he was going. He put his hand to his brow and sank roughly back to the earth to take a few more minutes of rest. The snake struck him in the shoulder and struck him again. Its coils turned dust into liquid light as they lashed. The strikes came like blows made by the thick, powerful arm of a young man.

"What then?" said Father Louis at the sudden stabbing pain and the blows that shook him. He first thought of mesquite thorns on a springy branch; they were long and, as he had often said, sharp as fangs, and their prick could fester if not treated. It occurred to him that this would be troublesome now, as he could hardly reach his own shoulder to wash, cut open the skin, and dig out the thorns if they had broken to stay in the flesh.

But he turned to see the branch that had attacked him, and saw the snake instead.

The snake was retreating. He could see its eye with its glaring drop of light. His heart began to beat hard. He had a surge of rage. He wanted to kill the snake, and actually rose to one knee and scraped the ground with his hands for something to attack with—a rock, a club of dead wood, anything—but he could find nothing. He sank down again and out of habit in any crisis brought his hands together with crossed thumbs in the attitude of prayer.

"No, no, no anger," he besought of himself with his eyes shut. He had just endured and come through a storm of his own pride, and he must not now create another. He opened his eyes and looked after the snake, and saw where it paused half in, half out of the dappled shade of the next bush.

"Go," he said to it.

What he meant by this came to be more and more clear through calm and struggle in the next hour or so. The snake, as though it heard him, resumed in infinite slowness the gliding flow of its retreat until it was lost to sight among the hot thickets where the insects still sang and sang.

"Yes, go," he repeated bitterly, and was ashamed to discover that he was trembling. It was the humanity in him that shook because death was coming. He fell over upon his face and put his cracked and dusty hands over his eyes. His mouth was open and he took into it the loose acid earth with his breath. His tears ran down his fingers. His heart was pounding rapidly upon the ground. It seemed to shake the earth. It told Father Louis that he was afraid.

"Afraid? Of what?" he thought. "Afraid of death? But I have dealt with it all my life and I have robbed it of its terrors for those who knew how to die. Is death the only victory of life? Or do we have to defeat life in its own terms? That depends. It depends upon whether sin is ever outside oneself, or always within. Yes, this is a very interesting matter."

He made himself lie quietly without thought for a moment. If, perhaps, he conserved his energy, he might by natural vitality, by pure goodness, defeat the murder that had been dealt him by the desert. He forced himself to relax, and promised that in a little while his head would be clearer, his heart would calm itself, and, moving with infinite caution, he would arise, mount his horse, and go slowly, steadily, cleverly, toward the long evening and come to the canyon where there must be a familiar trickle of water. A cool night with much prayer, a stout will, and tomorrow he would go forward and by the end of the day come to friends who would know how to make poultices and feed him and recover him to the use and enjoyment of many more years of duty, work, and acquired merit.

But the poison worked rapidly, and he felt it charging his mind with throbbing pain that confused him. Shining bars went across his vision behind his eyes like spokes of a great wheel. He was dazzled by their power. When he raised his head they took it with them, rolling and rolling until he fell down again upon the ground where his cheek was cut by little pebbles of gypsum. He tried to say,

"Let me not live for vanity, though, Lord."

Questions now became academic, for he went blind in his inner vision, and lay trembling as the terrible message that had been stricken into him traveled the course of his blood and reached him everywhere within.

Tied to his mesquite tree, Pancho stamped and waited.

Presently Father Louis believed that he awoke.

His mind was working sharply and with what seemed to him exquisite new ease and clarity. He saw all his thoughts as in crystal depths of cold fresh water. He knew he was in the mesquite thicket, and what had happened to him, and he possessed this knowledge with an elated purity such as he had always known in the state of grace, after receiving or administering the sacraments. It was more than mere physical well-being. It was a sense of delivery from the ordinary guilt of his own clay, and the exasperating weight of the world. It was the real meaning of communion with all that lay beyond himself. In such a state truth needed no seeking, and no definition. It was here, within, and it was there, without. It was everywhere. When all was known there could be no astonishment.

He was therefore not astonished now when right before him, lying at ease in the light of the sun, was the snake gazing at him with piercing sweetness. He spoke to it.

"I do not hate you. It is enough that I recognize you."

The snake replied, "That is my damnation."

"Yes," said Father Louis, "for when evil is recognized all other powers move together to defeat it."

"And yet they never do defeat it, do they? How do you explain that?"

"Ah. You and I do not see it in quite the same way. You conceive of the possible death of evil as being one, final end after which only goodness will survive."

"I do."

"That is your vanity. For the fact is that evil must be done to death over and over again, with every act of life. One might even say that this repeated act is a very condition for the survival of life itself. For only by acts of growth can more life be made, and if all evil, all acts of death, were ended once and for all, there would be nothing left for the soul to triumph over in repeated acts of growth."

The snake sighed despondently, and said, "Do you not permit me a comparable purpose and privilege? That is, of triumphing repeatedly over all acts of good, that is, of life, until only I remain?"

"I permit you your established role, but I do not admit the possibility of your triumphing repeatedly over all acts of life. I must point out that historically your premise is untenable."

"And yet I have played a part in every human life."

"Oh, admittedly. We are not discussing the fact that your powers exist; only the fact that they have their limits."

The snake smiled.

"This? From you?" it asked with ironic politeness.

"What do you mean, sir?"

"If my powers have their limits, then how is it that I have killed you? What greater power is there than that?"

Father Louis passed his hand across his face to hide his amusement.

"You have betrayed the weakness of your whole position," he replied, "for it appears to be impossible for you to know that the death of matter is of no importance, except to other matter. The materialist can see only destruction as the logical end of his powers. I, and my brothers, and my children, know that beyond matter lies spirit, and that it is there where answers are found, and truths become commonplace, and such efforts as yours, so restless, so ingenious, so full of torturing vanity, are seen for what they really are."

The snake frowned for a moment, but then shook off its irritation, and said, again with politeness, even with a charm and appeal that Father Louis was the first to admit, "Everyone must do that which his nature dictates."

"There again," said Father Louis with assumed gravity, "there is much behind the formation of that nature which you do not take into account."

"Oh, come, after all, I am a snake, I came from snakes, I do a snake's work, how could I behave like anything else but a snake?"

"The outer form is hardly the point. You can assume any form you choose, I believe?"

The snake hesitated before answering. A gleam of admiration went through its expression, and it marveled frankly for a moment at the astuteness of Father Louis.

"I must say, even if we are enemies, you force me to admire and like you," it said.

"Thank you," said Father Louis. "Viewed abstractly, you have great and beautiful qualities of your own."

"Do you really think so?"

"Oh, yes, I do. But I must add that they seem to me less important, in the end, than they do to you."

"You can also be very rude, you know."

"I do not think of it in that way," said Father Louis mildly. "Finally, it doesn't matter how things are said or done, it is what things are said or done.

For example, I really believe you can do things far more expertly than I can. But when it comes to what things, there I have you."

The snake looked away, far from pleased.

Father Louis resumed, "I can't assume any form, for example, as you can. I remain always what I am, a man, an old man, a dirty old man when water is scarce or I am busy, an old man full of pride and sin and vanity and all the rest of it; but nobody is ever in doubt about what I mean, or about what I think life means, and with all my mistakes in style and good form, the garden I scratch keeps growing."

"And I?"

"And you, sometimes you are a snake, and sometimes a whisper, and again, a daydream, a lump in the blood, a sweet face, an ambition, a scheme for making money, a task for an army. Sometimes you can even be a man and disarm everyone who cannot see your heart. But someone there is who always sees. Goodness is often performed without the slightest knowledge of its doing. But evil is always known."

"Yes, I think more people know me than the other thing."

"But don't congratulate yourself upon that," said Father Louis, "for it always means one of your uncountable defeats when you are known."

Father Louis saw that the snake would have to grow angry unless the subject were changed. The snake changed it.

"I wonder," it mused, "why I ever came to you today."

Father Louis shrugged.

"Sooner or later, we would have come together," he said.

"Did you expect me?"

"I have been expecting you all my life; though not exactly in this particular guise. You came to me in my sleep, like an evil dream."

"All I wanted was a little comfort. It was so hot, so dry."

Father Louis smiled in delight.

"You see? For comfort, even you have to appeal to the powers of goodness."

The snake habitually wore a scowling smile and now for a moment the smile disappeared leaving only the scowl. Then with an effort it restored the smile, and said,

"Why did you let me go?"

"I had no weapon."

"You could have stamped upon me."

"I do not believe in killing."

"Yet I am your enemy."

"Yes, you are. But I believe there are greater ways to dispose of you than in revenge."

"You do not have much time left, you know. Just think of all the time you would have left if I had not come to you. If you had seen me and killed me first."

"Yes, I have thought of that. But you speak as though time were my property. It is not. How can I count it? Or know how much of it is my share?"

The snake frowned and looked from side to side evasively. Unwillingly, against its own comfort, it asked,

"Who else can decide your share? Where do you get it? What do you refer to?"

The snake began uneasily to bring its coils together. There was anguish in its movement, slow as it was. It seemed to be obeying desire that was hurtful and yet impossible to deny.

"You do not really want to hear," said Father Louis tenderly.

"Oh, yes, I do, tell me," said the snake, with broken breath, already suffering under the answer it demanded.

Father Louis bent over the snake with compassion. There was torture in the creature, as with glittering sweet power it begged Father Louis to answer.

"Very well, my poor sinner," said Father Louis gravely. "I, and all creatures, draw our share of time in this life from God our Father in Heaven."

At these words the snake with speed of lightning knew convulsion in its dread coils and with mouth wide open and fangs exposed struck again and again at the earth where the dust rose like particles of gold and silver. Father Louis regarded it with pity as its paroxysm of hatred and chagrin spent itself. At last, gasping softly and stretched out in exhaustion, the snake said, sorrowfully,

"And so it was not by my will that you die now?"

"No."

"I was only the means."

"Only the means."

"Your hour was designated elsewhere?"

Father Louis looked upward. His face was radiant.

"My hour was fixed by our Heavenly Father."

The snake closed its eyes and shuddered reminiscently. Then it said, "And my hour?"

"You will die in your bodily form by His will."

"You're sure?"

"Yes. But you will live only on earth, no matter what form you assume."

The snake grew pale.

"Oh no."

"Yes," said Father Louis, as his argument drew to its close, "for there can be no evil in Heaven."

The snake lay with its mouth open, its tongue like a little tongue of fire flickering in despair, its eyes staring without sight. It was vanquished, destroyed, made trivial. Father Louis shook his head over it and wished it might not have suffered. Then he felt his brow where the diamondine lucidity of the past quarter of an hour seemed to be clouding over. His skull was cracking under blows that beat and beat there. How could he feel so ill after feeling so well?

"And now you must excuse me," he said, uncertainly, to the snake. "I have things to do, and actually, I do not feel too well, thank you, if you will just go now," and he looked to see if the snake was leaving, but the snake was already gone.

The battering pains in his head brought Father Louis from vision to consciousness.

"Oh, my God, my God," he said devoutly and with much effort, even with modesty, representing his trouble to Him whose suffering he had dwelt upon so deeply in a lifetime.

He looked around.

The air seemed entirely silent. This was because there was a ringing in his head so bewildering that he could no longer hear the myriad insects at their screaming celebration of the heat.

He saw Pancho tied to the tree.

"No, you must not stay with me," he said, and tried to stand up. He could barely stand, for his legs were weak as paralysis crept into them. And so he crawled across the open place among the thickets until he could hold to his stirrup, haul himself up, and lean with his head on the saddle for a moment.

"You need not die here, tied to a tree," he said. "Let me get my things, and you may go."

He fumbled with the buckles and straps until he was able to haul the saddle off the horse. It fell to the ground. He worked at the bridle until he had freed it enough to pull it over Pancho's head. The horsehair bridle hung from the thorny tree and trailed in the dust.

"Huya! Huya!" cried Father Louis, waving his hand at Pancho to make him trot away, as he so often had done after unsaddling the horse at the corral in Brownsville. But Pancho simply stood and regarded him.

"Very well, very well, in your own time, then," he said, and went down to his hands and knees, fondling a pouch on the saddle. Out of it into his hands came the objects he wished to hold once more. Holding them to his breast, he crawled back to his fatal shade across the clearing. The sun was almost down.

"Magnificat anima mea Dominum," he murmured while pain pierced him through and through, "et exultavit spiritus meus in Deo salutari meo," he said without knowing he spoke. But he brought a lifetime of prayer with him to death's door; and in a little while it entered there with him.

Pancho late the next evening finished finding his way through the brush back to the house of Encarnadino Guerra. The family saw that he was without his saddle and bridle. Guerra and his big sons went searching, and though they persevered for days found nothing in that wilderness of repeated clump and glaring shadow and lost sameness. They had to give up. Later that year when surveyors from an expedition of the United States Army came by his place on their way to Brownsville, Guerra told them the news, and asked them to see that it reached the proper authorities, along with the horse Pancho which he hoped they would take with them.

And then one day, eight years afterward, Guerra was on his way to San Ygnacio on the Rio Grande to see his new grandson, born to the household of his oldest boy who now lived there. Coming into a small clearing in the brush, he found quite by accident what he had looked for long ago. There was not much left, for the desert earth and sky were voracious. Coyotes and blowing sand, vultures and beating sunlight and wind had worked with the years on flesh and leather, French silk, parchment and homespun. Reverently Guerra took up the few bones that had not been scattered, and the few hard things that still stayed by them: the pewter chalice, a rosary of small seashells, three American silver dollars, the pair of green sunglasses, and, from a mesquite tree where it hung now off the ground, the horsehair bridle.

When he could, he made the journey to Brownsville bringing the relics of his old friend with him. He found his way to Father Pierre Arnoud.

"How these things speak to us!" said Father Pierre, after hearing the end of the story that had begun eight years before. He looked at Guerra and saw that this was a man who had lost a dear friend, who would understand anything said to him in the name of Father Louis. He added, "I am leaving soon for France. Do you know where that is?"

"Yes. He used to tell us much about it."

Father Pierre was making ready to obey a summons to return home to receive the dignity of bishop of a French diocese.

"I am going there to assume new work," he said. "These things, this sacrifice," he said, indicating what Guerra had brought, "will help me to do it better."

Guerra nodded.

"We will bury him here in the churchyard," continued Father Pierre, "and you must be present. As you were his friend, and have served him so well now, I would like to ask your permission to keep this."

He held up the little string of seashells.

"Yes," said Guerra, accepting with simplicity the power to dispose.

"I wonder how he died," murmured Father Pierre. "Indians? A heart attack?"

"No Indians."

"Why not?"

"They would not have let the horse go."

"True. What then?"

Guerra made a gesture with his mouth, putting his lips forward as though he would point to a place far from there and long ago. He saw the clearing in the thorny brush again, and he knew its nature, all of it.

"I think I know."

"How could you possibly?"

"He did not die suddenly."

"No?"

"No. He had time to free his horse."

"Ah."

"If he thought he could have saved himself, he would have come with the horse."

"Undoubtedly."

"But he did not come. He stayed. That means he knew there wasn't any use."

"And so?"

"Where I found him was just like the place where it would happen."

"What would happen?"

With his hand Guerra made in the air a slow, sinuous motion from side to side in an unmistakable imitation.

"No!" said Father Pierre. "A snake?"

Guerra nodded.

"I think so," he said.

Father Pierre shuddered at the nature of that fate, and then presently he kindled at the memory of an old weakness and an old strength.

"Do you know? I will tell you something," he said. "Our dear friend was an old man, tired, and ill, when he went on that last journey. For days before he left, I was supposed to tell him that he could not go. I tried, and I tried. But I could not tell him. Even on the last morning, I could not give the order."

Father Pierre put his hands together in emotion.

"What could I have saved him from? From dying at his work? That is how we—all of us—want to die, when our time comes."

He looked earnestly at Guerra, but if he thought he would find the abstract pardon of life there, he was mistaken. Guerra simply looked back at him with the impersonal judgment of the world.

"No, I could not give the order," resumed Father Pierre. "And do you know? I am sure he knew what I had to say. He would not let me say it. He gave the orders. Just to prove it, he even sent me upstairs to find his green sunglasses. I went, and I did not find them. When I came down again, there they were, he had them all the time."

Guerra laughed out loud at the crankiness this recalled, and what it meant. He bent over, took up the pair of green-glass spectacles with their rusted tin rims, and with a gleam of meaning, handed them to Father Pierre.

"Then keep these also," he said.

"Thank you," said the bishop-elect soberly.

6

EMMANUELE!
EMMANUELE!

Caroline Gordon

I

Robert Heyward glanced at his watch as he closed the door behind him and walked out onto the terrace: high noon. A waiter was passing. Heyward asked him to bring him writing materials and an apéritif. Before he sat down at a table he walked over to the balustrade and stood for some seconds looking out over the sea; the Hotel Alamède sat on an eminence not five hundred yards from the beach. The gardens of the hotel consisted of a series of terraces that ended in a cliff that rose straight out of the sea. The young American's eye left the wide, blue expanse to seek and find a line of dark growth that followed the cliff's curve: the orange and lemon trees that grew on the terraces gave way at the cliff's edge to ilex and pine. A path made of pinkish gravel ran the length of cliff. Bob had walked there yesterday with his employer, the famous French man of letters, Guillaume Fäy. At Fäy's suggestion they had left the path to go in under the shade of the orange trees. It had rained that morning and the sky was still overcast, but Bob, as he went stooping through the grove, had had the illusion that the sun shone on them: a profusion of golden globes that shone even in that dim light had hung over their heads. Fäy struck the trunk of one of the trees lightly with his stick. It was as richly colored as the pillars of the famous mosque at Córdoba, he said. A Sudanese Negro was sauntering along the path as they emerged from the grove. He was over six feet tall. The spray of white jasmine that he wore in his turban curled down over his cheek, giving him a look of languor that contrasted oddly with his brawny frame. When they came to the end of the green tunnel he grasped a handful of orange blossoms and held them in his hand a moment before he inserted the crushed petals into his nostrils.

The waiter had come back. Heyward walked over and sat down under the striped awning. He told himself that he would not touch his drink until he had written a page of his letter. But he did not begin writing at once. Instead, he stared at the door he had just closed.

It was a pale saffron color, like the walls of the hotel, but Bob fancied that the brownish yellow was here and there tinged with pink—the same pink that showed in the gravel walk on the cliff's edge. An ilex bough that drooped over the terrace cast a plume of almost black shadow on the door. A smile trembled on the young man's lips; it seemed almost incredible that the shadow should so faithfully reproduce the minute serrations that bordered each ilex leaf. He drew the sheet of paper toward him and began to write:

My Darling:

I got the job and have been at it for nearly a week. It is even easier than I had expected it to be. Fäy rises at eight every morning, drinks only a cup of tea, and is at work by nine. He is not ready for me before ten. I come in then and we work for two hours. He has an enormous correspondence, but he is already trusting me to write many of the letters, with only a memorandum for guide. He said yesterday that I seemed to know what he needed to have done without his telling me. So you see I am giving satisfaction!

Promptly at noon he sends me out of the room. It is his custom to write to his wife every day at this hour. He has been doing this for thirty years, he tells me, whenever he is separated from her. I am going to follow his example and write to you, too, every day, at this hour. Don't you think that it will bring us closer together if you know that every day at twelve o'clock I will be starting my letter to you?

The sound of footsteps made him look up from his writing. Two women stood only a few feet away from him. One of them, an elderly Frenchwoman, was evidently a servant. She stood a few paces behind the other, holding in each hand a string bag from which fruit and vegetables protruded.

The other woman stood with her hands resting on the back of a chair and contemplated the young man, her head a little on one side, a faint smile on her lips. Heyward, as he got to his feet and stood looking down on her, thought that he might have taken her for an American if he had not known that she had been born in France; she wore her broad black sun hat and gray cotton frock with a casual elegance that is not often found among elderly Frenchwomen. She was thin and a little stooped. The hands that grasped the chair back were still shapely but wrinkled and covered with sun spots. She fixed her large, gray-blue eyes on Heyward and said in a husky whisper, "And is *this* the way you work for Monsieur Fäy?"

Heyward got hurriedly to his feet. He was annoyed to find himself blushing. Mrs. Rensslaer, the widow of the historian Edgar Rensslaer, was a cousin of Guillaume Fäy's. Heyward's classmate, Forrest Blair, had taken Heyward to call upon her soon after he arrived in the city. It was Forrest who had discovered that Guillaume Fäy needed a secretary, Forrest who insisted that Heyward, with his unusually good command of French and his acquaintance with contemporary literature, was the man for the job. Mrs. Rensslaer had said negligently that she was sure that Guillaume would be fortunate to secure the services of Mr. Heyward. She would be delighted to write him a letter of introduction, but on one condition. Heyward must not let her cousin know that she was in the city. "I am not in the mood for Guillaume," she had said frankly.

Heyward, who had already written to thank her for her kind offices, told her now that he had been working for Fäy several days and found the work stimulating and delightful. He was about to say something else when Mrs. Rensslaer made a motion of her hand toward her maidservant that indicated that she was too pressed for time to share drinks with him. Casting a glance, which seemed to him tinged with mischief, at the door of Fäy's suite, she asked, "And what is Guillaume doing with himself this fine morning?"

Heyward replied simply that Monsieur Fäy was writing to his wife, adding, "He tells me that he has written to her at this hour, whenever they are separated, for thirty years."

Mrs. Rensslaer continued to eye him intently while he was speaking. When he finished she shook her head slowly from side to side, at the same time compressing her lips, then suddenly cast her remarkable eyes upward as if asking Heaven what it thought of that. An exclamation broke from her. Heyward did not think that it *could* have been "*Oo la la!*" and yet that was what it had sounded like.

"Can you dine with me tonight?" she asked. "Forrest is coming."

Heyward replied that he would be delighted to dine at Soleil d'Or any day, any hour she named. She told him to come at eight and, beckoning to her maid, went, with a step that struck him as surprisingly light for her years, down the stairs and onto the street.

Heyward sat down again and was about to resume his letter when he suddenly folded the sheet of paper and thrust it into his pocket. He would have to finish his letter later in the day; the door of Fäy's suite had opened. The great man stood for a second blinking in the Mediterranean sunshine before he saw his secretary and came swiftly toward him. He had been in his dressing gown when Heyward left him a few minutes ago. Now he wore a coffee-colored suit of some fine tropical weave and a Panama hat of equal fineness. Heyward was struck, not for the first time, by his air of extraordinary vitality. He wondered whether it was a family characteristic. Fäy was the same age as his cousin, Mrs. Rensslaer, and like her was tall and thin, but he was lither. As he came toward the young man his body actually seemed to sway from side to side out of a superabundance of vitality. He stopped and, settling his hat farther forward on his head, asked Heyward if he would like to walk with him to the marketplace. He had ordered a pair of gloves for his wife two weeks ago. They were to be ready today.

The vitality that animated his whole body found its chief expression in his eyes, Heyward thought. They were long, like his cousin's, capable of opening widely, and set under dark, level brows. Heyward had thought that they were a light hazel in color. This morning they were so lambent that they looked almost yellow. Fäy was smiling at the young man. His smile seemed to say that he realized that his conduct was unusual for an oldster. "But that can't be helped," the smile also said. "Here I am. You must take me as I am."

A scene from Heyward's childhood rose before him. A small boy, he had been helping his grandmother's old Negro gardener cut brush when a snake suddenly reared itself above a fallen bough. Its body was intricately patterned in rich shades of dark brown. Its head was copper-colored. From under the slanted lid an eye gleamed at him. He had put his hand out toward it when the old Negro, coming up behind him, struck it down: "Boy, don't you know a chunkhead when you see one?"

Heyward signified his desire to accompany Fäy to the marketplace. The two men began the descent of the long flight of steps. Fäy—who made a point of speaking English with his secretary—said that Muhammed Ali had been recommended to him as one of the best leather workers in the city. If the gloves he had ordered came up to his expectations he was of a mind to order another pair for his wife. "Her hands are one of her greatest beauties," he said. "Or were—until she ruined them with gardening—and the care of peasants—and animals." He turned his flashing gaze on Heyward. "I have seen her run out into the coldest weather, nothing on her head, a cloak falling off her shoulders, carrying a pan full of food. For whom? Stray cats, sick, mangy beasts that the farmers would let starve. In winter her hands are a pitiable sight, chapped, with raw places all over them. I give you my word I sometimes fear that she will succumb to an infection."

Heyward did not answer. There was something about the scene that struck him as unreal. He, Robert Durham Heyward, associate professor of English at Bonnell College, was receiving confidences from Guillaume Fäy—*Guillaume Fäy!* He thought helplessly that things had been happening too fast. His first volume of poems had been published only six months ago. Two months after that one of the great philanthropic foundations had awarded him the fellowship that had made possible his long-awaited trip to Paris. The day before he sailed the head of the English Department had summoned him to his office and had told him that the college had recently become the beneficiary of a sizable trust fund. The proceeds from it were to be devoted to securing scholars and artists as lecturers. "While you're over there you might fix something up for us," the administrator had said with a smile. When Forrest Blair, who was attached to the American consulate in a North African port, wrote that Guillaume Fäy was vacationing in the city, Heyward had hastily reckoned up his resources and had taken the next boat for Africa; it had seemed too good an opportunity to be missed. Forrest, he had felt sure, could get permission for him to call on Fäy. He might even have a little conversation with him while he was delivering the invitation to lecture. That had been the most he had hoped for, but now—and his heart beat faster at the thought—he lived under the same roof with the great man, in an association so intimate that Fäy discussed his wife with him, complained of her to him! Madame Fäy's picture stood on Fäy's desk in a heavily wrought silver frame; a young woman in a white dress, with her hair in a great coil on top of her head, gazing straight at you out of eyes that surely were dark. Heyward had a vision of her now, as slim as Fäy himself, her hair slipping from its coil, her cloak swinging behind her in the wind, as she ran across a courtyard, holding in her arms a great yellow cat. The Fäys lived in a chateau in Normandy. Mrs. Rensslaer had described it as a "cross between a museum and a menagerie." But Madame Fäy, he suddenly reminded himself, was not a young woman. Mrs. Rensslaer had told him that she was two years older than she herself was. She must then be seventy to her husband's sixty-eight.

They had come to the first landing in the long flight of steps. A narrow terrace bordered the stair on each side. At the right a marble bench stood under an orange tree. A gardener was taking oranges from the basket that he held on his arm and laying them down upon one end of the bench. There were varieties that Heyward had never seen before. One kind was as large as a muskmelon, another was shaped like an egg, and on top of the heap the gardener was scattering tangerines whose skins were a greenish yellow, faintly tinged with rose. Fäy had stopped, too. The two men stood looking down at the heap of fruit. Fäy gave a small shake of the head. "In France everything is gray," he said, "gray buildings, gray streets, gray light over everything. In Normandy we even have apples whose skin has a gray-ish cast!" His lean hand hovered for a moment over the heap before he selected a tangerine. It had been picked before it was quite ripe. The skin was a clear lemony green on one side, on the other a pale yellow, with a faint trace of color at the navel. Fäy held it in his hand and turned it so that it caught the light before he began stripping off the skin. "See!" he said. "The skin is as delicate, as pliable as those gloves that Muhammed Ali is making for my wife."

He sat down as he spoke. Heyward selected one of the larger oranges and sat down beside him. After they had eaten their fruit they sat on for a while, smoking. The harbor, almost elliptical in shape, lay directly below them. The sun beat straight down. The surface of the whole bay sparkled green. The depths beneath were bluer than any water Heyward had ever imagined. Fäy suddenly waved his hand.

"Does all this ever strike you as unreal?" he asked.

The young American slowly shook his head.

Fäy turned and gave him a fleeting glance. "How *does* it strike you, then?"

"Do you mean this particular scene?" Heyward asked.

"No," Fäy said impatiently. "I mean any scene, any landscape anywhere that is extraordinarily beautiful. Do you ever feel that it—does not exist?"

Heyward laughed. "No," he said. "I feel as if it had been there all along. The hell of it is that I didn't get there before!"

Fäy laughed, too. "Ah, you Americans!"

Somewhere below a clock struck. He rose and said that they must be on their way to the souks.

They left the great modern thoroughfare and turned off onto one of the older streets, cobbled and so narrow that the stick Fäy swung in his hand struck occasionally against the wall. He told Heyward that the last time he had been in the city was just after the winter rains. These walls had been mantled in green moss. The flowers planted on the edge of the terraces had overhung them like great baskets of flowers.

They emerged from the narrow passage into a square floored with cobblestones. From the dark stone fountain in its center interlacing plumes of water jetted high into the air. They went past the arched front entrance and passed through a narrow doorway shaded by a leaning jujube tree into an alley that led, Fäy said, into the saddlers' souks.

Heyward had never been in this part of the souks before. Fäy, striking his stick on stone, told him that when he first began to visit the city the alleyways all had earthen floors. On moonlight nights, Arabs and camels used to sleep against the walls of the mosque. Now the alleys all had sidewalks and policemen patrolled the square at all hours of the night. Heyward, as he walked, was gazing up over his head at the ceiling. Fäy pointed out to him the peculiar half-dark half-luminous light that bathed the stalls, the wares heaped on them, the figures stooping behind them. It was, he said, partly the effect of the whitewashed ceiling.

They had arrived at the stall he sought. The saddler, Muhammed Ali, his long legs crossed, was seated on a leather cushion, stitching a pair of gloves by the light that came in between the half-drawn curtains at the back of the stall. He laid his work aside when he saw Fäy and came forward. He wore a not very clean burnous. His turban was of some silky material striped with rose. Greetings were exchanged. He stopped and drew a parcel wrapped in tissue paper out from under the counter. His tawny eyes rested on Fäy's face for a second before he deftly whisked the wrappings away so that a pair of gloves was revealed.

Fäy stood in silence, eyeing the gloves. The leather had been dyed a dark red, almost the color of pomegranates. The texture of the leather was so fine as to be almost silky. As if obeying the kind of uncontrollable impulse that sometimes comes to children, Fäy put his finger out and touched one of the gloves, then turned to Heyward, showing his still strong, white teeth in a delighted smile. "Feel!" he said. "It is like the skin of the little oranges," and he brushed Heyward's cheek with the soft kidskin.

Muhammed Ali's tawny eyes gleamed. He said in fluent French that he was overjoyed to know that Monsieur was satisfied with his workmanship.

Fäy had held one of the gloves up and was studying the pattern of delicate stitching that ornamented the wrist when a shaft of blinding sunlight falling between suddenly parted curtains made both tourists look up. An Arab boy about fourteen entered, bearing a bundle of hides on his arm. He laid them down upon the floor at the back of the stall and, stepping over to Muhammed Ali's side, spoke to him in a low voice. Muhammed Ali nodded impatiently and, pointing to the end of the counter, said a few words in Arabic. The boy remained standing at his side for a second after he had spoken, staring straight ahead of him, then, as if he had all at once grasped the meaning of the answer that had been given him, he nodded and went to the end of the counter and, drawing out a bulky package, tucked it under his arm and left the shop. But not before his lustrous gaze rested first on one and then the other of the tourists. His eyes were unusually large, dark, and so lustrous that they seemed to brim in the head like water. Heyward had the feeling that some substance as tangible, as soft as the pliant kidskin had been drawn across his cheek. The curtain that had been pushed aside by the

97

boy's entrance had not swung back into place. As the boy turned away his cheek caught the light. Under a soft down it shone copper color, flushed with rose.

Fäy was still holding the glove in his hand. He did not move until the curtain had swung to behind the boy, then he laid the glove on the counter.

"Your son?" he asked.

The leather worker shook his head. "He is no son of mine," he said in an even, uninterested tone.

"Your apprentice?"

"He has been apprenticed to me," Muhammed Ali said indifferently. "It was his father's request. But I have doubts as to whether he will ever become proficient. He is not of the *caliber*." He added that time was when he would not have had a person of such low origins about him. "But what would you?" he asked. "In these days? If Monsieur will permit me to say so, the prevalence of foreigners in the city has not had an elevating influence upon the young. The boys make money too easily. It has been years since a respectable lad applied to apprentice himself to me. In the meantime, I must have somebody to fetch the hides from the warehouse and deliver the orders when they are accomplished. Hussein does that well enough. As Monsieur sees, he is well built, with a strong body and swift legs, if not a strong brain. What he does out of hours is Allah's concern, not mine."

A short sigh escaped Fäy. He picked the glove up again and held it in his hand, then extended it to Muhammed Ali. "The stitching!" he said. "It is so fine, so delicate! But would not a second row of stitching improve it?"

Muhammed Ali took the glove from him. With his finger he traced an imaginary line along the wrist of the glove, drawing his head back as if to study the effect. Finally he raised his tawny eyes to Fäy's face.

"If Monsieur wishes."

"When can I have them?" Fäy asked eagerly.

"Tuesday of next week?"

Fäy shook his head emphatically and, leaning over the counter, fixed his eyes on Muhammed Ali's face. "I leave within a week," he said. "An extra row of stitching—it could be executed within an hour. If one applied oneself. I should like to have the gloves today—this evening."

Muhammed Ali raised both his eyebrows and his shoulders. "Ah, but, monsieur . . . !"

Fäy suddenly laughed. He took his wallet out and, extracting a bill, laid it on the counter. "I should like to pay you in advance for the extra stitching," he said. "And I should like to order another pair of gloves. Exactly like these, only fawn color. Do you think you can deliver the gloves this evening?" As he spoke he raised the bill a few inches from the counter.

Muhammed Ali's brown hand shot out, closed over the bill. "At seven o'clock," he said. "Hussein will bring the gloves to the Alamède at seven o'clock. Will Monsieur be in at that hour?"

"Assuredly," Fäy told him and, crooking his stick jauntily over his arm, he laid his hand on Heyward's elbow and guided him at a rapid pace out of the great whitewashed mosque onto the square where the dark stone fountain still shot its crystalline jets into the blaze of the noonday sun.

II

"And with whom is Monsieur Guillaume Fäy dining tonight?" Mrs. Rensslaer asked.

"I don't know," Heyward said.

They had dined on an iced, rose-colored borscht, followed by breast of guinea hen basted in wine, with new potatoes the size of walnuts ranged about it, and a green salad in a great, dark wooden bowl. The dessert was a sherbet flavored with some fruit that Heywood had never tasted before. While they were eating their sherbets Marie, Mrs. Rensslaer's sharp-featured cook, had put her head in at the door to ask if Monsieur found the guinea hen as it should be. Mrs. Rensslaer explained that the *recette* was one which Forrest's aunt in Maryland had sent her at her request. Forrest must dine here often, Heyward thought, often enough, at any rate, to have his preferences in food consulted.

Immediately after dinner they had gone out on the terrace. Mrs. Rensslaer wore a long dress that she said was as old as the hills but was the same color as her eyes. As they passed through the hall she had caught up a white shawl, saying that it was likely to turn cool—thank God!—before the evening was over. She reclined now in her long garden chair that stood always beside the fountain. The little splash that Heyward heard every now and then was her hand dipping in and out of the water. Forrest Blair sat a few feet away from Mrs. Rensslaer in the shadow of the great mimosa tree. Heyward's chair was turned so that he faced the harbor.

The lights on the water, the shadowed terrace, the excellent food and wine which he had entrusted to his excellent digestion all contributed to his impression of having before him an agreeable evening. He said lazily to Forrest, "Before I forget, Fäy has let his visa run out and only told me about it this afternoon. Is there any head you could go over to and get it fixed up quick?"

"Take it to the new minister," Forrest said. "I met him at the Cortots last night. Seems a good guy."

Mrs. Rensslaer said, "Oh! Has Raoul Pleyol come? I hope he will come to see me."

"Could you take me to see him tomorrow?" Heyward asked boldly.

"Sure," Forrest said. "Eleven o'clock suit you?"

They agreed that Heyward should come to the consulate at eleven o'clock and that Forrest would then escort him to the ministry. Heyward, leaning back, felt a little of the same excitement he had felt that morning. All the world—all the world that seemed of any importance to him—knew of the correspondence which Guillaume Fäy and Raoul Pleyol, the poet-diplomat, had kept up over a period of years, in the high style so dear to French men of letters. The correspondence had ceased abruptly some years ago. It was probable that each man had become too engrossed in his own affairs to continue it. Still, it was strange that Fäy did not know that his old friend was to be the new minister.

"Is it true that Guillaume writes facing a mirror?" Forrest asked abruptly.

Heyward hesitated, seeing not only the oval mirror that hung over Fäy's desk but the face that opposed it. Fäy, he thought, was neither ignorant of nor indifferent to the deductions that might be drawn from this habit of his. "See this fellow," he had said once, pointing to the reflection of his long, saturnine face. "I have been holding a conversation with him for years. I will not say that he is always in the right, but one thing I can say of him: he never bores me," and he had struck the mirrored cheek a blow so light that it was like a caress. Heyward recalled now that the fact that Fäy wrote facing a mirror had been recorded in his published journal. There was therefore no secret for him to keep. He said gravely that in his employer's suite at the Hotel Alamède a mirror hung over the desk.

"Regular Gentleman of Shallot, isn't he?" Forrest said. "Gabrielle, what are you laughing at?"

"I was thinking of the first time we ever saw the mirror," Mrs. Rensslaer said. "Guillaume and I spent one whole summer at Crans. I was twelve, so he must have been twelve, too. Thérèse was fourteen. So was Edmond—that was Edmond Pribeaux, our cousin on the next estate."

"Bad as Alabama, for cousins," Forrest said.

Heyward said, "Thérèse?"

"She is Thérèse Gabrielle and I am Gabrielle Thérèse. I am named for her mother."

"*He* calls her Emmanuele."

"Yes. It is a name he gave her."

"What were you laughing at?" Forrest asked.

"The time we played *Peaux Rouges* on that island in the river. It was Edmond's idea, so he got to be . . ."

"Ok-äy?" Forrest asked.

"He was Ok-äy, naturally. Guillaume could have been Oon-ca but he only came and stood on the bank and looked at us and then went back to the house. So Thérèse was Oon-ca and I was Chin-gach-gook, which I didn't much like; he always seemed a bit of a bore, compared to the others. Still, we had a heavenly time. It was dark when we came home. Guillaume was sitting at his desk, with a mirror hung over it! We laughed till we rolled on the floor. All that summer we would laugh whenever we thought of it."

"Thérèse evidently didn't recognize her fate when she confronted it," Forrest said. "Why do you suppose she ever married the fellow?"

"I don't think it occurred to her that she had any choice in the matter," Mrs. Rensslaer said after a slight pause.

"Did the family make the match?" Heyward asked.

Mrs. Rensslaer said, "No," negligently, and all three were silent for several minutes. In the shadows Heyward could barely make out Mrs. Rensslaer's pale form half reclining on her long chair. There was a rustle among the pillows. She was sitting upright. Suddenly his cheeks were burning. Was it because her eyes fixed on his face? Was this woman subjecting him to a scrutiny more intense, more penetrating than she had hitherto found it worth her while to give him?

She leaned forward. She said, "I tried to break the match off. I tried to tell Thérèse something that I thought I knew about Guillaume. She silenced me by telling me something that *she* knew about him."

"That nobody else knows?" Forrest asked.

"That nobody else would believe."

"That makes it impossible for her to leave him?"

"I'm sure it has never occurred to her to leave Guillaume," Mrs. Rensslaer said. "She's very *bourgeoise* and she's also very devout."

"What *is* it she knows?" burst from Heyward.

"He suffers more than most people," Mrs. Rensslaer said.

"Of course," Heyward said drily. "The man's a genius."

"I don't think that makes any difference to her," Mrs. Rensslaer said. "It isn't that his capacity for suffering is greater than yours or mine. It's that it's—inevitable."

Forrest said, "For the Lord's sake! What *is* this doom that hangs over him?"

"He is possessed by a devil," Mrs. Rensslaer said.

There was a silence; then Forrest said, "How quaint! How long has he had it or how long has it had him?"

"I knew how that would sound to you young Americans!" Mrs. Rensslaer said. "He was able to tell Thérèse the moment it took hold of him—when he was quite young."

"Probably right after he made his first Communion!"

"He has never taken Communion. The Fäys are Protestants—or were. I do not think Guillaume professes any religion. But we Pribeaux have always been Catholic."

"So she's held to him by her religion—and her knowledge," Forrest mused. "Well, 'tis certain that fine women eat a crazy salad with their meat . . . !' "

Heyward said, "I wonder what it would be like to be inhabited by a devil."

"Nothing much," Mrs. Rensslaer said briskly.

"But the Devil is the Ancient Adversary."

"A created being who chose to be nothing rather than something—if I remember my catechism aright."

"The man suffers," Heyward said. "I've known him less than a week. But I can see that."

"Those Gadarene swine that rushed over the cliff must have had it tough," Forrest said. "Did they go over because they couldn't take it or did the devils hurl them to destruction?"

"Ah, I'm out of my depth now," Mrs. Rensslaer said. "But *you* ought not to be!" She laughed. "My husband used to say that ours was the first age in all history when the educated classes had no theology."

"Why does Fäy write to his wife every day?" Forrest asked. "What can he find to say to the woman?"

Heyward had recovered his self-possession and now felt an agreeable glow diffuse itself through his whole being. All the literary world knew that Guillaume Fäy's wife's name was never mentioned in his celebrated journal except casually. Even before he came abroad Heyward had heard that there was reason for this omission. It was rumored that the letters which the great man addressed to his wife whenever he was absent from her and which were not to be published until after his death would tell the real story of their life together, would, in effect, constitute another journal, a journal that was confidently expected to be even more startling than the already pub-lished journal.

He, Robert Heyward, knew something that nobody else knew! He could not tell his own wife, for he was a little ashamed of the way he had come by his knowledge. And yet he knew that if it were to do over again he would do exactly what he had done. Fäy had been called out of the room for a few minutes. The sheet of paper on which he had been writing lay where he had left it on the desk. Heyward had stepped over and read what was written there:

For you know, and you alone know, that if your name is not mentioned in my journal it is because I cannot trust myself to utter it. It is fatuous to say that I love you better than my life. You are my life. I have no existence except in and through you.

He looked out over the harbor. The lights of the city encircled it like a wreath of flowers flung down on the sand. The reflection of the lights extended only a little way out over the bay. The center of the vast body of water was dark blue, lusterless. From below the marble balustrade came a heady fragrance. On the terraces below, the mimosas were in full bloom. When he had told Mrs. Rensslaer about seeing the Sudanese crush the orange blossoms and insert them into his nostrils she had said that once in Paris, sitting with some friends at a café, she had seen a gigantic Sudanese walk past, holding a flower in his hand, and had burst into tears. She had added that she did not know that she would ever leave this part of the world again. Heyward had reported the conversation to Forrest, who had told him how Edgar Rensslaer, in his vigorous middle age, had been stricken with paralysis while on a vacation in this city. Those had been the days before airplane travel was common. The doctors had said that the journey back to Paris might have disastrous consequences. Rensslaer would not give up his work. His enormous library had been transported at considerable cost. And just as well, Forrest had said, for Edgar Rensslaer never left his bed again except for a wheelchair. After his death Mrs. Rensslaer had closed the villa and at the solicitation of friends had taken an apartment in Paris, but in two years' time she was back in the villa. She had told Blair that she could not bear being in places where her husband had never been, meeting people he had never known.

Heyward had asked Forrest if he had known Edgar Rensslaer. Forrest had replied in his slow way that he never had but he felt as if he had. He added that Mrs. Rensslaer had been very much in love with her husband.

Heyward bent his eyes now on his friend's half-shadowed face. Why was it that some men were swept all at once out into the current of life while others seemed fated to spend their lives in the shallows? He himself, poor as a church mouse, had been married at twenty-five, a father at twenty-six. Forrest, who had always had an income sufficient for his needs, was still unmarried at thirty-three. At St. Matthew's he had been in love with Sara Hall, who was two years older than he was and already going to dances at West Point. In college he had been in love with the wife of one of his professors. It was obvious that he was a little in love with Mrs. Rensslaer. She must have been an extraordinarily beautiful woman. Even now when she

103

turned those eyes on you it was like being proffered handfuls of violets. But even with the best will in the world what can a woman of sixty-eight do for a young man?

Somewhere within the recesses of the house a telephone bell pealed. Slow footsteps were heard in the hall. A voice said, "Madame. . . ." Mrs. Rensslaer said, "Oh . . . !" and got up and went into the house.

Heyward drew his chair up to the railing and sat leaning forward, his arms folded on the cold marble. On the terraces below the fragrances of the mimosa blossoms was almost overpowering. This villa was so high above the city that all the noises mingled to form one great humming sound—as if a gigantic bee hovered above the flowery lights. Occasionally another sound, heavy yet wailing, rose above the humming: the drums and singing from the casbah. Heyward, like all tourists, had visited the old city, strolling through it once with Forrest and going a few nights later with Fäy to a place that was half shop, half theater where pantomimes were enacted. As they made their way through the narrow streets Fäy had talked learnedly of the dances they were going to see. Obscenity was their distinguishing characteristic. They were forbidden by the police of every city except Constantinople and the city whose stones they now trod. The character whose amorous adventures constituted their subject matter appeared only at the Fast of Ramadan, when men's senses were sharpened by abstinence.

It had been, Heyward thought, a little like a New York nightclub, with its habitués, and its singer on whose popularity the show depended: a young boy who played a huge, vase-shaped drum and wore a heavy white blossom tucked over his ear. Fäy had whispered to Heyward that the shop was not a brothel but rather "a court of love." Those who made assignations here would have to go elsewhere to keep them. . . . The doorbell had rung promptly at seven o'clock this evening. The Arab boy stood there, holding a package in his hand. He had been about to pay him and dismiss him when Fäy called sharply from the inner room, "Is that Hussein? Let him come in here. I want to see him."

The passage was narrow. Heyward and the Arab boy had stood face to face before the boy slowly wheeled in the direction of Heyward's pointing finger. The Arab's eyes had been full on Heyward's face for a second and again Heyward had had that feeling of some infinitely soft substance being drawn lingeringly across his cheek.

Forrest Blair, as if he had been reading his friend's mind, asked suddenly, "Where *is* your old man tonight?"

"I don't know," Heyward said. He added coldly, "I am quite aware that Fäy's life is—irregular. At the same time I must say that his conduct toward me has been exemplary, both as man and employer."

Forrest laughed coarsely. "Maybe you don't ring his bell. I hear he likes 'em young."

"Is it because of his irregular life that Mrs. Rensslaer won't receive him?" Heyward asked after a pause.

"No," Forrest said thoughtfully, "I think it's those letters."

"You mean his correspondence with Raoul Pleyol?"

"No. The 'love' letters . . . the ones he writes his wife."

"Has she seen any of them?"

Forrest was silent so long that Heyward thought that he was not going to answer; then he said, "She thinks that the marriage has never been consummated. After all, she's in a position to know. Seems he tried to have a whirl with her after they were both married—before he began going after the Arab boys."

"Yes," Heyward said impatiently. "What's in the letters?"

"She thinks that they aren't written to Madame Fäy. . . ."

"I've never heard his name mentioned in connection with that of any other woman."

Forrest laughed again. "No . . . He writes them sitting in front of a mirror. That's what burns Gabrielle up."

"She's a charming woman who's just fed us a lot of delicious food," Heyward said hotly. "Guillaume Fäy's a genius. I don't believe she knows any more what goes into his letters than she knows what'll go into his next book."

"There she comes now," Forrest said in a low voice.

Mrs. Rensslaer emerged from the hall and stood in the doorway. "*Look!*" she said.

The moon had suddenly risen from behind a grove of ilex. It was at the full, as round as an orange and as yellow. But the light that fell upon the water was silver. In the broad track of light that it sent across the bay every wave was tipped with silver. Heyward got up and walked over to the balustrade. He was still thinking about his friend. When he had first known Forrest it was Forrest who had been the initiate and he the acolyte; it was in Forrest's rooms that he had first read Eliot and Pound and Mallarmé. But there was a gulf between them now, a gulf that was already widening. He remembered something that Fäy had written in one of his journals: "For five days now I have been *afraid* to work, yet always longing to!" Sometimes a man had to refrain from work simply because his mind was not supple enough to do what it would be called upon to do! To sit all day and look into a mirror might be the hardest thing a man was ever called upon to do. . . . Guillaume Fäy was obviously not like other men. A man, it might be, of unnatural loves. But is there not something mysterious in the very nature of love? And who is to say what love is natural, what love unnatural? *It is* they, *not* we, *who are strange*, he thought, and a sense of the almost insuperable difficulties that the artist confronts, of the immeasurable rewards he receives burst upon him and in his imagination mingled with the radiance spread upon the waters. At that moment he would not have changed places with any man.

All at once he was overcome by a longing for his wife. It seemed incredible that she should not be here beside him. Under the pretense of admiring the spectacle he walked over to the end of the terrace. At this moment she might be watching the same moon shed its rays over water. Their apartment in New York overhung the East River. After dinner he and Molly often turned off the lights and sat on the davenport to look out on the river. When he thought of her it was usually her eyes that came before him, brown eyes whose gaze was luminous but steady. Tonight he could not call up her eyes or her expression, could feel only the warmth and slightness of her in his arms.

"Gabrielle," Forrest said, "didn't you tell me that you were engaged to marry Guillaume Fäy once?"

Mrs. Rensslaer, laughing her silvery laugh, resumed her place on the chaise longue. "Don't hold it against me," she said. "Thérèse is older than I but I was—more precocious. It seemed natural that Guillaume should make love to me when we were at Crans together. And natural that I should accept him. After all, he was the first man who ever made love to me . . ." She shivered a little, as if the air had suddenly grown chill, and drew the shawl from the back of her chair and folded it about her.

"How long did the engagement last?" Forrest asked.

"A year," Mrs. Rensslaer said. "He was faithful to me for a year. At least I had no evidence that he was unfaithful."

"And yet you broke the engagement?"

"Yes," she said, and stifled a yawn. "He was keeping a journal even then."

The telephone bell pealed again. Footsteps were heard in the hall. "Bother!" Mrs. Rensslaer said. She rose and stood for a second, looking from one to the other of the young men who had risen too. "I was *gauche* in those days—heavens! But I knew that a man who keeps a journal makes a poor fiancé and a poorer husband."

"I suppose he just can't resist putting everything that happens to him into the journal," Forrest said reflectively.

"Or what doesn't happen to him!" Mrs. Rensslaer said, and went with her light step into the house.

III

When Heyward reached the consulate the next morning he found that Forrest had already attended to the matter of Fäy's visa. "But let's go over to the ministry anyhow," Forrest said. "I called Pleyol and he said he'd be glad to see you."

When they reached the ministry Forrest stopped to talk with a friend whom he met in an anteroom. Heyward was shown into an inner office.

Blinds drawn against the midday heat gave the room a pleasant gloom. It was sparsely furnished, with several heavy leather chairs, a black teakwood table drawn up beside one of them, and in the corner a huge desk behind which the minister sat.

Raoul Pleyol's peasant origins showed in his short, stocky body and round head. Heyward thought that he must be nearing seventy; his hair and bristling mustache were white, as were his shaggy eyebrows. He grasped Heyward's hand warmly and firmly and made a gesture which indicated that he should sit in a chair which had been drawn up beside the desk, and said with a smile, "The friend of my young friend. What do you do when you are at home?"

Heyward replied that he taught English literature in a college in New York and wrote poetry "on the side."

"What is the name of your volume of poetry?" Pleyol asked, and when Heyward answered, repeated the syllables after him musingly, then, nodding his shaggy head as if in approval, rose, and going to the window, pushed the blind aside so that he could look out on the square. "I have never been in America," he said, "but I should think that it would be good for a young American poet to live for a time in a country like this, a city like this one. Do you find that Africa speaks to you, Mr. Heyward?"

Bob said that in his mind there was no doubt that Africa spoke to him. "The trouble is that I haven't figured out yet what it's saying," he added, and then wished that that sentence had been better turned. But he found it hard to keep his mind on the conversation, he was so occupied in observing Pleyol. He was glad that the great man had risen at that moment. When he was seated at his desk he appeared taller than he actually was. Or did he give the impression that he was shorter than he actually was? His shoulders and arms were so large that the lower part of his body seemed to diminish in size when he stood. But it was the poet's head and neck that fascinated the young man. The big, round head was so set on the powerful neck that it seemed to flow out of it. One could hardly tell where the neck ended and the head began. The effect was of remarkable compactness, of leashed power. The man was, as it were, all of one piece, with all his members at his immediate disposal. Heyward remembered that in their correspondence Fäy had described Pleyol as being shaped like a hammer. He fancied that for all his age and bulk Pleyol would react in moments of stress faster than most men.

Pleyol, turning from the window, was asking him what poets he read. Heyward said that since he had been in Africa he had been rereading Rimbaud.

Pleyol nodded his head again. "When I first came to Africa to live I, too, reread Rimbaud. It was as if I had never read him before. . ."

Heyward said eagerly, "You feel that it was fated for him to come here. So much that he found here—the heat, the blossoms, the languors, even the diseases from which he suffered—they are all there in the early poems. It is as if he *had* to come here to find them."

Pleyol gave him a quick glance from under shaggy brows. He said, "I do not believe that Rimbaud was fated to be damned—any more than any other man."

Heyward felt the color rising in his cheeks. He spoke with the slight stammer that came over him in moments of excitement or confusion. "What I said about Rimbaud is hardly original, sir. Your confrère, Guillaume Fäy, said what amounted to the same thing the other day."

Pleyol said negligently, "Ah, Fäy. . . . There is no telling what notion will come into that head."

"You do not have any regard for Monsieur Fäy's critical opinion?" Heyward asked, somewhat taken aback.

Pleyol did not answer at once but looked at him intently. Heyward felt sweat start out on the palms of his hands. There was something minatory in the blue gaze, the slightly lowered head, the curious alertness of the stocky, powerful body. A phrase from one of Fäy's journals came into his mind: "*I wish that I had never met Raoul Pleyol!*" What could Fäy have meant by that? He pushed the question from him, heard himself talking at random: he had read the correspondence between Fäy and Pleyol, as who had not, and had been enormously stimulated by it. Pleyol must have been as pleased as he himself had been when he, Fäy, won the Monnier award last year. What made it so interesting was that Pleyol had won it the year before. Two such men of letters—men who had rendered service to letters which was at once disinterested and distinguished—had never before won the prize in two consecutive years. Did not Monsieur Pleyol regard this as a significant triumph?

Pleyol raised his shaggy head. "*No!*" he thundered. "The prize should have gone to an artist."

Heyward found himself stammering again. "You do not consider *Guillaume Fäy* an artist?"

Pleyol slowly shook his head.

"But, sir!" *La Fuite de Lemnos! Le Frère Prodigue!*"

Pleyol said, "Fäy cannot read mythology any better than he reads the Scriptures. *La Fuite de Lemnos* is a fantasy of the unconscious unresolved by art. *Le Frère Prodigue* is brilliant in passages but is a failure because of its inconclusive ending. Fäy himself does not know how his story turns out! There is an American expression that, to my mind, describes Fäy: 'He does not know what it is all about.' Fäy does not know what it is all about."

Heyward forgot his awe of the great man. He said, "Is not that the very source of his strength? He does not *know* but he has never stopped seeking. His journals alone . . ."

"What do you find in his journals?"

"A moral integrity that is an invaluable example to the younger writers. In his journals he dares face himself. It is more than most of us can do. . . ."

Pleyol said heavily, "It is more than any of us can do. . . . Do you think that a man sees himself when he looks into a mirror? He sees only the pose he has assumed. If you want to see yourself look into the eyes of your friends—or your enemies—who are made in the image of God."

Heyward said stubbornly, "An artist's first duty is to confront himself."

Pleyol brought his big hand down on the desk. "An artist's first duty is the same as any other man's—to serve, praise, and worship God."

"Do you not think that a poet, like yourself—or like Fäy—has responsibilities different from those of that pretty secretary who just showed me in here?"

"We have exactly the same responsibilities. The difference is in the methods we use to discharge them."

"And you wholly disapprove of the methods which Fäy uses to discharge his responsibilities?"

Pleyol said musingly, "Fäy is a poisoner. . . . What is strange is his influence. . . ." He looked up at the young man as if suddenly recalling his presence in the room. "I used to see a great deal of Fäy. That was before I learned of—the abyss in his life."

Heyward was trembling all over. "You profess to be a Christian. Yet you turn your back on him the minute you discover that he is unfortunate!"

Pleyol bent a piercing gaze upon him. When he spoke it was as if he were choosing his words with great care. "There is a fascination in heights. Fäy is not the first created being to feel it. I gave him up when I discovered that he loved the abyss better than life."

"But if a man goes down into the abyss for the sake of his fellow men?" Heyward asked. "Does not even *your* creed allow virtue in that?"

Pleyol shook his head. "He will have spent his life for nothing. There is nothing at the bottom of the abyss. . . ."

The two men sat staring at each other. Heyward never knew afterward what he would have said in answer. The pretty secretary put her head in at the door: Monsieur Bleeair was leaving. Did Monsieur Evard wish to accompany him?

Heyward got to his feet. He was about to leave with a murmured word of thanks, but Pleyol, making a gesture of assent to the girl, leaned over the desk to shake hands with him before letting him go. As Heyward felt the big, warm hand close over his he remembered the phrase with which Pleyol so often ended his letters to Fäy in the correspondence broken off twelve years ago: "I grasp your hand." And yet Pleyol evidently felt a real animosity toward Fäy. As he mounted the long flight of steps to the hotel he thought that it was strange that so much warmth and candor could exist side by side with envy. For in the last analysis, what but envy could have prompted Pleyol's displeasure over Fäy's receiving the Monnier award? He was still thinking of the two men as he let himself into his room. He came to the conclusion that Pleyol's attitude could only be explained by the notorious jealousy which French men of letters have always had for one another.

IV

"Her eyes have no perfume," Heyward wrote, and then crossed the words out.

Molly was not jealous by nature, but no woman, he thought, wants her husband waxing enthusiastic about another woman's eyes. Besides, when he wrote that sentence he had been thinking not of Madame Fäy's calm gray eyes but of Mrs. Rensslaer's eyes that always reminded him of crushed violets. She had spent a whole summer here when she was a girl. But that had been many years ago. It hardly seemed likely that her girlish ghost would haunt these old walls, these corridors, and yet ever since he had arrived at Crans he had found himself thinking, off and on, of Mrs. Rensslaer!

He must finish his letter! He and Fäy had arrived at Crans over a week ago and during that time he had written his wife only one short note. And yet he had written to her almost every day when he was in Africa. But it had been easy to write letters there. Every time he went out of his hotel he saw something he wanted to tell her about. It was different here. There was not much to see, and nothing going on—if there was anything going on it was not anything he could write her about.

He raised his head to stare through the open window. The view was monotonous and rather somber: wide, flat fields separated from each other by the avenues of beeches that in this region are planted to protect the houses from the winds that blow off the Channel. He had been a little disappointed, too, in the village. There were few old houses there. The dwellings were mostly cottages that had been erected a few years ago by a benevolent building association in which Madame Fäy had interested herself.

A breeze, laden with summer fragrances, came in through the open window at his back. He heard voices below. A laugh rang out. He had begun to type again, but he stopped, his hands suspended over the keys. The laugh sounded as if it might have come from a child who had laughed out in exuberance and might laugh again at any minute. He had seen only one child about the place, the cook's eight-year-old, black-haired granddaughter, who, whenever he passed her, stared at him, her finger in her mouth. He would not have thought that she could laugh with such exuberance. He got up and went to the window.

There were many magnificent trees on the wide lawn. Beech trees predominated. Some of them must be quite ancient. He had heard that the earth that surrounded beech trees was poisonous to other plants, that none except plants that were themselves poisonous would grow in their shade. Certainly, there was a wide ring of bare earth about the roots of each beech tree, but that would be the gardener's doing. He frowned. Pleyol had called Fäy "a poisoner." He wished that he had had an opportunity to know Pleyol better. He did not look like a man obsessed by jealousy—he himself had as great a reputation and had had as much public honor as Fäy—and yet what but jealousy could have inspired such a remark? Fäy, he thought, had as little jealousy as any man he had ever known, not even that jealousy which the old who are on their way out of life sometimes feel for the young who are coming into their strength.

Last night Heyward had read some of his poems aloud, at Fäy's request. In the salon after dinner, the old basset hound snoring in his chair, Madame Fäy, her knitting laid aside, sitting with her hands folded in her lap, her eyes fixed intently on his face. Fäy had sat a little apart from the others, beside a window. His hand shielded his eyes during the reading. Heyward had felt as if Fäy's whole intelligence was concentrated on the words that were being uttered—as if a great beacon had suddenly withdrawn its beams from the ocean to light a passer-by across a brook. When Heyward finished, Fäy looked up, let Heyward have his full, burning glance, then rose and came over and laid his hand on his shoulder. "You are a poet," he said.

Heyward thought now that Fäy couldn't have said anything to him that he would have liked better. But he frowned again and put his hand up and rubbed his forehead. He had not slept well last night and what little sleep he got had been broken by a long confused dream. He had been with Fäy in Africa or in some land beside a blue sea and Fäy had asked him to undertake a commission for him. "But you will have to go to. . ." he had said, and pronounced a name that Heyward had never heard before. Heyward's way had brought him to a long avenue bordered by beech trees. There was a house at the end of it and a woman was standing at the top of a long flight of marble stairs. She was neither young nor old and in answer to his questions would only smile and shake her head. "No, Monsieur Fäy is not here. . . . He has never been here. . . . No, Monsieur Guillaume Fäy is not here. . . ." "But he was to meet me here!" Heyward cried in anger, whereat the woman smiled and shook her head faster: "Not here . . . not here . . . He has never been here . . ." until Mrs. Rensslaer came and put her arm about the woman's shoulders and led her away.

"I'm a poet, all right," Heyward muttered, "or I wouldn't have such devilish dreams," and he took his handkerchief out and wiped the sweat from between his fingers.

On the right of the graveled drive a circle of fresh earth had been cut out of the turf. A man and a woman had just passed under his window and were crossing over to this bed. The man—one of whose arms ended in a steel hook—was dexterously guiding a wheelbarrow heaped high with loam. The woman who walked beside him carried a green shrub under her arm. She was not tall, rather broad in figure, and somewhat stooped. She wore a shapeless apron of some striped fabric over a black skirt and the sleeves of a gray pullover protruded from under the apron. A strand of her gray hair had come loose from the coil on top of her head and blew backward in the wind. She put a hand up to replace it and, turning to the old man, said something that brought a sour smile to his face, at which she laughed again. That, Heyward thought, was the most astonishing thing about Madame Fäy. He had become accustomed to the contrast between her appearance and that of her husband—she looked so much older than he did that he might have been taken for her son—and he no longer wondered at her rather long, weathered face whose withdrawn expression was enhanced rather than diminished by a pair of eyes of a very clear gray, but he had not yet heard her laugh without involuntarily looking around. It always seemed to him that that laugh might have come from a child hiding in the shrubbery. Or was it the laugh of an adult who remained in some ways immature? He had had an old maid aunt in North Carolina who laughed like that.

The old man took the little tree from the woman and set it firmly upright in the hole that had been made in the turf. She stooped her ungainly body and began vigorously throwing shovelfuls of earth about the shrub.

A young girl in a fawn-colored coat emerged from the house and stood watching them. Madame Fäy heard her footsteps on the gravel and, throwing one more shovelful of earth, turned and squatted on her heels to look up at the girl. "There is more consommé if the little Henri needs it," she said.

The girl shook her head and said, smiling, that Henri's temperature had been normal for two days. "The doctor says that this afternoon he may have *pommes purées*."

The girl, who looked more like a Provençal than a Norman, had an artificial rose pinned in the masses of her black hair. Heyward, noticing the awkward cut of the cloth coat, wondered if Madame Fäy had received, as he himself had received, an impression of something at once exotic and pathetic about her undeniable beauty. Just then Madame Fäy smiled and, detaining the girl with a gesture, rose heavily to her feet and went into the house.

The girl stood idly, balancing herself on shiny black heels. There was a large manila envelope under her arm. Heyward knew that it contained whatever material Fäy wanted typed that day. Soon after they had arrived at the chateau Fäy had informed his secretary that he was not to type any letters while he was there. "This is your first visit to Crans. Your boat sails all too soon. We will look upon you as a visitor. I know that you will not be able to work in the few days you have here. But meditation can sometimes be accomplished as well in a moment as in a month. Explore our grounds. They are not laid out on a grand scale, but I assure you they have their surprises. It would make me happy if while you are walking in our *allées* some vista down which you may gaze for years suddenly opened in your imagination. I should then feel that Emmanuele and I had our modest share in the fine poems you are sure to write."

Madame Fäy had come back. Heyward moved nearer to the window. She carried a package wrapped in tissue paper in her hand. The girl took it from her and slowly unwrapped it. Heyward leaned over farther in order to see what was in the package: a pair of gloves, dark red, almost the color of pomegranates. The girl's cry of pleasure floated up to the open window. Madame Fäy had watched the girl intently as she unwrapped the package. When she cried out she smiled, as if only now convinced that the gift had brought pleasure, laid her hand on the girl's arm for a second, shook it lightly, then turned back to her planting while the girl walked off down the drive.

A bell sounded. It was the custom at Crans as it had been at Heyward's grandfather's house in North Carolina, to sound a "warning bell" five or ten minutes before each meal. Madame Fäy put her shovel down and, still kneeling, leaned back on her heels again. Her hands, which even at this distance showed themselves stained with earth and swollen joints from arthritis, were clasped in front of her. She stared off through the trees.

The gardener finished tamping the last shovelful of earth about the little tree and straightened up. He made a sharp clicking sound with his teeth. Madame Fäy started and got up to her feet.

Heyward decided that he would finish his letter to his wife after luncheon and descended the curving staircase to the lower floor.

A small corridor opened off the main hall. Fäy's study was down that corridor. The door to the corridor was open. Heyward judged that Fäy had emerged for luncheon. He himself advanced up the hall and stood for a second before the open door of the *salon* for the pure pleasure of looking into the room. The parquet in here was lighter than the stair treads, almost honey-colored. The carpet was faintly colored in rose and green and fawn colors. Where the furniture was not covered with chintz it shone a dark mahogany. The *boiseries* were white.

A capacious chintz-covered armchair was drawn up to the empty fireplace. Sultan, the aged enormously fat basset hound, was sunk, as he often was at this hour, in its depths. He raised his domed head at the sound of footsteps and stared at Heyward out of red-rimmed eyes that reminded him of his uncle, Judge Walter Abbott of Winston-Salem.

In the dining room Fäy was already seated at the round table between two tall windows. The weather had been balmy since they had arrived at Crans but he complained frequently of the cold. For the last few days he had been wearing a white burnous that he had brought back from Africa over a corduroy jacket and flannel trousers. Heyward knew without looking that he still wore pantoufles though he had been up since seven o'clock.

He looked up as Heyward entered. "Heracles is on board!" he said.

An exclamation of delight broke from Heyward as he took his seat. "Heracles" was the name of the long poem that Guillaume Fäy had been working on for years. It had been Heyward's duty to type the lines Fäy had written while he was in Africa. The work had been rather a delight than a duty. Fäy, when he turned his manuscript over to Heyward, had had more the air of one man of letters asking the opinion of another man of letters than an employer assigning a task. When Heyward brought him back the carefully typed pages he always asked him if he had any comments to make and listened thoughtfully to whatever the young man said. And once he had showed Heyward where he had inserted an exclamation point at his suggestion.

Madame Fäy entered. She had removed her apron but she still wore the black skirt and gray pullover in which she had been gardening. Fäy half rose at her entrance, then, sinking back with a smile, let Heyward draw her chair out. The old manservant brought an omelette sprinkled with *fines herbes*, new asparagus, and a loaf of crusty bread made on the estate under Madame Fäy's supervision.

Fäy gave Heyward a look that seemed to say that they would resume their conversation later. His dark glance flickered over his wife's face. "What have you been doing this morning, Emmanuele?" he asked.

Madame Fäy smiled and said that she and Joseph had finished planting the third *pivoine de l'arbre* only a few minutes ago.

"Where?" Fäy demanded.

"One on each side of the drive and one a little farther back where it can be seen from your study window."

Fäy looked at her again and as hastily looked away. "That was very good of you, my dear. But you look flushed. Are you sure you have not been exerting yourself too much?"

Madame Fäy's fresh laugh rang out. "You know that the doctor has ordered me to exercise for my arthritis."

"But not necessarily with Joseph." He turned to Heyward. "Have you ever watched them together? Joseph stands like a statue. It is Emmanuele who does all the stooping, the carrying, the fetching."

"Joseph only has one hand," Madame Fäy said.

Heyward kept his eyes on his plate. *He has no existence except in and through her, and yet he leans a little forward when he addresses her, as if she were a stranger he is anxious to please, and his eyes seldom rest on her face and when they do will dart aside as though that placid countenance reflects the one thing he is not able to contemplate. . . . And when she spoke to him a moment ago her voice sank, as if to soften some blow that is preparing . . .*

" . . . with no education, no training, set himself up to be a veterinarian. God knows how many cows he has killed, to say nothing of dogs and cats, till he went to the war and came back with one hand—to become our gardener."

"Still, it is astonishing what he accomplishes with one hand," Madame Fäy said.

"Ah, but if he had two hands!"

"Then he could get a place anywhere as gardener."

Armand removed the larger plates and brought smaller ones. An epergne filled with apples stood in the center of the table. Armand proffered it first to Madame Fäy and then to the gentlemen. Fäy took a small, slightly misshapen apple from the dish and held it out toward Heyward. "Not much like our tangerines, *hein*? Did I not tell you that here we have apples that are of a grayness—actually of a grayness?"

Madame Fäy's eyes rested on her husband's face a moment, then sought the window.

Heyward felt a chill down his spine. *She does not see him! Is it because he is no longer there?*

Fäy's voice broke into his thoughts. "Can you not show them to him this afternoon, my dear? They were, after all, planted for your pleasure."

"What is that?" Heyward asked, confused.

"*Les pivoines de l'arbre*. Emmanuele and I brought them back from China, where we went on our honeymoon. We are transplanting some of them now to other parts of the grounds. But one has to go over there to the peony garden, behind the coach house, to see them in their full beauty. You will take Robert there this afternoon, Emmanuele?"

"Oh yes," Madame Fäy said. A maid was standing in the doorway. She arched her brows and in an audible whisper said something about "*le vieux Philippe*" and "*l'autobus.*"

Madame Fäy said, "Oh! He has come to get his medicine and he has to be back by three o'clock."

Fäy made an impatient gesture with his hand. "We will excuse you, my dear."

The old woman made off to the kitchen. Fäy laid his hand on Heyward's arm and walked slowly beside him out of the room. "My wife has become the veterinarian for the whole neighborhood," he said. "Joseph's influence, no doubt."

Heyward ignored the petulance in his tone. "I am glad you had such a good morning's work!" he said warmly.

"Ah! Heracles is on board!" Fäy said. "But will he sail? Will the nymph *let* him sail?" . . . His bony fingers closed on the young man's arm. "*If I had it to do over again I would not marry. Instead, I would go around the world . . . around . . . and around . . . and around!*"

Madame Fäy was waiting for Heyward under the porte cochere. They walked past the rabbit hutches and the poultry yard and on to the old stone building that now housed automobiles but was still called "the coach house." Back of the coach house the stable stood, encircled by a high brick wall. The gate was open. Heyward caught a glimpse of Joseph standing in the runway of the stable beside a black cow.

They passed the stable and were in a small wood that he had not entered before. A path wound between tall pines. The earth was brown with pine needles, except where ferns grew. Somewhere close by a brook was running. They walked slowly past the red-brown trunks and emerged in a hollow.

Heyward cried out. Confronting him was a rampart of massed blossoms. Pure white, delicate pink and lavender, pale yellow, scarlet, vermilion shading to clear crimson, dark red, even purple. He thought that he had never before seen so many colors in one place. The hollow formed a natural amphitheater. Three of its sides were covered with peonies. Many of them grew higher than Heyward's head.

Madame Fäy had sat down on a marble bench under a pine tree that stood at the edge of the clearing. He sat down beside her. The breeze brought the indefinable fragrance of the peonies to them. Heyward was remembering mornings in his grandmother's garden when, a small boy, he used to run and pick up the peony blossoms fallen on the ground after a night of spring rain and, breathing in their fragrance, asked himself what it was that peonies smelled like.

"You can smell them from here!" he said.

She told him that sometimes, riding in the mountains of northern China, she had smelled that faint fragrance and had known that when their ponies rounded a bend they would come upon a whole mountainside covered with the blossoms. She was silent a moment, then said dreamily, "It seemed strange to think that if nobody ever came that way again they would go on blooming."

Heyward said, "Paean to the god Apollo. You spent your honeymoon in a Greek temple!"

She said, "Guillaume remembered this hillside even then. The exposure was right but the soil was not suited to them. The first trees we imported died. Then Guillaume consulted someone at the Jardin des Plantes. They told him what to do. Today, when we want to transplant one of the trees we simply provide it with an ample supply of the soil from this hillside."

"He is an amazing man!" Heyward cried warmly. "The longer I know him, the more he astonishes me. I don't believe there's anything he couldn't do if he set his heart on it."

She turned her head. Her eyes met his. In the landscape of the face an eye is set like a lake, for exploration. He thought that her eyes were like those lakes that the hunter comes upon in the Carolina marshes at the end of a long day. The dog goes ahead, parts the reeds. The body of water shimmers palely in the rays of the setting sun. What is strange is to know that all the long day it has lain here unvisited and that after dog and man have made their way back to the road it will still lie here, reflecting nothing but the reeds along the bank and the sky above.

She said, "Yes. . . . If he sets his heart on anything."

There was a rustle on the path. A black-haired child in a checked pinafore stood before them. She said, "*Joseph a besoin de Madame.*"

Madame Fäy got to her feet. "You will excuse me? Evidently I am needed."

"I'll come, too," Heyward said, but did not immediately follow the old woman and the child up the path. He went over and stood in front of the rampart of blossoms. When one stood this close the fragrance came in almost tonic gusts. But the appeal to the eyes was even stronger. It was as if the sense of sight became another organ, plunged repeatedly, drunkenly, into depth on depth of color. A sob broke from him. He had to wait a moment before he regained his composure. And after he had started up the path he stopped short to stare at the brown pine needles. He had just realized with astonishment that all day long he had had an overpowering desire to see Mrs. Rensslaer.

He had not been in his room long before one of the maids informed him that Monsieur Fäy would like him to come to the study at his convenience. Heyward, as he washed his hands and brushed his hair, was smiling. The vision of Mrs. Rensslaer had faded before another vision, one which would always bring a smile to his lips, he thought. They had found Joseph standing beside the black cow, holding a quart measure in his hand. He beckoned to Madame Fäy peremptorily with his hook and, pointing to the child, said something in French so rapid—or colloquial—that Heyward could not follow it, then handed the measure to the child.

Madame Fäy smiled indulgently. "Her hands are not large enough, Joseph," she said and, stepping to the cow's side, she inserted the thumb and middle finger of each hand firmly into the flaring nostrils and drew the cow's head steadily upward. Joseph, meanwhile, braced himself against the cow's flank. There was a soughing noise, a surging backward of hindquarters promptly checked by Joseph. The beast opened her mouth and the child poured the draught down her throat.

Heyward, as he entered the little corridor that led to the study, was still thinking of the scene in the stable yard. After the drenching there had been some discussion of the cow's condition, then Joseph had said that he had a hundred cabbage plants to set out before nightfall and could attend to them if Madame would pick the raspberries for tonight's dinner. Madame replied that she would if Josette would help her. The three had made their way companionably to the garden while Heyward went back into the house. A strange woman, he thought, as he paused before the study door. As strange as her husband, perhaps, though in a different way. Perhaps even stranger.

Fäy was at his desk in a welter of papers. The old-fashioned wooden blinds and the jalousies that covered them had been drawn aside. The midafternoon sun poured through the window and made a little pool for motes to dance in on the carpet. Heyward thought that Fäy must have undergone a sharp change of mood since luncheon. He had discarded his burnous and sat erect behind his desk, basking in the sunlight. He turned glowing eyes on the young man and said, "I have written five more lines! At least I think I have."

"I *know* you have!" Heyward said jubilantly. "I can tell by looking at you."

He had come up to the side of the desk as he spoke. Fäy put a hand out and gave his shoulder an affectionate pressure. "Would you go quickly and ask Emmanuele for the key to the secretary? There is a phrase in a letter that I wrote her the other day which I think I can use. It goes. . . . But wait! You will see it in the poem."

Heyward hurried from the room. Halfway across the lawn he slowed his steps. In a few minutes he would hold in his hand the key not only to an old secretary but to a mystery. Fäy had announced years ago that the letters would supplement the mysterious omissions from the journal. What sort of man would emerge from the letters? What sort of woman? He stopped under a linden tree; a question beat in the air. He looked up as if his interlocutor were perched on the branch above his head. His lips formed words. *Yes. It is my duty to look at them if I get a chance. Surely I'll get a chance. . . .*

He ran on and arrived at the old walled vegetable garden. Joseph, squatting on his heels, trowel in hand, glanced up at him as he ran past. The child had disappeared. Madame Fäy was stooping along the raspberry rows at the end of the garden. He slackened his pace so as not to be out of breath when he approached her. He said, "Madame, Monsieur Fäy asks that you send him the key to the secretary in which his letters to you are kept. He wants to verify a phrase."

A blackbird flew down from the plum tree. Light dazzled off the raspberry leaves, a trailing branch quivered, then was still as the bird's claws took firmer hold of it. The woman's back was still toward him. The bulky body had not quivered but rather settled in on itself, as if to sustain a long-anticipated blow. She turned around. She looked at the basket she held in her hand, then up at him. She said, "I will go to him."

Was she going to refuse to give him the key? Was it possible that he might not see the letters, after all? He felt an insane desire to laugh out, to chatter nonsense. *It is not Bluebeard's key I ask for, madame! Merely the key to an old secretary.* Aloud he said, "If you could perhaps tell me where the key is kept?"

She did not seem to hear him. She had stooped clumsily to set her basket on the ground and now her hands came up to unfasten the apron that was tied about her waist. When she had untied the apron and had flung it on a raspberry bush she stood a second, looking down at her swollen, arthritic hands before they dropped to her sides, and she went with her old woman's gait down the raspberry rows and across the garden.

The blackbird left the raspberry bush and lit on the ground not far from Joseph. He made a menacing gesture with his hook and rose as the old woman approached. "*Madame* . . ." he began, then fell back as Madame Fäy walked past without looking at him.

They entered the house through the kitchen door, traversed two more rooms, and were in the back hall. Madame Fäy pushed aside the heavy velvet portieres that separated the back hall from the front and disappeared.

Heyward stayed where he was. It was always dark in here. He had never noticed before what a curious smell old velvet has. *I have been here a long time. . . . How long has it been since she pushed those curtains aside?* Somewhere on ahead there was a whimpering sound, such as might be made by a dog in distress . . . *or some other beast, that has thought to escape, being forced over a cliff?*

He pushed the curtains aside and tiptoed into the hall. The door to the corridor stood open. He tiptoed past it and down the hall. The door of the *salon* was open, too. The chintz-covered chair was drawn as usual up to the cold fireplace. The old basset hound who lay in its depths raised his head and stared at the young man a moment, then laid his head down on his paws.

Heyward heard footsteps behind him. Madame Fäy emerged from the corridor, passed him with a slight inclination of the head, went through the hall and out onto the front steps. Outdoors the sun was still bright, but on the horizon a few clouds glittered darkly. She spoke without turning her head: "It looks as if we might have rain later in the afternoon." "It looks as if we might," Heyward rejoined, and watched her go down the steps.

The whimpering had started again. He waited until the woman had disappeared into the shrubbery, then tiptoed into the corridor. A splinter of grayish light lay athwart it; Madame Fäy had not closed the door of the study when she left. The wailing broke off. A voice spoke in a whisper: "*We can never get them back. . . .*" Heyward's whole body grew rigid. "She *burned* them!" the voice said. There was a sob and then the whisper again: "*She* burned them!"

The young man's hands reached out on each side to touch the cold walls. Absently he noted that the shaft of grayish light had been blotted out; inside that room a body swayed from side to side. When he had left the room a few minutes ago it had been full of sunshine. Now it was dark. She must have drawn the blinds before she left. The old man's head and shoulders would show hunched against the pale-covered jalousies. Ever afterwards he was to think of that head as hooded, but the eyes, the eyes that had gleamed so merry, so mottled! They would be black now—twin prisons in which a creature that had once sported in the sun would sit forever in darkness.

7

THE DISPLACED PERSON

Flannery O'Connor

The peacock was following Mrs. Shortley up the road to the hill where she meant to stand. Moving one behind the other, they looked like a complete procession. Her arms were folded and as she mounted the prominence, she might have been the giant wife of the countryside, come out at some sign of danger to see what the trouble was. She stood on two tremendous legs, with the grand self-confidence of a mountain, and rose, up narrowing bulges of granite, to two icy blue points of light that pierced forward, surveying everything. She ignored the white afternoon sun that was creeping behind a ragged wall of cloud as if it pretended to be an intruder and cast her gaze down the red clay road that turned off from the highway.

The peacock stopped just behind her, his tail—glittering green-gold and blue in the sunlight—lifted just enough so that it would not touch the ground. It flowed out on either side like a floating train and his head on the long blue reed-like neck was drawn back as if his attention were fixed in the distance on something no one else could see.

Mrs. Shortley was watching a black car turn through the gate from the highway. Over by the toolshed, about fifteen feet away, the two Negroes, Astor and Sulk, had stopped work to watch. They were hidden by a mulberry tree but Mrs. Shortley knew they were there.

Mrs. McIntyre was coming down the steps of her house to meet the car. She had on her largest smile but Mrs. Shortley, even from her distance, could detect a nervous slide in it. These people who were coming were only hired help, like the Shortleys themselves or the Negroes. Yet here was the owner of the place out to welcome them. Here she was, wearing her best clothes and a string of beads, and now bounding forward with her mouth stretched.

The car stopped at the walk just as she did and the priest was the first to get out. He was a long-legged black-suited old man with a white hat on and a collar that he wore backward, which, Mrs. Shortley knew, was what priests did who wanted to be known as priests. It was this priest who had arranged for these people to come here. He opened the back door of the car and out jumped two children, a boy and a girl, and then, stepping more slowly, a woman in brown, shaped like a peanut. Then the front door opened and out stepped the man, the Displaced Person. He was short and a little sway-backed and wore gold-rimmed spectacles.

Mrs. Shortley's vision narrowed on him and then widened to include the woman and the two children in a group picture. The first thing that struck her as very peculiar was that they looked like other people. Every time she had seen them in her imagination, the image she had got was of the three bears, walking single file, with wooden shoes on like Dutchmen and sailor hats and bright coats with a lot of buttons. But the woman had on a dress she might have worn herself and the children were dressed like anybody from around. The man had on khaki pants and a blue shirt. Suddenly, as Mrs. McIntyre held out her hand to him, he bobbed down from the waist and kissed it.

Mrs. Shortley jerked her own hand up toward her mouth and then after a second brought it down and rubbed it vigorously on her seat. If Mr. Shortley had tried to kiss her hand, Mrs. McIntyre would have knocked him into the middle of next week, but then Mr. Shortley wouldn't have kissed her hand anyway. He didn't have time to mess around.

She looked closer, squinting. The boy was in the center of the group, talking. He was supposed to speak the most English because he had learned some in Poland and so he was to listen to his father's Polish and say it in English and then listen to Mrs. McIntyre's English and say that in Polish. The priest had told Mrs. McIntyre his name was Rudolph and he was twelve and the girl's name was Sledgewig and she was nine. Sledgewig sounded to Mrs. Shortley like something you would name a bug, or vice versa, as if you named a boy Bollweevil. All of them's last name was something that only they themselves and the priest could pronounce. All she could make out of it was Gobblehook. She and Mrs. McIntyre had been calling them the Gobblehooks all week while they got ready for them.

There had been a great deal to do to get ready for them because they didn't have anything of their own, not a stick of furniture or a sheet or a dish, and everything had had to be scraped together out of things that Mrs. McIntyre couldn't use any more herself. They had collected a piece of odd furniture here and a piece there and they had taken some flowered chicken feed sacks and made curtains for the windows, two red and one green, because they had not had enough of the red sacks to go around. Mrs. McIntyre said she was not made of money and she could not afford to buy curtains. "They can't talk," Mrs. Shortley said. "You reckon they'll know what colors even is?" and Mrs. McIntyre had said that after what those people had been through, they should be grateful for anything they could get. She said to think how lucky they were to escape from over there and come to a place like this.

Mrs. Shortley recalled a newsreel she had seen once of a small room piled high with bodies of dead naked people all in a heap, their arms and legs tangled together, a head thrust in here, a head there, a foot, a knee, a part that should have been covered up sticking out, a hand raised clutching nothing. Before you could realize that it was real and take it into your head, the picture changed and a hollow-sounding voice was saying, "Time marches on!" This was the kind of thing that was happening every day in Europe where they had not advanced as in this country, and watching from her vantage point, Mrs. Shortley had the sudden intuition that the Gobblehooks, like rats with typhoid fleas, could have carried all those murderous ways over the water with them directly to this place. If they had come from where that kind of thing was done to them, who was to say they were not the kind that would also do it to others? The width and breadth of this question nearly shook her. Her stomach trembled as if there had been a slight quake in the heart of the mountain and automatically she moved down from her elevation and went forward to be introduced to them, as if she meant to find out at once what they were capable of.

She approached, stomach foremost, head back, arms folded, boots flopping gently against her large legs. About fifteen feet from the gesticulating group, she stopped and made her presence felt by training her gaze on the back of Mrs. McIntyre's neck. Mrs. McIntyre was a small woman of sixty with a round wrinkled face and red bangs that came almost down to two high orange-colored penciled eyebrows. She had a little doll's mouth and eyes that were a soft blue when she opened them wide but more like steel or granite when she narrowed them to inspect a milk can. She had buried one husband and divorced two and Mrs. Shortley respected her as a person nobody had put anything over on yet—except, ha, ha, perhaps the Shortleys. She held out her arm in Mrs. Shortley's direction and said to the Rudolph boy, "And this is Mrs. Shortley. Mr. Shortley is my dairyman. Where's Mr. Shortley?" she asked as his wife began to approach again, her arms still folded. "I want him to meet the Guizacs."

Now it was Guizac. She wasn't calling them Gobblehook to their face. "Chancy's at the barn," Mrs. Shortley said. "He don't have time to rest himself in the bushes like them niggers over there."

Her look first grazed the tops of the displaced people's heads and then revolved downward slowly, the way a buzzard glides and drops in the air until it alights on the carcass. She stood far enough away so that the man would not be able to kiss her hand. He looked directly at her with little green eyes and gave her a broad grin that was toothless on one side. Mrs. Shortley, without smiling, turned her attention to the little girl who stood by the mother, swinging her shoulders from side to side. She had long braided hair in two looped pigtails and there was no denying she was a pretty child even if she did have a bug's name. She was better looking than either Annie Maude or Sarah Mae, Mrs. Shortley's two girls going on fifteen and seventeen but Annie Maude had never got her growth and Sarah Mae had a cast in her eye. She compared the foreign boy to her son, H.C., and H.C. came out far ahead. H.C. was twenty years old with her build and eyeglasses. He was going to Bible school now and when he finished he was going to start him a church. He had a strong sweet voice for hymns and could sell anything. Mrs. Shortley looked at the priest and was reminded that these people did not have an advanced religion. There was no telling what all they believed since none of the foolishness had been reformed out of it. Again she saw the room piled high with bodies.

The priest spoke in a foreign way himself, English but as if he had a throatful of hay. He had a big nose and a bald rectangular face and head. While she was observing him, his large mouth dropped open and with a stare behind her, he said, "Arrrrrr!" and pointed.

Mrs. Shortley spun around. The peacock was standing a few feet behind her, with its head slightly cocked.

"What a beauti-ful birdrrrd!" the priest murmured.

"Another mouth to feed," Mrs. McIntyre said, glancing in the peafowl's direction.

"And when does he raise his splendid tail?" asked the priest.

"Just when it suits him," she said. "There used to be twenty or thirty of those things on the place but I've let them die off. I don't like to hear them scream in the middle of the night."

"So beauti-ful," the priest said. "A tail full of suns," and he crept forward on tiptoe and looked down on the bird's back where the polished gold and green design began. The peacock stood still as if he had just come down from some sun-drenched height to be a vision for them all. The priest's homely red face hung over him, glowing with pleasure.

Mrs. Shortley's mouth had drawn acidly to one side. "Nothing but a peachicken," she muttered.

Mrs. McIntyre raised her orange eyebrows and exchanged a look with her to indicate that the old man was in his second childhood. "Well, we must show the Guizacs their new home," she said impatiently and she herded them into the car again. The peacock stepped off toward the mulberry tree where the two Negroes were hiding and the priest turned his absorbed face away and got in the car and drove the displaced people down to the shack they were to occupy.

Mrs. Shortley waited until the car was out of sight and then she made her way circuitously to the mulberry tree and stood about ten feet behind the two Negroes, one an old man holding a bucket half full of calf feed and the other a yellowish boy with a short woodchuck-like head pushed into a rounded felt hat. "Well," she said slowly, "yawl have looked long enough. What you think about them?"

The old man, Astor, raised himself. "We been watching," he said as if this would be news to her. "Who they now?"

"They come from over the water," Mrs. Shortley said with a wave of her arm. "They're what is called Displaced Persons."

"Displaced Persons," he said. "Well now, I declare. What do that mean?"

"It means they ain't where they were born at and there's nowhere for them to go—like if you was run out of here and wouldn't nobody have you."

"It seem like they here, though," the old man said in a reflective voice. "If they here, they somewhere."

"Sho is," the other agreed. "They here."

The illogic of Negro-thinking always irked Mrs. Shortley. "They ain't where they belong to be at," she said. "They belong to be back over yonder where everything is still like they been used to. Over here it's more advanced than where they come from. But yawl better look out now," she said and nodded her head. "There's about ten billion more just like them and I know what Mrs. McIntyre said."

"Say what?" the young one asked.

"Places are not easy to get nowadays, for white or black, but I reckon I heard what she stated to me," she said in a singsong voice.

"You liable to hear most anything," the old man remarked, leaning forward as if he were about to walk off but holding himself suspended.

"I heard her say, 'This is going to put the Fear of the Lord into those shiftless niggers!'" Mrs. Shortley said in a ringing voice.

The old man started off. "She say something like that every now and then," he said. "Ha. Ha. Yes indeed."

"You better get on in that barn and help Mr. Shortley," she said to the other one. "What you reckon she pays you for?"

"He the one sent me out," the Negro muttered. "He the one gimme something else to do."

"Well you better get to doing it then," she said and stood there until he moved off. Then she stood a while longer, reflecting, her unseeing eyes directly in front of the peacock's tail. He had jumped into the tree and his tail hung in front of her, full of fierce planets with eyes that were each ringed in green and set against a sun that was gold in one second's light and salmon-colored in the next. She might have been looking at a map of the universe but she didn't notice it any more than she did the spots of sky that cracked the dull green of the tree. She was having an inner vision instead. She was seeing the ten million billion of them pushing their way into new places over here and herself, a giant angel with wings as wide as a house, telling the Negroes that they would have to find another place. She turned herself in the direction of the barn, musing on this, her expression lofty and satisfied.

She approached the barn from an oblique angle that allowed her a look in the door before she could be seen herself. Mr. Chancey Shortley was adjusting the last milking machine on a large black and white spotted cow near the entrance, squatting at her heels. There was about a half-inch of cigarette adhering to the center of his lower lip. Mrs. Shortley observed it minutely for half a second. "If she seen or heard of you smoking in this barn, she would blow a fuse," she said.

Mr. Shortley raised a sharply rutted face containing a washout under each cheek and two long crevices eaten down both sides of his blistered mouth. "You gonna be the one to tell her?" he asked.

"She's got a nose of her own," Mrs. Shortley said.

Mr. Shortley, without appearing to give the feat any consideration, lifted the cigarette stub with the sharp end of his tongue, drew it into his mouth, closed his lips tightly, rose, stepped out, gave his wife a good round appreciative stare, and spit the smoldering butt into the grass.

"Aw Chancey," she said, "haw haw," and she dug a little hole for it with her toe and covered it up. This trick of Mr. Shortley's was actually his way of making love to her. When he had done his courting, he had not brought a guitar to strum or anything pretty for her to keep, but had sat on her porch steps, not saying a word, imitating a paralyzed man propped up to enjoy a cigarette. When the cigarette got the proper size, he would turn his eyes to her and open his mouth and draw in the butt and then sit there as if he had swallowed it, looking at her with the most loving look anybody could imagine. It nearly drove her wild and every time he did it, she wanted to pull his hat down over his eyes and hug him to death.

"Well," she said, going into the barn after him, "the Gobblehooks have come and she wants you to meet them, says, 'Where's Mr. Shortley?' and I says, 'He don't have time. . . .' "

"Tote up them weights," Mr. Shortley said, squatting to the cow again.

"You reckon he can drive a tractor when he don't know English?" she asked. "I don't think she's going to get her money's worth out of them. That boy can talk, but he looks delicate. The one can work can't talk and the one can talk can't work. She ain't any better off than if she had more niggers."

"I rather have a nigger if it was me," Mr. Shortley said.

"She says it's ten million more like them, Displaced Persons, she says that there priest can get her all she wants."

"She better quit messin' with that there priest," Mr. Shortley said.

"He don't look smart," Mrs. Shortley said, "—kind of foolish."

"I ain't going to have the Pope of Rome tell me how to run no dairy," Mr. Shortley said.

"They ain't Eye-talians, they're Poles," she said. "From Poland where all them bodies were stacked up at. You remember all them bodies?"

"I give them three weeks here," Mr. Shortley said.

Three weeks later Mrs. McIntyre and Mrs. Shortley drove to the cane bottom to see Mr. Guizac start to operate the silage cutter, a new machine that Mrs. McIntyre had just bought because she said, for the first time, she had somebody who could operate it. Mr. Guizac could drive a tractor, use the rotary hay-baler, the silage cutter, the combine, the letz mill, or any other machine she had on the place. He was an expert mechanic, a carpenter, and a mason. He was thrifty and energetic. Mrs. McIntyre said she figured he would save her twenty dollars a month on repair bills alone. She said getting him was the best day's work she had ever done in her life. He could work milking machines and he was scrupulously clean. He did not smoke.

She parked her car on the edge of the cane field and they got out. Sulk, the young Negro, was attaching the wagon to the cutter and Mr. Guizac was attaching the cutter to the tractor. He finished first and pushed the colored boy out of the way and attached the wagon to the cutter himself, gesticulating with a bright angry face when he wanted the hammer or the screwdriver. Nothing was done quick enough to suit him. The Negroes made him nervous.

The week before, he had come upon Sulk at the dinner hour, sneaking with a croker sack into the pen where the young turkeys were. He had watched him take a frying-size turkey from the lot and thrust it in the sack and put the sack under his coat. Then he had followed him around the barn, jumped on him, dragged him to Mrs. McIntyre's back door and had acted out the entire scene for her, while the Negro muttered and grumbled and said God might strike him dead if he had been stealing any turkey, he had only been taking it to put some black shoe polish on its head because it had the sorehead. God might strike him dead if that was not the truth before Jesus. Mrs. McIntyre told him to go put the turkey back and then she was a long time explaining to the Pole that all Negroes would steal. She finally had to call Rudolph and tell him in English and have him tell his father in Polish, and Mr. Guizac had gone off with a startled disappointed face.

Mrs. Shortley stood by hoping there would be trouble with the silage machine but there was none. All of Mr. Guizac's motions were quick and accurate. He jumped on the tractor like a monkey and maneuvered the big orange cutter into the cane; in a second the silage was spurting in a green jet out of the pipe into the wagon. He went jolting down the row until he disappeared from sight and the noise became remote.

Mrs. McIntyre sighed with pleasure. "At last," she said, "I've got somebody I can depend on. For years I've been fooling with sorry people. Sorry people. Poor white trash and niggers," she muttered. "They've drained me dry. Before you all came I had Ringfields and Collins and Jarrells and Perkins and Pinkins and Herrins and God knows what all else and not a one of them left without taking something off this place that didn't belong to them. Not a one!"

Mrs. Shortley could listen to this with composure because she knew that if Mrs. McIntyre had considered her trash, they couldn't have talked about trashy people together. Neither of them approved of trash. Mrs. McIntyre continued with the monologue that Mrs. Shortley had heard oftentimes before. "I've been running this place for thirty years," she said, looking with a deep frown out over the field, "and always just barely making it. People think you're made of money. I have taxes to pay. I have the insurance to keep up. I have the repair bills. I have the feed bills." It all gathered up and she stood with her chest lifted and her small hands gripped around her elbows. "Ever since the Judge died," she said, "I've barely been making ends meet and they all take something when they leave. The niggers don't leave—they stay and steal. A nigger thinks anybody is rich he can steal from and that white trash thinks anybody is rich who can afford to hire people as sorry as they are. And all I've got is the dirt under my feet!"

You hire and fire, Mrs. Shortley thought, but she didn't always say what she thought. She stood by and let Mrs. McIntyre say it all out to the end but this time it didn't end as usual. "But at last I'm saved!" Mrs. McIntyre said. "One fellow's misery is the other fellow's gain. That man there," and she pointed where the Displaced Person had disappeared, "—he has to work!

He wants to work!" She turned to Mrs. Shortley with her bright wrinkled face. "That man is my salvation!" she said.

Mrs. Shortley looked straight ahead as if her vision penetrated the cane and the hill and pierced through to the other side. "I would suspicion salvation got from the devil," she said in a slow detached way.

"Now what do you mean by that?" Mrs. McIntyre asked, looking at her sharply.

Mrs. Shortley wagged her head but would not say anything else. The fact was she had nothing else to say for this intuition had only at that instant come to her. She had never given much thought to the devil for she felt that religion was essentially for those people who didn't have the brains to avoid evil without it. For people like herself, for people of gumption, it was a social occasion providing the opportunity to sing; but if she had ever given it much thought she would have considered the devil the head of it and God the hanger-on. With the coming of these displaced people, she was obliged to give new thought to a good many things.

"I know what Sledgewig told Annie Maude," she said, and when Mrs. McIntyre carefully did not ask her what but reached down and broke off a sprig of sassafras to chew, she continued in a way to indicate she was not telling all, "that they wouldn't be able to live long, the four of them, on seventy dollars a month."

"He's worth raising," Mrs. McIntyre said. "He saves me money."

This was as much as to say that Chancey had never saved her money. Chancey got up at four in the morning to milk her cows, in winter wind and summer heat, and he had been doing it for the last two years. They had been with her the longest she had ever had anybody. The gratitude they got was these hints that she hadn't been saved any money.

"Is Mr. Shortley feeling better today?" Mrs. McIntyre asked.

Mrs. Shortley thought it was about time she was asking that question. Mr. Shortley had been in bed two days with an attack. Mr. Guizac had taken his place in the dairy in addition to doing his own work. "No he ain't," she said. "That doctor said he was suffering from over-exhaustion."

"If Mr. Shortley is over-exhausted," Mrs. McIntyre said, "then he must have a second job on the side," and she looked at Mrs. Shortley with almost closed eyes as if she were examining the bottom of a milk can.

Mrs. Shortley did not say a word but her dark suspicion grew like a black thundercloud. The fact was that Mr. Shortley did have a second job on the side and that, in a free country, this was none of Mrs. McIntyre's business. Mr. Shortley made whisky. He had a small still back in the farthest reaches of the place, on Mrs. McIntyre's land to be sure, but on land that she only owned and did not cultivate, on idle land that was not doing anybody any good. Mr. Shortley was not afraid of work. He got up at four in the morning and milked her cows and in the middle of the day when he was supposed to be resting, he was off attending to his still. Not every man would work like that. The Negroes knew about his still but he knew about theirs so there had never been any disagreeableness between them. But with foreigners on the place, with people who were all eyes and no understanding, who had come from a place continually fighting, where the religion had not been reformed—with this kind of people, you had to be on the lookout every minute. She thought that there ought to be a law against them. There was no reason they couldn't stay over there and take the places of some of the people who had been killed in their wars and butcherings.

"What's furthermore," she said suddenly, "Sledgewig said as soon as her papa saved the money, he was going to buy him a used car. Once they get them a used car, they'll leave you."

"I can't pay him enough for him to save money," Mrs. McIntyre said. "I'm not worrying about that. Of course," she said then, "if Mr. Shortley got incapacitated, I would have to use Mr. Guizac in the dairy all the time and I would have to pay him more. He doesn't smoke," she said, and it was the fifth time within the week that she had pointed this out.

"It is no man," Mrs. Shortley said emphatically, "that works as hard as Chancey, or is as easy with a cow, or is more of a Christian," and she folded her arms and her gaze pierced the distance. The noise of the tractor and cutter increased and Mr. Guizac appeared coming around the other side of the cane row. "Which can not be said about everybody," she muttered. She wondered whether, if the Pole found Chancey's still, he would know what it was. The trouble with these people was, you couldn't tell what they knew. Every time Mr. Guizac smiled, Europe stretched out in Mrs. Shortley's imagination, mysterious and evil, the devil's experiment station.

The tractor, the cutter, the wagon passed, rattling and rumbling and grinding before them. "Think how long that would have taken with men and mules to do it," Mrs. McIntyre shouted. "We'll get this whole bottom cut within two days at this rate."

"Maybe," Mrs. Shortley muttered, "if don't no terrible accident occur." She thought how the tractor had made mules worthless. Nowadays you couldn't give away a mule. The next thing to go, she reminded herself, will be niggers.

In the afternoon she explained what was going to happen to them to Astor and Sulk, who were in the cow lot, filling the manure spreader. She sat down next to the block of salt under a small shed, her stomach in her lap, her arms on top of it. "All you colored people better look out," she said. "You know how much you can get for a mule."

130

"Nothing, no indeed," the old man said, "not one thing."

"Before it was a tractor," she said, "it could be a mule. And before it was a Displaced Person, it could be a nigger. The time is going to come," she prophesied, "when it won't be no more occasion to speak of a nigger."

The old man laughed politely. "Yes indeed," he said. "Ha ha."

The young one didn't say anything. He only looked sullen but when she had gone in the house, he said, "Big Belly act like she know everything."

"Never mind," the old man said, "your place too low for anybody to dispute with you for it."

She didn't tell her fears about the still to Mr. Shortley until he was back on the job in the dairy. Then one night after they were in bed, she said, "That man prowls."

Mr. Shortley folded his hands on his bony chest and pretended he was a corpse.

"Prowls," she continued and gave him a sharp kick in the side with her knee. "Who's to say what they know and don't know? Who's to say if he found it he wouldn't go right to her and tell? How you know they don't make liquor in Europe? They drive tractors. They got them all kinds of machinery. Answer me."

"Don't worry me now," Mr. Shortley said. "I'm a dead man."

"It's them little eyes of his that's foreign," she muttered. "And that way he's got of shrugging." She drew her shoulders up and shrugged several times. "How come he's got anything to shrug about?" she asked.

"If everybody was as dead as I am, nobody would have no trouble," Mr. Shortley said.

"That priest," she muttered and was silent for a minute. Then she said, "In Europe they probably got some different way to make liquor but I reckon they know all the ways. They're full of crooked ways. They never have advanced or reformed. They got the same religion as a thousand years ago. It could only be the devil responsible for that. Always fighting amongst each other. Disputing. And then get us into it. Ain't they got us into it twict already and we ain't got no more sense than to go over there and settle it for them and then they come on back over here and snoop around and find your still and go straight to her. And liable to kiss her hand any minute. Do you hear me?"

"No," Mr. Shortley said.

"And I'll tell you another thing," she said. "I wouldn't be a tall surprised if he don't know everything you say, whether it be in English or not."

"I don't speak no other language," Mr. Shortley murmured.

"I suspect," she said, "that before long there won't be no more niggers on this place. And I tell you what. I'd rather have niggers than them Poles.

And what's furthermore, I aim to take up for the niggers when the time comes. When Gobblehook first come here, you recollect how he shook their hands, like he didn't know the difference, like he might have been as black as them, but when it come to finding out Sulk was taking turkeys, he gone on and told her. I known he was taking turkeys. I could have told her myself."

Mr. Shortley was breathing softly as if he were asleep.

"A nigger don't know when he has a friend," she said. "And I'll tell you another thing. I get a heap out of Sledgewig. Sledgewig said that in Poland they lived in a brick house and one night a man come and told them to get out of it before daylight. Do you believe they ever lived in a brick house?"

"Airs," she said. "That's just airs. A wooden house is good enough for me. Chancey," she said, "turn thisaway. I hate to see niggers mistreated and run out. I have a heap of pity for niggers and poor folks. Ain't I always had?" she asked. "I say ain't I always been a friend to niggers and poor folks?"

"When the time comes," she said, "I'll stand up for the niggers and that's that. I ain't going to see that priest drive out all the niggers."

Mrs. McIntyre bought a new drag harrow and a tractor with a power lift because she said, for the first time, she had someone who could handle machinery. She and Mrs. Shortley had driven to the backfield to inspect what he had harrowed the day before. "That's been done beautifully!" Mrs. McIntyre said, looking out over the red undulating ground.

Mrs. McIntyre had changed since the Displaced Person had been working for her and Mrs. Shortley had observed the change very closely: she had begun to act like somebody who was getting rich secretly and she didn't confide in Mrs. Shortley the way she used to. Mrs. Shortley suspected that the priest was at the bottom of the change. They were very slick. First he would get her into his Church and then he would get his hand in her pocketbook. Well, Mrs. Shortley thought, the more fool she! Mrs. Shortley had a secret herself. She knew something the Displaced Person was doing that would floor Mrs. McIntyre. "I still say he ain't going to work forever for seventy dollars a month," she murmured. She intended to keep her secret to herself and Mr. Shortley.

"Well," Mrs. McIntyre said, "I may have to get rid of some of this other help so I can pay him more."

Mrs. Shortley nodded to indicate she had known this for some time. "I'm not saying those niggers ain't had it coming," she said. "But they do the best they know how. You can always tell a nigger what to do and stand by until he does it."

"That's what the Judge said," Mrs. McIntyre said and looked at her with approval. The Judge was her first husband, the one who had left her the place. Mrs. Shortley had heard that she had married him when she was thirty and he was seventy-five, thinking she would be rich as soon as he died, but the old man was a scoundrel and when his estate was settled, they found he didn't have a nickel. All he left her were the fifty acres and the house. But she always spoke of him in a reverent way and quoted his sayings, such as "One fellow's misery is the other fellow's gain," and "The devil you know is better than the devil you don't."

"However," Mrs. Shortley remarked, "the devil you know is better than the devil you don't," and she had to turn away so that Mrs. McIntyre would not see her smile. She had found out what the Displaced Person was up to through the old man, Astor, and she had not told anybody but Mr. Shortley. Mr. Shortley had risen straight up in bed like Lazarus from the tomb.

"Shut your mouth!" he had said.

"Yes," she had said.

"Naw!" Mr. Shortley had said.

"Yes," she had said.

Mr. Shortley had fallen back flat.

"The Pole don't know any better," Mrs. Shortley had said. "I reckon that priest is putting him up to it is all. I blame the priest."

The priest came frequently to see the Guizacs and he would always stop in and visit Mrs. McIntyre too and they would walk around the place and she would point out her improvements and listen to his rattling talk. It suddenly came to Mrs. Shortley that he was trying to persuade her to bring another Polish family onto the place. With two of them here, there would be almost nothing spoken but Polish! The Negroes would be gone and there would be the two families against Mr. Shortley and herself! She began to imagine a war of words, to see the Polish words and the English words coming at each other, stalking forward, not sentences, just words, gabble gabble gabble, flung out high and shrill and stalking forward and then grappling with each other. She saw the Polish words, dirty and all-knowing and unreformed, flinging mud on the clean English words until everything was equally dirty. She saw them all piled up in a room, all the dead dirty words, theirs and hers too, piled up like the naked bodies in the newsreel. God save me, she cried silently, from the stinking power of Satan! And she started from that day to read her Bible with a new attention. She pored over the Apocalypse and began to quote from the Prophets and before long she had come to a deeper understanding of her existence. She saw plainly that the meaning of the world was a mystery that had been planned and she was not surprised to suspect that she had a special part in the plan because she was strong. She saw that the Lord God Almighty had created the strong people to do what had to be done and she felt that she would be ready when she was called. Right now she felt that her business was to watch the priest.

His visits irked her more and more. On the last one, he went about picking up feathers off the ground. He found two peacock feathers and four or five turkey feathers and an old brown hen feather and took them off with him like a bouquet. This foolish acting did not deceive Mrs. Shortley any. Here he was: leading foreigners over in hordes to places that were not theirs, to cause disputes, to uproot niggers, to plant the Whore of Babylon in the midst of the righteous! Whenever he came on the place, she hid herself behind something and watched until he left.

It was on a Sunday afternoon that she had her vision. She had gone to drive in the cows for Mr. Shortley who had a pain in his knee and she was walking slowly through the pasture, her arms folded, her eyes on the distant low-lying clouds that looked like rows and rows of white fish washed up on a great blue beach. She paused after an incline to heave a sigh of exhaustion for she had an immense weight to carry around and she was not as young as she used to be. At times she could feel her heart, like a child's fist, clenching and unclenching inside her chest, and when the feeling came, it stopped her thought altogether and she would go about like a large hull of herself, moving for no reason; but she gained this incline without a tremor and stood at the top of it, pleased with herself. Suddenly while she watched, the sky folded back in two pieces, like the curtain to a stage and a gigantic figure stood facing her. It was the color of the sun in the early afternoon, white-gold. It was of no definite shape but there were fiery wheels with fierce dark eyes in them, spinning rapidly all around it. She was not able to tell if the figure was going forward or backward because its magnificence was so great. She shut her eyes in order to look at it and it turned blood-red and the wheels turned white. A voice, very resonant, said the one word, "Prophesy!"

She stood there, tottering slightly but still upright, her eyes shut tight and her fists clenched and her straw sun hat low on her forehead. "The children of wicked nations will be butchered," she said in a loud voice. "Legs where arms should be, foot to face, ear in the palm of hand. Who will remain whole? Who will remain whole? Who?"

Presently she opened her eyes. The sky was full of white fish carried lazily on their sides by some invisible current and pieces of the sun, submerged some distance beyond them, appeared from time to time as though they were being washed in the opposite direction. Woodenly she planted one foot in front of the other until she had crossed the pasture and reached the lot. She walked through the barn like one in a daze and did not speak to Mr. Shortley. She continued up the road until she saw the priest's car parked in front of Mrs. McIntyre's house. "Here again," she muttered. "Come to destroy."

Mrs. McIntyre and the priest were walking in the yard. In order not to meet them face-to-face, she turned to the left and entered the feed house, a single-room shack piled on one side with flowered sacks of scratch feed. There were spilled oyster shells in one corner and a few old dirty calendars on the wall, advertising calf feed and various patent medicine remedies. One showed a bearded gentleman in a frock coat, holding up a bottle, and beneath his feet was the inscription, "I have been made regular by this marvelous discovery." Mrs. Shortley had always felt close to this man as if he were some distinguished person she was acquainted with but now her mind was on nothing but the dangerous presence of the priest. She stationed herself at a crack between two boards where she could look out and see him and Mrs. McIntyre strolling toward the turkey brooder, which was placed just outside the feed house.

"Arrrr!" he said as they approached the brooder. "Look at the little biddies!" and he stooped and squinted through the wire.

Mrs. Shortley's mouth twisted.

"Do you think the Guizacs will want to leave me?" Mrs. McIntyre asked. "Do you think they'll go to Chicago or some place like that?"

"And why should they do that now?" asked the priest, wiggling his finger at a turkey, his big nose close to the wire.

"Money," Mrs. McIntyre said.

"Arrrr, give them some morrre then," he said indifferently. "They have to get along."

"So do I," Mrs. Intyre muttered. "It means I'm going to have to get rid of some of these others."

"And arrre the Shortleys satisfactory?" he inquired, paying more attention to the turkeys than to her.

"Five times in the last month I've found Mr. Shortley smoking in the barn," Mrs. McIntyre said. "Five times."

"And arrre the Negroes any better?"

"They lie and steal and have to be watched all the time," she said.

"Tsk, tsk," he said. "Which will you discharge?"

"I've decided to give Mr. Shortley his month's notice tomorrow," Mrs. McIntyre said.

The priest scarcely seemed to hear her he was so busy wiggling his finger inside the wire. Mrs. Shortley sat down on an open sack of laying mash with a dead thump that sent feed dust clouding up around her. She found herself looking straight ahead at the opposite wall where the gentleman on the calendar was holding up his marvelous discovery but she didn't see him.

She looked ahead as if she saw nothing whatsoever. Then she rose and ran to her house. Her face was an almost volcanic red.

She opened all the drawers and dragged out boxes and old battered suitcases from under the bed. She began to unload the drawers into the boxes, all the time without pause, without taking off the sunhat she had on her head. She set the two girls to doing the same. When Mr. Shortley came in, she did not even look at him but merely pointed one arm at him while she packed with the other. "Bring the car around the back door," she said. "You ain't waiting to be fired!"

Mr. Shortley had never in his life doubted her omniscience. He perceived the entire situation in half a second and, with only a sour scowl, retreated out the door and went to drive the automobile around to the back.

They tied the two iron beds to the top of the car and the two rocking chairs inside the beds and rolled the two mattresses up between the rocking chairs. On top of this they tied a crate of chickens. They loaded the inside of the car with the old suitcases and boxes, leaving a small space for Annie Maude and Sarah Mae. It took them the rest of the afternoon and half the night to do this but Mrs. Shortley was determined that they would leave before four o'clock in the morning, that Mr. Shortley should not adjust another milking machine on this place. All the time she had been working, her face was changing rapidly from red to white and back again.

Just before dawn, as it began to drizzle rain, they were ready to leave. They all got in the car and sat there cramped up between boxes and bundles and rolls of bedding. The square black automobile moved off with more than its customary grinding noises as if it were protesting the load. In the back, the two long bony yellow-haired girls were sitting on a pile of boxes and there was a beagle hound puppy and a cat with two kittens somewhere under the blankets. The car moved slowly, like some overfreighted leaking ark, away from their shack and past the white house where Mrs. McIntyre was sleeping soundly—hardly guessing that her cows would not be milked by Mr. Shortley that morning—and past the Pole's shack on top of the hill and on down the road to the gate where the two Negroes were walking, one behind the other, on their way to help with the milking. They looked straight at the car and its occupants but even as the dim yellow headlights lit up their faces, they politely did not seem to see anything, or anyhow, to attach significance to what was there. The loaded car might have been passing mist in the early morning half-light. They continued up the road at the same even pace without looking back.

A dark yellow sun was beginning to rise in a sky that was the same slick dark gray as the highway. The fields stretched away, stiff and weedy, on either side. "Where we goin'?" Mr. Shortley asked for the first time.

Mrs. Shortley sat with one foot on a packing box so that her knee was pushed into her stomach. Mr. Shortley's elbow was almost under her nose and Sarah Mae's bare left foot was sticking over the front seat, touching her ear.

"Where we goin'?" Mr. Shortley repeated and when she didn't answer again, he turned and looked at her.

Fierce heat seemed to be swelling slowly and fully into her face as if it were welling up now for a final assault. She was sitting in an erect way in spite of the fact that one leg was twisted under her and one knee was almost into her neck, but there was a peculiar lack of light in her icy blue eyes. All the vision in them might have been turned around, looking inside her. She suddenly grabbed Mr. Shortley's elbow and Sarah Mae's foot at the same time and began to tug and pull on them as if she were trying to fit the two extra limbs onto herself.

Mr. Shortley began to curse and quickly stopped the car and Sarah Mae yelled to quit but Mrs. Shortley apparently intended to rearrange the whole car at once. She thrashed forward and backward, clutching at everything she could get her hands on and hugging it to herself, Mr. Shortley's head, Sarah Mae's leg, the cat, a wad of white bedding, her own big moon-like knee; then all at once her fierce expression faded into a look of astonishment and her grip on what she had loosened. One of her eyes drew near to the other and seemed to collapse quietly and she was still.

The two girls, who didn't know what had happened to her, began to say, "Where we goin', Ma? Where we goin'?" They thought she was playing a joke and that their father, staring straight ahead of her, was imitating a dead man. They didn't know that she had had a great experience or ever been displaced in the world from all that belonged to her. They were frightened by the gray slick road before them and they kept repeating in higher and higher voices, "Where we goin', Ma? Where we goin'?" while their mother, her huge body rolled back still against the seat and her eyes like blue-painted glass, seemed to contemplate for the first time the tremendous frontiers of her true country.

II

"Well," Mrs. McIntyre said to the old Negro, "we can get along without them. We've seen them come and seen them go—black and white." She was standing in the calf barn while he cleaned it and she held a rake in her hand and now and then pulled a corncob from a corner or pointed to a soggy spot that he had missed. When she discovered the Shortleys were gone, she was delighted as it meant she wouldn't have to fire them. The people she hired always left her—because they were that kind of people. Of all the families she had had, the Shortleys were the best if she didn't count the Displaced Person. They had been not quite trash; Mrs. Shortley was a good woman, and she would miss her but as the Judge used to say, you couldn't have your pie and eat it too, and she was satisfied with the D.P. "We've seen them come and seen them go," she repeated with satisfaction.

"And me and you," the old man said, stooping to drag his hoe under a feed rack, "is still here."

She caught exactly what he meant her to catch in his tone. Bars of sunlight fell from the cracked ceiling across his back and cut him in three distinct parts. She watched his long hands clenched around the hoe and his crooked old profile pushed close to them. You might have been here *before* I was, she said to herself, but it's mighty likely I'll be here when you're gone. "I've spent half my life fooling with worthless people," she said in a severe voice, "but now I'm through."

"Black and white," he said, "is the same."

"I am through," she repeated and gave her dark smock that she had thrown over her shoulders like a cape a quick snatch at the neck. She had on a broad-brimmed black straw hat that had cost her twenty dollars twenty years ago and that she used now for a sunhat. "Money is the root of all evil," she said. "The Judge said so every day. He said he deplored money. He said the reason you niggers were so uppity was because there was so much money in circulation."

The old Negro had known the Judge. "Judge say he long for the day when he be too poor to pay a nigger to work," he said. "Say when that day come, the world be back on its feet."

She leaned forward, her hands on her hips and her neck stretched and said, "Well that day has almost come around here and I'm telling each and every one of you: you better look sharp. I don't have to put up with foolishness any more. I have somebody now who *has* to work!"

The old man knew when to answer and when not. At length he said, "We seen them come and we seen them go."

"However, the Shortleys were not the worst by far," she said. "I well remember those Garrits."

"That was before them Collinses," he said.

"No, before the Ringfields."

"Sweet Lord, them Ringfields!" he murmured.

"None of that kind *want* to work," she said.

"We seen them come and we seen them go," he said as if this were a refrain. "But we ain't never had one before," he said, bending himself up until he faced her, "like what we got now." He was cinnamon-colored with eyes that were so blurred with age that they seemed to be hung behind cobwebs.

She gave him an intense stare and held it until, lowering his hands on the hoe, he bent down again and dragged a pile of shavings alongside the wheelbarrow. She said stiffly, "He can wash out that barn in the time it took Mr. Shortley to make up his mind he had to do it."

"He from Pole," the old man muttered.

"From Poland."

"In Pole it ain't like it is here," he said. "They got different ways of doing," and he began to mumble unintelligibly.

"What are you saying?" she said. "If you have anything to say about him, say it and say it aloud."

He was silent, bending his knees precariously and edging the rake along the underside of the trough.

"If you know anything he's done that he shouldn't, I expect you to report it to me," she said.

"It warn't like it was what he should ought or oughtn't," he muttered. "It was like what nobody else don't do."

"You don't have anything against him," she said shortly, "and he's here to stay."

"We ain't never had one like him before is all," he murmured and gave his polite laugh.

"Times are changing," she said. "Do you know what's happening to this world? It's swelling up. It's getting so full of people that only the smart thrifty energetic ones are going to survive," and she tapped the words, smart, thrifty, and energetic out on the palm of her hand. Through the far end of the stall she could see down the road to where the Displaced Person was standing in the open barn door with the green hose in his hand. There was a certain stiffness about his figure that seemed to make it necessary for her to approach him slowly, even in her thoughts. She had decided this was because she couldn't hold an easy conversation with him. Whenever she said anything to him, she found herself shouting and nodding extravagantly and she would be conscious that one of the Negroes was leaning behind the nearest shed, watching.

"No indeed!" she said, sitting down on one of the feed racks and folding her arms, "I've made up my mind that I've had enough trashy people on this place to last me a lifetime and I'm not going to spend my last years fooling with Shortleys and Ringfields and Collins when the world is full of people who *have* to work."

"Howcome they so many extra?" he asked.

"People are selfish," she said. "They have too many children. There's no sense in it any more."

He had picked up the wheelbarrow handles and was backing out the door and he paused, half in the sunlight and half out, and stood there chewing his gums as if he had forgotten which direction he wanted to move in.

"What you colored people don't realize," she said, "is that I'm the one around here who holds all the strings together. If you don't work, I don't make any money and I can't pay you. You're all dependent on me but you each and every one act like the shoe is on the other foot."

It was not possible to tell from his face if he heard her. Finally he backed out with the wheelbarrow. "Judge say the devil he know is better than the devil he don't," he said in a clear mutter and trundled off.

She got up and followed him, a deep vertical pit appearing suddenly in the center of her forehead, just under the red bangs. "The Judge has long since ceased to pay the bills around here," she called in a piercing voice.

He was the only one of her Negroes who had known the Judge and he thought this gave him title. He had had a low opinion of Mr. Crooms and Mr. McIntyre, her other husbands, and in his veiled polite way, he had congratulated her after each of her divorces. When he thought it necessary, he would work under a window where he knew she was sitting and talk to himself, a careful, roundabout discussion, question and answer and then refrain. Once she had got up silently and slammed the window down so hard that he had fallen backwards off his feet. Or occasionally he spoke with the peacock. The cock would follow him around the place, his steady eye on the ear of corn that stuck up from the old man's back pocket or he would sit near him and pick himself. Once from the open kitchen door, she had heard him say to the bird, "I remember when it was twenty of you walking about this place and now it's only you and two hens. Crooms it was twelve, McIntyre it was five. You and two hens now."

And that time she had stepped out of the door onto the porch and said, "MISTER Crooms and MISTER McIntyre! And I don't want to hear you call either of them anything else again. And you can understand this: when that peachicken dies there won't be any replacements."

She kept the peacock only out of a superstitious fear of annoying the Judge in his grave. He had liked to see them walking around the place for he said they made him feel rich. Of her three husbands, the Judge was the one most present to her although he was the only one she had buried. He was in the family graveyard, a little space fenced in the middle of the back cornfield, with his mother and father and grandfather and three great aunts and two infant cousins. Mr. Crooms, her second, was forty miles away in the state asylum and Mr. McIntyre, her last, was intoxicated, she supposed, in some hotel room in Florida. But the Judge, sunk in the cornfield with his family, was always at home.

She had married him when he was an old man and because of his money but there had been another reason that she would not admit then, even to herself: she had liked him. He was a dirty snuff-dipping Court House figure, famous all over the county for being rich, who wore hightop shoes, a string tie, a gray suit with a black stripe in it, and a yellowed panama hat, winter and summer. His teeth and hair were tobacco-colored and his face a clay pink pitted and tracked with mysterious prehistoric-looking marks as if he had been unearthed among fossils. There had been a peculiar odor about him of sweaty fondled bills but he never carried money on him or had a nickel to show. She was his secretary for a few months and the old man with his sharp eye had seen at once that here was a woman who admired him for himself. The three years that he lived after they married were the happiest and most prosperous of Mrs. McIntyre's life, but when he died his estate proved to be bankrupt. He left her a mortgaged house and fifty acres that he had managed to cut the timber off before he died. It was as if, as the final triumph of a successful life, he had been able to take everything with him.

But she had survived. She had survived a succession of tenant farmers and dairymen that the old man himself would have found hard to outdo, and she had been able to meet the constant drain of a tribe of moody unpredictable Negroes, and she had even managed to hold her own against the incidental bloodsuckers, the cattle dealers and lumber men and the buyers and sellers of anything who drove up in pieced-together trucks and honked in the yard.

She stood slightly reared back with her arms folded under her smock and a satisfied expression on her face as she watched the Displaced Person turn off the hose and disappear inside the barn. She was sorry that the poor man had been chased out of Poland and run across Europe and had had to take up in a tenant shack in a strange country, but she had not been responsible for any of this. She had had a hard time herself. She knew what it was to struggle. People ought to have to struggle. Mr. Guizac had probably had everything given to him all the way across Europe and over here. He had probably not had to struggle enough. She had given him a job. She didn't know if he was grateful or not. She didn't know anything about him except that he did the work. The truth was that he was not very real to her yet. He was a kind of miracle that she had seen happen and that she talked about but that she still didn't believe.

She watched as he came out of the barn and motioned to Sulk, who was coming around the back of the lot. He gesticulated and then took something out of his pocket and the two of them stood looking at it. She started down the lane toward them. The Negro's figure was slack and tall and he was craning his round head forward in his usual idiotic way. He was a little better than half-witted but when they were like that they were always good workers. The judge had said always hire you a half-witted nigger because they don't have sense enough to stop working. The Pole was gesticulating rapidly. He left something with the colored boy and then walked off and before she rounded the turn in the lane, she heard the tractor crank up. He was on his way to the field. The Negro was still hanging there, gaping at whatever he had in his hand.

She entered the lot and walked through the barn, looking with approval at the wet spotless concrete floor. It was only nine-thirty and Mr. Shortley had never got anything washed until eleven. As she came out at the other end, she saw the Negro moving very slowly in a diagonal path across the road in front of her, his eyes still on what Mr. Guizac had given him. He didn't see her and he paused and dipped his knees and leaned over his hand, his tongue describing little circles. He had a photograph. He lifted one finger and traced it lightly over the surface of the picture. Then he looked up and saw her and seemed to freeze, his mouth in a half-grin, his finger lifted.

"Why haven't you gone to the field?" she asked.

He raised one foot and opened his mouth wider while the hand with the photograph edged toward his back pocket.

"What's that?" she said.

"It ain't nothing," he muttered and handed it to her automatically.

It was a photograph of a girl of about twelve in a white dress. She had blond hair with a wreath in it and she looked forward out of light eyes that were bland and composed. "Who is this child?" Mrs. McIntyre asked.

"She his cousin," the boy said in a high voice.

"Well, what are you doing with it?" she asked.

"She going to mah me," he said in an even higher voice.

"Marry you!" she shrieked.

"I pays half to get her over here," he said. "I pays him three dollar a week. She bigger now. She his cousin. She don't care who she mah she so glad to get away from there." The high voice seemed to shoot up like a nervous jet of sound and then fall flat as he watched her face. Her eyes were the color of blue granite when the glare falls on it, but she was not looking at him. She was looking down the road where the distant sound of the tractor could be heard.

"I don't reckon she going to come nohow," the boy murmured.

"I'll see that you get every cent of your money back," she said in a toneless voice and turned and walked off, holding the photograph bent in two. There was nothing about her small stiff figure to indicate that she was shaken.

As soon as she got in the house, she lay down on her bed and shut her eyes and pressed her hand over her heart as if she were trying to keep it in place. Her mouth opened and she made two or three dry little sounds. Then after a minute she sat up and said aloud, "They're all the same. It's always been like this," and she fell back flat again. "Twenty years of being beaten and done in and they even robbed his grave!" and remembering that, she began to cry quietly, wiping her eyes every now and then with the hem of her smock.

What she had thought of was the angel over the Judge's grave. This had been a naked granite cherub that the old man had seen in the city one day in a tombstone store window. He had been taken with it at once, partly because its face reminded him of his wife and partly because he wanted a genuine work of art over his grave. He had come home with it sitting on the green plush train seat beside him. Mrs. McIntyre had never noticed the resemblance to herself. She had always thought it hideous but when the Herrins stole it off the old man's grave she was shocked and outraged. Mrs. Herrin had thought it very pretty and had walked to the graveyard frequently to see it, and when the Herrins left the angel left with them, all but its toes, for the ax old man Herrin had used to break it off with had struck slightly too high. Mrs. McIntyre had never been able to afford to have it replaced.

When she had cried all she could, she got up and went into the back hall, a closet-like space that was dark and quiet as a chapel and sat down on the edge of the Judge's black mechanical chair with her elbow on his desk. This was a giant rolltop piece of furniture pocked with pigeon holes full of dusty papers. Old bankbooks and ledgers were stacked in the half-open drawers and there was a small safe, empty but locked, set like a tabernacle in the center of it. She had left this part of the house unchanged since the old man's time. It was a kind of memorial to him, sacred because he had conducted his business here. With the slightest tilt one way or the other, the chair gave a rusty skeletal groan that sounded something like him when he had complained of his poverty. It had been his first principle to talk as if he were the poorest man in the world and she followed it, not only because he had but because it was true. When she sat with her intense constricted face turned toward the empty safe, she knew there was nobody poorer in the world than she was.

She sat motionless at the desk for ten or fifteen minutes and then as if she had gained some strength, she got up and got in her car and drove to the cornfield.

The road ran through a shadowy pine thicket and ended on top of a hill that rolled fan-wise down and up again in a broad expanse of tassled green. Mr. Guizac was cutting from the outside of the field in a circular path to the center where the graveyard was all but hidden by the corn, and she could see him on the high far side of the slope, mounted on the tractor with the cutter and wagon behind him. From time to time, he had to get off the tractor and climb in the wagon to spread the silage because the Negro had not arrived. She watched impatiently, standing in front of her black coupe with her arms folded under her smock, while he progressed slowly around the rim of the field, gradually getting close enough for her to wave to him to get down. He stopped the machine and jumped off and came running forward, wiping his red jaw with a piece of grease rag.

"I want to talk to you," she said and beckoned him to the edge of the thicket where it was shady. He took off the cap and followed her, smiling, but his smile faded when she turned and faced him. Her eyebrows, thin and fierce as a spider's leg, had drawn together ominously and the deep vertical pit had plunged down from under the red bangs into the bridge of her nose. She removed the bent picture from her pocket and handed it to him silently. Then she stepped back and said, "Mr. Guizac! You would bring this poor innocent child over here and try to marry her to a half-witted thieving black stinking nigger! What kind of a monster are you!"

He took the photograph with a slowly returning smile. "My cousin," he said. "She twelve here. First Communion. Six-ten now."

Monster! She said to herself and looked at him as if she were seeing him for the first time. His forehead and skull were white where they had been protected by his cap but the rest of his face was red and bristled with short yellow hairs. His eyes were like two bright nails behind his gold-rimmed spectacles that had been mended over the nose with haywire. His whole face looked as if it might have been patched together out of several others. "Mr. Guizac," she said, beginning slowly and then speaking faster until she ended breathless in the middle of a word, "that nigger cannot have a white wife from Europe. You can't talk to a nigger that way. You'll excite him and besides it can't be done. Maybe it can be done in Poland but it can't be done here and you'll have to stop. It's all foolishness. That nigger don't have a grain of sense and you'll excite . . ."

"She in camp three year," he said.

"Your cousin," she said in a positive voice, "cannot come over here and marry one of my Negroes."

"She six-ten year," he said. "From Poland. Mamma die, pappa die. She wait in camp. Three camp." He pulled a wallet from his pocket and fingered through it and took out another picture of the same girl, a few years older, dressed in something dark and shapeless. She was standing against a wall with a short woman who apparently had no teeth. "She mamma," he said, pointing to the woman. "She die in two camp."

"Mr. Guizac," Mrs. McIntyre said, pushing the picture back at him, "I will not have my niggers upset. I cannot run this place without my niggers. I can run it without you but not without them and if you mention this girl to Sulk again, you won't have a job with me. Do you understand?"

His face showed no comprehension. He seemed to be piecing all these words together in his mind to make a thought.

Mrs. McIntyre remembered Mrs. Shortley's words: "He understands everything, he only pretends he don't so as to do exactly as he pleases," and her face regained the look of shocked wrath she had begun with. "I cannot understand how a man who calls himself a Christian," she said, "could bring a poor innocent girl over here and marry her to something like that. I cannot understand it. I cannot!" And she shook her head and looked into the distance with a pained blue gaze.

After a second he shrugged and let his arms drop as if he were tired. "She no care black," he said. "She in camp three year."

Mrs. McIntyre felt a peculiar weakness behind her knees. "Mr. Guizac," she said, "I don't want to have to speak to you about this again. If I do, you'll have to find another place yourself. Do you understand?"

The patched face did not say. She had the impression that he didn't see her there. "This is my place," she said. "I say who will come here and who won't."

"Ya," he said and put back on his cap.

"I am not responsible for the world's misery," she said as an afterthought.

"Ya," he said.

"You have a good job. You should be grateful to be here," she added, "but I'm not sure you are."

"Ya," he said and gave his little shrug and turned back to the tractor.

She watched him get on and maneuver the machine into the corn again. When he had passed her and rounded the turn, she climbed to the top of the slope and stood with her arms folded and looked out grimly over the field. "They're all the same," she muttered, "whether they come from Poland or Tennessee. I've handled Herrins and Ringfields and Shortleys and I can handle a Guizac," and she narrowed her gaze until it closed entirely around the diminishing figure on the tractor as if she were watching him through a gunsight. All her life she had been fighting the world's overflow and now she had it in the form of a Pole. "You're just like all the rest of them," she said, "—only smart and thrifty and energetic but so am I. And this is my place," and she stood there, a small, black-hatted, black-smocked figure with an aging cherubic face, and folded her arms as if she were equal to anything. But her heart was beating as if some interior violence had already been done to her. She opened her eyes to include the whole field so that the figure on the tractor was no larger than a grasshopper in her widened view.

She stood there for some time. There was a slight breeze and the corn trembled in great waves on both sides of the slope. The big cutter, with its monotonous roar, continued to shoot it pulverized into the wagon in a steady spurt of fodder. By nightfall, the Displaced Person would have worked his way around and around until there would be nothing on either side of the two hills but the stubble, and down in the center, risen like a little island, the graveyard where the Judge lay grinning under his desecrated monument.

III

The priest, with his long bland face supported on one finger, had been talking for ten minutes about Purgatory, while Mrs. McIntyre squinted furiously at him from an opposite chair. They were drinking ginger ale on her front porch and she kept rattling the ice in her glass, rattling her beads, rattling her bracelet like an impatient pony jingling its harness. There is no moral obligation to keep him, she was saying under her breath, there is absolutely no moral obligation. Suddenly she lurched up and her voice fell across his brogue like a drill into a mechanical saw. "Listen," she said, "I'm not theological. I'm practical! I want to talk to you about something practical!"

"Arrrrrrr," he groaned, grating to a halt.

She had put at least a finger of whiskey in her own ginger ale so that she would be able to endure his full-length visit and she sat down awkwardly, finding the chair closer to her than she had expected. "Mr. Guizac is not satisfactory," she said.

The old man raised his eyebrows in mock wonder.

"He's extra," she said. "He doesn't fit in. I have to have somebody who fits in."

The priest carefully turned his hat on his knees. He had a little trick of waiting a second silently and then swinging the conversation back into his own paths. He was about eighty. She had never known a priest until she had gone to see this one on the business of getting her the Displaced Person. After he had got her the Pole, he had used the business introduction to try to convert her—just as she had supposed he would.

"Give him time," the old man said. "He'll learn to fit in. Where is that beautiful birrrrd of yours?" he asked and then said, "Arrr, I see him!" and stood up and looked out over the lawn where the peacock and the two hens were stepping at a strained attention, their long necks ruffled, the cock's violent blue and the hens' silver-green, glinting in the late afternoon sun.

"Mr. Guizac," Mrs. McIntyre continued, bearing down with a flat steady voice, "is very efficient. I'll admit that. But he doesn't understand how to get on with my niggers and they don't like him. I can't have my niggers run off. And I don't like his attitude. He's not the least grateful for being here."

The priest had his hand on the screen door and he opened it, ready to make his escape. "Arrrr, I must be off," he murmured.

"I tell you if I had a white man who understood the Negroes, I'd have to let Mr. Guizac go," she said and stood up again.

He turned then and looked her in the face. "He has nowhere to go," he said. Then he said, "Dear lady, I know you well enough to know you wouldn't turn him out for a trifle!" and without waiting for an answer, he raised his hand and gave her his blessing in a rumbling voice.

She smiled angrily and said, "I didn't create his situation, of course."

The priest let his eyes wander toward the birds. They had reached the middle of the lawn. The cock stopped suddenly and curving his neck backward, he raised his tail and spread it with a shimmering timbrous noise. Tiers of small pregnant suns floated in a green-gold haze over his head. The priest stood transfixed, his jaw slack. Mrs. McIntyre wondered where she had ever seen such an idiotic old man. "Christ will come like that!" he said in a loud gay voice and wiped his hand over his mouth and stood there, gaping.

Mrs. McIntyre's face assumed a set puritanical expression and she reddened. Christ in the conversation embarrassed her the way sex had her mother. "It is not my responsibility that Mr. Guizac has nowhere to go," she said. "I don't find myself responsible for all the extra people in the world."

The old man didn't seem to hear her. His attention was fixed on the cock who was taking minute steps backward, his head against the spread tail. "The Transfiguration," he murmured.

She had no idea what he was talking about. "Mr. Guizac didn't have to come here in the first place," she said, giving him a hard look.

The cock lowered his tail and began to pick grass.

"He didn't have to come in the first place," she repeated, emphasizing each word.

The old man smiled absently. "He came to redeem us," he said and blandly reached for her hand and shook it and said he must go.

If Mr. Shortley had not returned a few weeks later, she would have gone out looking for a new man to hire. She had not wanted him back but when she saw the familiar black automobile drive up the road and stop by the side of the house, she had the feeling that she was the one returning, after a long miserable trip, to her own place. She realized all at once that it was Mrs. Shortley she had been missing. She had had no one to talk to since Mrs. Shortley left, and she ran to the door, expecting to see her heaving herself up the steps.

Mr. Shortley stood there alone. He had on a black felt hat and a shirt with red and blue palm trees designed in it but the hollows in his long bitten blistered face were deeper than they had been a month ago.

"Well!" she said. "Where is Mrs. Shortley?"

Mr. Shortley didn't say anything. The change in his face seemed to have come from the inside; he looked like a man who had gone for a long time without water. "She was God's own angel," he said in a loud voice. "She was the sweetest woman in the world."

"Where is she?" Mrs. McIntyre murmured.

"Daid," he said. "She had herself a stroke on the day she left out of here." There was a corpse-like composure about his face. "I figure that Pole killed her," he said. "She seen through him from the first. She known he come from the devil. She told me so."

It took Mrs. McIntyre three days to get over Mrs. Shortley's death. She told herself that anyone would have thought they were kin. She rehired Mr. Shortley to do farm work though actually she didn't want him without his wife. She told him she was going to give thirty days' notice to the Displaced Person at the end of the month and that then he could have his job back in the dairy. Mr. Shortley preferred the dairy job but he was willing to wait. He said it would give him some satisfaction to see the Pole leave the place, and Mrs. McIntyre said it would give her a great deal of satisfaction. She confessed that she should have been content with the help she had in the first place and not have been reaching into other parts of the world for it. Mr. Shortley said he never had cared for foreigners since he had been in the first world's war and seen what they were like. He said he had seen all kinds then but that none of them were like us. He said he recalled the face of one man who had thrown a hand-grenade at him and that the man had had little round eyeglasses exactly like Mr. Guizac's.

"But Mr. Guizac is a Pole, he's not a German," Mrs. McIntyre said.

"It ain't a great deal of difference in them two kinds," Mr. Shortley had explained.

The Negroes were pleased to see Mr. Shortley back. The Displaced Person had expected them to work as hard as he worked himself, whereas Mr. Shortley recognized their limitations. He had never been a very good worker himself with Mrs. Shortley to keep him in line, but without her, he was even more forgetful and slow. The Pole worked as fiercely as ever and seemed to have no inkling that he was about to be fired. Mrs. McIntyre saw jobs done in a short time that she had thought would never get done at all. Still she was resolved to get rid of him. The sight of his small stiff figure moving quickly here and there had come to be the most irritating sight on the place for her, and she felt she had been tricked by the old priest. He had said there was no legal obligation for her to keep the Displaced Person if he was not satisfactory, but then he had brought up the moral one.

She meant to tell him that *her* moral obligation was to her own people, to Mr. Shortley, who had fought in the world war for his country and not to Mr. Guizac who had merely arrived here to take advantage of whatever he could. She felt she must have this out with the priest before she fired the Displaced Person. When the first of the month came and the priest hadn't called, she put off giving the Pole notice for a little longer.

Mr. Shortley told himself that he should have known all along that no woman was going to do what she said she was when she said she was. He didn't know how long he could afford to put up with her shilly-shallying. He thought himself that she was going soft and was afraid to turn the Pole out for fear he would have a hard time getting another place. He could tell her the truth about this: that if she let him go, in three years he would own his own house and have a television aerial sitting on top of it. As a matter of policy, Mr. Shortley began to come to her back door every evening to put certain facts before her. "A white man sometimes don't get the considera-tion a nigger gets," he said, "but that don't matter because he's still white, but sometimes," and here he would pause and look off into the distance, "a man that's fought and bled and died in the service of his native land don't get the consideration of one of them like he was fighting. I ast you: is that right?" When he asked her such questions he could watch her face and tell he was making an impression. She didn't look too well these days. He noticed lines around her eyes that hadn't been there when he and Mrs. Shortley had been the only white help on the place. Whenever he thought of Mrs. Shortley, he felt his heart go down like an old bucket into a dry well.

The old priest kept away as if he had been frightened by his last visit but finally, seeing that the Displaced Person had not been fired, he ventured to call again to take up giving Mrs. McIntyre instructions where he remem-bered leaving them off. She had not asked to be instructed but he instructed anyway, forcing a little definition of one of the sacraments or of some dogma into each conversation he had, no matter with whom. He sat on her porch, taking no notice of her partly mocking, partly outraged expression as she sat shaking her foot, waiting for an opportunity to drive a wedge into his talk. "For," he was saying, as if he spoke of something that had happened yester-day in town, "when God sent his Only Begotten Son, Jesus Christ Our Lord"—he slightly bowed his head—"as a Redeemer to mankind, He . . ."

"Father Flynn!" she said in a voice that made him jump. "I want to talk with you about something serious!"

The skin under the old man's right eye flinched.

"As far as I'm concerned," she said and glared at him fiercely, "Christ was just another D.P."

He raised his hands slightly and let them drop on his knees, "Arrrrr," he murmured as if he were considering this.

"I'm going to let that man go," she said. "I don't have any obligation to him. My obligation is to the people who've done something for their country, not to the ones who've just come over to take advantage of what they can get," and she began to talk rapidly, remembering all her arguments. The priest's attention seemed to retire to some private oratory to wait until she got through. Once or twice his gaze roved out onto the lawn as if he were hunting some means of escape but she didn't stop. She told him how she had been hanging onto this place for thirty years, always just barely making it against people who came from nowhere and were going nowhere, who didn't want anything but an automobile. She said she had found out they were the same whether they came from Poland or Tennessee. When the Guizacs got ready, she said, they would not hesitate to leave her. She told him how the people who looked rich were the poorest of all because they had the most to keep up. She asked him how he thought she paid her feed bills. She told him she would like to have her house done over but she couldn't afford it. She couldn't even afford to have the monument restored over her husband's grave. She asked him if he would like to guess what her insurance amounted to for the year. Finally she asked him if he thought she was made of money and the old man suddenly let out a great ugly bellow as if this were a comical question.

When the visit was over, she felt let down, though she had clearly triumphed over him. She made up her mind now that on the first of the month, she would give the Displaced Person his thirty days' notice and she told Mr. Shortley so.

Mr. Shortley didn't say anything. His wife had been the only woman he was ever acquainted with who was never scared off from doing what she said. She said the Pole had been sent by the devil and the priest. Mr. Shortley had no doubt that the priest had got some peculiar control over Mrs. McIntyre and that before long she would start attending his Masses. She looked as if something was wearing her down from the inside. She was thinner and more fidgety, and not as sharp as she used to be. She would look at a milk can now and not see how dirty it was and he had seen her lips move when she was not talking. The Pole never did anything the wrong way but all the same he was very irritating to her. Mr. Shortley himself did things as he pleased—not always her way—but she didn't seem to notice. She had noticed though that the Pole and all his family were getting fat; she pointed out to Mr. Shortley that the hollows had come out of their cheeks and that they saved every cent they made. "Yes'm, and one of these days he'll be able to buy and sell you out," Mr. Shortley had ventured to say, and he could tell that the statement had shaken her.

"I'm just waiting for the first," she had said.

Mr. Shortley waited too and the first came and went and she didn't fire him. He could have told anybody how it would be. He was not a violent man but he hated to see a woman done in by a foreigner. He felt that that was one thing a man couldn't stand by and see happen.

There was no reason Mrs. McIntyre should not fire Mr. Guizac at once but she put it off from day to day. She was worried about her bills and about her health. She didn't sleep at night or when she did she dreamed about the Displaced Person. She had never discharged anyone before; they had all left her. One night she dreamed that Mr. Guizac and his family were moving into her house and that she was moving in with Mr. Shortley. This was too much for her and she woke up and didn't sleep again for several nights; and one night she dreamed that the priest came to call and droned on and on saying, "Dear lady, I know your tender heart won't suffer you to turn the porrrrr man out. Think of the thousands of them, think of the ovens and the boxcars and the camps and the sick children and Christ Our Lord."

"He's extra and he's upset the balance around here," she said, "and I'm a logical practical woman and there are no ovens here and no camps and no Christ Our Lord and when he leaves, he'll make more money. He'll work at the mill and buy a car and don't talk to me—all they want is a car."

"The ovens and the boxcars and the sick children," droned the priest, "and our dear Lord."

"Just one too many," she said.

The next morning, she made up her mind while she was eating her breakfast that she would give him his notice at once, and she stood up and walked out of the kitchen and down the road with her table napkin still in her hand. Mr. Guizac was spraying the barn, standing in his swaybacked way with one hand on his hip. He turned off the hose and gave her an impatient kind of attention as if she were interfering with his work. She had not thought of what she would say to him, she had merely come. She stood in the barn door, looking severely at the wet spotless floor and the dripping stanchions. "Ya goot?" he said.

"Mr. Guizac," she said, "I can barely meet my obligations now." Then she said in a louder, stronger voice, emphasizing each word, "I have bills to pay."

"I too," Mr. Guizac said. "Much bills, little money," and he shrugged.

At the other end of the barn, she saw a long beak-nosed shadow glide like a snake halfway up the sunlit open door and stop; and somewhere behind her, she was aware of a silence where the sound of the Negroes shoveling had come a minute before. "This is my place," she said angrily, "All of you are extra. Each and every one of you are extra!"

"Ya," Mr. Guizac said, and turned the hose on again.

She wiped her mouth with the napkin she had in her hand and walked off, as if she had accomplished what she came for.

Mr. Shortley's shadow withdrew from the door and he leaned against the side of the barn and lit half of a cigarette that he took out of his pocket. There was nothing for him to do now but wait on the hand of God to strike, but he knew one thing: he was not going to wait with his mouth shut.

Starting that morning, he began to complain and to state his side of the case to every person he saw, black or white. He complained in the grocery store and at the courthouse and on the street corner and directly to Mrs. McIntyre herself, for there was nothing underhanded about him. If the Pole could have understood what he had to say, he would have said it to him too. "All men was created free and equal," he said to Mrs. McIntyre, "and I risked my life and limb to prove it. Gone over there and fought and bled and died and come back on over here and find out who's got my job—just exactly who I been fighting. It was a hand-grenade come that near to killing me and I seen who throwed it—little man with eyeglasses just like his. Might have bought them at the same store. Small world," and he gave a bitter little laugh. Since he didn't have Mrs. Shortley to do the talking any more, he had started doing it himself and had found that he had a gift for it. He had the power of making other people see his logic. He talked a good deal to the Negroes.

"Whyn't you go back to Africa?" he asked Sulk one morning as they were cleaning out the silo. "That's your country, ain't it?"

"I ain't goin' there," the boy said. "They might eat me up."

"Well, if you behave yourself it isn't any reason you can't stay here," Mr. Shortley said kindly. "Because you didn't run away from nowhere. Your granddaddy was bought. He didn't have a thing to do with coming. It's the people that run away from where they come from that I ain't got any use for."

"I never felt no need to travel," the Negro said.

"Well," Mr. Shortley said, "if I was going to travel again, it would be to either China or Africa. You go to either of them two places and you can tell right away what the difference is between you and them. You go to these other places and the only way you can tell is if they say something. And then you can't always tell because about half of them know the English language. That's where we make our mistake," he said, "—letting all them people onto English. There'd be a heap less trouble if everybody only knew his own language. My wife said knowing two languages was like having eyes in the back of your head. You couldn't put nothing over on her."

"You sho couldn't," the boy muttered, and then he added, "She was fine. She was sho fine. I never known a finer white woman than her."

Mr. Shortley turned in the opposite direction and worked silently for a while. After a few minutes he leaned up and tapped the colored boy on the shoulder with the handle of his shovel. For a second he only looked at him while a great deal of meaning gathered in his wet eyes. Then he said softly, "Revenge is mine, saith the Lord."

Mrs. McIntyre found that everybody in town knew Mr. Shortley's version of her business and that everyone was critical of her conduct. She began to understand that she had a moral obligation to fire the Pole and that she was shirking it because she found it hard to do. She could not stand the increasing guilt any longer and on a cold Saturday morning, she started off after breakfast to fire him. She walked down to the machine shed where she heard him cranking up the tractor.

There was a heavy frost on the ground that made the fields look like the rough backs of sheep; the sun was almost silver and the woods stuck up like dry bristles on the skyline. The countryside seemed to be receding from the little circle of noise around the shed. Mr. Guizac was squatting on the ground beside the small tractor, putting in a part. Mrs. McIntyre hoped to get the fields turned over while he still had thirty days to work for her. The colored boy was standing by with some tools in his hand and Mr. Shortley was under the shed about to get up on the large tractor and back it out. She meant to wait until he and the Negro got out of the way before she began her unpleasant duty.

She stood watching Mr. Guizac, stamping her feet on the hard ground, for the cold was climbing like a paralysis up her feet and legs. She had on a heavy black coat and a red head kerchief with her black hat pulled down on top of it to keep the glare out of her eyes. Under the black brim her face had an abstracted look and once or twice her lips moved silently. Mr. Guizac shouted over the noise of the tractor for the Negro to hand him a screwdriver and when he got it, he turned over on his back on the icy ground and reached up under the machine. She could not see his face, only his feet and legs and trunk sticking impudently out from the side of the tractor. He had on rubber boots that were cracked and splashed with mud. He raised one knee and then lowered it and turned himself slightly. Of all the things she resented about him, she resented most that he hadn't left on his own accord.

Mr. Shortley had got on the large tractor and was backing it out from under the shed. He seemed to be warmed by it as if its heat and strength sent impulses up through him that he obeyed instantly. He had headed it toward the small tractor but he braked it on a slight incline and jumped off and turned back toward the shed. Mrs. McIntyre was looking fixedly at Mr. Guizac's legs lying flat on the ground now. She heard the brake on the large tractor slip and, looking up, she saw it move forward, calculating its own path. Later she remembered that she had seen the Negro jump silently out of the way as if a spring in the earth had released him and that she had seen Mr. Shortley turn his head with incredible slowness and stare silently over his shoulder and that she had started to shout to the Displaced Person but that she had not. She had felt her eyes and Mr. Shortley's eyes and the Negro's eyes come together in one look that froze them in collusion forever, and she had heard the little noise the Pole made as the tractor wheel broke his backbone. The two men ran forward to help and she fainted.

She remembered, when she came to, running somewhere, perhaps into the house and out again but she could not remember what for or if she had fainted again when she got there. When she finally came back to where the tractors were, the ambulance had arrived. Mr. Guizac's body was covered with the bent bodies of his wife and two children and by a black one that hung over him, murmuring words she didn't understand. At first she thought this must be the doctor but then, with a feeling of annoyance, she recognized the priest, who had come with the ambulance and was slipping something into the crushed man's mouth. After a minute he stood up and she looked first at his bloody pants legs and then at his face that was not averted from her but was as withdrawn and expressionless as the rest of the countryside. She only stared at him for she was too shocked by her experience to be quite herself. Her mind was not taking hold of all that was happening. She felt she was in some foreign country where the people bent over the body were natives, and she watched like a stranger while the dead man was carried away in the ambulance.

That evening, Mr. Shortley left without notice to look for a new position and the Negro, Sulk, was taken with a sudden desire to see more of the world and set off for the southern part of the state. The old man Astor could not work without company. Mrs. McIntyre hardly noticed that she had no help left for she came down with a nervous affliction and had to go to the hospital. When she came back, she saw that the place would be too much for her to run now and she turned her cows over to a professional auctioneer (who sold them at a loss) and retired to live on what she had, while she tried to save her declining health. A numbness developed in one of her legs and her hands and head began to jiggle and eventually she had to stay in bed all the time with only a colored woman to wait on her. Her eyesight grew steadily worse and she lost her voice altogether. Not many people remembered to come out to the country to see her except the old priest. He came regularly once a week with a bag of breadcrumbs and, after he had fed these to the peacock, he would come in and sit by the side of her bed and explain the doctrines of the Church.

8

DAWN

J. F. Powers

Father Udovic placed the envelope before the Bishop and stepped back. He gave the Bishop more than enough time to read what was written on the envelope, time to digest *The Pope* and, down in the corner, the *Personal*, and then he stepped forward. "It was in the collection yesterday," he said. "At Cathedral."

"Peter's Pence, Father?"

Father Udovic nodded. He'd checked that. It had been in with the special Peter's Pence envelopes, and not with the regular Sunday ones.

"Well, then . . ." The Bishop's right hand opened over the envelope, then stopped, and came to roost again, uneasily, on the edge of the desk.

Father Udovic shifted a foot, popped a knuckle in his big toe. The envelope was a bad thing all right. They'd never received anything like it. The Bishop was doing what Father Udovic had done when confronted by the envelope, thinking twice, which was what Monsignor Renton at Cathedral had done, and his curates before him, and his housekeeper who counted the collection. In the end, each had seen the envelope as a hot potato and passed it on. But the Bishop couldn't do that. He didn't know *what* might be inside. Even Father Udovic, who had held it up to a strong light, didn't know. That was the hell of it.

The Bishop continued to stare at the envelope. He still hadn't touched it.

"It beats me," said Father Udovic, moving backwards. He sank down on the leather sofa.

"Was there something else, Father?"

Father Udovic got up quickly and went out of the office—wondering how the Bishop would handle the problem, disappointed that he evidently meant to handle it by himself. In a way, Father Udovic felt responsible. It had been his idea to popularize the age-old collection—"to personalize Peter's Pence"—by moving the day for it ahead a month so that the Bishop, who was going to Rome, would be able to present the proceeds to the Holy Father personally. There had been opposition from the very first. Monsignor Renton, the rector at Cathedral, and one of those at table when Father Udovic proposed his plan, was ill-disposed to it (as he was to Father Udovic himself) and had almost killed it with his comment, "Smart promotion, Bruno." (Monsignor Renton's superior attitude was understandable. He'd had Father Udovic's job, that of chancellor of the diocese, years ago, under an earlier bishop.) But Father Udovic had won out. The Bishop had written a letter incorporating Father Udovic's idea. The plan had been poorly received in some rectories, which was to be expected since it disturbed the routine schedule of special collections. Father Udovic, however, had been confident that the people, properly appealed to, could do better than in the past with Peter's Pence. And the first returns, which had reached him that afternoon, were reassuring—whatever the envelope might be.

It was still on the Bishop's desk the next day, off to one side, and it was there on the day after. On the following day, Thursday, it was in the "In" section of his file basket. On Friday it was still there, buried. Obviously the Bishop was stumped.

On Saturday morning, however, it was back on the desk. Father Udovic, called in for consultation, had a feeling, a really satisfying feeling, that the Bishop might have need of him. If so, he would be ready. He had a plan. He sat down on the sofa.

"It's about this," the Bishop said, glancing down at the envelope before him. "I wonder if you can locate the sender."

"I'll do my best," said Father Udovic. He paused to consider whether it would be better just to go and do his best, or to present his plan of operation to the Bishop for approval. But the Bishop, not turning to him at all, was outlining what he wanted done. And it was Father Udovic's own plan! The Cathedral priests at their Sunday Masses should request the sender of the envelope to report to the sacristy afterwards. The sender should be assured that the contents would be turned over to the Holy Father, if possible.

"Providing, of course," said Father Udovic, standing and trying to get into the act, "it's not something . . ."

"Providing it's possible to do so."

Father Udovic tried not to look sad. The Bishop might express himself better, but he was saying nothing that hadn't occurred to Father Udovic first, days before. It was pretty discouraging.

He retreated to the outer office and went to work on a memo of their conversation. Drafting letters and announcements was the hardest part of his job for him. He tended to go astray without a memo, to take up with the tempting clichés that came to him in the act of composition and sometimes perverted the Bishop's true meaning. Later that morning he called Monsignor Renton and read him the product of many revisions, the two sentences.

"Okay," said Monsignor Renton. "I'll stick it in the bulletin. Thanks a lot."

As soon as Father Udovic hung up, he doubted that that was what the Bishop wished. He consulted the memo. The Bishop was very anxious that "not too much be made of this matter." Naturally, Monsignor Renton wanted the item for his parish bulletin. He was hard up. At one time he had produced the best bulletin in the diocese, but now he was written out, quoting more and more from the magazines and even from the papal encyclicals. Father Udovic called Monsignor Renton back and asked that the announcement be kept out of print. It would be enough to read it once over lightly from the pulpit, using Father Udovic's version because it said enough without saying too much and was, he implied, authorized by the Bishop. Whoever the announcement concerned would comprehend it. If published, the announcement would be subject to study and private interpretation. "Announcements from the pulpit are soon forgotten," Father Udovic said. "I mean—by the people they don't concern."

"You were right the first time, Bruno," said Monsignor Renton. He sounded sore.

The next day—Sunday—Father Udovic stayed home, expecting a call from Monsignor Renton, or possibly even a visit. There was nothing. That evening he called the Cathedral rectory and got one of the curates. Monsignor Renton wasn't expected in until very late. The curate had made the announcement at his two Masses, but no one had come to him about it. "Yes, Father, as you say, it's quite possible someone came to Monsignor about it. Probably he didn't consider it important enough to call you about."

"*Not important!*"

"Not important enough to call *you* about, Father. On *Sunday*."

"I see," said Father Udovic mildly. It was good to know that the curate, after almost a year of listening to Monsignor Renton, was still respectful. Some of the men out in parishes said Father Udovic's job was a snap and maintained that he'd landed it only because he employed the touch system of typing. Before hanging up, Father Udovic stressed the importance of resolving the question of the envelope, but somehow (words played tricks on him) he sounded as though he were accusing the curate of indifference. What a change! The curate didn't take criticism very well, as became all too clear from his sullen silence, and he wasn't very loyal. When Father Udovic suggested that Monsignor Renton might have neglected to make the announcement at his Masses, the curate readily agreed. "Could've slipped his mind all right. I guess you know what that's like."

Early the next morning Father Udovic was in touch with Monsignor Renton, beginning significantly with a glowing report on the Peter's Pence collection, but the conversation languished, and finally he had to ask about the announcement.

"Nobody showed," Monsignor Renton said in an annoyed voice. "What d'ya want to do about it?"

"Nothing right now," said Father Udovic, and hung up. If there had been a failure in the line of communication, he thought he knew where it was.

The envelope had reposed on the Bishop's desk over the weekend and through most of Monday. But that afternoon Father Udovic, on one of his appearances in the Bishop's office, noticed that it was gone. As soon as the Bishop left for the day, Father Udovic rushed in, looking first in the waste-basket, then among the sealed outgoing letters, for a moment actually expecting to see a fat one addressed in the Bishop's hand to the Apostolic Delegate. When he uncovered the envelope in the "Out" section of the file basket, he wondered at himself for looking in the other places first. The envelope had to be filed somewhere—a separate folder would be best—but Father Udovic didn't file it. He carried it to his desk. There, sitting down to it in the gloom of the outer office, weighing, feeling, smelling the envelope, he succumbed entirely to his first fears. He remembered the parable of the cockle. "An enemy hath done this." An enemy was plotting to disturb the peace of the diocese, to employ the Bishop as an agent against himself, or against some other innocent person, some unsuspecting priest or nun—yes, against Father Udovic. Why him? Why not? Only a diseased mind would contemplate such a scheme, Father Udovic thought, but that didn't make it less likely. And the sender, whoever he was, doubtless anonymous and judging others by himself, would assume that the envelope had already been opened and that the announcement was calculated to catch him. Such a person would never come forward.

Father Udovic's fingers tightened on the envelope. He could rip it open, but he wouldn't. That evening, enjoying instant coffee in his room, he could steam it open. But he wouldn't. In the beginning, the envelope might have been opened. It would have been so easy, pardonable then. Monsignor Renton's housekeeper might have done it. With the Bishop honoring the name on the envelope and the intentions of whoever wrote it, up to a point anyway, there was now a principle operating that just couldn't be bucked. Monsignor Renton could have his way.

That evening Father Udovic called him and asked that the announcement appear in the bulletin.

"Okay. I'll stick it in. It wouldn't surprise me if we got some action now."

"I hope so," said Father Udovic, utterly convinced that Monsignor Renton had failed him before. "Do you mind taking it down verbatim this time?"

"Not at all."

In the next bulletin, an advance copy of which came to Father Udovic through the courtesy of Monsignor Renton, the announcement appeared in an expanded, unauthorized version.

The result on Sunday was no different.

During the following week, Father Udovic considered the possibility that the sender was a floater and thought of having the announcement broadcast from every pulpit in the diocese. He would need the Bishop's permission for that, though, and he didn't dare to ask for something he probably wouldn't get. The Bishop had instructed him not to make too much of the matter. The sender would have to be found at Cathedral, or not at all. If not at all, Father Udovic, having done his best, would understand that he wasn't supposed to know any more about the envelope than he did. He would file it away, and some other chancellor, some other bishop, perhaps, would inherit it. The envelope was most likely harmless anyway, but Father Udovic wasn't so much relieved as bored by the probability that some poor soul was trusting the Bishop to put the envelope into the hands of the Holy Father, hoping for rosary beads blessed by him, or for his autographed picture, and enclosing a small offering, perhaps a spiritual bouquet. Toward the end of the week, Father Udovic told the Bishop that he liked to think that the envelope contained a spiritual bouquet from a little child, and that its contents had already been delivered, so to speak, its prayers and communions already credited to the Holy Father's account in heaven.

"I must say I hadn't thought of that," said the Bishop.

Unfortunately for his peace of mind Father Udovic wasn't always able to believe that the sender was a little child.

The most persistent of those coming to him in reverie was a middle-aged woman saying she hadn't received a special Peter's Pence envelope, had been out of town a few weeks, and so hadn't heard or read the announcement. When Father Udovic tried her on the meaning of the *Personal* on the envelope, however, the woman just went away, and so did all the other suspects under questioning—except one. This was a rich old man suffering from scrupulosity. He wanted his alms to be in secret, as it said in Scripture, lest he be deprived of his eternal reward, but not *entirely* in secret. That was as far as Father Udovic could figure the old man. Who was he? An audacious old Protestant who hated communism, or could some future Knight of St. Gregory be taking his first awkward step? The old man was pretty hard to believe in, and the handwriting on the envelope sometimes struck Father Udovic as that of a woman. This wasn't necessarily bad. Women controlled the nation's wealth. He'd seen the figures on it. The explanation was simple: widows. Perhaps they hadn't taken the right tone in the announcement. Father Udovic's version had been safe and cold, Monsignor Renton's like a summons. It might have been emphasized that the Bishop, under certain circumstances, would *gladly* undertake to deliver the envelope. That might have made a difference. The sender would not only have to appreciate the difficulty of the Bishop's position, but abandon his own. That wouldn't be easy for the sort of person Father Udovic had in mind. He had a feeling that it wasn't going to happen. The Bishop would leave for Rome on the following Tuesday. So time was running out. The envelope could contain a check—quite the cruelest thought—on which payment would be stopped after a limited time by the donor, whom Father Udovic persistently saw as an old person not to be dictated to, or it could be nullified even sooner by untimely death. God, what a shame! In Rome, where the needs of the world, temporal as well as spiritual, were so well known, the Bishop would've been welcome as the flowers in May.

And then, having come full circle, Father Udovic would be hard on himself for dreaming and see the envelope as a whited sepulcher concealing all manner of filth, spelled out in letters snipped from newsprint and calculated to shake Rome's faith in him. It was then that he particularly liked to think of the sender as a little child. But soon the middle-aged woman would be back, and all the others, among whom the hottest suspect was a feeble-minded nun—devils all to pester him, and the last was always worse than the first. For he always ended up with the old man—and what if there was such an old man?

On Saturday, Father Udovic called Monsignor Renton and asked him to run the announcement again. It was all they could do, he said, and admitted that he had little hope of success.

"Don't let it throw you, Bruno. It's always darkest before dawn."

Father Udovic said he no longer cared. He said he liked to think that the envelope contained a spiritual bouquet from a little child, that its contents had already been delivered, its prayers and communions already . . .

"You should've been a nun, Bruno."

"Not sure I know what you mean," Father Udovic said, and hung up. He wished it were in his power to do something about Monsignor Renton. Some of the old ones got funny when they stayed too long in one place.

On Sunday, after the eight o'clock Mass, Father Udovic received a call from Monsignor Renton. "I told 'em if somebody didn't own up to the envelope, we'd open it. I guess I just got carried away." But it had worked. Monsignor Renton had just talked with the party responsible for the envelope—a Mrs. Anton—and she was on the way over to see Father Udovic.

"A woman, huh?"

"A widow. That's about all I know about her."

"A widow, huh? Did she say what was in it?"

"I'm afraid it's not what you thought, Bruno. It's money."

Father Udovic returned to the front parlor, where he had left Mrs. Anton. "The Bishop'll see you," he said, and sat down. She wasn't making a good impression on him. She could've used a shave. When she'd asked for the Bishop, Father Udovic had replied instinctively, "He's busy," but it hadn't convinced her. She had appeared quite capable of walking out on him. He invoked the Bishop's name again. "Now one of the things the Bishop'll want to know is why you didn't show up before this."

Mrs. Anton gazed at him, then past him, as she had when he'd tried to question her. He saw her starting to get up, and thought he was about to lose her. He hadn't heard the Bishop enter the room.

The Bishop waved Mrs. Anton down, seated himself near the doorway at some distance from them, and motioned to Father Udovic to continue.

To the Bishop it might sound like browbeating, but Father Udovic meant to go on being firm with Mrs. Anton. He hadn't forgotten that she'd responded to Monsignor Renton's threats. "Why'd you wait so long? You listen to the Sunday announcements, don't you?" If she persisted in ignoring him, she could make him look bad, of course, but he didn't look for her to do that, with the Bishop present.

Calmly Mrs. Anton spoke, but not to Father Udovic. "Call off your trip!"

The Bishop shook his head.

In Father Udovic's opinion, it was one of his functions to protect the Bishop from directness of that sort. "How do we know what's in here?" he demanded. Here, unfortunately, he reached up the wrong sleeve of his cassock for the envelope. Then he had it. "What's in here? Money?" He knew from Monsignor Renton that the envelope contained money, but he hadn't told the Bishop, and so it probably sounded rash to him. Father Udovic could feel the Bishop disapproving of him, and Mrs. Anton still hadn't answered the question.

"Maybe you should return the envelope to Mrs. Anton, Father," said the Bishop.

That did it for Mrs. Anton. "It's got a dollar in it," she said.

Father Udovic glanced at the Bishop. The Bishop was adjusting his cuffs. This was something he did at funerals and public gatherings. It meant that things had gone on too long. Father Udovic's fingers were sticking in the envelope. He still couldn't believe it. "Feels like there's more than that," he said.

"I wrapped it up good in paper."

"You didn't write a letter or anything?"

"Was I supposed to?"

Father Udovic came down on her. "You were supposed to do what everybody else did. You were supposed to use the envelopes we had printed up for the purpose." He went back a few steps in his mind. "You told Monsignor Renton what was in the envelope?"

"Yes."

"Did you tell him how much?"

"No."

"Why not?"

"*He* didn't ask me."

And *he* didn't have to, thought Father Udovic. One look at Mrs. Anton and Monsignor Renton would know. Parish priests got to know such things. They were like weight guessers, for whom it was only a question of ounces. Monsignor Renton shouldn't have passed Mrs. Anton on. He had opposed the plan to personalize Peter's Pence, but who would have thought he'd go to such lengths to get even with Father Udovic? It was sabotage. Father Udovic held out the envelope and pointed to the *Personal* on it. "What do you mean by that?" Here was where the creatures of his dreams had always gone away. He leaned forward for the answer.

Mrs. Anton leaned forward to give it. "I mean I don't want somebody else takin' all the credit with the Holy Father!"

Father Udovic sank back. It had been bad before, when she'd ignored him, but now it was worse. She was attacking the Bishop. If there were only a way to *prove* she was out of her mind, if only she'd say something that would make all her remarks acceptable in retrospect. "How's the Holy Father gonna know who this dollar came from if you didn't write anything?"

"I wrote my name and address in ink."

"All right, Father," said the Bishop. He stood up and almost went out of the room before he stopped and looked back at Mrs. Anton. "Why don't you send it by regular mail?"

"He'd never see it! That's why! Some flunky'd get hold of it! Same as here! Oh, don't I know!"

The Bishop walked out, leaving them together—with the envelope.

In the next few moments, although Father Udovic knew he had an obligation to instruct Mrs. Anton, and had the text for it—"When thou dost an alms-deed, sound not a trumpet before thee"—he despaired. He realized that they had needed each other to arrive at their sorry state. It seemed to him, sitting there saying nothing, that they saw each other as two people who'd sinned together on earth might see each other in hell, unchastened even then, only blaming each other for what had happened.

9

SILENT RETREATS

Philip F. Deaver

One Monday morning on the way to work, the traffic pausing behind
school buses, Martin Wolf was suddenly struck by the circularity of
life and began to sob. Or maybe it wasn't the circularity but something made
him sob and he thought that was it. The air, autumn cool, and the clear sky,
the nostalgia of the changing trees, the cars with their small rising trails of
exhaust, all conspired to give him existential doubt. He pulled onto a narrow shoulder along Roosevelt Road, two hundred feet from the big intersection at Glen Elyn Pike, slumped in his seat, and let himself go.

He'd gotten up too early that morning, reacting childishly to the mud-
dled rejections of his wife. In the dim light of the kitchen, he poached an
egg, half listening to the radio tuned to whatever station he inherited when
he turned it on. To keep from bothering her, he'd hit the shower in the
dark—strange experience: in the shower was a handbrush and as he
scrubbed his hands with it he was swept away with a recollection of watching his father scrubbing for surgery back when he was in high school. At
that time it was presumed Martin would be a doctor too someday. Now he
felt the bristles reddening his hands, and he brushed all the way to the
elbows to sustain the recollection. He dressed mostly in the available light
of a blue dawn—whatever of it could find its way past the pulled drapes of
the master bedroom. Then he'd read a while, sitting near the woodstove
in the den. Melissa Manchester and Jackson Browne were on WLS, their
love songs, their road songs. Martin pouted through the final routines of
tying his tie and finding his watch and keys, finally stepping out the back
door around 7:30. The vinyl of his car seat was stiff with the morning chill.

He worked as systems analyst at Argon Labs, a short commute. From the narrow shoulder on Roosevelt Road, he watched the cars go by and slowly turned the dial on the car radio, searching for the one station whose wave length he was already on. He looked intentionally into the passing cars. The drivers were looking ahead only as far as the back bumper of the car ahead of them, or, in extreme cases of foresight, as far as the Glen Elyn Pike cross-road. Stopped at the light, the men would pull the morning paper up out of the seat next to them and prop it on the steering wheel, take a sip of coffee from the cup balanced on the console; the women would sit perfectly still, waiting, or they would pull down their sunglasses—all the women wore sun-glasses—they would pull them down and check their makeup, cocking the rearview mirror toward themselves, cocking it back.

And all the while he watched, he couldn't stop crying. He sank deeper and deeper into his seat, the warmth and humidity of his tears steaming the car windows until the idling migration on Roosevelt Road finally became nothing but fog around him.

Maybe he fell asleep a few minutes—at least he lost touch. Presently he realized there was a car very close to his, stopped next to him, and he wiped a hand over the fogged-up window to look out. It was a woman, leaning from her driver's seat all the way across to the window on the passenger side, which was already down. Martin rolled down his window, trying to clear himself.

"Hello," she said, "is everything okay?" She had to talk loudly over the traffic.

"Right," Martin said. "Fine." He was trying to think if he knew her. He didn't.

"Are you sure? I have a CB here—I can make a call."

"I'm fine, thanks."

She looked right at him. "I have the feeling something's wrong—are you sure?"

"No," Martin said, answering the wrong question, rolling his window up again, "I mean yes, I'm sure," slumping down in his seat. When he looked back, she'd driven on.

He dropped a dime in the booth, and had to open the door again to bend down and pick it up. There were watermelon seeds, gravel bits, butts, brown stains in the corners. He heard his phone call go through.

"St. Michael's rectory." The voice spoke quickly but also seemed casual, a young man; the voice was deep, resonant, accustomed to speaking from the pulpit in modestly didactic sorties on the values of suburbanites.

"Hell." Martin was staring up the long street. From the booth, there was a gradual slope upward toward the outer suburbs presenting a linear retreating panorama of plastic franchise signs and the high-mounted signs of car dealers. The Radio Shack sign and the far off Dunkin' Donuts sign were turning; the tasteful bank sign, with gold bank logo on black, was giving digital readouts on the time, temperature, and interest rates, interspersed with ads and announcements.

"Anybody there?" the priest said. With the Chicago accent, he sounded like a cross between a LaSalle Street speculator and an Irish city cop: the practiced tone of an urban populist.

"I'm here. Yes. Sorry," Martin said.

"Don't apologize," the priest said. "It's just . . . you called me so you have to talk." There was a smile in the voice.

"Sorry," Martin said, then winced that he'd apologized again. But the priest was silent.

"Listen, Father, you don't know me," Martin said, conscious of the halting way he was speaking. "I'm actually not a Catholic anymore. I work out at the labs."

"Lots of Catholics survive working at the lab, pal. Are you in a booth?"

"Right," Martin said. A Triumph and a Camaro were doing a ritual revving at the stoplight, intersection of Roosevelt and U.S. 54.

"Sounds like the Daytona 500 out there. Roosevelt Road, right?"

"You got it," Martin said.

"Why not drop by if you have time. You know where we are? I've got some iced tea." The cars tore away from the mark. The Camaro left the Triumph after first gear, catching rubber in all four. "Mercy," the priest said when the noise relented.

"Sorry," Martin said.

"You know the Heiss family? Rick Heiss? Out at the labs?" Martin caught a sunbeam off a car bumper and it went all the way through his brain. "Heiss has a lovely family," the priest said. "He was a seminarian for a while, you know. They come to St. Mike's."

Martin was squinting, looking around through the grimy windows of the phone booth. "Look here, Father, I'm sorry to bother you this morning, but I'm on the way to work and I started wondering if . . ." He paused. Call a person "Father," it made you seem like the child, it made you seem innocent and the father all-knowing, like in the old days. It made life seem solid instead of liquid and gas. Intervention was possible; solutions existed and were only as far away as a rosary, a confessional, holy water. The tears were in his eyes. "I'm wondering if they still have silent retreats like they used to. I went on one with the Knights of Columbus once, when I was seventeen.

Down around St. Louis someplace. I figured if you guys might know if they still have things like that."

It was quiet at the other end. There was clicking in their connection.

"Hello? You there?"

"Well, usually they aren't silent anymore, to the best of my knowledge. But they do still have retreats. We've got marriage encounters and renewals, held at the old Maryknoll convent, you know? And the diocese has a retreat consultant come through from time to time, usually in conjunction with special diocese-level initiatives." The priest sighed. "The stress these days is on community. I guess the silent retreat stuff—they used to have retreats like that all the time—I guess the silent ones are considered self-indulgent. These days, in keeping with the community thing, community of the faith, of the faithful so to speak, these days at retreats they get in small groups, you know, and share perceptions, building a sense of community, you might say. That's the idea."

"Well, I'd like to go to a silent retreat," Martin said.

"I understand. You know, the new thinking, you see—I know you know what you want and pointing this out is a pain, but the new thinking is that silence like in those old retreats is a kind of self-indulgence—part of the problem, you get me?"

"Well." Martin felt a huge swell in his throat and chest, the fear of tears, the need for them to come on. "I don't know," he said. "I'll say this. I don't want to spend a week sitting around in small groups sharing, if that's what you're talking about, sharing perceptions and everybody getting a warm feeling inside. I know about that stuff and it's a big goddamned joke." He tried to wrestle himself back.

"Look," the priest said. "I've got some time this morning—why don't you drop by the rectory? You know where we are?"

"Nah, thanks. I only wanted to check on retreats, maybe get a schedule. I thought you could tell me if there are still the silent ones. I've gotta get to work."

It was cool in the booth and Martin's headache felt vaguely like hangovers he'd had.

"If you want, I could meet you over at the confessional or something. Keep it anonymous. No problem—whatever you want. You upset?"

"They think silence is self-indulgent? I'd be interested to know what they think of the Trappists. There's some real hedonistic guys. I swear," Martin said, and found his handkerchief. The tears were flowing freely and it was a relief for him not to have to hide it from the man on the phone.

"Look. Would you do something? Would you get out of the phone booth and drop by? I'm free all morning—we could just sit around and talk."

"Nah, I'm fine. I've been crying all morning, is all." Martin looked down the road. He could remember when he was a little boy. When he felt like this, there was someone who could make him feel better. "I appreciate your concern, Father, but . . ." Right then Martin noticed the turning bank sign. "Jesus! Nine o'clock! I've got to get to work." He wiped his eyes, almost laughing. "I can't do this all day—I don't have the energy. Excuse me a minute," he said, and clanked down the phone. He opened the door to the booth and blew his nose. "I'm coming apart here," he mumbled to himself away from the phone. He leaned back in and picked up the receiver.

"What's that?" the priest said.

"I'm sayin', I just wanted to get some information. Thanks for your help."

"What's so great about a silent retreat? They've got retreats for execs, they've got 'em for young marrieds and old marrieds and singles and psychologists. They've even got 'em for cod fishermen and neurotic priests." The priest laughed, tried to bring Martin along with his laugh. "No kidding. Retreats are still with us, it's just the silent ones that you don't see much."

"I understand."

"They even have retreats on educational TV. Do you have cable?"

"We're talking about two different things, Father. Are you aware of that? You're not talking about the kind of thing a person can go to and think."

There was no response from the priest. Martin decided he was a Franciscan. The Dominicans were parish priests, acculturated; Martin was thinking this guy sounded slightly more missionary, defying gravity with faith, so to speak. Suddenly, over the phone, Martin could hear the rectory doorbell.

"Hold on a minute," the priest said. "Seriously, hold on and maybe we can chat a little longer. I've got to get the door. While I'm up, I'll try to find the number for the Jebbie retreat house in Des Plaines."

Martin heard the priest go to the door. "Have a seat," he heard him say to someone, "I've got somebody on the phone. He's asking about retreats—you know the Jesuit place out north? Know anything about it?" The priest was talking to someone he knew well, someone who didn't know anything about the Des Plaines retreat house. Then Martin could hear pages turning. Then the priest was back. "Here we go. Call Father Hollins—661-3428. Gotta pen? 661-3428—no, wait a minute, that's the business office, hold it. Here we go: 661-3477. I think I know that Hollins guy—from Catholic Charities or something. Anyway, give him a call, ask him if he's got something in the way of silent retreats. Just tell him you don't want a bunch of sharing, you never can tell. That's all I can suggest."

"Thanks," Martin said. He didn't have a pen.

"I have to tell you, though," the priest said with something in his tone that indicated to Martin he wanted to level with him, "if you aren't going to mass and taking the sacraments a retreat won't help."

"Help what?" Martin said.

"Help."

"Well." Martin stared up the road. Traffic was relenting. "Thanks a lot for the numbers, Father."

"You see, a retreat might take some pressure off you, but what have you done for the Almighty lately, is my point." Martin had the feeling the priest was playing to the audience, this somebody who had come to the door and was now at least partially listening to the other end of the conversation while waiting. Martin pictured the rectory, holy water founts and gaudy sacred-heart renderings, crucifixes everywhere with small painted elaborations of Christ's blood and pain. "You see what I'm saying?" the priest said.

"I get it."

"I mean you can retreat all the way to Milwaukee and back, you get me? But if you aren't going to mass, if you aren't with the program, you aren't pointed in the right direction to solve anything."

"I get it. I said I get it and I get it." Martin clawed at his tie, getting it loose.

"You ought to start coming to mass. Do you have children?"

"What's this, the pitch? Right here on the telephone?"

"It's all we've got, you and me. Sorry."

"Don't apologize," Martin said, and before he could quite control it he popped the phone back onto its cradle, the bell inside it singing from the impact. "Think about it, you jerk," Martin said to himself, and left the booth, stuffing his handkerchief in his back pocket.

He pulled up in front of the school. He was self-conscious because the windows on this side of the building provided him with a cross-section of all elementary grades in the school, each of which was partly distracted by him when he pulled up and parked in the drop-off zone. He was trying to remember his son's teacher's name, Solomon, Lamb, Kennedy, something like that.

The school was low-slung, brick and windows. He walked in the north end, hoping that as he walked by the classrooms a name would hit him. The teachers' names were in little frames on the blond classroom doors. He wanted to see his little boy through the narrow windows, watch him a minute just to watch. The long, narrow yellow-tile hall depressed him even worse, Bauhaus education. Gone the bell tower and the tower clock and the small teacher-student ratio of his own Catholic elementary school days.

Back to basics, walls and halls, floors and doors. Cut-out autumn leaves were taped to the blond bricks. Each leaf had a name on it, scrawled in a hopeful hand. He heard a child coughing as he passed one room, low murmur of the teacher as he passed another. His child, Jeff—pressed into this mass process. This was where he learned reading and writing, and, out on the playground, the recently unveiled revision of "Yankee Doodle" (". . . stuck a feather up his butt and called it . . ."). Martin noticed a sign on a door. Mrs. Rudolph, that was it, his son's teacher.

He peered through the window, and all he could see were the backs of children's heads as they bent over their seat work in the beige light. Despite all the windows, at nearly noon on this clear day the whole idea of the out-of-doors seemed to evaporate in this building. The teacher at the rear of the classroom was grading papers at her desk. Occasionally a child would lean over to sneak a comment to a friend across the aisle. There was Daren, his son's friend, and there was his son, blond boy, blessed. Martin watched him, and the tears were there again, unexplainable.

"Excuse me," somebody said from behind. "Have you been to the office yet?"

It was a little lady with dark gray hair, tightly bound. "You have to go to the office and check in—it's right down there, take a left." She smiled.

"I have to what?" Martin said, hastily. They were talking just above a whisper.

"To check in," she answered. "Down there." She turned and pointed down the hall. "My sister-in-law has allergies, too," she said, observant.

"I was hoping to . . . my son wasn't feeling well this morning and I thought I'd just look in on him," Martin said. "I don't want to bother him in class . . . I just wanted to lay my eyes on him, you know?"

"Of course," she said. "They have an intercom in the office."

"No need for any of that," he said.

She stood there insistently as he went back to peering in the window. He sensed that she was impatient with him. "Listen," he said, "you seem like a pleasant enough lady. Why don't I just break the rules and take a look at my boy for another thirty seconds, and then I'll head out the same door I just walked in, no problem."

"This, sir, is a city school here. We have to control who comes and goes. Besides they have a visitor's packet for you in the office, and they can call your son from there, on the intercom. Or you could wait," she said. "In a few minutes, they'll be coming to the gymnasium for lunch." She was still smiling, perhaps a little more forcibly. Martin wanted to punch her in her soft little jaw. "The PTA worked very hard on the packet. It's got their newsletter and the financial report."

"Please," he said. "I don't want the PTA newsletter. I want a moment's peace here, looking at my little boy. I don't want to mess over school policy, but this is a little thing, not big. I'll be out of here in a minute." Martin leaned down to whisper something in the lady's ear. "I'm just not in the mood for the visitor's packet. Frankly," he said, still talking in a loud whisper, and he winked, "I'm afraid it will piss me off." He stood back and looked at her, his arms up. "I might go berserk right there in the principal's office."

The woman turned and hurried down the hall to tattle. She wore matronly black-heeled shoes that clacked as she went. At one point as she hurried, she looked back over her shoulder.

A wave of restlessness seemed to sweep through the school. The big round clocks were signaling to everyone that the morning segment of confinement was close to over. Then Martin noticed another lady coming down the hall, approaching somehow warily but with a big smile.

"Good morning," she said. "Can I help you? I'm Dr. Cousins—Alberta Cousins—I'm the principal here. Is your boy in this room?"

"Yes," Martin said, looking through the window. "I was just looking at him."

"Which child is it?" She came close to look through the same small window as he pointed.

"The white-haired boy with the pencil in his mouth. Chews the erasers."

"I hear you just encountered our librarian, Mrs. Redding."

"Yes." Martin continued to look through the window.

"She probably seems like an old biddy to you, but she's a real pro in the classroom, I can tell you."

"That's good," Martin said. "Very loyal of you to mention it."

"Want me to get your boy out here?—It's no problem at all." Before he could answer, she ducked past him and opened the door. She signaled to Mrs. Rudolph, a very tall, made-up woman, straight-backed, perhaps forty-five. "Jeff's father has come to see him—could we have him a moment?"

Then Jeff was out in the hall, a little bewildered. He grinned up at his dad, cheeky face, eyes like his mom. "Hey," Martin said to him.

"Hey," the boy said back.

"If you don't mind," the principal said to Martin, "would you take your walk out the north door? In four minutes the halls will be filled with masses of children, marginally controlled and very hungry." She smiled warmly. "And," she said, "I don't know whether our librarian mentioned it, but when you're finished we have a visitor's register for you to sign and a packet of materials for you, in the office."

"She mentioned it."

The lady faded off, back down the hall.

"How you doin'?" Martin said to Jeff when they were alone. Jeff was in the first grade.

"Fine," he said. As they walked toward the north door, they were holding hands, both looking at the floor. Martin was fighting another swell of emotion. "We goin' home now?" Jeff asked.

"What're you studying in there?" Martin said in a low voice.

"Nothin'."

"C'mon."

"Vegetables."

"Vegetables, great. Which ones?"

"We had to write out our favorite ones."

"That must have been tough. Which ones are your favorites?"

"Carrots, root beer, and grape juice."

"Real good, fresh produce. I saw Daren—he's almost as tall as you are now."

"We had a army guy today." They arrived at the north door.

"Yeah? A real one?"

"He let us sit in his jeep. Army guys aren't to kill people—they under-arrest 'em."

"Did you sign up?"

"Sign up for what?" Jeff said.

"Hey, Jeffrey. I just thought of something." They were sitting on the north step in warm sunlight. "Remember when we played baseball last spring? When we played together in the park where the ducks are? Remember?"

"Yip."

"Know what that made me think of?"

"Nope."

"I thought of when my dad first played baseball with me." Tears welled up.

"How come?" Jeff said. He squinched up his nose.

"How come what?" The handkerchief.

"Daaa-ud, I mean how come you thought of that?"

"I don't know—I just did. Once Dad and I were playing burn-out—you know?—When you throw back and forth real hard trying to make the other guy say ouch. And I threw this one real hard and it skipped off his glove and gave him a black eye. Playing baseball with you, it made me think of playing with my own dad and it made me happy. Back then, when I was playing with him, I never knew there'd be a you."

"Your dad died, right?"

"That's right, but that's not what I'm talking about. I'm talking about before that. When I was little like you are. Little kids don't realize you were little once too. It just . . ." Martin could feel the point laboring down to nothing, but he kept wanting to say something magic. "It just seems real . . . real interesting to me that my dad played baseball with me and then I played it with you years and years later. And you and him, you never met. You're flesh and blood, but you never met. I'm the bridge between you."

Jeff was looking out toward the playground. "Hey, Dad . . ." Martin waited. "Wanna see the gym? It's time for lunch."

Martin stood up, hurt. "Nah. I gotta go to work." He kissed Jeff on top of his blond head and squeezed him a good one. "I love you, boy," he told him, and Jeff's eyes wandered back toward the north door.

"I love you too, Poppsy," Jeff said, still looking away. "I don't get it. Why did you come to school?"

Martin was heading back toward the car. "I needed to know about vegetables. Grown-ups don't know everything, you know."

"Hey, Dad," Jeff shouted as he pulled open the door to the school, "guess what?"

"What?" Martin spoke over the top of his car and across part of the school yard.

"Daren's got poison oak."

"It'll go away." Martin smiled, getting into the car. When he looked back that way, Jeff had gone into the school.

What an odd state of mind, Martin thought, to wander through the suburbs in broad daylight, drifting with the radio and the flow of traffic. These disc jockeys, they had the city mood perfectly calibrated with their rattling jokes and timed, practiced chaos. At the stoplights, he watched the other drivers. How many of them too were wandering? He came across the north side, all the way to Lake Michigan, and drove a short distance south on Lake Shore Drive until he came to Belmont Harbor.

He parked at the far end of the parking lot and, in the wind and long shadows, sat motionless. There was a woman he knew and he thought of her now, because she always talked to him about being lonely and maybe she was alone now for all he knew, and she had talked to him about keeping a bottle of gin under the bed for nighttime, whether because she was afraid or because she was bored or because she needed love and had no chance of ever having it. It had been a revelation to hear her talk about being alone. She'd been in every kind of therapy known to woman, she'd even been Rolfed in a motel room in Danville, all for the company of it, because other possibilities seemed to have expired. She'd raised her children—they were gone from her except for desperate phone calls they'd make to her in the night, the kind that brought up the heartbeat and made sleep impossible for nights afterward; because she was nearly forty-seven, she felt she was about to slip darkly, alone, into the hole.

Today Martin knew how she felt, as he watched the October waves on the lake. The sun dropped just behind the tall bank of apartment buildings west of Lake Shore Drive, and a chill sat him up. He'd met her, this woman, in a strange town. In a Mexican restaurant they talked with their heads close so even now he could remember the glitter in her makeup, the slightly caked mascara in her eyelashes when she'd cried a couple of times, the warning she gave him about being unfaithful, voice of experience: "I'm not married any-more because of something like this," she said to him. "I found out he was seeing someone else and I left him inside the hour. I took the kids." She was staring right at him. She knew what she was saying to him, the sign she was giving. "If you love a person and the person isn't faithful, there's no hurt like it." She made him think hard about that.

There was a phone booth in the lobby of the Drake Hotel, not far from Belmont Harbor.

"South Ridge Legal Services," a voice said at the other end of the line.

"I'm calling a guy named Skidmore."

"I'm sorry," the voice said, "we're closed. Can I take a message?"

"Closed?"

"Yessir," said the voice, flat, bored, unapologetic.

"I just wanted to tell this guy Skidmore . . . I wanted to tell him what to do with a red hot poker."

"I see. That doesn't sound too nice, sir. May I say who called?" The man on the other end spoke in a monotone.

"Tell him this is your old pal and worst enemy from when you were twelve."

"I see. That's nice. That sounds very nice, I would say." Skidmore would not sound surprised nor break character. "What shall I tell him you are up to these days?"

"Tell him it's none of his business."

"I see," Skidmore said. "That doesn't sound very nice. Where should I tell him you are calling from?"

"Las Vegas, on the strip."

"Nice. That's nice. Say hello to Wayne Newton for him." They both laughed. "Shall I tell him you were drunk when you called, like you usually are?"

"I don't recognize the accent," Martin told him. "It isn't quite British, is it?"

"Kind of a mix, I'd say," Skidmore said. "Sophisticated, don't you think?"

"Not really."

"You were in a religious thing last time you called, seems like. Drunk and very religious. We talked about baseball and the absence of an afterlife."

"I don't remember," Martin said.

"Drunk." Skidmore mumbled it away from the phone.

"Your letters," Martin said, "are meaner than usual lately."

"Don't start it. I'm not mean."

"I'm not the only one who thinks you are."

"I know. Let's not get into it, wha'dya say?"

"How's legal services for the poor in Nebraska?"

"Terrible. I'm not such a great lawyer, I'm afraid. McFarland says I hate Indians and won't admit it."

"I expect he's right."

"Cut the crap, you don't know. You don't know me anymore. Every cell in my body has turned over once since way back the hell when—the old days."

"Some things don't turn over with the cells," Martin said. He heard a resolute sigh on the other end.

Skidmore changed the subject. "I'm living in this trailer—in my office, you know? And I've got this Indian woman around here somewhere. Fifty years old. I just saw her go by the window here a minute ago, chasing a blue jay with a goddamned tomahawk." The low familiar mean laugh.

"Fifty," Martin said.

"Nothing like it. We like to rassle," Skidmore said in his best boys-will-be-boys central Illinois idiom, but with the subsequent affectations of Australia crowding in.

"Rassle?" Martin said, and he laughed in spite of himself.

The wires buzzed. Maybe this would be the last time they would ever talk. Letters were easier than phone calls. Nowhere in this world could Martin quite find the Skidmore he knew a long time ago, but the handwriting, it had never changed. Always, on the brink of making a call to Skidmore, he noticed his motivations. It was always a wave of feeling alone, wanting to be friends again.

"Ken Boyer died."

"Yup," Skidmore said. Cardinal third baseman, their old common hero. "How's the wife and kid, Rod or whatever his name is?"

"His name is Jeff."

"Right. How's he? Gonna have a bunch more?"

"Everyone's fine. Thanks for asking," Martin said.

Again the phone line buzzed.

"Rough old world," Martin said. Maybe he could convey something by suggestion.

"Plenty rough," Skidmore said. Silence. Then he said, "God. What a laughable jerk."

Quiet again.

"I always think, if I could just put together the right set of words or something," Martin said.

"Well, outgrow it," Skidmore said. "It's pitiful."

Now the full flood of sadness was coming up again on Martin, and he let the phone call die. The buzz in his ear remained, and there was nothing from Skidmore to stop it. Trying to keep his voice flat, Martin said, "There isn't any friendship anymore. Or something."

"I know," Skidmore said. "Go home. Vegas is no place for a man in your frame of mind."

"Shit. It was built by people in my frame of mind. Anyway, I'm in Chicago."

"I gotta go. I'm an attorney. Time is money. Get off the sauce and go home, is my advice. Play catch with Rod." Skidmore hung up.

Martin responded to the operator by feeding in the change, and then opened the door just a little to shut the ceiling light off. Across the lobby, through the front doors, he watched a Mercedes being unloaded by two bellmen. The sun was almost down.

Nine o'clock. The hotel lobby's colors seemed faster when he was coming out of the smoky lounge than they had seemed when he went in. The phone booth was still in approximately the same place, give or take. The floor sloped in a way Martin hadn't noticed earlier. For three hours he'd hung suspended in a vision of himself in a mirror, through some upside-down glasses hanging in a rack behind the bar. This time he called collect.

"Hello," she said.

"Hello."

She paused, recognizing the voice. "Well. Where might you be?"

"I'm downtown at the Drake Hotel, case someone asks. I'm okay."

"Sure you are."

"I am."

"This is getting to be a regular thing."

"I wouldn't say that," Martin muttered.

"You what?"

"I took a drive," he said. "Just ended up down here."

"You took a drive? Is that what you want me to believe?"

"You don't know shit about men," he said.

"I see."

He didn't think she quite did see yet. "Do you understand what I'm saying? You don't know shit about men." His voice banged against the wall of the phone booth, banged back into his own ears. "I've been meaning to tell you that."

"I think I've pretty much got it," she said. She didn't say anything for a moment and neither did Martin. Finally she said, "What's to understand? I missed a meeting tonight because of this and I'm in a lousy mood. You stay downtown 'til you either get it straight or sleep it off. You got somebody to drive you?"

"I'll be home in an hour or so."

"Who'll drive?" she said.

"Look, I'm resoundingly alone and shall do the driving," Martin said.

"Delightful."

The phone line was quiet for a while. "Do you understand me, about what I was saying?" he finally asked.

"Which was?"

Martin momentarily forgot. This was not a good situation.

She said, "Jeffrey finally mentioned around bedtime that you'd been to school to see him. So I called Charlotte Rudolph and she said you'd terrorized the librarian in the school hall at lunch—threatened to tear the principal's office to pieces or something. Do you ever think about anyone else?"

"Like who?"

"Like your son."

"He was fine. We had a nice chat. Don't use him—he was fine. Don't use him on me because you missed a sales meeting. You miss those all the time. You hate those goddamned sales meetings."

"He was embarrassed. He told me so."

"He did not. He wasn't embarrassed."

"He was," she said. "You embarrassed him."

Martin thought about that. Maybe it was true.

"Look," she said. "I've been worried. I need to know what's going on so I can make some plans for myself. What's going on? Is this the great midlife crisis?"

"That would be the easy conclusion, my dear," he said. "Or the pre-midlife fore-crisis. I called them about silent retreats. He asked me what I've done for the Almighty lately."

"Are there any silent retreats anymore?"

"Yes, but they ain't silent and they ain't retreats. I told him I can have an encounter any time I want one, but I can't get silence when I need it. He said silence is self-indulgent, something like that."

"What's wrong with self-indulgence, or did he say?"

"We didn't talk very long." He took a deep breath. He was buzzing, the line was buzzing, the colors in the hotel lobby were buzzing. "I'll drive with maximum carefulness and caution."

"To the extent you can differentiate," she said.

Martin hung it up. "I'm having a willful adventure here," he said to the hung-up phone. A lady in a glittering gown and jewelry buzzed across the lobby. He opened the door of the booth just long enough to let the ceiling light go out, and from the dark observed her. He could imagine what her aloof, urbane arms would feel like around him, what look in her self-absorbed eye there would be if they were together.

It was ten-thirty when he pulled up in front of the rectory at St. Michael's in Wheaton. The front right tire of the car jumped the curb. Martin, accepting chaos as a way of life, left it that way. He crossed the wide amber-lighted street, walked into the shadows up the front walk, felt the chill around his ankles as he carefully climbed the shadowed front porch steps and knocked on the door. The porch light came on, yellow. A Franciscan priest cracked the door and looked out, then flipped the chain lock and opened it wide. "Yes, can I help you?" he said, his hands deep in his long brown habit, the white ropes dangling far down.

"Bless me, Father—for I am drunk."

"Funny," the priest said. "But I've heard funnier. You must be Silent Retreats himself. I think I recognize the voice."

"I doubt it. Every cell in my body has turned over since this morning."

The priest gestured for Martin to come in, and Martin bowed past him, walking carefully so as not to fall. The priest indicated a parlor-like room off to the right, and Martin went in there.

"Looks like you've been trying to work out your own redemption."

"Are you going to keep saying things like that all the time I'm here?"

"Sorry. Have a seat."

When Martin sat down, he noticed that the priest was pulling a pistol out of his habit and setting in on the umbrella stand behind the front door.

"Sorry," the priest said. "Not very attractive, a man of the cloth bearing arms. Some joker robbed us last month—got the Bishop's Relief Fund collection. Scared hell out of the Monsignor."

"I'm serious," Martin said. "You gonna blow somebody away with that thing? Blow him out of his socks right on your front porch?"

"Yeah, I know—I probably won't shoot anybody."

"Don't you guys carry insurance for the Bishop's collection or whatever?" Martin rubbed his face. The beard was back. "You know, you might consider a dog. Experience tells me you can keep the poor from crowding in on you if you simply buy a large, well-trained killer dog." Martin's head was buzzing. "I think if I kept a .38 around I'd be afraid I'd use it on myself, and I'm not even celibate on purpose. I would never use a killer dog on myself, no matter how loathsome things got."

"You have a number of interesting points there," the priest said. "How about some coffee?"

"Tell me the truth. Is that thing loaded?"

"Hey—touché on the gun, okay? I'm sorry I met you at the door with a gun."

"No, no, don't apologize to me," Martin said. "Black and no sugar. I'll just sit here a while. Semi-upright. On this couch."

"That would be fine," the priest said. He headed for the kitchen. Martin stared at the picture of Christ on the wall. It was an ordinary picture of a man, only Martin knew it was Christ because of how the guy was holding his hands. When had they stopped painting halos so you knew who was holy?

The priest was back with a huge mug of coffee and two aspirin. "For the hangover," he said. "I don't know your name still. I'm Thomas Simon." He seemed to have a regular chair, and he relaxed in it and let Martin sip at the scalding coffee. The floors of the whole house were bare gleaming hardwood, dark. The warm glow of the low light bent down on them and made the hour seem very late. The priest watched him, and Martin was aware he was watching. Martin had a flash of the woman that morning, leaning over toward him, shouting through the window that she'd help. He tried to think about her. Stopping, that was a nice thing she did. Then she was completely gone. He wanted to run an ad in the paper that might find her. What would the ad say?

"You don't have to tell me your name if you don't want to," the priest said.

"Are we gonna start sharing now?" Martin said. The furniture was spare, the floor dark and clean, the lights dimmer and dimmer, and the house was completely still.

10

KEEPSAKES

Jon Hassler

Roger rode to town on a wagonload of sweet corn. Rocking with the load and baking under the high August sun, he lay on his stomach with his hands between his face and the rough cobs.

At the top of the first hill his father stopped the tractor to talk with a neighbor, Martin Palmer, who was returning from town with an empty wagon. Roger sat up and edged forward on the corn to hear what the two men were saying from one idling tractor to another.

"They're paying what they paid last year," Martin Palmer shouted over the clatter of the engines. "But it takes more to make a ton this summer." He took off his floppy straw hat and wiped the sweatband with a red handkerchief.

"I figured it would," said Roger's father. "There doesn't seem to be any heft to the cob this year. Lack of moisture."

"I had this wagon piled high as she'd go—you see the sideboards." Palmer poked his thumb over his shoulder. "Still wasn't quite two and a half tons."

Roger's father pulled a crooked cigarette out of his shirt pocket and lit it with a stick match. "Lack of moisture," he said, blowing out smoke.

Palmer looked up at Roger and said, "If you're planning to have the boy weighed in with the load, it won't work."

Both men laughed.

"I'm taking him into town to help Father Fogarty pack. Father's leaving next week, you know."

"I know. None too soon," said Palmer.

Roger's father picked hairs of corn silk off the front of his flannel shirt.

"They left him here too long," Palmer said. "He's a crabby old man."

"Twenty-three years," said Roger's father. "He came the year I was confirmed."

"How did your boy get hooked into working for him?"

"Roger serves Mass. The servers are taking turns helping him this week. Roger's turn is this afternoon."

"Well, pitch in and do your best," Palmer shouted up at Roger. "The sooner Father Fogarty is on the road, the better."

Roger nodded. His father put the tractor in gear, waved to Martin Palmer, and started down the long hill to the creek bottom.

Two miles ahead at the top of the next hill stood the elm-covered town, and Roger could see the water tower, the smokestack of the canning factory, and the steeple of St. Henry's Church glinting above the trees. On his left and right, gold and green fields of ripening corn rolled away to the sky, every stalk motionless in the still heat. In the distance the short daily train approached from the city of Rochester, its cloud of smoke rising from the steam locomotive. Roger crawled back to the slight depression he had made on top of the load and settled on his stomach again, moving two or three cobs that stuck him in the ribs.

Helping Father Fogarty pack his belongings was not Roger's idea. Each altar boy was asked to help for one afternoon and Roger's parents gave him no choice. Father Fogarty was a strong old man with a hard mouth. Only last week Father Fogarty had slapped him, and Roger had made an oath under his breath that he would never again serve Mass or speak to the priest.

On a broad windowsill of the sacristy stood a flowerpot that Father Fogarty used for an ashtray whenever he entered church smoking a cigar or a pipe. He smoked only occasionally, and there were a number of forgotten cigar butts and half-filled pipes lying at the stem of the dead geranium in the pot. Last week Roger and his partner Lloyd Deming had served evening Benediction on the Feast of Assumption, and after the service while Father Fogarty disrobed at one end of the sacristy, Roger and Lloyd packed one of the pipes full of pebbly brown sacramental incense and ran outside to the big elm near the rectory. They were both farm boys and they had to hurry to catch their rides. Behind the broad trunk of the elm, Lloyd, who always carried matches, lit the pipe. He drew hard through the stem and the incense crackled and turned red in the twilight. He blew out a mouthful of smoke too heavy to dissolve in the air, almost too heavy to rise. It hung about their heads and made their eyes water. Lloyd handed the pipe to Roger, who sucked timidly and blew a slight puff of smoke through his nostrils. It stung and made his head throb with a sudden ache. Lloyd took the pipe again and twice he drew deeply, bringing the incense to a bright glow in the bowl. On the third draw he inhaled and as the smoke struck his windpipe he coughed and retched and dropped the pipe at Roger's feet. When he recovered his breath, he ran around the corner of the church to his parent's car. Roger, too, was about to run when he saw Father Fogarty come out of the sacristy door and walk toward the rectory. Roger stood still, straining to be invisible in the gloaming. Halfway to his kitchen door, Father Fogarty raised his head and stopped. He stepped off the sidewalk and followed his nose to Roger, who stood by the pillar of smoke that rose from the grass and spread into the leaves of the elm. Father Fogarty looked down at Roger, and Roger looked down at the pipe. Father Fogarty said nothing and Roger, fearing his silence as much as punishment, prepared to say he was sorry and that it was Lloyd Deming's idea, but when he looked up at the priest and saw his mouth set hard and tight like a trap, Roger couldn't say a word. So he stooped and picked the pipe out of the grass, burning his thumb on the bowl, and handed it to Father Fogarty, who took it by the stem and with his free hand slapped Roger high on the left cheek. Father Fogarty nodded, as if to dismiss him, as if to say "Case closed," and Roger ran to the car and climbed in the back seat. It was getting quite dark now and his parents did not notice his tears, nor did his two younger brothers notice, who were wrestling and giggling at his feet. His father drove out of town. "What a strong smell of incense," said his mother without looking into the back seat. "Your clothes must be full of smoke." As Roger rode in the dark, his little brothers butting their heads against his shins, he vowed never again to return to church as a server and never again to speak to Father Fogarty. "It's a good smell," his father said as they drove along the gravel road, raising dust in the dark, coasting into two valleys and climbing two hills to the farm.

Roger was rocked almost to sleep by the wagonload of sweet corn following the tractor downhill, but he was aware even with his eyes closed that he was passing under the shade of the willows that lined the creek bottom. His father stopped the tractor, turned off the engine, and walked ahead to the narrow bridge. Roger climbed off the load and followed him. They leaned side by side over the iron bridge railing and looked at the mud.

"I don't remember when there wasn't at least a trickle in the creek," his father said.

"Me neither."

"Lucky we had rain early. June was wet enough to carry us."

Roger had heard his father say this dozens of times during the dry weeks, but always to his mother or to the mailman or to the vet. Now he was saying it to Roger, and although Roger knew how crucial a wet June was, he was honored to be told about it. His father spoke to him very little and this was like being handed a truth to cherish. Wishing to pay his father back in kind, Roger said, "Not many people like Father Fogarty."

His father glanced at him, then lit a cigarette. "You know what I say about that."

Roger nodded, waiting for him to say it anyhow.

"Don't talk about priests."

Again Roger nodded. With his thumbnail he peeled flakes of rust off the angle-iron railing as his father smoked. It was cool in the shade of the willows.

"Martin Palmer hasn't had any time for Father Fogarty since the day his mother-in-law went to confession for the last time," his father said, squinting back at the hilltop where they had met Palmer. "I suppose you heard about it?"

Roger shook his head.

"No. I don't suppose you did. It was some years ago. It's no story for kids."

They stood on the bridge for several minutes but they said no more. The sound of a cicada rose in the willows and a crow called from a great distance. Then his father flicked his cigarette into the creek bed where it lay smoking on the hardening mud, and Roger crawled up on the load of corn. His father started the tractor and they climbed the hill to town.

The gravel road became tar at the village limits, and Roger sat up under arching elms. Scattered along the wide and quiet street lay corn that had spilled from other wagons. White houses, four or five to the block, stood behind tall flowers and large porches. The lawns were spacious and brown. A group of small children were gathering up cobs that hadn't been flattened by tractors and putting them in a small red wagon. Roger waved and they shouted something he could not hear over the noise of the tractor. He held up a cob and they ran after the load, skipping and shouting, until he dropped it over the side. They stood where the cob landed and watched him ride away. Had he been riding an elephant, they could not have been more envious. They watched until he was out of sight.

At the center of town the sun beat down on the street and on the few shoppers and loiterers who stepped out here and there from under faded storefront awnings. Roger's father stopped in the middle of the wide street and left the tractor idling while he went into the post office. Roger slid down off the corn and sat on a fender of the tractor.

An old man he had often seen in church stepped off the sidewalk and asked where his father was. Roger pointed to the post office.

"I've got to see him about Father Fogarty's going-away present," the old man shouted above the noise of the engine.

Roger's father appeared in the sun with the postmaster, and the old man joined them at the curb. Roger could not hear their conversation, but it was clear the postmaster was excited, for he was shaking his finger as he spoke. The three men approached the tractor.

"It's my wife he always picks on," the postmaster was saying, close enough now for Roger to hear. "And you expect a contribution from me? I tell you that priest is not civil. I sometimes think he's not in his right mind."

"Nobody's forcing you to give anything," said the old man. "You suit yourself about that. But it seems to me and some others I've talked to that he deserves something from us."

"Not after what he did last Sunday," said the postmaster.

"Not after giving us twenty-three years of his life?" asked the old man.

"Last Sunday morning—ask anybody that went to early Mass, they saw it—he stopped in the middle of his sermon and ordered everybody to pay attention. I was in a pew near the back with my wife and she was reading her prayer book like she always does while he preaches. She says she gets more out of her prayer book than she does out of his crazy sermons. So she wasn't listening and I had no idea he was talking to her, and the first thing you know he comes down out of the pulpit and runs clear down the aisle, vestments flying ever-which-way, to where we're sitting and he reaches over and pulls the prayer book right out of my wife's hands." The postmaster stepped back and waited for comment. A tractor curved around him, pulling a load of sweet corn.

Roger's father said, "I've got to get to the factory before there's a waiting line," and he climbed up to his seat and put the tractor in gear. The postmaster and the old man backed away to the curb.

Roger rode on the fender and when they were again under a canopy of arching elms, he asked his father, "Are you going to give money for the going-away present?"

"Yup," his father said.

A block short of St. Henry's Church, Roger's father turned left off Main Street and stopped the tractor. "When you're done at Father's you can start walking home," he said. "I'll probably meet you along the way. I plan to keep hauling till dark."

Roger jumped to the ground and his father chugged off toward the canning factory.

Roger ran to the rectory and opened the door to the airtight front porch. He stepped over a pile of ragged books and torn window shades and rang the front doorbell. With all the windows closed the porch was an oven, and packed wall-to-wall with junk from the attic and the basement it smelled musty. Roger rang twice more, then went around to the back door. He knocked and peered through the screen door to the kitchen, but he could see no one. He looked in the garage where Father Fogarty's black Oldsmobile was surrounded by a dozen large wooden crates. The priest was not in the garage, nor was he in the small grove of oak trees that stood behind the rectory and the church. Walking through the grove, Roger came upon a pile of trash between an incinerator and a crooked outhouse, the latter abandoned since the day plumbing came down the street some ten years earlier.

Roger entered the church by the sacristy door and saw Father Fogarty in the sanctuary, kneeling at the prie dieu that he had pulled up to the foot of the altar. Father Fogarty gave him a quick glance and turned a page in his breviary. Roger backed out of sight and sat on a high stool in the sacristy next to the dead geranium. After a minute of perfect silence Father Fogarty left his prayers and strode into the sacristy. Roger jumped off the stool and Father Fogarty peered at him closely through his rimless glasses. Roger was ashamed, both of interrupting him and of having smoked incense.

"What do you want?" asked the priest.

"I'm here to help you pack, Father."

"Who asked you?"

"You did, Father. You called my dad."

"You're a server, are you?"

"Yes, Father."

"The packing is done. Your job is cleaning up the trash."

"Yes, Father."

"Start on the porch."

Father Fogarty wore a collarless black shirt open at the top, and Roger studied the cords in his long, withered neck as he waited for further instructions. There were none. Father Fogarty returned to the altar and Roger went outside.

In a minute Roger came back. He walked through the sacristy and onto the carpet of the cool, dark sanctuary, where several bronze saints stood in the shadows looking up at the crucifix over the altar and a lone candle flickered in a red glass cylinder.

"Where shall I put the trash?" he whispered to Father Finn.

"You know where the old outhouse is?"

Roger nodded.

"Pile it by the old outhouse. Now don't bother me again. I'll be out soon enough."

It was a half-block from the front porch to the outhouse in the grove of oaks, and Roger had to stop halfway with his first boxful of junk because it was too heavy. He emptied part of his load on the lawn and continued with the rest to the grove. He tipped the cardboard box and out tumbled newspapers, ledgers, loose sheets of paper covered on both sides with handwriting, and a set of small red books with gilt-edged pages. Roger picked up several of the loose sheets. "Brethren," it said at the top of one. That was the word signaling the start of a thirty-minute sermon every Sunday morning. Roger tried to read what followed but the handwriting, like Father Fogarty's preaching, was untidy and sharp and hard to understand.

He dropped the loose pages and picked up one of the small red books. He opened it to the page marked by a black ribbon and recognized the first sentence that caught his eye: "Where the carrion is, there the eagles will gather." It was a sentence the priest was fond of. Whenever the sentence occurred in the Gospel he read from the pulpit, Father Fogerty would look up with a scowl and add, "Where the mutton is, there the English will gather." Whatever he meant by the remark was lost on his parishioners, for, unlike Father Fogarty, they were native-born Americans and unaware of the simmering resentment for the English he had brought with him from Dublin. All the same, the remark became a byword of the parish, often repeated jokingly when neighbors gathered for a meal together. "Here's the mutton, where's the English?" Roger's father might say as he prepared to carve the beef roast at a festive dinner. Roger read the passage again: "Where the carrion is, there the eagles will gather." He scanned the rest of the page and the one following, but he could not find the sentence about the mutton and the English.

He dropped the book and turned over several newspapers with his foot. They were aged the color of toast and they had no pictures.

He went back to the pile he had left on the grass and packed it into his cardboard box, pausing several times to read lyrics on scraps of old sheet music. "Red Sails in the Sunset" was a song he had heard and the notes looked easy enough to play with a little practice. On the cover was a sailboat silhouetted against the sun, which upon closer examination turned into the round face of Laura Cronin, "The Lark of the Airwaves." The pile also contained more of the small red books and Sunday sermons and a stack of magazines that smelled like wet fur. He took it all to the grove and dumped it.

It took him five trips to make a sizeable clearing between the porch door and the inner door. From there he began clearing a path lengthwise down the center of the porch. Again and again he filled the cardboard box with as much as he could lift, carried it to the grove of oaks, and dumped it between the outhouse and the incinerator. Once, at the sound of scratching in a load of rags and pamphlets, he dropped the box, tumbling everything onto the grass, including a mouse that ran and hid behind a root of the big elm tree. Once, loading the box, he grabbed a rubbery handful of small dead bats. Twice he tripped on roots and vines in the grove and left the junk where it spilled. A slight breeze rose from the east, drying the sweat in his shirt and hair as he walked to and from the stifling front porch.

After clearing a path the length of the porch, he could reach the bird-cages piled six feet high against the wall. By curling his fingers through the wire, he was able to carry two in each hand. The cages came in all styles, some simple and rusty with only a wire swing by way of accommodations, some ornate and equipped with jeweled mirrors and dollhouse furniture. He piled them in the grove.

On his sixth and final birdcage trip, Roger found Father Fogarty sitting on a kitchen chair next to the incinerator. He was reading the pictureless newspapers with his back turned, and Roger tried not to distract him as he set the cages in the weeds. Father Fogarty turned and scowled.

"You see this?" He held a newspaper above his head with a trembling hand.

"Yes, Father."

"*Tidings* it was called." He pointed to the banner on the front page. "Step closer, boy, and see the date. July 3, 1917." He opened the paper and read from the masthead: "*Tidings*. Official organ of the Diocese of Winona. Right Reverend John Peter Boyle, Bishop. Father Francis Fogarty, Editor." He looked at Roger.

"That was you, Father?"

"That was me."

"You were editor then."

"I was the first editor, son. I was editor for twelve years." He paged through the paper, scanning the headlines. "*Tidings* lasted almost thirty years. It died about the time you were learning to read. A few years ago Bishop Lawrence got an inspiration one day and put the seminarians in charge of the paper. That was long after my time, of course. 'Why not let the boys in the seminary edit the paper?' he said. 'What better way for them to learn the affairs of the diocese?' That's the way Bishop Lawrence thinks. 'Why don't you put your trust in the youth?' he asks us old veterans all the time."

Roger tried to avoid the priest's intense eyes by looking beyond him at a ragged cobweb in the crotch of a tree.

"*Tidings* died of youth," said Father Fogarty. "A malady as fatal as old age." He crumpled the paper and dropped it into the incinerator.

After what he considered a respectful pause, Roger turned to make another trip.

"Is that the last of the birdcages?" the priest asked.

"Yes, Father."

Father Fogarty rose and walked around the pile, wiping his throat with a white handkerchief. "Look at that, would you. Ever see so many?"

"No, Father."

"I had a housekeeper once—in the days when I could abide house-keepers—who was crazy about canaries. She kept one in her room and one in the kitchen. There were two birds in the house at all times. And whenever she found a canary dead in its cage—she was always caring for other people's sick canaries—she would bury the bird and put the cage in the basement." He stooped to look closely at Roger. "For every new bird, she had to have a new cage. Spent half her salary on cages." He picked up a small yellow cage with a cardboard floor. "She couldn't stand 'deathbed cages.' That's what she called them, 'deathbed cages!' Have you ever known what it is to be fond of a bird?"

"You mean like a pet?"

"Yes, like a pet."

"No, Father."

"Neither have I," said Father Fogarty, and with one strong sure motion he kicked the small yellow cage over the roof of the outhouse.

"I'll have someone with a pickup haul them to the dump."

He returned to his straight-backed chair and after filling his pipe and lighting it, he touched the match to the paper in the incinerator. He dropped more newspapers into the fire, one by one, then did the same with the stack of sheet music.

"Could I have one of these songs?" Roger asked.

"Help yourself." Father Fogarty shifted his attention to the small red books. "Here, take one of these, too. It's the Douay New Testament. Bishop Lawrence says, 'Get the New American Bible and burn your Douay translation.' "

Roger took a book from the priest and laid it with "Red Sails in the Sunset" at the base of an oak. Father Fogarty dropped the remaining books into the fire and the overhanging leaves curled as the flames grew.

When Roger arrived with his next load, mostly chipped plates and rusty paint cans, the incinerator was burning with a roar and Father Fogarty had moved his chair some distance away. He was reading passages from old sermons.

"Sit down, son," he said without looking up. "You're doing a man's work. We'll have a drink of soda pop."

Roger sank into the weeds under an oak. Father Fogarty picked up the loose pages at his feet and shielding his face with them he approached the incinerator and threw them all into the fire. He went back to his chair and picked up a ledger, in which he became so engrossed he didn't notice when Roger got up to resume his work.

Ten minutes later as Roger dumped a boxful of ringing tobacco cans near the birdcages, Father Fogarty stood up and threw the ledger into the dying fire.

"Sit on my chair," he said, "we'll have a drink of soda pop." He went to the kitchen and Roger sat on the chair surrounded by junk.

"It's ninety-four in the shade," Father Fogarty said, returning with another chair and two bottles of Squirt. "Thank God for the breeze." He put the chair down several times before he found level ground, then he sat and handed a bottle to Roger. He raised his bottle and said, "Here's to the Douay translation."

They took a long drink.

"And here's to *Tidings*. Died five years ago, Christmas issue."

They drank again.

"You've been working hard, son. Are you played out?"

"Not yet, Father."

"You're used to work."

"This isn't as hard as loading hay."

Above them the oak leaves rustled fitfully as the breeze rose and fell.

"A good summer for hay?" asked the priest.

"The first crop was good. The second one won't amount to much."

"How's the corn?"

"Corn's not bad, considering how dry it's been. June was wet enough to carry us."

"Here's to the corn."

They finished the pop and Roger rubbed his hands, cool from the bottle, over his forehead and cheeks, leaving muddy streaks on his face. Father Fogarty reached under Roger's chair for a copy of *Tidings*.

"Here's something I ran across. A poem I forgot I wrote." He tore out a corner of a brittle page and handed it to Roger, who strained to understand what he read. The first few lines told of a hawk soaring high over a valley, but after three readings that was all he could understand.

"When did you write that, Father?"

The priest consulted the front page. "Nineteen twenty-two." He crumpled the paper and threw it into the incinerator where it lay on the ashes a few seconds, then flared into flame.

Roger handed him the poem but Father Fogarty said, "No, put it with your sheet music. Read it again someday when you're grown up."

"But you might want it for a keepsake."

"Keepsake? Nonsense." The priest stared at the small fire and Roger did the same. "All my life I've been keeping things," said the priest. "Notes and papers and gifts and letters." He continued to watch the burning newspaper curl into itself and sink to ashes. "I've been stashing my past away in trunks and closets, down in the cellar and up in the attic. I've kept diaries and snapshots and roadmaps—and I have a filing cabinet in my office packed with personal papers." He turned to look at Roger. "All that stuff is what I'm letting go of today. With your help."

He filled his pipe with shaking hands.

"The paper will burn, except for a few pieces caught by the wind and carried into someone's pasture or barnyard. Burned or not, the paper will dissolve into the earth in the first heavy rain. The birdcages and knick-knacks will rust and chip and dissolve, too, after a few seasons."

The oak leaves stirred noisily in a sudden gust of wind.

"It's time to discard my keepsakes. All through the years I hoarded up my past as though the part you could put on paper was worth something to somebody. I guess there was no harm in it, but two weeks ago I suddenly realized the time had come to discard it all. I was talking with Bishop Lawrence after confirmation and he said, 'Francis, how would you like to be chaplain at St. Mary's Convent? The sisters asked me for a priest and I thought of you. St. Henry's is pretty large for a man your age.' 'How old do you think I am?' I asked him. 'Seventy-four,' he said. Knew more about me than I thought he did."

The guest of wind died and the leaves hung limp. Roger was suddenly very tired.

"I smell rain," said Father Fogarty. "Rain before dark." He lit his pipe. "I must admit St. Mary's Convent sounded pretty attractive. It's down in the river valley five miles from the nearest town. Great place for hiking and fishing. They have a few old codgers about the place, I understand—a gardener and a carpenter and I don't know what all. I'll have a room there with a view over the river and all the time in the world to read and pray and try to save my soul. For twenty-three years I've been trying to save the souls around St. Henry's and I haven't been tending to my own. St. Mary's Convent would be the place to tend to it. Next best thing to a monastery.

"As far as I know, it was the first good idea Bishop Lawrence ever had, but I didn't want to seem eager. 'You mean I'm to spend the rest of my life hearing nuns' confessions?' I said to him. 'What kind of reward is that for a lifetime shepherding flocks?' He laughed at that. 'I'll have the chancery office make the announcement,' he said. 'Can you move by the first week of September?'

"That's when I decided to burn my bridges. The thought of sorting and moving all that stuff by the first of September was what did it. Burn it and be done with it. Besides, who would want it? The nuns at St. Mary's? What do they care about my keepsakes?"

Roger felt sleepy.

"The next pastor at St. Henry's? Nonsense! My nephews? Ha! I doubt if my nephews know how to read. And they're all making grand money each year. My wealthiest nephew made his fortune servicing jukeboxes and gum-ball machines. Do you imagine a man like that would be interested in a life-time collection of sermons? Do you imagine his brother, who sells artificial flowers to widows for their husbands' graves would be interested in my diaries?

"So for two weeks now I've been pulling out drawers and emptying boxes and throwing the whole mess on the front porch. How much is left?"

"Not much, Father. Mostly old clothes and books."

"The old clothes and books go to the garage. You'll find crates out there for them. The bishop can dispose of them as he wishes."

With a great effort, Roger picked up his cardboard box and walked to the front porch. The sky was hazy now and the shadows across the lawn less sharp, but the heat of the sun was more intense. Emerging from the shade of the oaks, Roger had to squint, for the white hazy light seemed to emanate from trees and buildings as well as from the sky. Even the brown, dying grass cast up a hot light.

Roger gradually recovered the rhythm of his work. He made several trips to the garage and transferred the clothes and books from his cardboard box to the wooden crates. With his last load of books his box fell apart. He dragged the cardboard back to the grove and told Father Fogarty that the porch was empty.

"Good work. I thought it would take another day." He looked at his watch. "The part of your past that you can get on paper takes about one afternoon to dispose of. The part that isn't on paper lasts for eternity. What time are you due home?"

"We eat at six usually."

"Just time enough for the filing cabinet."

Father Fogarty led Roger through the kitchen to his office, and he showed him which cabinet to empty. "All except the bottom drawer," he said. "The bottom drawer is full of parish records. Of course, in the end church records won't be worth as much as a man's keepsakes. Do you suppose at the end of the world God is going to examine the parish files like an auditor? You don't think that, do you?"

"No, Father."

"Nor do I."

They carried out a stack of manila folders heavy with letters. Father Fogarty pulled his chair up to the incinerator and threw in the letters, one at a time.

After emptying the filing cabinet, Roger stood by the priest's chair, waiting to be dismissed. The haze had turned to clouds and Roger felt a drop of rain on his face.

"Look at this," said Father Fogarty, delicately holding a letter by one corner as though it were flypaper. "If I save one letter out of these hundreds, I suppose it should be this one. It's a humbling letter."

Roger read it.

Dec. 25, 1936

Dear Fr. Fogarty:
May almight God, at the moment of your
death deliver you into the hands of Satin.

Yours truely,
Corinne Jones

Father Fogarty said, "A man should tack that up on his wall and pray every day for the writer and the reader. That was from Martin Palmer's mother-in-law. Do you know Martin Palmer?"

"He's our neighbor."

"Well, his mother-in-law's long dead now, poor soul. She used to live with Martin Palmer and his wife when they were first married. Think how full of hate she was the day she wrote that, Christmas Day. There was little joy in Martin Palmer's house for a good many years. She had spells when she turned into a terrible old bitch, screaming and cursing. I do believe she was possessed. Yes, I do believe it now." He touched a match to the cinders in the bowl of his pipe.

"One day she had a spell in confession. It was Christmas season with a long line waiting and as soon as I opened the slot to hear her confession she cursed in my ear. I'll never know what she had against me. When I tried to quiet her down she got louder. Scandalous language. So I stepped out and drew back the curtain where she was kneeling. She wouldn't budge. I had to drag her out by the elbow. Martin Palmer was waiting in line and he was embarrassed fit to die. I told him to take her to a doctor and if it kept up to call me, for she might be in need of exorcism. That little episode was what brought on this letter. Well, as long as she lived he never took her to a doctor and he never called me. If fact, he turned against me himself. Quit taking the Sacraments. He didn't even let me in the house a few years later when I heard she was dying."

Father Fogarty read the letter aloud.

"Maybe that Christmas Day after she wrote this note and got it off her mind, there might have been a bit of peace in Martin Palmer's house for a few hours. I hope so."

As he dropped the letter into the fire, he felt rain on his hand and he looked up through the oak leaves. "Only a sprinkle. Before it comes down hard I'll have these letters burned and you'll be home for supper."

The rain clouds were a mercy, for Roger had been dreading the hot walk home; if his father did not meet him along the way it would be five miles, counting the mile from St. Henry's to the east edge of town. He picked up the sheet music and the small red book, into which he had put the poem about the hawk. Father Fogarty led him into his office and opened a large, hardcover checkbook.

"Will ten dollars do?" he asked.

"Ten dollars? I never made ten dollars before."

"It will do then." The priest scribbled.

"It's more than I earned, Father."

"What's your name?"

"Roger Rudy."

Father Fogarty wrote the name and tore out the check. He gave it to Roger as he saw him out through the bare front porch.

"It's nearly six, so hurry home."

"Goodbye, Father."

"Goodbye." He put his hand on Roger's shoulder. "Show the new pastor your best side."

"I will."

Father Fogarty shut the door.

At the restaurant next to the post office Roger cashed his check and drank a Coke. Then he walked down Main Street under the moving elms and out of town on the gravel road. At the bottom of the long hill he rested on the bridge under the willows. Leaning on the iron railing, he took out the yellowed scrap of paper and read the poem again. He folded it back into the book and set off up the hill.

At the crest Roger saw his father approaching with another load of corn. The dust raised by the tractor and wagon was swept off the road by the east wind. The low clouds over the fields were turning lavender.

"I made ten dollars," he said to his father when they met.

"Did you earn it?" his father asked, certain he had, for the boy looked dirty and exhausted.

"Father Fogarty is going to St. Mary's Convent," Roger said over the noise of the tractor. "He burned all his letters and sermons. He burned everything he had. Except these." He handed the book and the sheet music up to his father, who turned them over in his hands and read the cover of each.

"It's not much, is it?" said his father, handing them back.

"I guess not."

"Climb up on the load. You can ride to town and back."

"It's only two miles home. I think I'll get home and eat."

"Suit yourself." His father shifted in his seat and prepared to drive off.

"Dad, can you take me to St. Mary's Convent someday?"

"What for?"

"To see Father Fogarty."

"What for?"

The tractor noise was too loud for explaining. Roger stepped back and waved. His father waved and drove off.

On Sunday evening at Father Fogarty's reception in the church base-ment, Roger put two dollars in the basket for his going-away present and signed the card. He stood in the line that slowly worked its way up to Father Fogarty, but when it was his turn to shake the priest's hand Father Fogarty did not recognize him.

"Goodbye," said Roger.

"Thank you," said Father Fogarty, looking sternly at the far wall.

In October, as part of a letter-writing unit in English class, Roger wrote a page of news to Father Fogarty. He got his address from the new pastor after serving Sunday Mass. A week later the letter came back with the word DECEASED stamped on the envelope.

Roger took the letter to his room and put it in the bottom drawer of his dresser where he kept the red book, the sheet music, and the poem about the hawk.

11

RESIDENT PRIEST

Jon Hassler

Ernie Booker, the hunchback of St. Mary's Convent, unhooked the grasscatcher from the lawn mower and carried it to the edge of the cliff. He knelt and held it low over the side of the cliff to empty it, so that the breeze off the water wouldn't catch the grass and dump it back on the lawn he was mowing. Ernie believed that leaving clippings on the grass made for a healthier lawn, but after nearly ten years with the sisters, he wasn't one to argue. "Dead grass chokes live grass, Mr. Booker," Sister Simon had told him his first summer at the convent. He'd just finished mowing for the first time—and what a scraggly, bumpy piece of ground it was back then—when Sister Simon, appearing from out of nowhere, handed him a rake. "But the clippings give nourishment to the sod," he declared, and she repeated, as though he hadn't caught it the first time, "Dead grass chokes live grass, Mr. Booker—so my brother says." Her tone of voice he resented at first, but now, having heard it almost daily for a decade, sometimes directed at himself but more often at the sisters in her charge, he'd come to depend on it. It left no question unanswered. It was like the closing of a heavy door.

Ernie watched the grass tumble and lodge and tumble again to the rocks at the base of the cliff, where the lazy current of the river divided and lapped along both sides of Kettle Island. He took off his floppy straw hat, sat back on his heels and wiped his brow with a large blue handkerchief. On the near side of the river—the Minnesota side—the afternoon Northbound Limited glittered orange and blue between the trees and left a trail of black smoke as it chugged along the base of a bluff. On the Wisconsin side where the highway ran close to the river Ernie could see the glinting silver specks of cars and trucks reflecting the high summer sun through the soft August haze.

In spite of the breeze it was hot. It had been hot and dry since mid-June and what with the expanded flower beds and the acre of grass, Ernie with his hoses and sprinklers had all he could do to fight off the tendency in all growing things to wilt. In fact, it was more than a tendency in some places. It was a malicious trick, Ernie was convinced, on the part of the six tomato plants and the bed of asters by the back door of the convent to droop whenever he turned his back. Ernie had grown the tomato plants from the seeds Sister Simon gave him during Holy Week. They came in the mail from her brother in Iowa. "I would like these by the kitchen door when the time comes to move them outside, Mr. Booker." Ernie said they might do better in the vegetable garden, the soil by the kitchen door running pretty much to sand. "They'll grow in sand if they have water, Mr. Booker." So that's where he put them and that's where he was directing enough water every morning and evening to satisfy a herd of thirsty cows. Thank God we haven't gone into dairying like the monks at Marydale, thought Ernie, certain that the additional demands of a single cow would push him to the point of collapse.

Ernie Booker ran the handkerchief over the top of his bald head and around the inside of his hatband. The bell in the tower rang three times, calling the sisters to chapel and announcing a fifteen-minute respite for Ernie if he wanted it, and today he did. Ordinarily he worked his slow, steady pace through rain or drought, through lauds or vespers, with little care whether the sisters were watching or praying or working or whatever in the name of heaven they did those many hours when they were closed up in the house. But now he would rest, for the heat was oppressive and a sternwheeler was coming into view through the haze upstream. He laid his hat in the grass-catcher and moved into the shade of the huge oak that leaned out over the upstream point of the island like the prow of a ship. He glanced around at the pinnacled, turreted, steepled house to make sure all fourteen sisters were about their chapel business before he pulled a pinch of stringy tobacco out of his shirt pocket and stuffed it carefully under his tongue. He sat on the ground with his spindly legs crossed and his hunch against the rough bark of the oak. He glanced around him at the grass, none of it pale and spikey as one might expect in August of a dry year, all of it dark green and level where he had been mowing. He leaned forward to spit over the edge of the cliff, then settled back to watch the sternwheeler approach, barges first. The breeze felt cool in the sweaty fringe of white hair above his ears.

"Mr. Booker. Mr. Booker." Ernie opened his eyes to wave at the silhouette in the pilothouse, wondering how a pilot happened to know him by name, but the sternwheeler was gone. "Mr. Booker." It was Sister Henrietta standing in the front porch waving a red-checkered tablecloth. If the sisters were out of chapel and the tea was ready, he must have slept for twenty minutes. He jumped to his feet, put on his hat and hooked the grasscatcher to the lawn mower. Halfway to the house he stooped and pretended to dig something out of the grass, his back to the porch so the sisters wouldn't see him spit out the little ball of tobacco.

He climbed the steps to the spacious open porch and took his place at one end of a table so long that two tablecloths, end to end, barely covered it. Most of the sisters were already seated. They nodded and smiled and murmured his name. They never called him Ernie, not even the teenager, Sister Henrietta, who romped about the grounds like a fat lamb and helped him with the weeding and sprinkling every chance she got. Not even Sister Robert, who trimmed his hair and called him from his chores when her fresh bread was cool enough to slice. Sister Robert, the oldest, the least educated, the hardest working, the most like Ernie of all the sisters, never once called him Ernie. And because all his life he thought of himself as Ernie, this formal title among the sisters puffed him up. Never in fifty years before coming to Kettle Island had he been called Mr. Booker. Now the title was a considerable fringe benefit that went with his job.

"Won't you have ice in your tea this afternoon, Mr. Booker? I'll see to it if you wish."

Ernie looked up from his hat in his lap and smiled at Sister Henrietta, whose coif always seemed too small for her plump face.

"No, thanks."

"Stop your fussing, Sister," said Sister Simon from the other end of the table. "You know Mr. Booker takes his tea hot winter and summer. Why would you wish to make Mr. Booker unpredictable?"

Sister Robert appeared with the tea. She balanced the icy pitcher on her tray while she poured hot water in Ernie's cup from a teapot. Two sisters followed with glasses and a bucket of ice and took their places at the table.

Ernie drew his pipe from a pocket. The sisters stirred, nodded, tasted, and talked.

"Excellent tea, Sister Robert."

"I believe it's a warmer day than yesterday."

"Tay is tay."

"Is it warmer than yesterday, Mr. Booker?"

"Warmer by two degrees," said Ernie, who always kept his chair at a slight angle from the table, as though he expected to be suddenly called away. "Ninety-four when I looked at noon."

"And even warmer now, most likely."

"Do I taste a bit of mint, Sister Robert?"

"Well, there are few enough warm days left to us. Tomorrow is September."

"And First Friday."

"Doesn't it seem the tomatoes are all ripening at once, Mr. Booker?"

"And have you ever seen bigger cabbages, Mr. Booker?"

"There's half a bushel of tomatoes to be picked this afternoon," said Ernie. "And I believe there's a tomato ripening on one of the plants by the back door." He did not look at Sister Simon.

"The plants by the back door are a late-bearing variety," said Sister Simon from the head of the table. "They will bear into October with proper care."

As was the custom when Sister Simon spoke, a hush fell over the table. Ernie stuffed his pipe with several pinches of tobacco that he drew out of his shirt pocket.

Gradually the conversation resumed. It was the same conversation as yesterday's and it would be repeated after supper, but the sisters took delight in it, for they were permitted such sociability only twice each day. Ernie, wreathed in smoke, looked across the lawn to the river and listened to the small high voices along the table much the way he listened to birds as he worked in the garden, deeply pleased by the light sound rising and falling like a fountain, yet only half aware of it.

"Such a haze."

"Isn't there more river traffic than last summer?"

"So much coal going north."

"Father Parker says the channel is shifting and the buoys may have to be moved before winter."

"Shifting which way, Sister?"

"Father didn't say."

"Will Father Parker be able to say our Mass tomorrow, Sister Simon?" Again a hush.

Tomorrow? thought Ernie. Oh yes, tomorrow, September first is First Friday.

"I assume he will be here. He has not called to say otherwise."

The sisters nodded silently. Father Parker served the Kettle Island sisters from his pastorate at Sandy Point, but because of the distance—twenty-six miles of poor road—he was obliged by the bishop to visit the convent only on Sundays and holy days. On his own, he had made it a practice each First Friday of driving to the island for a Mass at six in the morning, but in March and July he'd had funerals in Sandy Point and so he didn't come, and every year during the spring breakup of early April the causeway connecting the island to the Minnesota shore was impassable for a week or more until the wind hardened the earth sufficiently to hold up a car. So three times this year the sisters' First Friday novena had been broken.

"I had intended to announce this at supper, but since we are on the subject I shall tell you now. Sunday Father Parker will say his last Mass on the island." Sister Simon examined each face to see if anyone was not duly amazed. "The bishop is giving us our own priest."

What followed was the convent version of a cheer. Ernie, who hadn't been listening, dropped his pipe.

"His name is Father Fogarty. He comes to us from Gunnars Bluff on Monday evening, and he shall have the east room next to the chapel. Sister Robert and Sister Henrietta will ready the room tomorrow. Scrub the woodwork, sisters, and Mr. Booker will varnish it."

"Is he the same Father Fogarty that used to edit the bishop's newspaper?"

"My mother lives near Gunnars Bluff. She spoke of him in her letter this year."

"Imagine, Mass every morning."

"Is he retiring from parish work?"

"Mr. Booker, perhaps you will have a fishing companion again."

"Our time is up," said Sister Simon, rising from her chair and looking at the porch ceiling. "I believe you will have to do some scraping and painting out here this fall, Mr. Booker." Ernie studied the ceiling, drawing short thoughtful puffs from his pipe while the sisters silently cleared the table of cups and napkins. Then they scurried inside.

Over the weekend a cold wind sailed downriver, trailing with it a hard rain. Ernie couldn't remember a heavier rain. After it let up on Sunday afternoon, the earth continued to soften as it drew the water deeper and deeper through the clay to the sandy subsoil. The causeway, passable Sunday morning for Father Parker's last Mass, was soupy by Monday morning and a mire by Monday afternoon. Because the causeway was connected to the wooded end of Kettle Island a quarter mile from the convent, the sisters and Ernie were not aware of its condition until, during tea on Monday afternoon, they heard the honking of an automobile horn. It was still chilly and cloudy after the rain, and the sisters, wrapped in heavy black shawls and warming their hands on their teacups, were telling each other what a blessed relief the cool weather was when the horn interrupted their chatter, first with a long honk that Ernie mistook for a sternwheeler, then with several short, impatient toots.

"Could that be our resident priest?" asked Sister Henrietta. "We weren't expecting him until this evening, were we?"

"We've been expecting him for six years," said Sister Simon, standing. "Father Scone's been dead six years."

Again the horn.

"Mr. Booker, that is an approaching automobile, is it not?"

"It's a car all right, but it ain't approaching, I'm afraid. Sounds like it's stuck."

The possibility of Father Fogarty getting stuck hadn't occurred to the sisters and Ernie's words came as a relief to several of them, including Sister Simon, who for a moment imagined the approach of a flamboyant priest honking his horn to announce his arrival.

"Mr. Booker, you shall bring him to my office. Through the front door, mind you. Sister Robert, clear the table. Sisters, to your duties. You shall be introduced at supper."

Ernie Booker bounced down the porch steps and hurried around to the back of the house where the gravel road twisted through the woods to the causeway. At a pace more like a waddle than a run, though he went his fastest, he weaved down the road, sidestepping puddles and low-hanging boughs and muttering each time the horn sounded, "Hold your horses, priest."

Before emerging from the woods, Ernie stopped and studied the priest's predicament. Halfway across the causeway the priest sat in a 1935 Oldsmobile that was up to its axles in mud. The two fresh ruts behind it from the Minnesota shore curved from one side of the embankment to the other, indicating the priest had taken such a run at the causeway that he barely kept the car from swerving over the banks. Ernie wouldn't have attempted such a thing, for there were no guardrails, and he wondered if the priest was brave or foolhardy.

The horn sounded.

There was no hope of moving the car till the road dried. The priest would have to walk the rest of the way through the slop and he seemed to be needing encouragement. Ernie waddled down to the causeway, took off his shoes and socks and waded into the mud. On his right the river swirled against the embankment and gurgled as it passed through the culverts under the road.

Father Fogarty opened his door and stood on the running board, over which mud was oozing.

"What are you doing?" he shouted.

Ernie, assuming what he was doing was apparent, stopped to consider his reply.

"I'm coming to get you," he said finally.

"Can't you call a wrecker?"

"Road's too bad," said Ernie and he began trudging again. There was a sucking smack each time he lifted a foot out of the cold mud.

"Go back," shouted the priest. "I'll come along."

Ernie, reaching a hard grassy spot on the edge of the embankment, stood waiting for the priest, who had returned to the front seat.

In a minute the priest got out of the car with his pants rolled up to his knees, a small black bag in one hand and his shoes in the other. With an elbow he tried to slam the door, but the mud was over the sill and it remained ajar. He started walking. To Ernie he looked like a ghost in a black suit, his pale face and white hair above a wide white collar, his long shins like white sticks churning through the slop, his height beyond anything Ernie had seen on the island in ten years. He reached the grassy spot, panting with a trace of color rising in his cheeks and forehead, and he set down his bag but not his shoes.

"You might have phoned to say the road was out," said the priest, not offering his hand.

"I'm sorry, Father. We didn't know. It's hardly ever out except in the spring." Ernie stood his tallest, which brought him up to the priest's Adam's apple.

"Lead on then. It's no day for going barefoot."

Ernie took Father Fogarty's black bag and led the way to the island. The tracks they made in the mud quickly filled with water.

On the bank of the island with the oak boughs waving above them they washed their feet in the river.

"The water feels warm," said Father Fogarty, shivering.

"Yes, the river's always warmer than the air during a cold snap."

"I'm getting the feeling back in my toes. That mud was like ice."

"Yes, the water's warmer than the air today."

Ernie stuffed his socks in a pocket and put on his shoes. The priest sat on a rock to tug his socks on over his wet feet; as he laced his shoes, Ernie lit his pipe.

The priest stood, then quickly sat again and hung his head. Ernie stood at his side, silent for a few moments, then he asked if anything was wrong.

The priest held his head and shook it slowly. He stood and raised an arm over his head and massaged the shoulder.

"Plain tired out," said Father Fogarty, turning to Ernie. "Just last week I started having these tired spells. Tired to the marrow of my bones. It's from moving and all the fuss that goes with it." His voice was low, hardly as loud as the murmur of oak leaves hanging over the water. "But it doesn't last long. Give me five minutes."

He sat on the rock again.

Ernie squatted by his side and broke twigs into little pieces, flipping them into the river.

"Sounds to me like you could use a few days' rest," said Ernie.

"That's exactly what I'm here for, my man," said Father Fogarty, looking across the water at his car, up to its bumper in mud. "The bishop came to the same conclusion as you have, but it took him longer. And instead of recommending a few days' rest he has decided I shall rest for the rest of my life." There was a tremor in his voice and Ernie glanced at him.

"My name is Father Fogarty and yours . . . ?"

"Ernie Booker, Father."

They both watched the river as they spoke.

"Let it be known that, having been sent to Kettle Island to rest, the first thing I did upon my arrival was to sit on a rock and rest. I see my biographer using that as an illustration of my obedience."

Ernie gave him a serious nod.

"Please pardon me if I seem to be taking myself seriously. You see, I'm traveling light. I've discarded my past, except for whatever shred I could pack in my trunk. And my skull." The priest tapped his temple.

Like old Father Scone, thought Ernie; his mind seems at loose ends, forced away from its moorings and floating sideways in a strong current.

"So it's an important time for me. On a par, I'd say, with being assigned my first pastorate."

The priest's voice was gaining strength and Ernie was relieved. He would obviously prove to be quite a talker—already he was rambling—but Ernie didn't mind. If the priest required a listener, there was no better listener on the island than Ernie.

They watched a leaf float by in the wrong direction, for the current doubled back upstream along the bank above the culverts. The clouds pulled apart in several places and a spot of sunlight moved across the face of a distant bluff.

"In case I fail to mention it when we're better acquainted," said Father Fogarty, "I'm glad to be here."

"We're happy to have you. The sisters have been in a sweat for a resident priest ever since Father Scone died. You'll get pretty good treatment. And me, of course, I'm happy to have another fellow around the place."

"You're the only man on the island, Mr. Booker?"

"The only one."

"I thought there were two men, a gardener and a carpenter. I was told that."

"No. I'm the gardener and the carpenter and the painter and so on. There used to be another fellow here and I guess he was a jack-knife carpenter all right, but he was more or less a charity case. He had a room like mine. Comfortable enough. But he decided to move on. Found himself a place closer to town. Closer to the Sandy Point Bar, if you want to know the truth."

"Well, I'll be depending on you, then, to teach me the tricks of convent living."

"No tricks to it. Don't eat the crab apples that grow by the pumphouse and don't argue with Sister Simon. That's all I can tell you about convent living."

"Who's Sister Simon?"

"The boss."

Father Fogarty stood. He put his hand to his forehead and said he was dizzy.

"Maybe you need to rest more," said Ernie, stepping around to look him in the eye.

"Not here. Show me my room, Mr. Booker."

Father Fogarty did not feel up to meeting Sister Simon. As they approached the house, he asked if Ernie could show him to his room through the back door.

"Sister said I have to bring you in through the front door. She's waiting in the office."

Father Fogarty shrugged and followed Ernie around the house. At the top of the porch steps and again in the front hall he paused. He had never felt such fatigue. He turned and looked outside through the long glass of the front door to hide his alarm. He wanted to lie on the floor and close his eyes.

Hearing the men enter, Sister Simon rose from her desk and stood waiting to greet them. When they did not appear in the office doorway, she peered down the hall to see what was keeping them. Mr. Booker, in profile, looked like a tramp, his long thin jacket hanging from his hunch like a towel on a globe. What looked like the toe of a dirty white sock protruded from a back pocket. And the tall man with his back turned—could he be the priest, his pants rolled halfway up to his knees? She approached them.

"Here's Father Fogarty, Sister," said Ernie, "and he ain't himself. We had trouble in the mud."

Father Fogarty turned and took the hand Sister Simon offered. She hadn't seen a face so pale since Sister Cyril died at the convent three and a half years before. In the blank north light of the front hall his flesh looked as white as his collar and hair.

"You don't know what a happy occasion this is for St. Mary's Convent," said Sister Simon. "I'm sorry for the difficulty you had on the road."

"Yes. I can see how your road discourages visitors. I came the last fifty yards barefoot through the mud." Father Fogarty drew a long breath and put his hand on Ernie's shoulder for support. "I'm afraid it's left me a bit weak."

Sister Simon looked sternly at Ernie. "Mr. Booker, couldn't you have done something?"

"Well, the road is downright . . ."

"He did his best to play St. Christopher," Father Fogarty said, "but his size was against him."

"I'm so ashamed, Father. If we had known . . ."

"With your permission, I feel I must be shown to my room. I need to lie down."

"Of course. It's all ready for you. Mr. Booker will show you the way. And when you are rested the sisters will be anxious to meet you."

"Thank you. I look forward to getting acquainted, but I wonder if we might save the introductions until morning."

"Of course. Mr. Booker, the east room. You are among friends here, Father."

Ernie led Father Fogarty down the hall past several closed doors bright with varnish. They met two sisters who stopped in a sort of obsequious crouch with silent smiles so broad they looked foolish. At a double door Ernie stopped and held one side open. "Here's the chapel, Father. Just so you know in the morning."

They looked down the short aisle between the light oak pews. The sanctuary candle in gold-tinted glass hung on a golden chain from the ceiling and flickered in front of the large crucifix over the altar. The chapel, full of gilt statues and candlelight and scrubbed varnish, was gold and warm.

"What time?"

"Six has been the custom, Father. If six is too early, I'm sure . . ."

"Six it will be."

Ernie shut the chapel door and opened the next one down the hall.

"Here's your room, Father, next to the chapel."

Father Fogarty noticed the fine view from his window; the late afternoon sun was spotting the distant Wisconsin bluffs; but now he was more interested in his bed. He sat on it and thanked Ernie for his trouble.

"Pooh," said Ernie.

Father Fogarty reached to shake Ernie's hand. "It's good to be among friends."

Ernie lingered at the door.

"Father, there's a matter I'm wondering about. It's been the custom that I serve Mass. And I hope you'll want me to continue."

"Of course, Mr. Booker. I'd be grateful."

Ernie bowed and closed the door.

At five-thirty he returned and knocked. Father Fogarty woke to a faint high hum that came through his wall. He was groggy.

"Who is it?"

"Ernie."

"Come in, Mr. Booker." He propped himself up on an elbow.

Ernie opened the door, then closed it to a crack when he saw the priest in bed.

"The sisters asked me to tell you supper is at six if you want to eat with them." He spoke through the crack. "Or I can bring it to your room."

"No supper for me, Mr. Booker."

"Yes, Father. Sorry to disturb you."

"Mr. Booker."

"Yes?"

"Wake me in the morning at five."

"Yes, Father."

"And Mr. Booker."

"Yes?"

"What's that noise?"

Ernie listened. "It's the sisters in the chapel, Father. It's their chant."

"I thought it was mosquitoes."

"Yes, Father." Ernie closed the door.

Father Fogarty dropped back to sleep immediately.

Later he heard someone speak in the hall and he opened his eyes. It was dark and before he could figure out where he was he was asleep again.

Still later he was vaguely aware of the humming. He was in the gold chapel walking barefoot through the mud of the aisle toward the altar. Each step was a mighty effort, and his feet were freezing. Hour after hour he plodded up the short aisle.

Father Fogarty died as Ernie came down the hall to rouse him for Mass.

12

GENESEO

Philip F. Deaver

At dawn Jerome Slater came down the tall, chipping stairs of the carriage house apartment, down to the idling white Camaro in the drive. Behind the wheel, Janet messed with her gloves and he saw the frail blue-white skin of her hands. In the short time he'd known her, a few months, this was what he always noticed—her pallid, almost transparent color. The skin of a woman can make you wonder what you don't know about her.

Sometimes she would stay the night, and if she did she always dressed very early in the morning, and, thinking he was still asleep, she'd slide out the front door and soundlessly descend the rickety stairs. He would climb the ladder to the skylight and watch her as she hurried down the long back sidewalk through the trees, furtive and alone like a neighborhood cat.

He climbed into the car.

"Morning." He pulled the car door shut and slid down into the bucket seat.

"What's the matter?" she said. "You still up for this?"

"You've got rust on the back quarter-panel."

"You're speaking of the car?" She looked at him, smiled. "It's old, give me a break. Do you still want to go?"

"Tell you later," he said. She registered alarm, so he quickly leaned over and kissed her. "Yes, I still do."

They went down to Scott Street, turned right onto Main, rumbled north past the college and into Tuscola's business district. The streets were brick and combined with the steel belts in Janet's radials to create a washboard effect. At the four-way stop downtown, Janet said, "Last call." She spoke staring straight ahead. "I'll whip a U-ey and you'll be home in sixty seconds."

"Don't make me keep reassuring you," he said. "I'm going."

Downtown was deserted except for a cluster of cars at the donut shop. She drove on.

Jerome had first met her at Gabby's, a tavern out on the township line. Out there they called her Geneseo because that's how she had introduced herself. He'd observed her from a distance then, as she charmed construction crews and the guys from the chemical plant, the few professors from the college who ever went out there and, of course, the farmers' sons and all their country girlfriends. She told them long stories about rock and roll, and sometimes she'd even bring her twelve-string and sing old protest songs.

But also sometimes she would get too much to drink and she'd cry, her hair dragging in the water puddles left by her last four bottles of beer. Or halfway through the evening she would make a telltale switch to vodka, retreat to a corner. She had, it turned out, regrets about her former life—whether for having lived it or having lost it, Jerome was not always too clear.

Her former life: Janet had lived in what she called an "intentional community" for quite a number of years; within the past year, she had come to Tuscola to live, leaving her husband and daughter behind.

"Look at it like this," she had said, very good-naturedly. "Remember when communes were in? Back to nature, all that? Someone must have joined them, right?"

Fact was, Jerome knew several people out of New York who'd joined Virginia and Tennessee communes.

"The place was called Geneseo," she said. "On that land the women were called places. I was an early one there and was named after that very place. Make sense?"

When he first met her, Jerome probably didn't believe half the things she said. Yet she sort of grew on him over the months. She was so soft and likable, and so feisty. Who knew where she'd been in her forty years, or who she'd been with? Who knew where her stories ended and the truth began, as she rambled on about things? Her clothes betrayed an obsession with her life many years ago, beads and shawls, jeans and workshirts. She held him with a kind of desperate, childlike "help me" stare, very level because of the sharp, even browline against the pale skin. He knew someday he was going to draw those sparse lines of hers and remember her forever.

Now, Janet was heading back to Geneseo to reclaim her daughter, Barbara, and she seemed reassured that Jerome was willing to go, too, and they were heading north out of town. At the hardroad she turned left—the gates were down at the Illinois Central crossing. In a few moments a slick chrome Amtrak flew by.

"That's the famous City of New Orleans," she said. "Steve Goodman's dead, did you know that?"

"No," Jerome said.

"Don't you like music?" Janet turned onto Highway 45. She handed him the map. "You're the copilot—get me there. It's along the river."

Jerome wasn't used to getting up this early. "What river would that be?" he said.

Janet laughed, slammed a Beatles tape into the tape player. *Abbey Road*, pretty loud. Jerome pulled it out again. "What river?"

"The Mississippi, dorkus. Maybe *I* better navigate."

He put the cassette in its case, the case in its holder on the console, and went back to scanning the map. For a while they were quiet, and Janet put the first miles behind them at sixty-five.

"How about Steppenwolf—I've got everything they ever did in that box."

The vent window on his side whistled, and Jerome tried tightening it. Then he found himself forgetting the map and watching the barns fly past. Each barn was a different weathered color and bent shape, bent into its surroundings. Janet slammed in a Richie Havens tape. *Alarm Clock*. Here comes the sun. Recently Jerome had taught a summer class in painting at the college. "Don't bring me pictures of barns," he told them.

"Goddamn," he muttered.

"What's wrong?"

"I forgot the thermos. I had it ready. Walked off without it."

"Big hairy deal. Who needs it," she said, reaching behind Jerome's seat, "when we have each other." She pulled two cans of Stroh's out of a Styrofoam cooler, set his on the console, opened hers. "Cheers, my friend! We're on the road!"

It was a good state, Illinois: the middle. Here was the future population of California, Bimini, New England, Alaska, the cities of Texas, being nurtured up in these little farming towns: Strawn, Forrest, Neoga, Watseka, Kankakee, Urbana, Rockford, Plainfield. In the city Jerome had known many artists and Soho-dwellers who'd come from towns like these in the middle states. In fact, his ex-wife, a New York architect, had been raised in Waverly, Iowa.

"There's a picnic table on the spot. Find Galesburg . . ." Janet was reaching over and pointing at the map, trying to hold her beer and drive with the other hand. They swerved a little. "Then find a little town named Joy—it's west of Joy—and don't say 'Aren't we all,' because I've heard all possible Joy jokes. Find the picnic table."

"I found Geneseo."

"That's Geneseo the town, not the commune. The commune isn't on the map. Look for a picnic table on the river."

"Now we have three Geneseos?"

"It's a bitch, right? Can you handle it?" She laughed.

He traced the river north from Hannibal with his index finger. "I fixed that damned thermos and then forgot it."

"You're unusual, all right," she said, turning up the music.

The plan was to bring Janet's little girl back to Tuscola to live with her. There were unknowns. For instance, Janet didn't know how things were going at Geneseo these days.

"When I think of places like this, I keep thinking of Jonestown—the congressman's films and all that," he said.

"Of course, you do," Janet said. "How 'bout the commune in *Easy Rider*, remember it? That was a *real* beaut."

She sipped her beer. "The CIA has a plot going with the news media to make these pinko communities look pinko." She laughed. "I love this. You're gonna learn so much." She was smiling and gestured big, a joyful arm wave that let the car swerve again.

"So tell me about it," he said, reaching back to locate the seat belt. He fastened it.

"My husband, Will . . . I've told you about him, right? He's something. I just hope he's sensible about this. God, that just reminded me of my dream last night." She was staring straight ahead.

"Wonderful."

"You think I talk too much, right?" She smiled right at him. "Tell you what, this was a strange dream. I woke up to a knocking on the door downstairs. Three or four raps, then a pause. Three or four more, pause. No telling how long it had been going on while I was asleep. So I woke up then—I wasn't really awake, just in the dream—and I went to Barbara's room and woke her up. I said, 'Barbara, someone's knocking at the door in the middle of the night.' And she sat up. There she was, except she was about fourteen. I saw what my little eight-year-old will look like when she's a teenager—this is weird."

"No kidding."

"Barbara was sleeping in this guest room in this strange part of the apartment I've never been in—it doesn't exist, actually. She wasn't wearing any clothes." Janet stared ahead as though she were back in the dream. "Amazing."

"Incest," Jerome said, jokingly. He turned down the music.

She looked over at him but then she went back to it. She had her fore-arms resting over the top of the steering wheel, leaning forward. "She was under a blanket or bedspread or something. I was glad that she was with me again, even though so much time had gone by and she was older and I'd missed—you know—a time in her life."

"Guilt," Jerome said.

She gave him another look.

"Sorry."

"I said, 'Someone's knocking on the door and it's the middle of the night.' Her bed had a window right above it. We could look out and see down in the front yard, but we couldn't see the porch because the porch roof hid who was down there knocking. A couple of more times the knocking came, and we lay on the bed together, real low, watching out the window. Then the knocking stopped and we saw this young woman. She was dressed like—I don't know—like Florence Nightingale or something, that kind of era—the bonnet, you know?—and all in black? She was hurrying away, I mean walking real fast, through the shadows and stuff—where could she have been going?—so fast I almost couldn't see her in the dark, almost couldn't focus on her, but I saw that she was carrying these flowers and they were black. Black flowers."

Janet was quiet for a while. She stared up the road. Finally, Jerome said, "Guilt. And death."

She punched him on the leg good-naturedly, then opened her window and chucked the can, rolled the window back up, and opened another beer.

He looked up the highway, trying to think of a way to change the sub-ject. "Why didn't you bring Barbara with you when you left the place?"

"I didn't know what in hell I was doing—I was just getting out." Janet ran her fingers through her hair, shook her head. "I don't know. Don't ask me that. I was nuts."

The road was narrow, the old kind. The grass grew right up to the edge. The land was fairly flat, so the road was straight. In his mind, Jerome sketched it, stick and ink, the very subtle contours of the retreating tree lines and pastures, the clusters of houses, the receding road in the flatness. He wrestled with the colors in his mind, trying to paint it. In this season, the values were close, tans and grays, blacks and browns. In art school he'd drawn and painted a lot of landscapes, efforts he had long ago ditched.

Janet cut back the heat. She reached up on the dashboard and found a picture, which she handed to him. It was a wrinkled-up Polaroid of a lit-tle blond girl next to a tire swing. "I need this little girl in my life." Now there were tears. "Anyway," she said, wiping them, "Geneseo's an anarchist community, founded by libertarians. That was the name of the game in 1969 or whenever. The main guy's still there—Stephen Boyce."

Jerome was still looking at the picture.

"These communities, if you're wondering, aren't all drugs and free love like the CIA says. They often turn out to be more rigid than ordinary society or whatever. Believe that?"

Someone passed them in a van, honking. She stared into the cab as they went by. "Speed on, hell ain't half full." She toasted them with her beer. "Sometimes we'd get kids from Chicago or St. Louis, and they'd think they wanted to join. But they wouldn't work. We'd always split over what to do about it. One side believed that if these creeps wouldn't work they should be gone. And you had these other people over here who believed in the 'process' of anarchism. Very big idea. They believed the kids should be allowed to stay and that the process of community would convert them to work and the cooperative life."

They went on up the road a while. They were coming into the west side of Champaign. Jerome said, "So tell me about Stephen Boyce."

"He's like . . . the main person."

They shot under a sign for Interstate 74, and Jerome pointed her onto the cloverleaf. The van ahead of them was gone. Janet rolled down her window and chucked the can.

"As he gets older, he settles down more and more. He's a father figure there now. Beard's getting gray, that sort of thing." She smiled. "He's a literature buff, however, and big on Kafka, so anything can happen. He makes money for us by giving speeches about community and communes and stuff."

They were passing an enormous salvage yard with piles of old cars.

"I have a friend there named Clay City. Forgot her real name. May seem odd to you, but she's just Clay City to me, plain as day. She runs the school. Has a son there about Barbara's age. She and I were tight—she used to be a teacher, in the world."

Jerome put the picture of Barbara back on the dashboard. "A very pretty little girl," he said. He reached to cut the heat, discovered she'd already done it, and cracked his window. He heard her pop another Stroh's.

"She had been a teacher—out in Kansas somewhere. A terrible thing happened to her."

"Isn't that usually the deal? Something terrible has happened, so people join a commune?"

"You're so smart," she said, raising her can in a toast, smiling at him. "You're going to learn so much."

"Will I learn how the old hippie rationalizes throwing these cans out on the highway?"

She looked over at him. "Sorry," she said. She took a deep breath. "*Anyway.*" She smiled at him. "So anyway, Clay City was living with her sister, both of them teaching. But Clay City was dating someone, and one day she found out that she was pregnant. And listen, this wasn't any of that sexual revolution 1960's shit—it's just something that happened, you know? Like it happens?" She stared at Jerome. The car swerved again. "Men don't understand this stuff, and I'm not kidding. Why do I bother? Anyway, she was ashamed, and you can bet she was never going to get an abortion, and so she headed back to her parents' home—somewhere, I forget—leaving her sister in Kansas to teach. She'd be back when the baby was born. Well, it's incredible, but while she was home having her baby, her sister, alone back in Kansas, twenty-seven years old, something like that, died. Believe it?"

Janet looked over at Jerome. "She just died in bed. Do you believe it? What kind of luck is that? Very rare virus, the doctor said." Janet wiped the rim of her beer can with the elbow of her jacket. "Well, of course, Clay City had a theory that God was getting her for her sin. A sort of divine scarlet letter, only hardball." She gulped down some beer. "I'd think it myself, and I'm not Catholic, never been to church a day in my life. Anyway, she reacts by following some extreme religious guys, a bunch of movements and groups. She was up in Winnipeg for a while, following some wise man named Murray. Then she heard about Geneseo and it sounded a little broader in scope, but was still shelter. So she packed up the kid and came. Stay there 'til she dies, too."

Jerome stared up the highway.

"The community group is very logical for some people," she said.

"You didn't find that, though."

She gulped her beer. "Actually, I did for a while. But like Will says, 'Some folks don't fit nowhere.' I kinda stopped fitting."

They drove north and west. Sometimes they were quiet for a while, and it seemed to Jerome like Janet was averaging ten minutes per beer. A couple of more times she swerved, so he suggested they stop at a Burger Chef for coffee. They arrived about the same time as a chartered bus loaded with Illinois State University students. Feeling rowdy, Janet exchanged one-liners with some of the boys. While she went to the bathroom, Jerome carried their coffee to the car, splashing it on his hand and shirt. He decided he would do the driving unless she argued against it, and sat behind the wheel. He dabbed at the spilled coffee with napkins. Traveling with Janet made him feel married to her. Jerome's ex-wife, Erica, still lived in the city with their little boy, and for some reason now he was missing them both terribly. He wondered how anyone in his generation ever stayed married.

He watched Janet come across the Burger Chef driveway. She knew he was watching, and it changed something in how she held her shoulders, the expression at the corners of her mouth.

The warmth of the coffee seemed to refresh Jerome, but Janet leaned her head back against the headrest, looking out the window away from him. Finally, she was asleep. The day had become warmer with the last warm weather of the year. He tried to imagine what to expect when they arrived and to prepare for it. After a while she was awake again, but still they said nothing for nearly an hour. Then they were coming through the town of Joy. Hovering just above the town's business district was a large steel ball propped atop four legs—the water tower. "Joy" was painted on it in big black block-type letters that loomed over an IGA, post office, drugstore, and police station. They parked in front of a Rexall drugstore, and Janet ran inside for aspirin. Outside, leaning against the car, Jerome watched the pantomime of Janet in the drugstore through the front window.

When she came out, she wanted to drive. They pulled away from the curb and in a moment they were back in the country. "Will's a good person," she said after a while. "He'll let her come with us."

They turned onto a country road and white gravel dust flew up behind them. The land was now very hilly. They plunged into a parklike area, deep in beech trees and shade, with ravines first on one side of the road, then the other. They crossed ravines on old iron bridges. Old farmhouses were decaying in every hollow.

"There's your picnic table, from the map," she told him when they came into a picnic ground. "Geneseo community maintains this for the state. Pretty good job, eh?"

Soon they came up out of the trees. There was a gate and a simple handpainted sign: "Geneseo, Intentional Community, founded 1968." Several kids came running to the gate. Jerome was now leaning forward in his seat, watching. Two swung it open and the others clamored up around the car, smiling and shouting at Janet.

"Hi, Mick," Janet said to one of them. "Is Stephen here today?" The air felt so good coming in through Janet's window that Jerome rolled his own down. As he did so, he heard the gate swinging and craned his neck just in time to see it latch shut again behind them.

The little boy pointed toward several barns clustered in the distance, off to the right across the grassy field. "At the dairy barn," he said.

"Thank you. You're getting very big," she told him. "Where's Barbara?" she asked, and the boy gestured back in a different direction. "Thanks, Mick," she said to him.

All the buildings seemed scaled down. There was something new about most of them. They were made of rough-sawn wood on the outside, stained dark, with decorative detail that seemed almost nineteenth century in style. Janet was driving across the large field toward the barns on a two-rutted grass path, grasshoppers jumping on the hood and butterflies scattering. The grass was brushing hard underneath the car. It was nearly noon and the sun was warm, the sky blue as crystal. For a distance the children chased along behind them, laughing loudly. Jerome could hear a bell ringing, like the yard bells they used to have on farms.

Presently Janet pulled up to one of the barns and stopped the car. She stared at the big double doors, closed, and took a deep breath. "He's in there," she said. "I'll be back in a minute."

She climbed out, disappeared into the cool, abrupt shade of the building. The sunlight on the windshield and dash was so bright Jerome couldn't look toward the barn. He stared off to his right, to a stand of trees in the distance.

After a few moments, a tall clean-shaven man came out with Janet. He seemed very friendly to her, chatting as they walked toward the car, laughing warmly at one point, his hand on her shoulder, her arm around his waist. He came to Jerome's side of the car and leaned down.

"Hi. I'm Stephen. Brought Janet back to us, looks like." They shook hands. Jerome didn't say anything, but smiled cordially at him. "Maybe you'd like to come in and get some water or something, look around? We've got to head over and find Barbara and her dad."

"I'd like him to come along," Janet said.

"Look," Stephen said to Janet, speaking over the roof of the car, "this is a family thing, Geneseo. There's no problem with Barbara leaving. But it's Will—we should be sensitive to how he feels about this."

For a moment everyone was still, saying nothing and not moving. Then Stephen opened Jerome's door, and Jerome found himself almost automatically climbing out of the car, Stephen sliding in. He looked up at Jerome. "Half an hour, give us. We won't be long."

Over the top of the car, Janet told Jerome, "I'll be right back." He was looking for some signal from her. Nothing came. She was absorbed now.

He stood outside the barn. Stephen looked large in the passenger seat, next to a very thin and frail Janet. He leaned back, his arm reaching all the way behind her on the back of the seat. The white Camaro slowly turned around in deep grass and headed off the way it had come, the exhaust rising up out of the grass behind it.

Jerome went into the barn. Inside were several cows, and on the other side it was open to a large pasture where many more dairy cattle were grazing.

There was a pump and a tin cup like he hadn't seen in years. He pumped himself a drink of cold water, then a second one, washing away the sour taste of the morning beer and coffee. The cows watched him as he looked around. After a while he went outside. The south side of the barn had a painting of John Lennon on it, painted in dots like a Lichtenstein, only in black and white. "In Memoriam" was printed at the lower edge. Each dot was the size of a silver dollar. Jerome needed to get off a ways in order to really see the picture. He decided to head toward the clump of trees. The sun was warm on his back as he walked. Erica, his ex-wife, came into his mind. If they had lived in a situation like this, maybe they'd have survived. No, he thought, she depended on the city, and, really, so had he back then. Judging from the amount of work he was getting done these days, maybe he still did. He thought of the painting he had going right now, felt a wave of discouragement about it. Right now it felt a little irrelevant.

At the edge of the clump of trees he looked back at the Lennon painting on the barn. It was a close-up of the last Lennon we knew, gaunt, amazed at being forty, wire rims on the long bony nose, singing into the microphone, eyes half shut.

Looking into the woods, Jerome spotted a small pond among the trees and a house on the other side. The house seemed large and peculiarly modern, but sunken in among the foliage as though it too had grown there from roots. He sat in tall grass at the edge of the pond, in a large square of sunlight blazing down, high noon. He watched the house and occasionally looked back toward the barn, half a mile behind him, to see if the car had returned. He thought about little Barbara. This was what she knew, had always known. It was sad to be a part of showing her the larger world. It was bound to disappoint.

Presently Jerome heard the bell again, ringing off beyond the barns, and soon after two men came out of the house and hurried along a path that led right toward him. He couldn't tell whether they had seen him or not. His heart sped up, and he bent farther down until he thought he might be completely obscured by the tan grass. The two men passed him, heading out across the field. They seemed like monks, their hair short, their work clothes ill-fitting. And there was something about their silence as they walked fast, side by side, first among the tall trees, then out into the sunlight, crossing the field toward the distant rise.

He walked closer to the house. It was a large cottage, older than the other buildings. As he approached, a woman came out. Right away he thought he might know who she was. She was wearing an old dress that was long.

"Hello," Jerome said, going to meet her. "I'm here with Janet."

"I know," the woman said. "I can see the gate from the other side of the lodge. Her famous white car." A smile. The two of them were standing under gray beeches, oaks red and brown. Jerome could sense their branches arching high above him.

"Am I trespassing? That bell rang and I thought . . ."

"The bell is how we put out word if someone is needed," she said. "You aren't trespassing. I love the sound of it, don't you? You can hear it for miles. Stephen got it from a school that was being torn down in Rockford. It was made in the Netherlands. The new school probably uses buzzers." She looked at him. "Did you find Stephen?" Maybe there was some tension in the question.

A woman appeared in shadows on the steps of the cottage, another at the window. Jerome felt as though he'd come into a herd of deer, gentle, wary. Any sudden move might cause them to leap away.

"Well . . ." He gestured back toward the dairy barn. "Stephen and Janet went off that way somewhere, to find Janet's husband, I think. Stephen was at the barn—they went off that way." Jerome pointed again. "They wanted me to wait."

"We all know to find Stephen at the dairy barn if it's a workday," she said.

"Why's that?"

"It's just true. The cattle are his project. Will's not well, I assume they told you." She extended her hand to him. "My name is Madeline Eisley. I'm called Clay City here." She smiled. "It's so your old boyfriends won't ever find you. That's what we always say among ourselves."

"Like Sister Mary Fatima?"

"Exactly," she said. She looked around. She gestured toward the other women, watching from the cottage. "We almost never get visitors. Can you tell?" She tried to wave them out into the yard, but they wouldn't come. "Janet's name here was Geneseo. Somehow it fit. You get used to things."

In the awkward pauses, Jerome looked out over the pond. Clay City looked back toward the cottage, where her friends continued to watch.

"We know you're here for Barbara," she said. "Is that right?"

Jerome nodded. "Yes."

"It took Janet longer to come for her than we thought it would."

"Yes," Jerome said. "She missed you all."

"She was unhappy here. What's your name?" This directness was much like the assuming way Stephen Boyce had taken Jerome's seat in Janet's car. When Jerome paused a beat too long, she went on. "I don't know what all Janet's told you . . ."

"I'm Jerome. She's talked about her daughter—and, of course, her husband. She talks a lot about the old days, this place. She misses this life, I think."

Clay City looked over her shoulder to the women watching. She stared out at the pond.

"Don't let me keep you from anything," Jerome said. "Maybe I'll walk back to the barn. I'd have stayed but the cows made me self-conscious. Those big brown eyes." They both laughed.

"Will's been having trouble lately. I don't know how much you know."

There was no telling what this lady meant or what she was assuming. Jerome watched her eyes, and what he saw was that she was watching his. After a while he pointed out over the pond, down a long slope to a cluster of rough shacks. "What's that?" The ground around the shacks had been cut up, bulldozed.

"We've been doing some clearing down there," she said. "When visitors come—or 'temporaries,' we call them, somebody who might want to join—they stay there. Might end up down there several weeks before they're allowed to come up and stay in the lodge." She indicated the house. "That's the lodge. A lot of kinds of people used to think they wanted to live here . . ." She smiled again. "And we, of course, would never know if we wanted them. Now nobody's coming at all," she added after a moment. "Mostly, we're losing people." She avoided his eyes. "Some of them, when they leave it's in the middle of the night. Like they feel they've failed." The pond whipped up a little in an afternoon breeze. She led him down to the edge of the water, where there was a sort of log bench. "Mostly we would get the young ones. They would always be disappointed that certain things here were about the same as in the world."

"Such as?"

"Such as the raggedy ways people relate."

The woods were very quiet except for the gentle wind. He checked back toward the barn.

"You go through times when this life out here is all you need." She shyly laughed at herself.

"I can understand why someone might want to come here to live," he said.

"We're awfully isolated."

"Isolation can be good sometimes, can't it?" He realized as he said it that he'd never lived in any real isolation in his life.

"Stephen thinks we're almost gone. He compares us to an endangered species—he says that at some point the animal gets the hint and begins to aid in the process of its own extinction." She stood up. "Want to look at the river?"

"Maybe I'll walk back to the barn," he said. "I think we should stay close."

"It is close," she said.

A cat came out of some bushes nearby, a small gray cat, carrying in its mouth a baby rabbit. The rabbit was kicking. The cat found some soft grass and sat holding the rabbit tight until finally the kicking stopped and it stretched out softly in a bent U-shape hanging from the cat's mouth.

"C'mon. It'll pass the time," she said, and she turned to the women who were still watching from the lodge. "I'm going to the gazebo," she called to them. She kicked off her leather sandals and tossed them toward the porch. The women disappeared inside.

The path arched around the pond and deeper into the woods. "The pond is quite important here at Geneseo," Clay City was saying. She was walking ahead of Jerome, her soft old dress flowing off her hips and down almost to the ground. It dragged among the burrs and scrub, and when something caught on the skirt it pulled away, revealing for a moment her bare feet, reddish and rough.

"Little places like this depend heavily on symbols, and the pond is one of ours. So's the bell, I guess. The pond is spring-fed. The spring is back there in the trees somewhere. Stephen and some of the other early ones used to give talks at the pond. The idea was to inspire the group to the ideas that founded us. One guy taped most of the pond talks and typed them up. Some have actually been published in magazines. I've never read them, but so they say. This is the cemetery." She indicated off to the left of the path. "We don't mark the graves. One man got sick or something, way back when. There's two babies, and some others. We buried a soldier out here in 1974. He arrived in one of those aluminum cans. Nobody knows who he was. They had an extra body, I think."

As he listened, Jerome thought of the sad story of Clay City that Janet had told him. He sensed that the immediacy of the death of her sister was gone. He looked back into the woods. The dead moldered under this ancient stand of trees.

"Owl," she said. A big bird lifted up out of the treetops to their right. Its shadow passed over. She was talking straight ahead of her. They came into an area of birches, a wonderland of white and yellow amazingly different from the part of the woods they'd just been in. The birchwood, she called it. Then they came out of the trees high above the river. The gazebo was a round, porchlike structure, covered, enclosed at the back. The walls were a gleaming white wood lattice letting the light through in small diamond shapes that gleamed on the green floor.

"We just repainted it last week. Isn't it stunning?" she said "I wanted to show it to you because Will built it. He's our best builder. He has all the best ideas." From the gazebo platform, she pointed out over the river to the village of New Boston, and the other way toward what she called Lock 17, a dam.

Jerome sat on the bench in the gazebo and looked out on the river.

"Did you see the sign?" she said. There was a small hand-painted plaque over the threshold of the gazebo, on the inside. It said "Save the Earth." "Seems a little dated now. When he came, he was one of these big ecology people. You can about estimate the date of his arrival knowing that—1972, right? He had T-shirts with that green ecology flag, remember? Turned out he was more complicated than that. But we're glad he came to us. For a long time he and Geneseo were very close—but he got worse. He beat her up." She looked at Jerome. "Janet—when things started coming apart with Will and all, so did she. She's an alcoholic. Has she told you all this?"

"No," he said.

"Maybe I should shut up. I'm sorry—I keep wondering how you fit in."

Good question, Jerome thought but didn't say.

She laughed. "You're friends with Janet? That's all?"

Jerome shrugged, feeling a little helpless. "I don't mean to be coy, but isn't being friends enough?"

"Yes." She said it quietly. "I mean," she said, "I guess. We'll see."

"I paint," he said. "I've been teaching some out at the college, in Tuscola. And I do a little carpentry with a local construction crew, to pay the rent. I'm not a craftsman like this guy, though." He indicated the gazebo.

"Well, you must have noticed that Janet drinks a lot. People die of it when they have it like she does."

Jerome stared out across the river from the bluff where they were standing. Iowa.

"Tell me," she said. "Do you think she's stable enough for Barbara to be with her?"

Jerome sat there. He did not answer her. He wondered if they hadn't now struck upon the whole reason for this walk.

"What's Janet doing to eat? Does she have a job?"

Again he said nothing.

"Look," Clay City said, "we love this little girl. She's frail, like her mother. She has a lot of friends here who are as close as brothers and sisters. We can take care of her. Don't take her if Janet isn't ready yet." When he didn't say anything, she pressed on. "I'm trying to talk sense with you. We love Barbara very much. We don't know where she's going."

"I understand you," he said. He held up his hand for her to stop. She stepped away from the gazebo and stood looking out on the river. He wanted her to trust him, and he knew she didn't at all. He felt accused of being a party to Janet's problems. He had to think about that one. He realized he would like to have been a friend of Clay City, wouldn't ever be.

"There are only twenty-seven on this land now," Clay City said. "Nine children. There are eleven men and seven women. We've lost eight in two years. We're definitely the whooping crane."

Jerome looked at her. He tried to imagine her, how she'd look and what she'd be like if this commune had not been part of her life.

"A couple of the originals are here. Stephen is the main one. He says he'll be the one to close the door and turn off the lights." She smiled, perhaps having noted that Jerome's guard was up and trying to relax him. "Well, anyway, that's the Mississippi. There are other pretty places I could show you if you had the time. A painter could love this area. I suspect you don't have time, right?" Her tone was cooler now.

Down below, the river stretched before them. At that distance there was no sense of the water flowing, although in the sunlight it gleamed and flashed between colors of blue and brown. She was leading him back toward the lodge, a different route. For some distance, they were climbing uphill. At one point, she passed between Jerome and the sun. He caught a flash of her brown hair in the wind and saw the silhouette of her legs through the veil of thin cotton she wore around her. From the top of the high bank they had climbed, he saw that the Camaro had pulled up to the edge of the trees. Stephen and Janet were sitting on the log next to the pond. Standing off from them, along the edge of the pond, was Barbara. On the hood of the car was a large cloth bag.

When they got to the pond, Clay City hugged Janet, held her a long time. Janet had been crying, and now she was again. Her hair was messed. She was utterly apart from Jerome—it was clear that he didn't belong there at all.

"They'll be taking Barbara," Stephen said.

Clay City looked at him. "Of course they will," she said.

She took Janet's arm gently and they walked together toward the lodge, the other women coming into the yard to meet them. Janet's blue jeans were a contrast to the long old dresses. Jerome was standing several feet from Stephen, and neither of them said anything. Barbara was on the bench, her arms folded tightly around herself. She was taller than in the picture Jerome had seen, and her nose was sunburned and peeled. Some of the other children had gathered there, too. Jerome could see Janet talking with people in the lodge. All he could hear was the wind.

When they came out of the house, Janet and Clay City were arm-in-arm, walking close, talking quietly. They went down to the edge of the pond and bent down over Barbara.

"How did it go?" Jerome asked Stephen.

"This is his daughter."

Jerome tried to hear friendliness in the tone, but he wasn't sure there was any.

"Will knows it's better this way. He's been confused for days, you know. Not because of this. He had a bad war." Stephen bent down, pulled a long blade of grass. "Janet's terrified of him. He's in a room and won't come out. She tried to talk to him. Forget it. It's a bad time, everything at once." Stephen paused a moment. Then he said, "You're an artist, didn't Janet say?"

Jerome nodded.

"We have several here, artists. Quite a number through the years. One older gentleman here helps the whole community financially with his work. He sells through a gallery on the near northside, New Town, in Chicago."

"Is he the one who did the Lennon on the barn?"

"Nah, one of our people put that up there when John was shot." He turned so that he could see it, and Jerome looked back that way, too. "I always think of the eye-doctor billboard in *Gatsby*. The way it stares out across the field. 'In Memoriam.' I guess I haven't really looked at it for a long time. We aren't ordinarily grim around here. Listen," he said then, talking straight at Jerome but not looking at him, speaking quieter to keep from being heard by anyone else. "We want this girl taken care of. If Janet has problems, you let us know, will you? We can come down and get Barbara. We can come and get them both, although I don't think Janet wants to come back. This little girl—she's part of us almost as much as she's part of Janet. We care about her, I'm trying to say. You must let us know. Call me— I'll send money—anything."

"I understand," Jerome said. Again, as with Clay City, he had the impulse to show Stephen that he could fit in here, that he was likable in the terms of this community. But it was a futile notion. He watched the women at the edge of the pond.

Stephen spoke in a southern accent, strong and steady. "They call this an anarchist community." Now he was looking right at Jerome, smiling. "To my way of thinking, you got most of the anarchy out where you live."

"No argument on that," Jerome said. He and Stephen shook hands.

The women walked back up to them, bringing Barbara along, their hands on her shoulders. Barbara had the same kind of wide-open face and level stare, but she also had that pale, frail blue-white skin, blue veins in her forehead and temples, at the corners of her eyes.

"I'll be coming back, won't I?" she was asking her mom.

"Maybe so," Janet said.

"No," Stephen said, and he squatted down to her. "You stay with your mother. We love you, but you stay with your mom, Barbara. Okay?" She was crying, and Stephen hugged her. The bell, far off, was ringing again. "I've got to go," Stephen said, standing up and turning to Janet. He embraced her, saying something to her no one else could hear. Then he waved again and jogged toward the barns, heading for where the tolling sound of the bell had come from.

"Will I see Daddy anymore?" the little girl said.

Janet put Barbara's cloth bag in the front seat of the car. "You will," she said. "Of course you will." She and Barbara both got in the back seat. Jerome started the car and slowly, driving on dry leaves, pulled out from under the oaks. In the rearview mirror there was Clay City waving. Barbara was waving, too, through the back window.

Suddenly Jerome was thinking about where they were going. A time or two he'd stayed the night at Janet's rented trailer when they'd dragged in late from Gabby's. The feeling was desperate and temporary. The trailer was dark inside, and damp—so damp that the borrowed couch smelled and the dark walnut-print contact paper on the bathroom wall was peeling off in a sheet. The little grass that might have separated Janet's from the next trailer down had long ago been fried away by the sun.

"What did Stephen say to you?" Jerome asked.

"He said good-bye. He said Geneseo's going down. It was like he was apologizing. He said it isn't a failure just because it doesn't last forever."

Clay City came forward out of the shade into the afternoon sun. As they went down the long two-rutted grassy path toward the gate, Jerome could see her, still waving. The children had taken a shortcut and met the car near the gate. One of the older boys swung it open wide. He said "See you, Barbara" as the car went by him.

Barbara was crying quietly, her head down in her mother's lap. Once on the road just beyond Geneseo's gate, Jerome looked back toward the clump of trees, and now he could see where the lodge was, and down the hill to the shacks where the visitors stayed, and deep in the trees he saw Clay City one last time, watching them drive away toward the main highway.

13

PLAYLAND

Ron Hansen

After the agricultural exhibit of 1918, some partners in a real-estate development firm purchased the cattle barns, the gymkhana, the experimental alfalfas and sorghums, the paddocks and pear orchards, and converted one thousand acres into an amusement park called Playland. A landscape architect from Sardinia was persuaded to oversee garden construction, and the newspapers made much of his steamship passage and arrival by train in a December snow, wearing a white suit and boater. Upon arrival he'd said, "It is chilly," a sentence he'd practiced for two hundred miles.

He invented gardens as crammed as flower shops, glades that were like dark green parlors, ponds that gently overlipped themselves so that water sheeted down to another pond, and trickle streams that issued from secret pipes sunk in the crannies of rocks. Goldfish with tails like orange scarves hung in the pools fluttering gill fins or rising for crumbs that children sprinkled down. South American and African birds were freighted to Playland, each so shockingly colored that a perceiver's eyes blinked as from a photographer's flash. They screamed and mimicked and battered down onto ladies' hats or the perch of an index finger, while sly yellow canaries performed tricks of arithmetic with green peas and ivory thimbles. Cats were removed from the premises, dogs had to be leashed, policemen were instructed to whistle as they patrolled "so as not to surprise visitors to the park at moments of intimacy."

The corn pavilion was transformed into trinket shops, two clothing stores, a bank, a bakery where large chocolate-chip cookies were sold while still hot from the oven, and a restaurant that served cottage-fried potatoes with catfish that diners could snag out of a galvanized tank. The carnival galleries were made slightly orange with electric arc lights overhead, as was the miniature golf course with its undulating green carpets—each hole a foreign country represented by a fjord, pagoda, minaret, windmill, pyramid, or the like. The Ferris wheels and merry-go-rounds were turned by diesel truck engines that were framed with small barns and insulated lest they allow more than a grandfatherly noise; paddlewheel craft with bicycle pedals chopped down a slow, meandering river. Operas and starlight concerts were staged from April to October, and the exhibition place was redecorated at great cost for weekend dances at which evening gowns and tuxedos were frequently required. A pretty ice-skating star dedicated the ballroom, cutting the ribbon in a hooded white mink coat that was so long it dragged dance wax onto the burgundy carpet. A newspaper claimed she'd been tipsy, that she'd said, "You got a saloon in this place?" But after a week's controversy an editor determined that the word she'd used was *salon*, and later the entire incident was denied, the reporter was quietly sent away, and the newspaper grandly apologized to the Playland management.

Lovers strolled on the swept brick sidewalks and roamed on resilient lawns that cushioned their shoes like a mattress, and at night they leaned against the cast-iron lampposts, whispering promises and nicely interlocking their fingers. Pebbled roads led to nooks where couples were roomed by exotic plants and resplendent flowers whose scent was considered an aphrodisiac, so that placards suggesting temperance and restraint were tamped into the pansy beds.

The park speedily rose to preeminence as the one place in America for outings, holidays, company picnics, second honeymoons, but its reputation wasn't truly international until the creation of the giant swimming pool.

Construction took fourteen months. Horse stables were converted to cabanas, steam-powered earth movers sloped the racetrack into a saucer, the shallows and beach were paved, and over twenty thousand railroad cars of Caribbean sand were hauled in on a spur. The pool was nearly one mile long, more than half of that in width, and thirty-six feet deep in its center, where the water was still so pellucid that a swimmer could see a nickel wink sunlight from the bottom. Twelve thousand gallons of water evaporated each summer day and were replaced by six artesian wells feeding six green fountains on which schooling brass fish spouted water from open mouths as they seemed to flop and spawn from a roiling upheaval.

And the beach was a marvel. The sand was as fine as that in hotel ashtrays, so white that lifeguards sometimes became snow-blind, and so deep near the soda-pop stands that a magician could be buried in it standing up, and it took precious minutes for a crew with spades to pull him out when his stunt failed—he gasped, "A roaring noise. A furnace. Suffocation." Gymnasts exercised on silver rings and pommel horses and chalked parallel bars, volleyball tournaments were played there, oiled muscle men pumped dumbbells and posed, and in August girls in saucy bathing suits and high heels walked a gangway to compete for the Miss Playland title. Admission prices increased each season, and yet two million people and more pushed through the turnstiles at Playland during the summers. Playland was considered pleasing and inexpensive entertainment, it represented gracious fellowship, polite surprise, good cheer. The Depression never hurt Playland, cold weather only increased candy sales, rains never seemed to persist for long, and even the periodic scares—typhoid in the water, poisonous snakes in sand burrows, piranha near the diving platform—couldn't shrink the crowds. Nothing closed Playland, not even the war.

Soldiers on furlough or medical release were allowed free entrance, and at USO stations on the beach, happy women volunteers dispensed potato chips and hot dogs on paper plates, sodas without ice, and pink towels just large enough to scrunch up on near the water. Young men would queue up next to the spiked iron fence at six o'clock in the morning when a camp bus dropped them off, and they'd lounge and smoke and squat on the sidewalk reading newspapers, perhaps whistling at pretty girls as the streetcars screeched past. As the golden gates whirred open, the GIs collided and jostled through, a sailor slapped a petty officer's cap off, and little children raced to the teeter-totters and swings as Playland's nursemaids applauded their speed.

The precise date was never recorded, but one morning a corporal named Gordon limped out of the bathhouse and was astonished to see an enormous pelican on the prow of the lifeguard's rowboat. The pelican's eyes were blue beads, and she swung her considerable beak to the right and left to regard Gordon and blink, then she flapped down to the beach and waddled toward him, her wings amorously fanning out to a span of ten feet or more as she struck herself thumpingly on the breast with her beak until a spot of red blood appeared on her feathers. The corporal retreated to the bathhouse door and flung sand at the bird and said, "Shoo!" and the pelican seemed to resign herself and lurched up into eastward flight, her wings loudly swooping the air with a noise like a broom socking dust from a rug on a clothesline.

More guests drifted out of the bathhouse. Children carried tin shovels and sand pails. Married women with bare legs and terry-cloth jackets walked in pairs to the shade trees, sharing the heft of a picnic basket's straw handle. Pregnant women sat on benches in cotton print dresses. Girls emerged into the sun, giggling about silly nothings, their young breasts in the squeeze of crossed arms. On gardened terraces rich people were oiled and massaged by stocky women who spoke no English. Dark waiters in pink jackets carried iced highballs out on trays. A perplexed man in an ascot and navy-blue blazer stood near the overflowing food carts with a dark cigarette, staring down at the pool. Red and yellow hot-air balloons rose up from the apricot orchard and carried in the wind. A rocket ship with zigzag fins and sparkling runners and a science-fiction arsenal screamed by on an elevated rail. Children were at the portholes, their noses squashed to the window glass like snails.

A girl of seventeen sat on the beach with her chin in her hands, looking at the mall. Her name was Bijou. A rubber pillow was bunched under her chest and it made her feel romantic. She watched as her boyfriend, the corporal named Gordon, limped barefoot away from a USO stand in khaki pants belted high at his ribs, a pink towel yoking his neck, a cane in his left hand. He dropped his towel next to Bijou's and squared it with his cane's rubber tip. He huffed as he sat and scratched at the knee of his pants. He'd been a messenger between commanders' posts in Africa and rode a camouflaged motorcycle. A mine explosion ruined his walk. Bijou wondered if she was still in love with him. She guessed that she was.

Bijou knelt on her beach blanket and dribbled baby oil onto her thighs. Her white swimming suit was pleated at her breasts but scooped revealingly under her shoulder blades so that pale men wading near her had paused to memorize her prettiness, and a man with a battleship tattoo on his arm had sloshed up onto the hot sand and sucked in his stomach. But Gordon glowered and flicked his cane in a dispatching manner and the man walked over to a girls' badminton game and those in the water lurched on.

"My nose itches," Bijou said. "That means someone's going to visit me, doesn't it?"

"After that pelican I don't need any more surprises," Gordon replied, and then he saw an impressive shadow fluctuate along the sand, and he looked heavenward to see an airplane dip its wings and turn, then lower its flaps and slowly descend from the west, just over a splashing fountain. His eyes smarted from the silver glare of the steel and porthole windows. The airplane slapped down in a sudden spray of water, wakes rolling outward from canoe floats as it cut back its engines and swung around. The propellers chopped and then idled, and a door flapped open as a skinny young man in a pink double-breasted suit stepped down to a rocking lifeguard's boat.

"Must be some bigwig," said Gordon.

The airplane taxied around, and Bijou could see the pilot check the steering and magnetos and instruments, then plunge the throttle forward, ski across the water, and wobble off. The rowboat with the airplane's passenger rode up on the beach and retreated some before it was hauled up by a gang of boys. The man in the pink suit slipped a dollar to a lifeguard and hopped onto the sand, sinking to his ankles. As he walked toward Bijou he removed a pack of cigarettes and a lighter from his shirt pocket. His pants were wide and pleated and he'd cocked a white Panama hat on his head. He laid a cigarette on his lip and grinned at Bijou, and arrested his stride when he was over her.

"Don't you recognize your cousin?"

She shaded her eyes. "Frankie?"

He clinked his cigarette lighter closed and smiled as smoke issued from his nose. "I wanted to see how little Bijou turned out, how this and that developed."

"I couldn't be more surprised."

He'd ignored the corporal, so Gordon got up, brushing sand from his khakis, and introduced himself. "My name's Gordon. Bijou's boyfriend."

"Charmed," Frankie said. He removed his hat and wiped his brow with a handkerchief. His wavy hair was black and fragrantly oiled and he had a mustache like William Powell's. He had been a radio actor in New York. He asked if they served drinks on the beach, and Gordon offered to fetch him something, slogging off to a soda-pop stand.

"Sweet guy," Frankie said. "What's he got, polio or something?"

"He was wounded in the war."

"The dope," Frankie said. He unlaced his white shoes and unsnapped his silk socks from calf garters and removed them. He slumped down on Gordon's towel, unbuttoning his coat.

"You're so handsome, Frankie!"

"Ya think so?"

"I can't get over it. How'd you find me at Playland?"

"You're not that hard to pick out," Frankie said, and he gave his cousin the once-over. "You look like Betty Grable in that suit."

"You don't think it's too immodest?"

"You're a feast for the eyes."

The corporal returned with an orange soda and a straw. Frankie accepted it without thanks and dug in his pocket for a folded dollar bill. "Here, here's a simoleon for your trouble."

"Nah," Gordon said. "You can get the next round."

Frankie sighed as if bored and poked the dollar bill into the sand near Gordon's bare left foot. He leaned back on his elbows and winked at someone in the pool. "Somebody wants you, Sarge."

"Say again?"

"Two dames in a boat."

A rowboat had scraped bottom, and two adolescent girls with jammy lipstick, Gordon's sister and her girlfriend, motioned for him to come over. Gordon waded to where the water was warm at his calves and climbed darkly up his pant legs. "What're you doing, Sis?"

"Having fun. Where's Bijou?"

"On the beach, Goofy."

His sister strained to see around him. "*Where?*"

He turned. Bijou and Frankie had disappeared.

Frankie strolled the hot white sand with his cousin and sipped orange soda through the straw. Hecklers repeatedly whistled at Bijou and Frankie winked at them. "Hear that? You're the berries, kid. You're driving these wiseacres off their nut."

"Oh, those wolves do that to any female."

"Baloney!" He was about to make a statement but became cautious and revised it. "What am I, nine years older than you?"

"I think so," Bijou said.

"And what about GI Joe?"

Bijou glanced over her shoulder and saw her boyfriend hunting someone on the beach. Gordon squinted at her and she waved, but he seemed to look past her. "He's twenty-one," she said.

"Four years older. What's he doing with a kid like you for his bim?"

"He's mad about me, Stupid."

Frankie snickered. He crossed his ankles and settled down in the bathhouse shade. Bijou sat next to him. Frankie pushed his cigarette down in the sand and lit another, clinking his lighter closed. "Do you and Gordo smooch?"

Bijou prodded sand from between her toes. "Occasionally."

"How shall I put it? You still Daddy's little girl?"

"You're making me uncomfortable, Frankie."

"Nah, I'm just giving you the needle."

The corporal was confused. His nose and shoulders were sunburned and his legs ached and Bijou and Frankie had flat out evaporated. His sister and her girlfriend stroked the rowboat ahead and Gordon sat on the rim board near a forward oarlock, scouting the immeasurable Playland beach. Soon his sister complained that she was tired and bored and blistered, and

Gordon said, "All right already. Cripes—don't think about me. Do what you want to do."

After a while Frankie clammed up and then decided he wanted a little exercise and removed his tie and pink coat as he walked past the USO stand to the gym equipment. He performed two pull-ups on the chalked high bar, biting his cigarette, then amused a nurse in the first-aid station with his impressions of Peter Lorre, Ronald Colman, Lionel Barrymore.

"I love hearing men talk," the nurse said. "That's what I miss most."

"Maybe I could close this door," Frankie said.

"You can't kiss me, if that's what you're thinking. I'm not fast."

"Maybe I should amscray, then."

"No!" the nurse said, and shocked herself with her insistence. "Oh, shoot." She turned her back and walked to the sickbed. "Go ahead and close the door."

Anchored in Playland's twenty-foot waters were five diving platforms fixed as star points radiating out from a giant red diving tower with swooping steel buttresses and three levels, the topmost being a crow's nest that was flagged with snapping red pennants. It reached one hundred feet above the surface and was closed off except for the professionals paid to somersault dangerously from the perch at two and four in the afternoon, nine o'clock at night.

And there Gordon had his sister and her girlfriend row him after he'd wearied of looking for Bijou. The boat banged into a steel brace, and the corporal left his cane and walked off the board seat to a ladder slat. He ascended to the first elevation and saw only shivering children who leaned to see that the bottom was unpopulated, then worked up their courage and leapt, shouting paratrooper jump calls. At the second elevation was a short man with gray hair and a very brief suit and skin nearly chocolate brown. The man paused at the edge, adjusting his toes, and then jackknifed off, and Gordon bent out to see him veer into the water sixty feet down. Gordon wanted to recoup, to do something masculine and reckless and death defying. He yelled to the platform below him, "Anybody down there?" and there was no answer. Then he saw a woman in a white bathing suit like Bijou's underwater near the tower. Her blond hair eddied as she tarried there below the surface. Gordon grinned.

His sister and her girlfriend were spellbound. They saw Gordon carefully roll up his pant cuffs and yank his belt tight through his brass buckle clasp. They saw him simply walk off the second level into a careening drop that lasted almost two seconds. A geyser shot up twenty feet when he smacked the water, then the surface ironed out and his sister worried; finally he burst up near the boat.

"Something's down there!"

"What is?"

"Don't know!" Gordon swam over, wincing with pain, and when he gripped the boat, blood braided down his fist.

Bijou strapped on a white rubber bathing cap and pushed her hair under it as she tiptoed on the hot sand. She splashed water onto her arms and chest, and then crouched into the pool and swam overhand toward a rocking diving platform. It floated on groaning red drums that lifted and smacked down and lifted again as boys dived from the boards. Bijou climbed a ladder and dangled her legs from a diving platform carpeted with drenched rope. She removed her cap, tossed her blond hair, ignored the oglers who hung near the ladder. Her breasts ached and she wished Gordon could somehow rub them without making her crazy.

The diving platform had sloped because a crowd took up a corner, staring toward the diving tower. Bijou saw that the ferry had stopped and that its passengers had gathered at the rail under the canopy, gaping in the same direction. Four lifeguards hung on a rowboat, struggling with something, as a policeman with a gaff hook stood in the boat and Gordon clinched the anchor lock with a bandaged right hand. Gordon! Two swimmers disappeared under water, and the policeman hooked the gaff and they heaved up a black snapping turtle as large as a manhole cover and so heavy that the gaff bowed like a fishing rod. The turtle's thorny neck hooked madly about and its beak clicked as it struck at the gaff and its clawed webs snagged at whatever they could, as if they wanted to rake out an eye. Bijou's boyfriend manipulated a canvas mailbag over the turtle's head and nicked it over the turtle's horned shell. The policeman heard a woman shriek, then saw the hubbub and the astonished crowds on the ferry and diving platforms, and he kicked the turtle onto the boat's bottom and said, "Hide it. Hurry up, hide it."

That night the exhibition palace burned so many light bulbs that signs at the gate warned visitors not to linger too close to the marquee or stare at the electrical dazzle without the green cellophane sunglasses available at the ticket booth. Limousines seeped along an asphalt cul-de-sac that was redolent with honeysuckle, violets, and dahlias, and at least forty taxicabs idled against the curb, the drivers hanging elbows out or sitting against their fenders. Gordon stood on a sidewalk imbedded with gold sparkle and laced his unbandaged fingers with Bijou's as Frankie ostentatiously paid for their admission. Then Bijou left for the powder room with her evening gown in a string-tied box, a pair of white pumps in her hand.

Frankie sauntered inside with Gordon, commenting on the sponge of the burgundy lobby carpet, the vast dance floor's uncommon polish, the vapored fragrances shot overhead from jet instruments tucked into the ceiling's scrolled molding. Bijou's two escorts selected a corner cocktail table and listened to the Butch Seaton Orchestra in sleepy, mopey solitude, without criticism or remark. Then Bijou glided down the ballroom stairs in her glamorous white gown, looking like Playland's last and best creation, Playland's finishing touch, and the men rose up like dukes.

Gordon danced with her and Frankie cut in. Frankie murmured at her ear over sodas, and Gordon asked Bijou to accompany him to the dance floor. The three bandied conversations during breaks, then music would start and they'd detach again. Male hands sought Bijou's hands as she sat; songs were solicited for her from the orchestra; Gordon fanned a napkin near her when it warmed.

By ten o'clock the great ballroom was jammed. Young Marines introduced themselves and danced with uneasy strangers, a sergeant danced with a hatcheck girl, some women danced with each other as the Butch Seaton Orchestra played "Undecided," "Boo Hoo," "Tangerine." Bijou stood near the stage, her boyfriend's hand at her back, his thumb independently diddling her zipper as a crooner sang, "I love you, there's nothing to hide. It's better than burning inside. I love you, no use to pretend. There! I've said it again!" Sheet music turned. A man licked his saxophone reed. The crooner retreated from the microphone as woodwinds took over for a measure. A mirrored sunburst globe rotated on the ceiling, wiping light spots across a man's shoulder, a woman's face, a tasseled drape, a chair. The orchestra members wore white tuxedos with red paper roses in their lapels. Gordon's fingers gingered up Bijou's bare back to her neck, where fine blonde hairs had come undone from an ivory barrette. Bijou shivered and then gently swiveled into Gordon, not meaning to dance but moving with him when he did. His shoes nudged hers, his khaki uniform smelled of a spicy aftershave that Bijou regretted, his pressure against her body made her feel secure and loving.

The music stopped and Gordon said, "Let's ditch your cousin."

"How mean!"

"The guy gives me the creeps."

"Still."

Gordon thumped his cane on the floor and weighed his hankerings. "How about if you kissed me a big sloppy one right on my ear?"

Bijou giggled. "Not *here*."

"Maybe later, okay?"

Butch Seaton gripped his baton in both hands and bent into a microphone as a woman in a red evening dress with spangles on it like fish scales crossed to the microphone that the crooner was readjusting lower with a wing nut. The orchestra leader suggested, "And now, Audrey, how about Duke Ellington's soulful tune, 'Mood Indigo'?"

Audrey seemed amenable.

Bijou asked, "I wonder where Frankie is."

"Maybe he was mixing with his kind and somebody flushed him away." The corporal's little joke pleased him, and he was near a guffaw when his nose began to bleed. He spattered drops on his bandaged hand and Bijou's wrist and shoe before he could slump, embarrassed, on a chair with a handkerchief pressed to his nostrils. He remarked, "This day is one for the record books, Bijou. This has been a really weird day."

Bijou complained that she was yukky with Gordon's blood, and she slipped off to the powder room. Gordon watched her disappear among the couples on the dance floor, and then Frankie flopped down on a folding chair next to him.

"How's the schnozzola?" Frankie asked. Gordon removed the handkerchief, and Frankie peered like a vaudeville doctor. "Looks dammed up to me." He slapped Gordon's crippled knee. "I hereby declare you in perfect health. Come on, let's drink to it."

Frankie showed him to a gentleman's saloon, and Gordon paid for a rye whiskey and a Coca-Cola with a simoleon that had grains of sand stuck to it. The Playland glassware was, of course, unblemished with water spots.

Frankie said, "I was a radio actor in New York before the war. I'm coming back from a screen test in Hollywood. Another gangster part. That's about all I do: gunsels, crooks, schlemiels."

"No kidding," the corporal said. He rebandaged his right hand and sulked about his miserable afternoon.

Frankie stared at an eighteenth-century painting of a prissy hunter with two spaniels sniffing at his white leggings, a turkey strangled in his fist. "What a jerk, huh? Here I am, horning in on your girl, and I expect chitchat from you."

"Well, don't expect me to be palsy-walsy. I'll shoot the breeze, okay. But I'm not about to be your pal just because you're Bijou's cousin from Hollywood and radio land."

Frankie scrooched forward on his bar stool. "You oughta see things with my eyes. You take Bijou, for instance. She's a dish, a real hot patootie in anybody's book, but she ain't all she wrote, Gordo, not by a long shot. You and Bijou, you come to Playland, you dance to the music, swallow all this phonusbalonus, and you think you've experienced life to the hilt. Well, I got news for you, GI. You haven't even licked the spoon. You don't know what's out there, what's available." Frankie slid off the bar stool and hitched up his pink pleated pants. "You want a clue, you want a little taste of the hot stuff, you call on Cousin Frankie. I gotta go to the can."

Gordon hunched over his Coca-Cola glass and scowled down into the ice, then swiveled to call to Frankie as he left the saloon, but the schlemiel wasn't there.

Gordon was loitering in the burgundy lobby, slapping his garrison cap in his hand, when Bijou came out of the powder room. He asked, "Do you want to see the moon?"

"Where's Frankie?"

"Who cares?"

A great crush of partygoers was pushing against the lobby's glass doors, yelling to get in, each wearing green cellophane sunglasses. Gordon and Bijou exited and a couple was admitted; screams rose and then subsided as the big door closed.

The two strolled past a penny arcade, a calliope, a gypsy fortuneteller's tent, a lavender emporium where chimpanzees in toddler clothes rollerskated and shambled. At a booth labeled Delights, Bijou observed a man spin apples in hot caramel and place them on cupcake papers to cool, and she seemed so fascinated that the corporal bought her one. Bijou chewed the candied apple as they ambled past the stopped rocket ship, an empty French café, a darkened wedding chapel. They walked near pools where great frogs croaked on green lily pads that were as large as place mats, and gorgeous flowers like white cereal bowls drifted in slow turns. The couple strolled into gardens of petunias, loblolly, blue iris, philodendrons, black orchids. Exciting perfumes craved attention, petals detached and fluttered down, a white carnation shattered at the brush of Bijou's hem and piled in shreds on the walk, the air hummed and hushed and whined. Cat's-eye marbles layered a path that veered off into gardens with lurid green leaves overhead, and this walk they took with nervous stomachs and the near panic of erotic desires. The moon vanished and the night cooled. Creepers overtook lampposts and curled up over benches; the wind made the weeping willows sigh like a child in sleep. Playland was everywhere they looked, insisting on itself.

Then Gordon and Bijou were boxed in by black foliage. The corporal involved himself with Bijou and they kissed as they heard the orchestra playing the last dance. Bijou shivered and moved to the music and her boyfriend woodenly followed, his cane slung from a belt loop, his bandaged right hand on her hip. Her cheek nuzzled into his shoulder. His shoes scruffed the grass in a two-step. The music was clarinets and trombones and the crooner singing about heartache, but under that, as from a cellar, Bijou could pick out chilling noises, so secret that they could barely be noticed: of flesh ripped from bone, claws scratching madly at wood, the clink of a cigarette lighter.

Bijou felt the corporal bridle and cease dancing, and then start up again. He danced her around slowly until she could see what he'd seen, but Bijou closed her eyes and said, "Forget about him. Pretend he's not there."

14

THE DEVIL AND IRV CHERNISKE

T. Coraghessan Boyle

Just outside the sleepy little commuter village of Irvington, New York, there stands a subdivision of half-million-dollar homes, each riding its own sculpted acre like a ship at sea and separated from its neighbors by patches of scrub and the forlorn-looking beeches that lend a certain pricey and vestigial air to the place. The stockbrokers, lawyers, doctors, and software salesmen who live here with their families know their community as Beechwood, in deference to the legend hammered into the slab of pink marble at the entrance of Beechwood Drive. This slab was erected by the developer, Sal Maggio, in the late nineteen-sixties, though there are few here now who can remember that far back. For better or worse, Beechwood is the sort of community in which the neighbors don't know one another and don't really care to, though they do survey each other's gardeners and automobiles with all the perspicacity of appraisers, and while the proper names of the people next door may escape them, they are quick to invent such colorful sobriquets as the Geeks, the Hackers, the Volvos, and the Chinks by way of compensation.

For the most part, the handsome sweeping macadam streets go untrodden but for the occasional backward jogger, and the patches of wood are ignored to the point at which they've begun to revert to the condition of the distant past, to the time before Maggio's bulldozer, when the trees stretched unbroken all the way to Ardsley. Fieldmice make their home in these woods, moths, spiders, sparrows, and squirrels. In the late afternoon, garter snakes

239

silently thread the high, rank, thick-stemmed morass of bluegrass gone wild, and toads thump from one fetid puddle to another. An unpropitious place, these woods. A forgotten place. But it was here, in one of these primordial pockets, beneath a wind-ravaged maple and within earshot of the chit-chit-chit of the gray squirrel, that Irv Cherniske made the deal of his life.

Irv was one of the senior residents of Beechwood, having moved into his buff-and-chocolate Tudor with the imitation flagstone façade some three years earlier. He was a hard-nosed cynic in his early forties, a big-headed, heavy-paunched, irascible stock trader who'd seen it all—and then some. The characteristic tone of his voice was an unmodulated roar, but this was only the daintiest of counterpoint to the stentorian bellow of his wife, Tish. The two fought so often and at such a pitch that their young sons, Shane and Morgan, often took refuge in the basement game room while the battle raged over their heads and out across the placid rolling lawns of Beechwood Estates. To the neighbors, these battles were a source of rueful amusement: separately, yet unanimously, they had devised their own pet nickname for the Cherniskes. A torn, ragged cry would cut the air around dinnertime each evening, and someone would lift a watery gimlet to his lips and remark, with a sigh, that the Screechers were at it again.

One evening, after a particularly bracing confrontation with his wife over the question of who had last emptied the trash receptacle in the guest room, Irv was out in the twilit backyard, practicing his chip shot and swatting mosquitoes. It was the tail end of a long Fourth of July weekend, and an unearthly stillness had settled over Beechwood, punctuated now and again by the distant muffled pop of leftover fireworks. The air was muggy and hot, a fiery breath of the tropics more suitable to Rangoon than New York. Irv bent in the fading light to address a neon-orange Titleist. Behind him, in the house which seemed almost to sink under the weight of its mortgage, Tish and his sons were watching TV, the muted sounds of conflict and sorrow carrying fitfully to where he stood in the damp grass, awash in birdsong. He raised the nine-iron, dropped it in a fluid rush, and watched the ball rise mightily into the darkening belly of the sky. Unfortunately, he overshot the makeshift flag he'd set up at the foot of the lawn and carried on into the ragged clump of trees beyond it.

With a curse, Irv trundled down the hill and pushed his way through the mounds of cuttings the gardener had piled up like breastworks at the edge of the woods and a moment later found himself in the hushed and shadowy stand of beeches. An odor of slow rot assaulted his nostrils. Crickets chirruped. There was no sign of the ball. He was kicking aimlessly through the leaves, all but certain it was gone for good—two-and-a-half bucks down the drain—when he was startled by a noise from the gloom up ahead.

Something—or someone—was coming toward him, a presence announced by the crush of brittle leaves and the hiss of uncut grass. "Who is it?" he demanded, and the crickets fell silent. "Is someone there?"

The shape of a man began to emerge gradually from the shadows—head and shoulders first, then a torso that kept getting bigger. And bigger. His skin was dark—so dark Irv at first took him to be a Negro—and a wild feral shock of hair stood up jaggedly from his crown like the mane of a hyena. The man said nothing.

Irv was not easily daunted. He believed in the Darwinian struggle, believed, against all signs to the contrary, that he'd arisen to the top of the pack and that the choicest morsels of the feast of life were his for the taking. And though he wasn't nearly the bruiser he'd been when he started at nose tackle for Fox Lane High, he was used to wielding his paunch like a weapon and blustering his way through practically anything, from a potential mugging right on down to putting a snooty maître d' in his place. For all that, though, when he saw the size of the man, when he factored in his complexion and considered the oddness of the circumstances, he felt uncertain of himself. Felt as if the parameters of the world as he knew it had suddenly shifted. Felt, unaccountably, that he was in deep trouble. Characteristically, he fell back on bluster. "Who in hell are you?'?" he demanded.

The stranger, he now saw, wasn't black at all. Or, rather, he wasn't a Negro as he'd first supposed, but something else altogether. Swarthy, that's what he was. Like a Sicilian or a Greek. Or maybe an Arab. He saw too that the man was dressed almost identically to himself, in a Lacoste shirt, plaid slacks, and white Adidas. But this was no golf club dangling from the stranger's fingertips—it was a chainsaw. "Hell?" the big man echoed, his voice starting down low and then rising in mockery. "I don't believe it. Did you actually say 'Who in hell are you?'" He began to laugh in a shallow, breathy, and decidedly unsettling way.

It was getting darker by the minute, the trunks of the trees receding into the shadows, stars dimly visible now in the dome of the sky. There was a distant sound of fireworks and a sharp sudden smell of gunpowder on the air. "Are you . . . are you somebody's gardener or something?" Irv asked, glancing uncomfortably at the chainsaw.

This got the stranger laughing so hard he had to pound his breastbone and wipe the tears from his eyes. "Gardener?" he hooted, stamping around in the undergrowth and clutching his sides with the sheer hilarity of it. "You've got to be kidding. Come on, tell me you're kidding."

Irv felt himself growing annoyed. "I mean, because if you're not," he said, struggling to control his voice, "then I want to know what you're doing back here with that saw. This is private property, you know."

Abruptly, the big man stopped laughing. When he spoke, all trace of amusement had faded from his voice. "Oh?" he growled. "And just who does it belong to, then—it wouldn't be yours, by any chance, would it?"

It wasn't. As Irv well knew. In fact, he'd done a little title-searching six months back, when Tish had wanted to mow down the beeches and put in an ornamental koi pond with little pink bridges and mechanical waterfalls. The property, useless as it was, belonged to the old bird next door—"the Geek" was the only name Irv knew him by. Irv thought of bluffing, but the look in the stranger's eye made him think better of it. "It belongs to the old guy next door—Beltzer, I think his name is. Bitzer. Something like that."

The stranger was smiling now, but the smile wasn't a comforting one. "I see," he said. "So I guess you're trespassing too."

Irv had had enough. "We'll let the police decide that," he snapped, turning to stalk back up the lawn.

"Hey, Irv," the stranger said suddenly, "don't get huffy—old man Belcher won't be needing this plot anymore. You can hide all the golf balls you want down here."

The gloom thickened. Somewhere a dog began to howl. Irv felt the tight hairs at the base of his neck begin to stiffen. "How do you know my name?" he said, whirling around. "And how do you know what Belcher needs or doesn't need?" All of a sudden, Irv had the odd feeling that he'd seen this stranger somewhere before—real estate, wasn't it?

"Because he'll be dead five minutes from now, that's how." The big man let out a disgusted sigh. "Let's quit pissing around here—you know damn well who I am, Irv." He paused. "October twenty-two, 1955, Our Lady of the Immaculate Heart Church in Mount Kisco. Monsignor O'Kane. The topic is the transubstantiation of the flesh and you're screwing around with Alfred LaFarga in the back pew, talking 'Saturday Night Creature Features.' 'Did you see it when the mummy pulled that guy's eyes out?' you whispered. Alfred was this ratty little clown, looked like his shoulders were going to fall through his chest—now making a killing in grain futures in Des Moines, by the way—and he says, 'That wasn't his eye, shit-for-brains, it was his tongue.'"

Irv was stunned. Shocked silent for maybe the first time in his life. He'd seen it all, yes—but not this. It was incredible, it really was. He'd given up on all that God and Devil business the minute he left parochial school—no percentage in it—and now here it was, staring him in the face. It took him about thirty seconds to reinvent the world, and then he was thinking there might just be something in it for him. "All right," he said, "all right, yeah, I know who you are. Question is, what do you want with me?"

The stranger's face was consumed in shadow now, but Irv could sense that he was grinning. "Smart, Irv," the big man said, all the persuasion of a born closer creeping into his voice. "What's in it for me, right? Let's make a deal, right? The wife isn't working, the kids need designer jeans, PCs, and dirt bikes, and the mortgage has you on the run, am I right?"

He was right—of course he was right. How many times, bullying some loser over the phone or wheedling a few extra bucks out of some grasping old hag's retirement account, had Irv wondered if it was all worth it? How many times had he shoved his way through a knot of pink-haired punks on the subway only to get home all the sooner to his wife's nagging and his sons' pale, frightened faces? How many times had he told himself he deserved more, much more—ease and elegance, regular visits to the track and the Caribbean, his own firm, the two or maybe three million he needed to bail himself out for good? He folded his arms. The stranger, suddenly, was no more disturbing than sweet-faced Ben Franklin gazing up benevolently from a mountain of C-notes. "Talk to me," Irv said.

The big man took him by the arm and leaned forward to whisper in his ear. He wanted the usual deal, nothing less, and he held out to Irv the twin temptations of preternatural business success and filthy lucre. The lucre was buried right there in that shabby patch of woods, a hoard of Krugerrands, bullion, and silver candlesticks socked away by old man Belcher as a hedge against runaway inflation. The business success would result from the collusion of his silent partner—who was leaning into him now and giving off an odor oddly like that of a Szechuan kitchen—and it would take that initial stake and double and redouble it till it grew beyond counting. "What do you say, Irv?" the stranger crooned.

Irv said nothing. He was no fool. Poker face, he told himself. Never look eager. "I got to think about it," he said. He was wondering vaguely if he could rent a metal detector or something and kiss the creep off. "Give me twenty-four hours."

The big man drew away from him. "Hmph," he grunted contemptuously. "You think I come around every day? This is the deal of a lifetime I'm talking here, Irv." He paused a moment to let this sink in. "You don't want it, I can always go to Joe Luck across the street over there."

Irv was horrified. "You mean the Chinks?"

At that moment, the porch light winked on in the house behind him. The yellowish light caught the big man's face, bronzing it like a statue. He nodded. "Import/export. Joe's got connections with the big boys in Taiwan—and believe me, it isn't just backscratchers he's bringing in in those crates.

But I happen to know he's hard up for capital right now, and I think he'd jump at the chance—"

Irv cut him off. "Okay, okay," he said. "But how do I know you're the real thing? I mean, what proof do I have? Anybody could've talked to Alfred LaFarga."

The big man snorted. Then, with a flick of his wrist, he fired up the chainsaw. *Rrrrrrrrow*, it sang as he turned to the nearest tree and sent it home. Chips and sawdust flew off into the darkness as he guided the saw up and down, back and across, carving something into the bark, some message. Irv edged forward. Though the light was bad, he could just make out the jagged uppercase *B*, and then the *E* that followed it. When the big man reached the *L*, Irv anticipated him, but waited, arms folded, for the sequel. The stranger spelled out *BELCHER*, then sliced into the base of the tree; in the next moment the tree was toppling into the gloom with a shriek of clawing branches.

Irv waited till the growl of the saw died to a sputter. "Yeah?" he said. "So what does that prove?"

The big man merely grinned, his face hideous in the yellow light. Then he reached out and pressed his thumb to Irv's forehead and Irv could hear the sizzle and feel the sting of his own flesh burning. "There's my mark," the stranger said. "Tomorrow night, seven o'clock. Don't be late." And then he strode off into the shadows, the great hulk of him halved in an instant, and then halved again, as if he were sinking down into the earth itself.

The first thing Tish said to him as he stepped in the door was "Where the hell have you been? I've been shouting myself hoarse. There's an ambulance out front of the neighbor's place."

Irv shoved past her and parted the living-room curtains. Sure enough, there it was, red lights revolving and casting an infernal glow over the scene. There were voices, shouts, a flurry of people clustered round a stretcher and a pair of quick-legged men in hospital whites. "It's nothing," he said, a savage joy rising in his chest—it was true, true after all, and he was going to be rich—"just the old fart next door kicking off."

Tish gave him a hard look. She was a year younger than he—his college sweetheart, in fact—but she'd let herself go. She wasn't so much obese as muscular, big, broad-beamed—every inch her husband's match. "What's that on your forehead?" she asked, her voice pinched with suspicion.

He lifted his hand absently to the spot. The flesh seemed rough and abraded, raised in an annealed disc the size of a quarter. "Oh, this?" he said, feigning nonchalance. "Hit my head on the barbecue."

She was having none of it. With a move so sudden it would have surprised a cat, she shot forward and seized his arm. "And what's that I smell—

Chinese food?" Her eyes leapt at him; her jaw clenched. "I suppose the enchiladas weren't good enough for you, huh?"

He jerked his arm away. "Oh, yeah, I know—you really slaved over those enchiladas, didn't you? Christ, you might have chipped a nail or something tearing the package open and shoving them in the microwave."

"Don't give me that shit," she snarled, snatching his arm back and digging her nails in for emphasis. "The mark on your head, the Chinese food, that stupid grin on your face when you saw the ambulance—I know you. Something's up, isn't it?" She clung to his arm like some inescapable force of nature, like the tar in the La Brea pits or the undertow at Rockaway Beach. "Isn't it?"

Irv Cherniske was not a man to confide in his wife. He regarded marriage as an arbitrary and essentially adversarial relationship, akin to the yoking of prisoners on the chain gang. But this once, because the circumstances were so arresting and the stranger's proposal so unique (not to mention final), he relented and let her in on his secret.

At first, she wouldn't believe it. It was another of his lies, he was covering something up—*devils*: did he think she was born yesterday? But when she saw how solemn he was, how shaken, how feverish with lust over the prospect of laying his hands on the loot, she began to come around. By midnight she was urging him to go back and seal the bargain. "You fool. You idiot. What do you need twenty-four hours for? Go. Go now."

Though Irv had every intention of doing just that—in his own time, of course—he wasn't about to let her push him into anything. "You think I'm going to damn myself forever just to please you?" he sneered.

Tish took it for half a beat, then she sprang up from the sofa as if it were electrified. "All right," she snapped. "I'll find the son of a bitch myself and we'll both roast—but I tell you I want those Krugerrands and all the rest of it too. And I want it now."

A moment later, she was gone—out the back door and into the soft suburban night. Let her go, Irv thought in disgust, but despite himself he sat back to wait for her. For better than an hour he sat there in his mortgaged living room, dreaming of crushing his enemies and ascending the high-flown corridors of power, envisioning the cut-glass decanter in the bar of the Rolls and breakfast on the yacht, but at last he found himself nodding and decided to call it a day. He rose, stretched, and then padded through the dining room and kitchen to the back porch. He swung open the door and halfheartedly called his wife's name. There was no answer. He shrugged, retraced his steps, and wearily mounted the stairs to the bedroom: devil or no devil, he had a train to catch in the morning.

Tish was sullen at breakfast. She looked sorrowful and haggard and there were bits of twig and leaf caught in her hair. The boys bent silently over their caramel crunchies, waiflike in the khaki jerseys and oversized shorts they wore to camp. Irv studied his watch while gulping coffee. "Well," he said, addressing his stone-faced wife, "any luck?"

At first she wouldn't answer him. And when she did, it was in a voice so constricted with rage she sounded as if she were being throttled. Yes, she'd found the sorry son of a bitch, all right—after traipsing all over hell and back for half the night—and after all that he'd had the gall to turn his back on her. He wasn't in the mood, he said. But if she were to come back at noon with a peace offering—something worth talking about, something to show she was serious—he'd see what he could do for her. That's how he'd put it.

For a moment Irv was seized with jealousy and resentment—was she trying to cut him out, was that it?—but then he remembered how the stranger had singled him out, had come to him, and he relaxed. He had nothing to worry about. It was Tish. She just didn't know how to bargain, that was all. Her idea of a give and take was to reiterate her demands, over and over, each time in a shriller tone than the last. She'd probably pushed and pushed till even the devil wouldn't have her. "I'll be home early," he said, and then he was driving through a soft misting rain to the station.

It was past seven when finally he did get home. He pulled into the driveway and was surprised to see his sons sitting glumly on the front stoop, their legs drawn up under them, rain drooling steadily from the eaves. "Where's your mother?" he asked, hurrying up the steps in alarm. The elder, Shane, a pudgy, startled-looking boy of eight, whose misfortune it was to favor Tish about the nose and eyes, began to whimper. "She, she never came back," he blubbered, smearing snot across his lip.

Filled with apprehension—and a strange, airy exhilaration too: maybe she was gone, gone for good!—Irv dialed his mother. "Ma?" he shouted into the phone. "Can you come over and watch the kids? It's Tish. She's missing." He'd no sooner set the phone down than he noticed the blank space on the wall above the sideboard. The painting was gone. He'd always hated the thing—a gloomy dark swirl of howling faces with the legend "Cancer Dreams" scrawled in red across the bottom, a small monstrosity Tish had insisted on buying when he could barely make the car payments—but it was worth a bundle, that much he knew. And the moment he saw that empty space on the wall he knew she'd taken it to the big man in the woods—but what else had she taken? While the boys sat listlessly before the TV with a bag of taco chips, he tore through the house. Her jewelry would have been the first thing to go, and he wasn't surprised to see that it had disappeared, teak box and all. But in growing consternation he discovered that his coin collection was gone too, as were his fly rod and his hip waders and the bottle of V.S.O.P. he'd been saving for the World Series. The whole business had apparently been bundled up in the Irish-linen cloth that had shrouded the dining-room table for as long as he could remember.

Irv stood there a moment over the denuded table, overcome with grief and rage. She *was* cutting him out, the bitch. She and the big man were probably down there right now, dancing round a gaping black hole in the earth. Or worse, she was on the train to New York with every last Krugerrand of Belcher's hoard, heading for the Caymans in a chartered yacht, hurtling out of Kennedy in a big 747, two huge, bursting, indescribably heavy trunks nestled safely in the baggage compartment beneath her. Irv rushed to the window. There were the woods: still, silent, slick with wet. He saw nothing but trees.

In the next instant, he was out the back door, down the grassy slope, and into the damp fastness of the woods. He'd forgotten all about the kids, his mother, the house at his back—all he knew was that he had to find Tish. He kicked through dead leaves and rotting branches, tore at the welter of grapevine and sumac that seemed to rise up like a barrier before him. "Tish!" he bawled.

The drizzle had turned to a steady, pelting rain. Irv's face and hands were scratched and insect-bitten and the hair clung to his scalp like some strange species of mold. His suit—all four hundred bucks' worth—was ruined. He was staggering through a stubborn tangle of briars, his mind veering sharply toward the homicidal end of the spectrum, when a movement up ahead made him catch his breath. Stumbling forward, he flushed a great black carrion bird from the bushes; as it rose silently into the darkening sky, he spotted the tablecloth. Still laden, it hung from the lower branches of a pocked and leprous oak. Irv looked round him cautiously. All was still, no sound but for the hiss of rain in the leaves. He straightened up and lumbered toward the pale damp sack, thinking at least to recover his property.

No such luck. When he lifted the bundle down, he was disappointed by its weight; when he opened it, he was shocked to the roots of his hair. The tablecloth contained two things only: a bloody heart and a bloody liver. His own heart was beating so hard he thought his temples would burst; in horror he flung the thing to the ground. Only then did he notice that the undergrowth round the base of the tree was beaten down and trampled, as if a scuffle had taken place beneath it. There was a fandango of footprints in the mud and clumps of stiff black hair were scattered about like confetti—and wasn't that blood on the bark of the tree?

"Irv," murmured a voice at his back, and he whirled round in a panic. There he was, the big man, his swarthy features hooded in shadow. This time he was wearing a business suit in a muted gray check, a power-yellow tie, and an immaculate trenchcoat. In place of the chainsaw, he carried a shovel, which he'd flung carelessly over one shoulder. "Whoa," he said, holding up a massive palm, "I didn't mean to startle you." He took a step forward and Irv could see that he was grinning. "All's I want to know is do we have a deal or not?"

"Where's Tish?" Irv demanded, his voice quavering. But even as he spoke he saw the angry red welt running the length of the big man's jaw and disappearing into the hair at his temple, and he knew.

The big man shrugged. "What do you care? She's gone, that's all that matters. Hey, no more of that nagging whiny voice, no more money down the drain on face cream and high heels—just think, you'll never have to wake up again to that bitchy pout and those nasty red little eyes. You're free, Irv. I did you a favor."

Irv regarded the stranger with awe. Tish was no mean adversary, and judging from the look of the poor devil's face, she'd gone down fighting.

The big man dropped his shovel to the ground and there was a clink of metal on metal. "Right here, Irv," he whispered. "Half a million easy. Cash. Tax-free. And with my help you'll watch it grow to fifty times that."

Irv glanced at the bloody tablecloth and then back up at the big man in the trenchcoat. A slow grin spread across his lips.

Coming to terms wasn't so easy, however, and it was past dark before they'd concluded their bargain. At first the stranger insisted on Irv's going into one of the big Hollywood talent agencies, but when Irv balked, he said he figured the legal profession was just about as good—but you needed a degree for that, and begging Irv's pardon, he was a bit old to be going back to school, wasn't he? "Why can't I stay where I am," Irv countered, "in stocks and bonds? With all this cash I could quit Tiller Ponzi and set up my own office."

The big man scratched his chin and laid a thoughtful finger alongside his nose. "Yeah," he murmured after a moment, "yeah, I hadn't thought of that. But I like it. You could promise them thirty percent and then play the futures market and gouge them till they bleed."

Irv came alive at the prospect. "Bleed 'em dry," he hooted. "I'll scalp and bucket and buy off the CFTC investigators, and then I'll set up an offshore company to hide the profits." He paused, overcome with the beauty of it. "I'll screw them right and left."

"Deal?" the devil said.

Irv took the big, callused hand in his own. "Deal."

Ten years later, Irv Cherniske was one of the wealthiest men in New York. He talked widows into giving him their retirement funds to invest in ironclad securities and sure bets, lost them four or five hundred thousand, and charged half that again in commissions. With preternatural luck his own investments paid off time and again and he eventually set up an inside-trading scheme that made guesswork superfluous. The police, of course, had been curious about Tish's disappearance, but Irv showed them the grisly tablecloth and the crude hole in which the killer had no doubt tried to bury her, and they launched an intensive manhunt that dragged on for months but produced neither corpse nor perpetrator. The boys he shunted off to his mother's, and when they were old enough, to a military school in Tangiers. Two months after his wife's disappearance, the newspapers uncovered a series of ritual beheadings in Connecticut and dropped all mention of the "suburban ghoul," as they'd dubbed Tish's killer; a week after that, Tish was forgotten and Beechwood went back to sleep.

It was in the flush of his success, when he had everything he'd ever wanted—the yacht, the sweet and compliant young mistress, the pair of Rolls Corniches, and the houses in the Bahamas and Aspen, not to mention the new wing he'd added to the old homestead in Beechwood—that Irv began to have second thoughts about the deal he'd made. Eternity was a long time, yes, but when he'd met the stranger in the woods that night it had seemed a long way off too. Now he was in his fifties, heavier than ever, with soaring blood pressure and flat feet, and the end of his career in this vale of profits was drawing uncomfortably near. It was only natural that he should begin to cast about for a loophole.

And so it was that he returned to the church—not the Roman church, to which he'd belonged as a boy, but the Church of the Open Palm, Reverend Jimmy, Pastor. He came to Reverend Jimmy one rainy winter night with a fire in his gut and an immortal longing in his heart. He sat through a three-hour sermon in which Reverend Jimmy spat fire, spoke in tongues, healed the lame, and lectured on the sanctity of the one and only God— profit—and then distributed copies of the *Reverend Jimmy Church–Sponsored Investment Guide* with the chili and barbecue recipes on the back page.

After the service, Irv found his way to Reverend Jimmy's office at the back of the church. He waited his turn among the other supplicants with growing impatience, but he reminded himself that the way to salvation lay through humility and forbearance. At long last he was ushered into the presence of the Reverend himself. "What can I do for you, brother?" Reverend Jimmy asked. Though he was from Staten Island, Reverend Jimmy spoke in the Alabama hog-farmer's dialect peculiar to his tribe.

"I need help, Reverend," Irv confessed, flinging himself down on a leather sofa worn smooth by the buttocks of the faithful.

Reverend Jimmy made a small pyramid of his fingers and leaned back in his adjustable chair. He was a youngish man—no older than thirty-five or so, Irv guessed—and he was dressed in a flannel shirt, penny loafers, and a plaid fishing hat that masked his glassy blue eyes. "Speak to me, brother," he said.

Irv looked down at the floor, then shot a quick glance round the office—an office uncannily like his own, right down to the computer terminal, mahogany desk, and potted palms—and then whispered, "You're probably not going to believe this."

Reverend Jimmy lit himself a cigarette and shook out the match with a snap of his wrist. "Try me," he drawled.

When Irv had finished pouring out his heart, Reverend Jimmy leaned forward with a beatific smile on his face. "Brother," he said, "believe me, your story's nothin' new—I handle just as bad and sometimes worser ever day. Cheer up, brother: salvation is on the way!"

Then Reverend Jimmy made a number of pointed inquiries into Irv's financial status and fixed the dollar amount of his tithe—to be paid weekly in small bills, no checks please. Next, with a practiced flourish, he produced a copy of Adam Smith's *Wealth of Nations*, the text of which was interspersed with biblical quotes in support of its guiding theses, and pronounced Irv saved. "You got your holy book," the Reverend Jimmy boomed as Irv ducked gratefully out the door, "—y'all keep it with you ever day, through sleet and snow and dark of night, and old Satan he'll be paarless against you."

And so it was. Irv gained in years and gained in wealth. He tithed the Church of the Open Palm, and he kept the holy book with him at all times. One day, just after his sixtieth birthday, his son Shane came to the house to see him. It was a Sunday and the market was closed, but after an early-morning dalliance with Sushoo, his adept and oracular mistress, he'd placed a half dozen calls to Hong Kong, betting on an impending monsoon in Burma to drive the price of rice through the ceiling. He was in the Blue Room, as he liked to call the salon in the west wing, eating a bit of poached salmon and looking over a coded letter from Butram, his deep man in the SEC. The holy book lay on the desk beside him.

Shane was a bloated young lout in his late twenties, a sorrowful, shameless leech who'd flunked out of half a dozen schools and had never held a job in his life—unlike Morgan, who'd parlayed the small stake his father had given him into the biggest used-car dealership in the country. Unwashed, unshaven, the gut he'd inherited from his father peeping out from beneath a Hawaiian shirt so lurid it looked as if it had been used to stanch wounds at the emergency ward, Shane loomed over his father's desk. "I need twenty big ones," he grunted, giving his father a look of beery disdain. "Bad week at the track."

Irv looked up from his salmon and saw Tish's nose, Tish's eyes, saw the greedy, worthless, contemptible slob his son had become. In a sudden rage he shot from the chair and hammered the desk so hard the plate jumped six inches. "I'll be damned if I give you another cent," he roared.

Just then there was a knock at the door. His face contorted with rage, Irv shoved past his son and stormed across the room, a curse on his lips for Magdalena, the maid, who should have known better than to bother him at a time like this. He tore open the door only to find that it wasn't Magdalena at all, but his acquaintance of long ago, the big black man with the wild mane of hair and the vague odor of stir-fry on his clothes. "Time's up, Irv," the big man said gruffly. In vain did Irv look over his shoulder to where the Reverend Jimmy's holy book sat forlorn on the desk beside the plate of salmon that was already growing cold. The big man took his arm in a grip of steel and whisked him through the hallway, down the stairs, and out across the lawn to where a black BMW with smoked windows sat running at the curb. Irv turned his pale fleshy face to the house and saw his son staring down at him from above, and then the big man laid an implacable hand on his shoulder and shoved him into the car.

The following day, of course, as is usual in these cases, all of Irv's liquid assets—his stocks and bonds, his Swiss and Bahamian bankbooks, even the wads of new-minted hundred dollar bills he kept stashed in safe-deposit boxes all over the country—turned to cinders. Almost simultaneously, the house was gutted by a fire of mysterious origin, and both Rolls-Royces were destroyed. Joe Luck, who shuffled out on his lawn in a silk dressing gown at the height of the blaze, claimed to have seen a great black bird emerge from the patch of woods behind the house and mount into the sky high above the roiling billows of steam and smoke, but for some reason, no one else seemed to have shared his vision.

The big refurbished house on Beechwood Drive has a new resident now, a corporate lawyer by the name of O'Faolain. If he's bothered by the unfortunate history of the place—or even, for that matter, aware of it—no one can say. He knows his immediate neighbors as the Chinks, the Fat Family, and the Turf Builders. They know him as the Shyster.

15

THE RICH BROTHER
Tobias Wolff

There were two brothers, Pete and Donald.

Pete, the older brother, was in real estate. He and his wife had a Century 21 franchise in Santa Cruz. Pete worked hard and made a lot of money, but not any more than he thought he deserved. He had two daughters, a sailboat, a house from which he could see a thin slice of the ocean, and friends doing well enough in their own lives not to wish bad luck on him. Donald, the younger brother, was still single. He lived alone, painted houses when he found the work, and got deeper in debt to Pete when he didn't.

No one would have taken them for brothers. Where Pete was stout and hearty and at home in the world, Donald was bony, grave, and obsessed with the fate of his soul. Over the years Donald had worn the images of two different Perfect Masters around his neck. Out of devotion to the second of these he entered an ashram in Berkeley, where he nearly died of undiagnosed hepatitis. By the time Pete finished paying the medical bills Donald had become a Christian. He drifted from church to church, then joined a pentecostal community that met somewhere in the Mission District to sing in tongues and swap prophecies.

Pete couldn't make sense of it. Their parents were both dead, but while they were alive neither of them had found it necessary to believe in anything. They managed to be decent people without making fools of themselves, and Pete had the same ambition. He thought that the whole thing was an excuse for Donald to take himself seriously.

The trouble was that Donald couldn't content himself with worrying about his own soul. He had to worry about everyone else's, and especially Pete's. He handed down his judgments in ways that he seemed to consider subtle: through significant silence, innuendo, looks of mild despair that said, *Brother, what have you come to?* What Pete had come to, as far as he could tell, was prosperity. That was the real issue between them. Pete prospered and Donald did not prosper.

At the age of forty Pete took up skydiving. He made his first jump with two friends who'd started only a few months earlier and were already doing stunts. They were both coked to the gills when they jumped but Pete wanted to do it straight, at least the first time, and he was glad that he did. He would never have used the word "mystical," but that was how Pete felt about the experience. Later he made the mistake of trying to describe it to Donald, who kept asking how much it cost and then acted appalled when Pete told him.

"At least I'm trying something new," Pete said. "At least I'm breaking the pattern."

Not long after that conversation Donald also broke the pattern, by going to live on a farm outside of Paso Robles. The farm was owned by several members of Donald's community, who had bought it and moved there with the idea of forming a family of faith. That was how Donald explained it in the first letter he sent. Every week Pete heard how happy Donald was, how "in the Lord." He told Pete that he was praying for him, he and the rest of Pete's brothers and sisters on the farm.

"I only have one brother," Pete wanted to answer, "and that's enough." But he kept this thought to himself.

In November the letters stopped. Pete didn't worry about this at first, but when he called Donald at Thanksgiving Donald was grim. He tried to sound upbeat but he didn't try hard enough to make it convincing. "Now listen," Pete said, "you don't have to stay in that place if you don't want to."

"I'll be all right," Donald answered.

"That's not the point. Being all right is not the point. If you don't like what's going on up there, then get out."

"I'm all right," Donald said again, more firmly. "I'm doing fine."

But he called Pete a week later and said that he was quitting the farm. When Pete asked him where he intended to go, Donald admitted that he had no plan. His car had been repossessed just before he left the city, and he was flat broke.

"I'll guess you'll have to stay with us," Pete said.

Donald put up a show of resistance. Then he gave in. "Just until I get my feet on the ground," he said.

"Right," Pete said. "Check out your options." He told Donald he'd send him money for a bus ticket, but as they were about to hang up Pete changed his mind. He knew that Donald would try hitchhiking to save the fare. Pete didn't want him out on the road all alone where some head case could pick him up, where anything could happen to him.

"Better yet," he said. "I'll come and get you."

"You don't have to do that. I didn't expect you to do that," Donald said. He added, "It's a pretty long drive."

"Just tell me how to get there."

But Donald wouldn't give him directions. He said that the farm was too depressing, that Pete wouldn't like it. Instead, he insisted on meeting Pete at a service station called Jonathan's Mechanical Emporium.

"You must be kidding," Pete said.

"It's close to the highway," Donald said. "I didn't name it."

"That's one for the collection," Pete said.

The day before he left to bring Donald home, Pete received a letter from a man who described himself as "head of household" at the farm where Donald had been living. From this letter Pete learned that Donald had not quit the farm, but had been asked to leave. The letter was written on the back of a mimeographed survey form asking people to record their response to a ceremony of some kind. The last question said:

What did you feel during the liturgy?
a) Being
b) Becoming
c) Being and Becoming
d) None of the Above
e) All of the Above

Pete tried to forget the letter. But of course he couldn't. Each time he thought of it he felt crowded and breathless, a feeling that came over him again when he drove into the service station and saw Donald sitting against a wall with his head on his knees. It was late afternoon. A paper cup tumbled slowly past Donald's feet, pushed by the damp wind.

Pete honked and Donald raised his head. He smiled at Pete, then stood and stretched. His arms were long and thin and white. He wore a red bandanna across his forehead, a T-shirt with a couple of words on the front. Pete couldn't read them because the letters were inverted.

"Grow up," Pete yelled. "Get a Mercedes."

Donald came up to the window. He bent down and said, "Thanks for coming. You must be totally whipped."

"I'll make it." Pete pointed at Donald's T-shirt. "What's that supposed to say?"

Donald looked down at his shirtfront. "Try God. I guess I put it on backwards. Pete, could I borrow a couple of dollars? I owe these people for coffee and sandwiches."

Pete took five twenties from his wallet and held them out the window.

Donald stepped back as if horrified. "I don't need that much."

"I can't keep track of all these nickels and dimes," Pete said. "Just pay me back when your ship comes in." He waved the bills impatiently. "Go on—take it."

"Only for now." Donald took the money and went into the service station office. He came out carrying two orange sodas, one of which he gave Pete as he got into the car. "My treat," he said.

"No bags?"

"Wow, thanks for reminding me," Donald said. He balanced his drink on the dashboard, but the slight rocking of the car as he got out tipped it onto the passenger's seat, where half its contents foamed over before Pete could snatch it up again. Donald looked on while Pete held the bottle out the window, soda running down his fingers.

"Wipe it up," Pete told him. "Quick!"

"With what?"

Pete stared at Donald. "That shirt. Use the shirt."

Donald pulled a long face but did as he was told, his pale skin puckering against the wind.

"Great, just great," Pete said. "We haven't even left the gas station yet."

Afterward, on the highway, Donald said, "This is a new car, isn't it?"

"Yes. This is a new car."

"Is that why you're so upset about the seat?"

"Forget it, okay? Let's just forget about it."

"I said I was sorry."

Pete said, "I just wish you'd be more careful. These seats are made of leather. That stain won't come out, not to mention the smell. I don't see why I can't have leather seats that smell like leather instead of orange pop."

"What was wrong with the other car?"

Pete glanced over at Donald. Donald had raised the hood of the blue sweatshirt he'd put on. The peaked hood above his gaunt, watchful face gave him the look of an inquisitor.

"There wasn't anything wrong with it," Pete said. "I just happened to like this one better."

Donald nodded.

There was a long silence between them as Pete drove on and the day darkened toward evening. On either side of the road lay stubble-covered fields. A line of low hills ran along the horizon, topped here and there with trees black against the gray sky. In the approaching line of cars a driver turned on his headlights. Pete did the same.

"So what happened?" he asked. "Farm life not your bag?"

Donald took some time to answer, and at last he said, simply, "It was my fault."

"What was your fault?"

"The whole thing. Don't play dumb, Pete. I know they wrote to you." Donald looked at Pete, then stared out the windshield again.

"I'm not playing dumb."

Donald shrugged.

"All I really know is they asked you to leave," Pete went on. "I don't know any of the particulars."

"I blew it," Donald said. "Believe me, you don't want to hear the gory details."

"Sure I do," Pete said. He added, "Everybody likes the gory details."

"You mean everybody likes to hear how someone else messed up."

"Right," Pete said. "That's the way it is here on Spaceship Earth."

Donald bent one knee onto the front seat and leaned against the door so that he was facing Pete instead of the windshield. Pete was aware of Donald's scrutiny. He waited. Night was coming on in a rush now, filling the hollows of the land. Donald's long cheeks and deep-set eyes were dark with shadow. His brow was white. "Do you ever dream about me?" Donald asked.

"Do I ever dream about you? What kind of question is that? Of course I don't dream about you," Pete said, untruthfully.

"What do you dream about?"

"Sex and money. Mostly money. A nightmare is when I dream I don't have any."

"You're just making that up," Donald said.

Pete smiled.

"Sometimes I wake up at night," Donald went on, "and I can tell you're dreaming about me."

"We were talking about the farm," Pete said. "Let's finish that conversation and then we can talk about our various out-of-body experiences and the interesting things we did during previous incarnations."

For a moment Donald looked like a grinning skull; then he turned serious again. "There's not much to tell," he said. "I just didn't do anything right."

"That's a little vague," Pete said.

"Well, like the groceries. Whenever it was my turn to get the groceries I'd blow it somehow. I'd bring the groceries home and half of them would be missing, or I'd have all the wrong things, the wrong kind of flour or the wrong kind of chocolate or whatever. One time I gave them away. It's not funny, Pete."

Pete said, "Who did you give the groceries to?"

"Just some people I picked up on the way home. Some field-workers. They had about eight kids with them and they didn't even speak English—just nodded their heads. Still, I shouldn't have given away the groceries. Not all of them, anyway. I really learned my lesson about that. You have to be practical. You have to be fair to yourself." Donald leaned forward, and Pete could sense his excitement. "There's nothing actually wrong with being in business," he said. "As long as you're fair to other people, you can still be fair to yourself. I'm thinking of going into business, Pete."

"We'll talk about it," Pete said. "So, that's the story? There isn't any more to it than that?"

"What did they tell you?" Donald asked.

"Nothing."

"They must have told you something."

Pete shook his head.

"They didn't tell you about the fire?" When Pete shook his head again Donald regarded him for a time, then said, "I don't know. It was stupid. I just completely lost it." He folded his arms across his chest and slumped back into the corner. "Everybody had to take turns cooking dinner. I usually did tuna casserole or spaghetti with garlic bread. But this one night I thought I'd do something different, something really interesting." Donald looked sharply at Pete. "It's all a big laugh to you, isn't it?"

"I'm sorry," Pete said.

"You don't know when to quit. You just keep hitting away."

"Tell me about the fire, Donald."

Donald kept watching him. "You have this compulsion to make me look foolish."

"Come off it, Donald. Don't make a big thing out of this."

"I know why you do it. It's because you don't have any purpose in life. You're afraid to relate to people who do, so you make fun of them."

"Relate," Pete said softly.

"You're basically a very frightened individual," Donald said. "Very threatened. You've always been like that. Do you remember when you used to try to kill me?"

"I don't have any compulsion to make you look foolish, Donald—You do it yourself. You're doing it right now."

"You can't tell me you don't remember," Donald said. "It was after my operation. You remember that."

"Sort of." Pete shrugged. "Not really."

"Oh yes." Donald said. "Do you want to see the scar?"

"I remember you had an operation. I don't remember the specifics, that's all. And I sure as hell don't remember trying to kill you."

"Oh yes," Donald repeated, maddeningly. "You bet your life you did. All the time. The thing was, I couldn't have anything happen to me where they sewed me up because then my intestines would come apart again and poison me. That was a big issue, Pete. Mom was always in a state about me climbing trees and so on. And you used to hit me there every chance you got."

"Mom was in a state every time you burped," Pete said. "I don't know. Maybe I bumped into you accidentally once or twice. I never did it deliberately."

"Every chance you got," Donald said. "Like when the folks went out at night and left you to baby-sit. I'd hear them say good night, and then I'd hear the car start up, and when they were gone I'd lie there and listen. After a while I would hear you coming down the hall, and I would close my eyes and pretend to be asleep. There were nights when you would stand outside the door, just stand there, and then go away again. But most nights you'd open the door and I would hear you in the room with me, breathing. You'd come over and sit next to me on the bed—you remember, Pete, you have to—you'd sit next to me on the bed and pull the sheets back. If I was on my stomach you'd roll me over. Then you would lift up my pajama shirt and start hitting me on my stitches. You'd hit me as hard as you could, over and over. And I would just keep lying there with my eyes closed. I was afraid that you'd get mad if you knew I was awake. Is that strange or what? I was afraid that you'd get mad if you found out that I knew you were trying to kill me." Donald laughed. "Come on, you can't tell me you don't remember that."

"It might have happened once or twice. Kids do those things. I can't get all excited about something I maybe did twenty-five years ago."

"No maybe about it. You did it."

Pete said, "You're wearing me out with this stuff. We've got a long drive ahead of us and if you don't back off pretty soon we aren't going to make it. You aren't, anyway."

Donald turned away.

"I'm doing my best," Pete said. The self-pity in his own voice made the words sound like a lie. But they weren't a lie! He was doing his best.

The car topped a rise. In the distance Pete saw a cluster of lights that blinked out when he started downhill. There was no moon. The sky was low and black.

"Come to think of it," Pete said, "I did have a dream about you the other night." Then he added, impatiently, as if Donald were badgering him. "A couple of other nights too. I'm getting hungry," he said.

"The same dream?"

"Different dreams. I only remember one of them well. There was something wrong with me, and you were helping out. Taking care of me. Just the two of us. I don't know where everybody else was supposed to be."

Pete left it at that. He didn't tell Donald that in this dream he was blind.

"I wonder if that was when I woke up," Donald said. He added, "I'm sorry I got into that thing about my scar. I keep trying to forget it but I guess I never will. Not really. It was pretty strange, having someone around all the time who wanted to get rid of me."

"Kid stuff," Pete said. "Ancient history."

They ate dinner at a Denny's on the other side of King City. As Pete was paying the check he heard a man behind him say, "Excuse me, but I wonder if I might ask which way you're going?" and Donald answered, "Santa Cruz."

"Perfect," the man said.

Pete could see him in the fish-eye mirror above the cash register: a red blazer with some kind of crest on the pocket, little black mustache, glossy black hair combed down on his forehead like a Roman emperor's. A rug, Pete thought. Definitely a rug.

Pete got his change and turned. "Why is that perfect?" he asked.

The man looked at Pete. He had a soft ruddy face that was doing its best to express pleasant surprise, as if this new wrinkle were all he could have wished for, but the eyes behind the aviator glasses showed signs of regret. His lips were moist and shiny. "I take it you're together," he said.

"You got it," Pete told him.

"All the better, then," the man went on. "It so happens I'm going to Santa Cruz myself. Had a spot of car trouble down the road. The old Caddy let me down."

"What kind of trouble?" Pete asked.

"Engine trouble," the man said. "I'm afraid it's a bit urgent. My daughter is sick. Urgently sick. I've got a telegram here." He patted the breast pocket of his blazer.

Pete grinned. Amazing, he thought, the old sick daughter ploy, but before he could say anything Donald got into the act again. "No problem," Donald said. "We've got tons of room."

"Not that much room," Pete said.

Donald nodded. "I'll put my things in the trunk."

"The trunk's full," Pete told him.

"It so happens I'm traveling light," the man said. "This leg of the trip anyway. In fact I don't have any luggage at this particular time."

Pete said, "Left it in the old Caddy, did you?"

"Exactly," the man said.

"No problem," Donald repeated. He walked outside and the man went with him. Together they strolled across the parking lot, Pete following at a distance. When they reached Pete's car Donald raised his face to the sky, and the man did the same. They stood there looking up. "Dark night," Donald said.

"Stygian," the man said.

Pete still had it in mind to brush him off, but he didn't do that. Instead he unlocked the door for him. He wanted to see what would happen. It was an adventure, but not a dangerous adventure. The man might steal Pete's ashtrays but he wouldn't kill him. If Pete got killed on the road it would be by some spiritual person in a sweatsuit, someone with his eyes on the far horizon and a wet Try God T-shirt in his duffel bag.

As soon as they left the parking lot the man lit a cigar. He blew a cloud of smoke over Pete's shoulder and sighed with pleasure. "Put it out," Pete told him.

"Of course," the man said. Pete looked into the rear-view mirror and saw the man take another long puff before dropping the cigar out the window. "Forgive me," he said. "I should have asked. Name's Webster, by the way."

Donald turned and looked back at him. "First name or last?"

The man hesitated. "Last," he said finally.

"I know a Webster," Donald said. "Mick Webster."

"There are many of us," Webster said.

"Big fellow, wooden leg," Pete said.

Donald gave Pete a look.

Webster shook his head. "Doesn't ring a bell. Still, I wouldn't deny the connection. Might be one of the cousinry."

"What's your daughter got?" Pete asked.

"That isn't clear," Webster answered. "It appears to be a female complaint of some nature. Then again it may be tropical." He was quiet for a moment and then added: "If indeed it *is* tropical, I will have to assume some of the blame myself. It was my own vaulting ambition that first led us to the tropics and kept us in the tropics all those many years, exposed to every evil. Truly I have much to answer for. I left my wife there."

Donald said quietly, "You mean she died?"

"I buried her with these hands. The earth will be repaid, gold for gold."

"Which tropics?" Pete asked.

"The tropics of Peru."

"What part of Peru are they in?"

"The lowlands," Webster said.

Pete nodded. "What's it like down there?"

"Another world," Webster said. His tone was sepulchral. "A world better imagined than described."

"Far out," Pete said.

The three men rode in silence for a time. A line of trucks went past in the other direction, trailers festooned with running lights, engines roaring.

"Yes," Webster said at last, "I have much to answer for."

Pete smiled at Donald, but Donald turned in his seat again and was gazing at Webster. "I'm sorry about your wife," Donald said.

"What did she die of?" Pete asked.

"A wasting illness," Webster said. "The doctors have no name for it, but I do." He leaned forward and said, fiercely, "*Greed.*" Then he slumped back against his seat. "My greed, not hers. She wanted no part of it."

Pete bit his lip. Webster was a find and Pete didn't want to scare him off by hooting at him. In a voice low and innocent of knowingness, he asked, "What took you there?"

"It's difficult for me to talk about."

"Try," Pete told him.

"A cigar would make it easier."

Donald turned to Pete and said, "It's okay with me."

"All right," Pete said. "Go ahead. Just keep the window rolled down."

"Much obliged." A match flared. There were eager sucking sounds.

"Let's hear it," Pete said.

"I am by training an engineer," Webster began. "My work has exposed me to all but one of the continents, to desert and alp and forest, to every terrain and season of earth. Some years ago I was hired by the Peruvian government to search for tungsten in the tropics. My wife and daughter accompanied me. We were the only white people for a thousand miles in any direction, and we had no choice but to live as the Indians lived—to share their food and drink and even their culture."

Pete said, "You knew the lingo, did you?"

"We picked it up." The ember of the cigar bobbed up and down. "We were used to learning as necessity decreed. At any rate, it became evident after a couple of years that there was no tungsten to be found. My wife had fallen ill and was pleading to be taken home. But I was deaf to her pleas, because by then I was on the trail of another metal—a metal far more valuable than tungsten."

"Let me guess," Pete said. "Gold?"

Donald looked at Pete, then back at Webster.

"Gold," Webster said. "A vein of gold greater than the Mother Lode itself. After I found the first traces of it nothing could tear me away from my search—not the sickness of my wife nor anything else. I was determined to uncover the vein, and so I did—but not before I laid my wife to rest. As I say, the earth will be repaid."

Webster was quiet. Then he said, "But life must go on. In the years since my wife's death I have been making the arrangements necessary to open the mine. I could have done it immediately, of course, enriching myself beyond measure, but I knew what that would mean—the exploitation of our beloved Indians, the brutal destruction of their environment. I felt I had too much to atone for already." Webster paused, and when he spoke again his voice was dull and rushed, as if he had used up all the interest he had in his own words. "Instead I drew up a program for returning the bulk of the wealth to the Indians themselves. A kind of trust fund. The interest alone will allow them to secure their ancient lands and rights in perpetuity. At the same time, our investors will be rewarded a thousandfold. Two thousandfold. Everyone will prosper together."

"That's great," Donald said. "That's the way it ought to be."

Pete said, "I'm willing to bet that you just happen to have a few shares left. Am I right?"

Webster made no reply.

"Well?" Pete knew that Webster was on to him now, but he didn't care. The story had bored him. He'd expected something different, something original, and Webster had let him down. He hadn't even tried. Pete felt sour and stale. His eyes burned from cigar smoke and the high beams of road-hogging truckers. "Douse the stogie," he said to Webster. "I told you to keep the window down."

"Got a little nippy back there."

Donald said, "Hey, Pete. Lighten up."

"Douse it!"

Webster sighed. He got rid of the cigar.

"I'm a wreck," Pete said to Donald. "You want to drive for a while?"

Donald nodded.

Pete pulled over and they changed places.

Webster kept his counsel in the back seat. Donald hummed while he drove, until Pete told him to stop. Then everything was quiet.

Donald was humming again when Pete woke up. Pete stared sullenly at the road, at the white lines sliding past the car. After a few moments of this he turned and said, "How long have I been out?"

Donald glanced at him. "Twenty, twenty-five minutes."

Pete looked behind him and saw that Webster was gone. "Where's our friend?"

"You just missed him. He got out in Soledad. He told me to say thanks and goodbye."

"Soledad? What about his sick daughter? How did he explain her away?" Pete leaned over the seat. Both ashtrays were still in place. Floor mats. Door handles.

"He has a brother living there. He's going to borrow a car from him and drive the rest of the way in the morning."

"I'll bet his brother's living there," Pete said. "Doing fifty concurrent life sentences. His brother and his sister and his mom and his dad."

"I kind of liked him," Donald said.

"I'm sure you did," Pete said wearily.

"He was interesting. He'd been places."

"His cigars had been places, I'll give you that."

"Come on, Pete."

"Come on yourself. What a phony."

"You don't know that."

"Sure I do."

"How? How do you know?"

Pete stretched. "Brother, there are some things you're just born knowing. What's the gas situation?"

"We're a little low."

"Then why didn't you get some more?"

"I wish you wouldn't snap at me like that," Donald said.

"Then why don't you use your head? What if we run out?"

"We'll make it," Donald said. "I'm pretty sure we've got enough to make it. You didn't have to be so rude to him," Donald added.

Pete took a deep breath. "I don't feel like running out of gas tonight, okay?"

Donald pulled in at the next station they came to and filled the tank while Pete went to the men's room. When Pete came back, Donald was sitting in the passenger's seat. The attendant came up to the driver's window as Pete got in behind the wheel. He bent down and said, "Twenty-two fifty-five."

"You heard the man," Pete said to Donald.

Donald looked straight ahead. He didn't move.

"Cough up," Pete said. "This trip's on you."

Donald said, softly, "I can't."

"Sure you can. Break out that wad."

Donald glanced up at the attendant, then at Pete. "Please," he said. "Pete, I don't have it anymore."

Pete took this in. He nodded, and paid the attendant.

Donald began to speak when they left the station but Pete cut him off. He said, "I don't want to hear from you right now. You just keep quiet or I swear to God I won't be responsible."

They left the fields and entered a tunnel of tall trees. The trees went on and on. "Let me get this straight," Pete said at last. "You don't have the money I gave you."

"You treated him like a bug or something," Donald said.

"You don't have the money," Pete said again.

Donald shook his head.

"Since I bought dinner, and since we didn't stop anywhere in between, I assume you gave it to Webster. Is that right? Is that what you did with it?"

"Yes."

Pete looked at Donald. His face was dark under the hood but he still managed to convey a sense of remove, as if none of this had anything to do with him.

"Why?" Pete asked. "Why did you give it to him?" When Donald didn't answer, Pete said, "A hundred dollars. Gone. Just like that. I *worked* for that money, Donald."

"I know, I know," Donald said.

"You don't know! How could you? You get money by holding out your hand."

"I work too," Donald said.

"You work too. Don't kid yourself, brother."

Donald leaned toward Pete, about to say something, but Pete cut him off again.

"You're not the only one on the payroll, Donald. I don't think you understand that. I have a family."

"Pete, I'll pay you back."

"Like hell you will. A hundred dollars!" Pete hit the steering wheel with the palm of his hand. "Just because you think I hurt some goofball's feelings. Jesus, Donald."

"That's not the reason," Donald said. "And I didn't just *give* him the money."

"What do you call it, then? What do you call what you did?"

"I *invested* it. I wanted a share, Pete." When Pete looked over at him Donald nodded and said again, "I wanted a share."

Pete said, "I take it you're referring to the gold mine in Peru."

"Yes," Donald said.

"You believe that such a gold mine exists?"

Donald looked at Pete, and Pete could see him just beginning to catch on. "You'll believe anything," Pete said. "Won't you? You really will believe anything at all."

"I'm sorry," Donald said, and turned away.

Pete drove on between the trees and considered the truth of what he had just said—that Donald would believe anything at all. And it came to him that it would be just like this unfair life for Donald to come out ahead in the end, by believing in some outrageous promise that would turn out to be true and that he, Pete, would reject out of hand because he was too wised up to listen to anybody's pitch anymore except for laughs. What a joke. What a joke if there really was a blessing to be had, and the blessing didn't come to the one who deserved it, the one who did all the work, but to the other.

And as if this had already happened Pete felt a shadow move upon him, darkening his thoughts. After a time he said, "I can see where all this is going, Donald."

"I'll pay you back," Donald said.

"No," Pete said. "You won't pay me back. You can't. You don't know how. All you've ever done is take. All your life."

Donald shook his head.

"I see exactly where this is going," Pete went on. "You can't work, you can't take care of yourself, you believe anything anyone tells you. I'm stuck with you, aren't I?" He looked over at Donald. "I've got you on my hands for good."

Donald pressed his fingers against the dashboard as if to brace himself. "I'll get out," he said.

Pete kept driving.

"Let me out," Donald said. "I mean it, Pete."

"Do you?"

Donald hesitated. "Yes," he said.

"Be sure," Pete told him. "This is it. This is for keeps."

"I mean it."

"All right. You made the choice." Pete braked the car sharply and swung it to the shoulder of the road. He turned off the engine and got out. Trees loomed on both sides, shutting out the sky. The air was cold and musty. Pete took Donald's duffel bag from the back seat and set it down behind the car. He stood there, facing Donald in the red glow of the taillights. "It's better this way," Pete said.

Donald just looked at him.

"Better for you," Pete said.

Donald hugged himself. He was shaking. "You don't have to say all that," he told Pete. "I don't blame you."

"Blame me? What the hell are you talking about? Blame me for what?"

"For anything," Donald said.

"I want to know what you mean by blame me."

"Nothing. Nothing, Pete. You'd better get going. God bless you."

"That's it," Pete said. He dropped to one knee, searching the packed dirt with his hands. He didn't know what he was looking for; his hands would know when they found it.

Donald touched Pete's shoulder. "You'd better go," he said.

Somewhere in the trees Pete heard a branch snap. He stood up. He looked at Donald, then went back to the car and drove away. He drove fast, hunched over the wheel, conscious of the way he was hunched and the shallowness of his breathing, refusing to look at the mirror above his head until there was nothing behind him but darkness.

Then he said, "A hundred dollars," as if there were someone to hear.

The trees gave way to fields. Metal fences ran beside the road, plastered with windblown scraps of paper. Tule fog hung above the ditches, spilling into the road, dimming the ghostly halogen lights that burned in the yards of the farms Pete passed. The fog left beads of water rolling up the windshield.

Pete rummaged among his cassettes. He found Pachelbel's Canon and pushed it into the tape deck. When the violins began to play he leaned back and assumed an attentive expression as if he were really listening to them. He smiled to himself like a man at liberty to enjoy music, a man who has finished his work and settled his debts, done all things meet and due.

And in this way, smiling, nodding to the music, he went another mile or so and pretended that he was not already slowing down, that he was not going to turn back, that he would be able to drive on like this, alone, and have the right answer when his wife stood before him in the doorway of his home and asked, Where is he? Where is your brother?

16

MRS. CASSIDY'S LAST YEAR

Mary Gordon

Mr. Cassidy knew he couldn't go to Communion. He had sinned against charity. He had wanted his wife dead.

The intention had been his, and the desire. She would not go back to bed. She had lifted the table that held her breakfast (it was unfair, it was unfair to all of them, that the old woman should be so strong and so immobile). She had lifted the table above her head and sent it crashing to the floor in front of him.

"Rose," he had said, bending, wondering how he would get scrambled egg, coffee, cranberry juice (which she had said she liked, the color of it) out of the garden pattern on the carpet. That was the sort of thing she knew but would not tell him now. She would laugh, wicked and bland-faced as an egg, when he did the wrong thing. But never say what was right, although she knew it, and her tongue was not dead for curses, for reports of crimes.

"Shithawk," she would shout at him from her bedroom. "Bastard son of a whore." Or more mildly, "Pimp," or "Fathead fart."

Old words, curses heard from soldiers on the boat or somebody's street children. Never spoken by her until now. Punishing him, though he had kept his promise.

He was trying to pick up the scrambled eggs with a paper napkin. The napkin broke, then shredded when he tried to squeeze the egg into what was left of it. He was on his knees on the carpet, scraping egg, white shreds of paper, purple fuzz from the trees in the carpet.

"Shitscraper," she laughed at him on his knees.

And then he wished in his heart most purely for the woman to be dead.

The doorbell rang. His son and his son's wife. Shame that they should see him so, kneeling, bearing curses, cursing in his heart.

"Pa," said Toni, kneeling next to him. "You see what we mean."

"She's too much for you," said Mr. Cassidy's son Tom. Self-made man, thought Mr. Cassidy. Good time Charlie. Every joke a punchline like a whip.

No one would say his wife was too much for him.

"Swear," she had said, lying next to him in bed when they were each no more than thirty. Her eyes were wild then. What had made her think of it? No sickness near them, and fearful age some continent like Africa, with no one they knew well. What had put the thought to her, and the wildness, so that her nails bit into his palm, as if she knew small pain would preserve his memory.

"Swear you will let me die in my own bed. Swear you won't let them take me away."

He swore, her nails making dents in his palms, a dull shallow pain, not sharp, blue-green or purplish.

He had sworn.

On his knees now beside his daughter-in-law, his son.

"She is not too much for me. She is my wife."

"Leave him then, Toni," said Tom. "Let him do it himself if it's so goddamn easy. Serve him right. Let him learn the hard way. He couldn't do it if he didn't have us, the slobs around the corner."

Years of hatred now come out, punishing for not being loved best, of the family's children not most prized. Nothing is forgiven, thought the old man, rising to his feet, his hand on his daughter-in-law's squarish shoulder.

He knelt before the altar of God. The young priest, bright-haired, faced them, arms open, a good little son.

No sons priests. He thought how he was old enough now to have a priest a grandson. This boy before him, vested and ordained, could have been one of the ones who followed behind holding tools. When there was time. He thought of Tom looking down at his father who knelt trying to pick up food. Tom for whom there had been no time. Families were this: the bulk, the knot of memory, wounds remembered not only because they had set on the soft, the pliable wax of childhood, motherhood, fatherhood, closeness to death. Wounds most deeply set and best remembered because families are days, the sameness of days and words, hammer blows, smothering, breath grabbed, memory on the soft skull, in the lungs, not once only but again and again the same. The words and the starvation.

Tom would not forget, would not forgive him. Children thought themselves the only wounded.

Should we let ourselves in for it, year after year, he asked in prayer, believing God did not hear him.

Tom would not forgive him for being the man he was. A man who paid debts, kept promises. Mr. Cassidy knelt up straighter, proud of himself before God.

Because of the way he had to be. He knelt back again, not proud. As much sense to be proud of the color of his hair. As much choice.

It was his wife who was the proud one. As if she thought it could have been some other way. The house, the children. He knew, being who they were they must have a house like that, children like that. Being who they were to the world. Having their faces.

As if she thought with some wrong turning these things might have been wasted. Herself a slattern, him drunk, them living in a tin shack, children dead or missing.

One was dead. John, the favorite, lost somewhere in a plane. The war dead. There was his name on the plaque near the altar. With the other town boys. And she had never forgiven him. For what he did not know. For helping bring that child into the world? Better, she said, to have borne none than the pain of losing this one, the most beautiful, the bravest. She turned from him then, letting some shelf drop, like a merchant at the hour of closing. And Tom had not forgotten the grief at his brother's death, knowing he could not have closed his mother's heart like that.

Mr. Cassidy saw they were all so unhappy, hated each other so because they thought things could be different. As he had thought of his wife. He had imagined she could be different if she wanted to. Which had angered him. Which was not, was almost never, the truth about things.

Things were as they were going to be, he thought, watching the boy-faced priest giving out Communion. Who were the others not receiving? Teenagers, pimpled, believing themselves in sin. He wanted to tell them they were not. He was sure they were not. Mothers with babies. Not going to Communion because they took the pill, it must be. He thought they should not stay away, although he thought they should not do what they had been told not to. He knew that the others in their seats were there for the heat of their bodies. While he sat back for the coldness of his heart, a heart that had wished his wife dead. He had wished the one dead he had promised he would love forever.

The boy priest blessed the congregation. Including Mr. Cassidy himself.

"Pa," said Tom, walking beside his father, opening the car door for him. "You see what we mean about her?"

"It was my fault. I forgot."

"Forgot what?" said Tom, emptying his car ashtray onto the church parking lot. Not my son, thought Mr. Cassidy, turning his head.

"How she is," said Mr. Cassidy. "I lost my temper."

"Pa, you're not God," said Tom. His hands were on the steering wheel, angry. His mother's.

"Okay," said Toni. "But look, Pa, you've been a saint to her. But she's not the woman she was. Not the woman we knew."

"She's the woman I married."

"Not any more," said Toni, wife of her husband.

If not, then who? People were the same. They kept their bodies. They did not become someone else. Rose was the woman he had married, a green girl, high-colored, with beautifully cut nostrils, hair that fell down always, hair she pinned up swiftly, with anger. She had been a housemaid and he a chauffeur. He had taken her to the ocean. They wore straw hats. They were not different people now. She was the girl he had seen first, the woman he had married, the mother of his children, the woman he had promised: Don't let them take me. Let me die in my own bed.

"Supposing it was yourself and Tom, then, Toni," said Mr. Cassidy, remembering himself a gentleman. "What would you want him to do? Would you want him to break his promise?"

"I hope I'd make him promise anything like that," said Toni.

"But if you did?"

"I don't believe in those kinds of promises."

"My father thinks he's God. You have to understand. There's no two ways about anything."

For what was his son now refusing to forgive him? He was silent now, sitting in the back of the car. He looked at the top of his daughter-in-law's head, blond now, like some kind of circus candy. She had never been blond. Why did they do it? Try to be what they were not born to. Rose did not.

"What I wish you'd get through your head, Pa, is that it's me and Toni carrying the load. I suppose you forget where all the suppers come from?"

"I don't forget."

"Why don't you think of Toni for once?"

"I think of her, Tom, and you too. I know what you do. I'm very grateful. Mom is grateful, too, or she would be."

But first I think of my wife to whom I made vows. And whom I promised.

"The doctor thinks you're nuts, you know that, don't you?" said Tom. "Rafferty think you're nuts to try and keep her. He thinks we're nuts to go along with you. He says he washes his hands of the whole bunch of us."

The doctor washes his hands, thought Mr. Cassidy, seeing Leo Rafferty, hale as a dog, at his office sink.

The important thing was not to forget she was the woman he had married.

So he could leave the house, so he could leave her alone, he strapped her into the bed. Her curses were the worst when he released her. She had grown a beard this last year, like a goat.

Like a man?

No.

He remembered her as she was when she was first his wife. A white nightgown, then as now. So she was the same. He'd been told it smelled different, a virgin's first time. And never that way again. Some blood. Not much. As if she hadn't minded.

He sat her in the chair in front of the television. They had Mass now on television for sick people, people like her. She pushed the button on the little box that could change channels from across the room. One of their grandsons was a TV repairman. He had done it for them when she got sick. She pushed the button to a station that showed cartoons. Mice in capes, cats outraged. Some stories now with colored children. He boiled an egg for her lunch.

She sat chewing, looking at the television. What was that look in her eyes now? Why did he want to call it wickedness? Because it was blank and hateful. Because there was no light. Eyes should have light. There should be something behind them. That was dangerous, nothing behind her eyes but hate. Sullen like a bull kept from a cow. Sex mad. Why did that look make him think of sex? Sometimes he was afraid she wanted it.

He did not know what he would do.

She slept. He slept in the chair across from her.

The clock went off for her medicine. He got up from the chair, gauging the weather. Sometimes the sky was green this time of year. It was warm when it should not be. He didn't like that. The mixup made him shaky. It made him say to himself, "Now I am old."

He brought her the medicine. Three pills, red and gray, red and yellow, dark pink. Two just to keep her quiet. Sometimes she sucked them and spat them out when they melted and she got the bad taste. She thought they were candy. It was their fault for making them those colors. But it was something else he had to think about. He had to make sure she swallowed them right away.

Today she was not going to swallow. He could see that by the way her eyes looked at the television. The way she set her mouth so he could see what she had done with the pills, kept them in a pocket in her cheek, as if for storage.

"Rose," he said, stepping between her and the television, breaking her gaze. "You've got to swallow the pills. They cost money."

She tried to look over his shoulder. On the screen an ostrich, dressed in colored stockings, danced down the road. He could see she was not listening to him. And he tried to remember what the young priest had said when he came to bring Communion, what his daughter June had said. Be patient with her. Humor her. She can't help what she does. She's not the woman she once was.

She is the same.

"Hey, my Rose, won't you just swallow the pills for me. Like my girl."

She pushed him out of the way. So she could go on watching the television. He knelt down next to her.

"Come on, girleen. It's the pills make you better."

She gazed over the top of his head. He stood up, remembering what was done to animals.

He stroked her throat as he had stroked the throats of dogs and horses, a boy on the farm. He stroked the old woman's loose, papery throat, and said, "Swallow, then, just swallow."

She looked over his shoulder at the television. She kept the pills in a corner of her mouth.

It was making him angry. He put one finger above her lip under her nose and one below her chin, so that she would not be able to open her mouth. She breathed through her nose like a patient animal. She went on looking at the television. She did not swallow.

"You swallow them, Rose, this instant," he said, clamping her mouth shut. "They cost money. The doctor says you must. You're throwing good money down the drain."

Now she was watching a lion and a polar bear dancing. There were pianos in their cages.

He knew he must move away or his anger would make him do something. He had promised he would not be angry. He would remember who she was.

He went into the kitchen with a new idea. He would give her something sweet that would make her want to swallow. There was ice cream in the refrigerator. Strawberry that she liked. He removed each strawberry and placed it in the sink so she would not chew and then get the taste of the medicine. And then spit it out, leaving him, leaving them both no better than when they began.

He brought the dish of ice cream to her in the living room. She was sitting staring at the television with her mouth open. Perhaps she had opened her mouth to laugh? At what? At what was this grown woman laughing? A zebra was playing a xylophone while his zebra wife hung striped pajamas on a line.

In opening her mouth, she had let the pills fall together onto her lap. He saw the three of them, wet, stuck together, at the center of her lap. He thought he would take the pills and simply hide them in the ice cream. He bent to fish them from the valley of her lap.

And then she screamed at him. And then she stood up.

He was astonished at her power. She had not stood by herself for seven months. She put one arm in front of her breasts and raised the other against him, knocking him heavily to the floor.

"No," she shouted, her voice younger, stronger, the voice of a well young man. "Don't think you can have it now. That's what you're after. That's what you're always after. You want to get into it. I'm not one of your whores. You always thought it was such a great prize. I wish you'd have it cut off. I'd like to cut it off."

And she walked out of the house. He could see her wandering up and down the street in the darkness.

He dragged himself over to the chair and propped himself against it so he could watch her through the window. But he knew he could not move any farther. His leg was light and foolish underneath him, and burning with pain. He could not move any more, not even to the telephone that was half a yard away from him. He could see her body, visible through her night-gown, as she walked the street in front of the house.

He wondered if he should call out or be silent. He did not know how far she would walk. He could imagine her walking until the land stopped, and then into the water. He could not stop her. He would not raise his voice.

There was that pain in his leg that absorbed him strangely, as if it were the pain of someone else. He knew the leg was broken. "I have broken my leg," he kept saying to himself, trying to connect the words and the burning.

But then he remembered what it meant. He would not be able to walk. He would not be able to take care of her.

"Rose," he shouted, trying to move toward the window.

And then, knowing he could not move and she could not hear him, "Help."

He could see the green numbers on the clock, alive as cat's eyes. He could see his wife walking in the middle of the street. At least she was not walking far. But no one was coming to help her.

He would have to call for help. And he knew what it meant: they would take her away somewhere. No one would take care of her in the house if he did not. And he could not move.

No one could hear him shouting. No one but he could see his wife, wandering up and down the street in her nightgown.

They would take her away. He could see it; he could hear the noises. Policemen in blue, car radios reporting other disasters, young boys writing his words down in notebooks. And doctors, white coats, white shoes, wheeling her out. Her strapped. She would curse him. She would curse him rightly for having broken his promise. And the young men would wheel her out. Almost everyone was younger than he now. And he could hear how she would be as they wheeled her past him, rightly cursing.

Now he could see her weaving in the middle of the street. He heard a car slam on its brakes to avoid her. He thought someone would have to stop then. But he heard the car go on down to the corner.

No one could hear him shouting in the living room. The windows were shut; it was late October. There was a high bulk of grey cloud, showing islands of fierce, acidic blue. He would have to do something to get someone's attention before the sky became utterly dark and the drivers could not see her wandering before their cars. He could see her wandering; he could see the set of her angry back. She was wearing only her nightgown. He would have to get someone to bring her in before she died of cold.

The only objects he could reach were the figurines that covered the low table beside him. He picked one up: a bust of Robert Kennedy. He threw it through the window. The breaking glass made a violent, disgraceful noise. It was the sound of disaster he wanted. It must bring help.

He lay still for ten minutes, waiting, looking at the clock. He could see her walking, cursing. She could not hear him. He was afraid no one could hear him. He picked up another figurine, a bicentennial eagle and threw it through the window next to the one he had just broken. Then he picked up another and threw it through the window next to that. He went on: six windows. He went on until he had broken every window in the front of the house.

He had ruined his house. The one surprising thing of his long lifetime. The broken glass winked like green jewels, hard sea creatures, on the purple carpet. He looked at what he had destroyed. He would never have done it; it was something he would never have done. But he would not have believed he was a man who could not keep his promise.

In the dark he lay and prayed that someone would come and get her. That was the only thing now to pray for; the one thing he had asked God to keep back. A car stopped in front of the house. He heard his son's voice speaking to his mother. He could see the two of them; Tom had his arm around her. She was walking into the house now as if she had always meant to.

Mr. Cassidy lay back for the last moment of darkness. Soon the room would be full.

His son turned on the light.

17

THE WHORE'S CHILD

Richard Russo

Sister Ursula belonged to an all but extinct order of Belgian nuns who conducted what little spiritual business remained to them in a decrepit old house purchased by the diocese seemingly because it was unlikely to out-last them. Since it was on Forest Avenue, a block from our house, I'd seen Sister Ursula many times before the night she turned up in class, but we never had spoken. She drove a rusted-out station wagon that was always crowded with elderly nuns who needed assistance getting in and out. Though St. Francis Church was only a few blocks away, that was too far to walk for any of them except Sister Ursula, her gait awkward but relentless. "You should go over there and introduce yourself someday," Gail, my wife, suggested more than once. "Those old women have been left all alone." Her suspicion was later confirmed by Sister Ursula herself. "They are waiting for us to die," she confessed. "Impatient of how we clutch to our miserable existences."

"I'm sure you don't mean that," I said, an observation that was to become my mantra with her, and she, in turn, seemed to enjoy hearing me say it.

She appeared in class that first night and settled herself at the very center of the seminar despite the fact that her name did not appear on my computer printout. Fiction writing classes are popular and invariably oversubscribed at most universities, and never more so than when the writing teacher has recently published a book, as I had done the past spring. Publishing the kind of book that's displayed in strip-mall bookstores bestows a celebrity on aca-demic writers and separates them from their scholar colleagues, whose books resemble the sort of dubious specialty items found only in boutiques and health food stores. I'd gotten quite a lot of press on my recent book, my first in over a decade, and my fleeting celebrity might have explained Sister Ursula's presence in my classroom the first chilly evening of the fall semester, though she gave no indication of this, or that she recognized me as her neighbor.

No, Sister Ursula seemed innocent not only of me but also of all department and university protocol. When informed that students petitioned to take the advanced fiction writing class by means of a manuscript submission the previous term, and that its prerequisites were beginning and intermediate courses, Sister Ursula disputed neither the existence nor the wisdom of these procedures. Nor did she gather her things and leave, which left me in an odd position. Normally it's my policy not to allow unregistered students to remain in class, because doing so encourages their mistaken belief that they can wheedle, cajole or flatter their way in. In the past I'd shown even football players the door without the slightest courtesy or ceremony, but this was a different challenge entirely. Sister Ursula herself was nearly as big as a linebacker, yet more persuasive than this was her body language, which suggested that once settled, she was not used to moving. And since she was clearly settled, I let her stay.

After class, however, I did explain why it would be highly unprofessional of me to allow her to remain in the advanced fiction workshop. After all, she freely admitted she'd never attempted to write a story before, which, I explained, put her at an extreme disadvantage. My mistake was in not leaving the matter there. Instead I went on. "This is a storytelling class, Sister. We're all liars here. The whole purpose of our enterprise is to become skilled in making things up, of substituting our own truth for *the* truth. In this class we actually prefer a well-told lie," I concluded, certain that this would dissuade her.

She patted my hand, as you might the hand of a child. "Never you mind," she then assured me, adjusting her wimple for the journey home. "My whole life has been a lie."

"I'm sure you don't mean that," I told her.

In the convent, Sister Ursula's first submission began, *I was known as the whore's child*.

Nice opening, I wrote in the margin, as if to imply that her choice had been a purely artistic one. It wasn't, of course. She was simply starting with what was for her the beginning of her torment. She was writing—and would continue to write—a memoir. By mid-semester I would give up asking her to invent things.

The first installment weighed in at a robust twenty-five pages, which detailed the suffering of a young girl taken to live in a Belgian convent school where the treatment of children was determined by the social and financial status of the parents who had abandoned them there. As a charity case and the daughter of a prostitute, young Sister Ursula (for there could be no doubt that she *was* the first-person narrator) found herself at the very bottom of the ecclesiastical food chain. What little wealth she possessed—some pens and paper her father had purchased for her the day before they left the city, along with a pretty new dress—was taken from her, and she was informed that henceforth she would have no use for such pitiful possessions. Her needs—food, a uniform and a single pair of shoes—would be provided for her, though she would doubtless prove unworthy to receive them. The shoes she was given were two sizes too small, an accident, Sister Ursula imagined, until she asked if she might exchange them for the shoes of a younger girl that were two sizes too large, only to be scorned for her impertinence. So before long she developed the tortured gait of a cripple, which was much imitated by the other children, who immediately perceived in her a suitable object for their cruelest derision.

The mockery of her classmates was something Sister Ursula quickly accommodated, by shunning their companionship. In time she grew accustomed to being referred to as "the whore's child," and she hoped that the children would eventually tire of calling her this if she could manage to conceal how deeply it wounded her. During periods of recreation in the convent courtyard she perfected the art of becoming invisible, avoiding all games and contests when, she knew, even those on her own team would turn on her. What she was not prepared for was the cruelty she suffered at the hands of the nuns, who seemed to derive nearly as much satisfaction from tormenting her as their charges—beginning with her request to exchange shoes. She had not merely been told that this would not be permitted, but was given a horrible explanation as to why this was so. The chafing of the too small shoes had caused her heels to bleed into her coarse white socks and then into the shoes themselves. Only a wicked child, Sister Veronique explained, would foul the shoes she'd been given with her blood, then beg to exchange them for the shoes of an innocent child. Did she think it fair, the old nun wondered out loud, that another child, one who had not only a virtuous mother but also a father, be asked to wear the polluted shoes of a whore's child?

Worse than the sting of the old nun's suggestion that anything Sister Ursula touched immediately became contaminated was the inference that trailed in the wake of her other remark. The innocent girl had not only a virtuous mother—Sister Ursula knew what this meant—*but also a father,* which seemed to imply that she herself didn't have one. Of course she knew that she did have a father, a tall, handsome father who had promised to rescue her from this place as soon as he could find work. Indeed, it was her father who had brought her to the convent, who had assured Mother Superior that she was a good girl and not at all wicked. How then had sister Veronique concluded that she had no father? The young girl tried to reason it through but became confused. She knew from experience that evil, by its very nature, counted for more in the world than good. And she understood that her mother's being a prostitute made her "the whore's child," that her mother's wickedness diminished her father's value, but did it negate his very existence? How could such a thing be? She dared not ask, and so the old nun's remark burrowed even deeper, intensifying a misery that already bordered on despair.

Sister Ursula's first installment ended here, and her fellow students approached the discussion of it as one would an alien spacecraft. Several had attended Catholic schools where they'd been tutored by nuns, and they weren't sure, despite my encouragement, that they were allowed to be critical of this one. The material itself was foreign to them; they'd never encountered anything like it in the workshop. On the plus side, Sister Ursula's story had a character in it, and the character was placed in a dire situation, and those were good things for stories to do. On the other hand, the old nun's idiom was imperfect, her style stiff and old-fashioned, and the story seemed to be moving forward without exactly getting anywhere. It reminded them of stories they'd heard other elderly people tell, tales that even the tellers eventually managed to forget the point of, narratives that would gradually peter out with the weak insistence that all these events really did happen. "It's a victim story," one student recognized. "The character is being acted on by outside forces, but she has no choices, which means there can be no consequences to anything she does. If she doesn't participate in her own destiny, where's the story?"

Not having taken the beginning and intermediate courses, Sister Ursula was much enlightened by these unanticipated critiques, and she took feverish notes on everything that was said. "I liked it, though," added the student who'd identified it as a victim story. "It's different." By which he seemed to mean that Sister Ursula herself was different.

The old nun stopped by my office the day after, and it was clear she was still mulling the workshop over. "To be so much . . . a victim," she said, searching for the right words, "it is not good?"

"No," I smiled. Not in stories, not in life, I was about to add, until I remembered that Sister Ursula still wasn't making this distinction, and my doing so would probably confuse her further. "But maybe in the next installment?" I suggested.

She looked at me hopefully.

"Maybe your character will have some choices of her own as your story continues?" I prodded.

Sister Ursula considered this possibility for a long time, and I could tell by looking at her that the past wasn't nearly as flexible as she might have wished.

She was about to leave when she noticed the photograph of my daughter that I keep on my desk. "Your little girl," she said, "is a great beauty?"

"Yes," I said, indicating that it was okay to pick up the photo if she wanted to.

"Sometimes I see her when I am driving by," she explained. When I didn't say anything, she added, "Sometimes I don't see her anymore?"

"She and her mother are gone now," I explained, the sentence feeling syntactically strange, as if English were my second language, too. "They're living in another state."

Sister Ursula nodded uncertainly, as if deliberating whether "state" meant a condition or a place, then said, "She will return to this state?"

It was my turn to nod. "I hope so, Sister."

And so I became a Catholic, began the second installment of Sister Ursula's story, and again I scribbled *nice opening* in the left margin before hunkering down. I'd had students like Sister Ursula before, and they'd inspired the strictly enforced twenty-five page limit in all my workshops. I noted that for this second submission she had narrowed her margins, fiddled with the font, wedging the letters closer together. The spacing didn't look quite double, maybe 1.7. Venial sins.

Having had no religious training prior to entering the convent, Sister Ursula was for some time unable to recite prayers with the other children, further evidence, if any were needed, of the moral depravity inherent to being the offspring of a whore. She discovered it was not an easy task, learning prayers to the cadence of public ridicule, but learn them she did, and though the rote recitation was, in the beginning, a torment, it eventually became a comfort. Most of the prayers she fought to memorize were adamant about the existence of a God who, at least in the person of the crucified Christ, was infinitely more loving and understanding and forgiving than the women He'd led to the altar as His brides.

To be loved and understood and forgiven seemed to Sister Ursula the ultimate indulgence, and thus she became a denizen of the convent chapel, retreating there at every opportunity from the taunts and jeers of the other children and the constant crowlike reprimands of the nuns. She liked the smell of the place—damp and cool and clean—especially when she had it to herself, when it wasn't filled with the bodies of stale old nuns and sweaty children. Often she could hide in the chapel for an hour or more before one of the side doors would finally creak open, momentarily flooding the floor with bright light. Then the long dark shadow of a nun would fall across Sister Ursula where she knelt in prayer at the foot of the cross, and she would have no choice but to rise and be led back to her torment, often by a twisted ear.

In addition to the authorized prayers she'd memorized, Sister Ursula composed others of her own. She prayed that Sister Veronique, who had suggested that she had no father and who worked in the convent stable, might be kicked in the head by a horse and paralyzed for life. She prayed that Sister Joseph, who used her command of the kitchen to ensure that charity children were given the poorest food in the smallest quantities, might one day slip and fall into one of her boiling vats. Required herself to spend most holidays at the convent, Sister Ursula prayed that the children who were allowed to go home might perish in railway accidents. Sometimes, in an economical mood, she prayed that the convent might burn to the ground, and the air fill with black ash. She saw nothing wrong with offering such prayers, particularly since none of them, no matter how urgent, were ever answered. She felt a gentle trust in the Jesus of the Cross who hung above the main altar of the convent chapel. He seemed to know everything that was in her heart and to understand that nothing dwelt there that wasn't absolutely necessary to her survival. He would not begrudge her these prayers.

In truth, Jesus on the cross reminded Sister Ursula of her father who she knew had never wanted to see her packed off to the convent, and who missed her every day, just as she missed him. Like Jesus, her father was slender and handsome and sad; and unable to find work and married to a woman who was his shame. He was, like Jesus, stuck where he was. Yet if the prayer she had struggled to memorize were true, there was hope. Had not Jesus shed His crown of thorns, stepped down from the cross to become the light and salvation of the world, raising up with Him the lowly and the true of heart? Sister Ursula, when she wasn't praying that a horse kick Sister Veronique in the head, fervently prayed that her father might one day be free. The first thing he would do, she felt certain, was come for her, and so every time the chapel's side door opened, she turned toward the harsh light with a mixture of hope and fear, and though it was always a nun whose dark silhouette filled the doorway, she held tenaciously to the belief that soon it would be her father standing there.

One Christmas season—was it her third year at the convent school?— Sister Ursula was summoned to the chamber of Mother Superior, who told her to ready herself for a journey. This was a full week before any of the other students would be permitted to leave for the Christmas holiday, and Sister Ursula was instructed to tell no one of her impending departure. Indeed, Mother Superior seemed flustered, and this gave Sister Ursula heart. During her years of secret, vengeful prayer she'd indulged many fantasies of dramatic liberation, and often imagined her father's arrival on horseback, his angry pounding at the main gate, his purposeful stride through the courtyard and into the chapel. Perhaps Mother Superior's anxiety stemmed from the fact that her father was already on his way to effect just such a rescue.

At the appointed hour, Sister Ursula waited, as instructed, by the main gate, beyond which no men save priests were permitted entry, and awaited her father's arrival. She hoped he would come by a coach or carriage that then would convey them to the village train station, but if necessary she was more than happy to make the journey on foot, so long as she and her father were together. She had better shoes now, though she still hobbled like a cripple. And so when a carriage came into view in the dusty road beyond the iron gate, her heart leapt up—until she recognized it as the one belonging to the convent. Inside sat not her father but Sister Veronique, who had not been kicked in the head by a horse despite three years' worth of Sister Ursula's dogged prayers. When the carriage drew to a halt, Sister Ursula understood that her hopes had been led astray by her need and that she was to be banished from the convent, not rescued from it. She did not fear a worse existence than her present one, because a worse existence was not within her powers of imagination. Rather, what frightened her was the possibility that if she was taken from the convent school, her father no longer would know where to find her when the time came. This terrible fear she kept to herself. She and Sister Veronique did not speak a word on the long journey to the city.

Late that evening they arrived at a hospital and were taken to the charity ward, only to learn that Sister Ursula's mother had expired just after they had left the convent that morning. A nun dressed all in white informed Sister Veronique that it would be far better for the child not to see the deceased, and a look passed between them. All that was left by way of a keepsake was a brittle, curling, scallop-edged photograph, which the white nun gave to Sister Ursula, who had offered no reaction to the news that her mother was dead. Since arriving at the hospital, Sister Ursula had lapsed into a state of paralytic fear that it was her father who had fallen ill there. Instead, it seemed at least one of her prayers had been answered: her father was free.

But where was he? When she summoned the courage to ask, the two nuns exchanged another glance, in which it was plain that the white nun shared Sister Veronique's belief that she had no father, and Sister Ursula saw, too, that it would be useless for her, a child, to try to convince the white nun otherwise. Her fury supported her during their train ride, but then, when the convent came into view from the carriage, Sister Ursula broke down and began to sob. To her surprise, if not comfort, Sister Veronique placed a rough, calloused hand on her shoulder and said softly, "Never mind child. You will become one of us now." In response Sister Ursula slid as far away from the old nun as she could and sobbed even harder, knowing it must be true.

"Are we ever going to meet the father?" one student wanted to know. "I mean, she yearns for him, and he gets compared to Christ, but we never see him directly. We're, like, *told* how to feel about him. If he doesn't ever show up, I'm going to feel cheated."

Sister Ursula dutifully noted this criticism, but you had only to look at the old woman to know that the father was not going to show up. Anybody who felt cheated by this could just join the club.

The day after Sister Ursula's second workshop, my doorbell rang at seven-thirty in the morning. I struggled out of bed, put on a robe and went to the door. Sister Ursula stood on the porch, clearly agitated. The forlorn station wagon idled at the curb with its full cargo of curious, myopic nuns, returning, I guessed, from morning Mass. The yard was strewn with dry, unraked November leaves, several of which had attached themselves to the bottom of Sister Ursula's flowing habit.

"Must he be in the story? Must he return?" Sister Ursula wanted to know. As badly as she had wanted her father to appear in life, she needed, for some reason, to exclude him from the narrative version.

"He's already in the story," I pointed out, cinching my robe tightly at the waist.

"But I never saw him after she died. This is what my story is about."

"How about a flashback?" I suggested. "You mentioned there was one Christmas holiday . . ."

But she was no longer listening. Her eyes, slate gray, had gone hard. "She died of syphilis."

I nodded, feeling something harden in me too. Behind me I heard the bathroom door open and close, and I thought I saw Sister Ursula's gaze flicker for an instant. She might have caught a glimpse of Jane, the woman I was involved with, and I found myself hoping she had.

"My father's heart was broken."

"How do you know that, if you never saw him again?"

"He loved her," she explained. "She was his ruin."

It was my hatred that drew me deeper into the Church, began Sister Ursula's third installment, the words cramped even more tightly on exactly twenty-five pages, and this elicited my now standard comment in the margin. As a writer of opening sentences, Sister Ursula was without peer among my students.

In the months following her mother's death, an explanation had occurred to Sister Ursula. Her father, most likely, had booked passage to America to search for work. Such journeys, she knew, were fraught with unimaginable peril, and perhaps he now lay at the bottom of the ocean. So it was that she gradually came to accept the inevitability of Sister Veronique's cruel prophecy. She would become one of those whom she detested. Ironically, this fate was hastened by the prophet's untimely death when she was kicked by a horse, not in the head as Sister Ursula had prayed, but in the chest, causing severe internal hemorrhaging and creating an opening in the stable. During her long sojourn at the convent, Sister Ursula had learned to prefer the company of animals to that of humans, and so at the age of sixteen, already a large, full woman like her mother, she became herself a bride of Christ.

Sister Ursula's chronicle of the years following her vows, largely a description of her duties in the stable, featured several brief recollections of the single week she'd spent at home in the city during the Christmas holiday of that first year she entered the convent school. During that holiday she'd seen very little of her mother—a relief, since Sister Ursula dreaded the heat of her mother's embrace and the cloying stench of her whore's perfume. Rather, her beloved father took her with him on his rounds, placing her on a convenient bench outside the dark buildings he entered, telling her how long he would be, how high a number she would have to count to before he would return. Only a few times did she have to count higher. "Did you find work, Father?" she asked each time he reappeared. It seemed to Sister Ursula that in buildings as large and dark as the ones he entered, with so many other men entering and exiting, there should have been work in one of them, but there was none. Still, that they were together was joy enough. Her father took her to the wharf to see the boats, to a small carnival where a man her father knew let her ride a pony for free and finally to a bitter cold picnic in the country where they ate warm bread and cheese. At the end of each of these excursions her father promised again that she would not have to remain much longer in the convent school, that another Christmas would find them together.

The installment ended with Sister Ursula taking her final vows in the same chapel that for years had been her refuge from the taunts of children for whom she would always be the whore's child. There, at the very altar of God, Sister Ursula, like a reluctant bride at an arranged marriage, indulged her fantasy of rescue right up to the last moment. When asked to proclaim her irrevocable devotion to God and the one true Church, she paused and turned toward the side door of the chapel, the one she'd always imagined her father would throw open, and willed her father's shadow to emerge from the blinding light and scatter these useless women and hateful children before him.

But the door remained shut, the chapel dark except for the flickering of a hundred candles, and so Sister Ursula became a bride.

"Isn't there a lot of misogyny in this story?" observed a male student who I happened to know was taking a course with the English department's sole radical feminist, and was therefore alert to all of misogyny's insidious manifestations. By stating this opinion in the form of a question, perhaps he was indicating that the distrust and even hatred of women evident in Sister Ursula's memoir might be okay in this instance because the author was, sort of, a woman.

At any rate, he was right to be cautious. What would you expect, a chorus of his female classmates sang out. The whole thing takes place in a girls' school. There were only two men in the story and one was Jesus, so the statistical sample was bound to be skewed. No, read correctly, Sister Ursula was clearly a feminist.

"I *would* like to see more of the mother, though," one young woman conceded. "It was a major cop-out for her to die before they could get to the hospital."

"You wanted a deathbed scene?" said another. "Wouldn't that be sort of melodramatic?"

Here the discussion faltered. Melodrama was a bad thing, almost as bad as misogyny.

"Why was the daughter sent for?" wondered someone else. "If the mother didn't love her, why send for her?"

"Maybe the father sent for her?"

"Then why wasn't he there himself?"

"I know I was the one," interrupted another, "who wanted to see more of the father after the last submission, but now I think I was wrong. All that stuff with her father over the Christmas holiday? It was like we kept hearing what we already knew. And *then* he's not there at the hospital when the mother dies. I'm confused." He turned to me. "Aren't you?"

"Maybe somebody in the hospital contacted the convent," another student suggested, letting me off the hook.

"For a dying prostitute in a charity ward? How would they even know where the daughter was unless the mother told them?"

Everyone now turned to Sister Ursula, who under this barrage of questions seemed to have slipped into a trance.

"I don't care," said another student, one of the loners in the back of the room. "I *like* this story. It feels real."

The fourth and final installment of Sister Ursula's story was only six-and-a-half pages long with regular margins, normal fonts, and standard double spacing.

My life as a nun has been one of terrible hatred and bitterness, it began. I considered writing, *You don't mean that*, in the margin, but refrained. Sister Ursula always meant what she said. It was now late November, and she hadn't veered a centimeter from literal truth since Labor Day. These last, perfunctory pages summarized her remaining years in the convent until the school was partially destroyed by fire. It was then that Sister Ursula came to America. Still a relatively young woman, she nonetheless entertained no thoughts of leaving the order she had always despised. She had become, as Sister Veronique predicted, one of them.

Once, in her late forties, she had returned to Belgium to search for her father, but she had little money and found no trace of him. It was as if, as Sister Veronique had always maintained, the man had never existed. When her funds were exhausted, Sister Ursula gave up and returned to America to live out what remained of her life among the other orphans of her order. This was her first college course, she explained, and she wanted the other students to know that she had enjoyed meeting them and reading their stories, and thanked them for helping her with hers. All of this was contained in the final paragraph of the story, an unconsciously postmodern gesture.

"This last part sort of fizzled out," one student admitted, clearly pained to say this after its author had thanked her readers for their help. "But it's one of the best stories we've read all semester."

"I liked it too," said another, whose voice didn't fall quite right.

Everyone seemed to understand that there was more to say, but no one knew what it might be. Sister Ursula stopped taking notes and silence descended on the room. For some time I'd been watching a young woman who'd said next to nothing all term, but who wrote long, detailed reports on all the stories. She'd caught my attention now because her eyes were brimming with tears. I sent her an urgent telepathic plea. No. Please don't.

"But the girl in the story never *got* it," she protested.

The other students, including Sister Ursula, all turned toward her. "Got what?"

"About the father," she said. "He was the mother's pimp, right? Is there another explanation?"

"So," Sister Ursula said sadly, "I was writing what you call a fictional story after all."

It was now mid-December, my grades were due, and I was puzzling over what to do about Sister Ursula's. She had not turned in a final portfolio of revised work to be evaluated, nor had she returned to class after her final workshop, and no matter how hard I tried, I couldn't erase from my memory the image of the old nun that had haunted me for weeks, of her face coming apart in terrible recognition of the willful lie she'd told herself over a lifetime.

So I'd decided to pay her a visit at the old house where she and five other elderly nuns had been quartered now for nearly a decade in anticipation of their order's dissolution. I had brought the gift of a Christmas tree ornament, only to discover that they had no tree, unless you counted the nine-inch plastic one on the mantel in the living room. Talk about failures of imagination. In a house inhabited by infirm, elderly women, who did I suppose would have put up and decorated a tree?

Sister Ursula seemed surprised to see me standing there on her sloping porch, but she led me into a small parlor off the main hall. "We must be very still," she said softly. "Sister Patrice has fallen ill. I am her nurse, you see. I am nurse to all of them."

In the little room we took seats opposite each other across a small gate-leg table. I must have looked uncomfortable, because Sister Ursula said, "You have always been very nervous of me, and you should not. What harm was in me has wasted away with my flesh."

"It's just that I was bitten by a nun as a child," I explained.

Sister Ursula, who'd said so many horrible things about nuns, looked momentarily shocked. Then she smiled. "Oh, I understand that you made a joke," she said. "I thought that you might be . . . what was that word the boy in our class used to describe those like me?"

I had to think a minute. "Oh, a misogynist?"

"Yes, that. Would you tell me the truth if I asked you do you like women?"

"Yes, I do. Very much."

"And I men, so we are the same. We each like the opposite from us."

Which made me smile. And perhaps because she had confided so much about herself, I felt a sudden, irrational urge to confide something in return. Something terrible, perhaps. Something I believed to be true. That my wife had left because she had discovered my involvement with a woman I did not love, who I had taken up with, I now realized, because I felt cheated when the book I'd published in the spring had not done well, cheated because my publisher had been irresponsibly optimistic, claiming the book would make me rich and famous, and because I'd been irresponsibly willing to believe it, so that when it provided neither fame nor fortune, I began to look around for a consolation prize and found her. I am not a good man, I might have told Sister Ursula. I have not only failed but also betrayed those I love. If I said such things to Sister Ursula, maybe she would find some inconsistency in my tale, some flaw. Maybe she'd conclude that I was judging myself too harshly and find it in her heart to say, "You don't mean that."

But I kept my truths to myself, because she was right. I *was* "nervous of her."

After an awkward moment of silence, she said, "I would like to show you something, if you would like to see it?"

Sister Ursula struggled heavily to her feet and left the room, returning almost immediately. The old photograph was pretty much as described— brown and curled at its scalloped edges, the womanly image at its center faded nearly into white. But still beautiful. It might have been the photo of a young Sister Ursula, but of course it wasn't. Since there was nothing to say, I said nothing, merely put it down on the small table between us.

"You? You had loving parents?"

I nodded. "Yes."

"You are kind. This visit is to make sure that I am all right, I understand. But I am wondering for a long time. You also knew the meaning of my story?"

I nodded.

"From the beginning?"

"No, not from the beginning."

"But the young woman was correct? Based on the things that I wrote, there could be no other . . . interpretation?"

"Not that I could see."

"And yet *I* could not see."

There was a sound then, a small, dull thud from directly overhead. "Sister Patrice," Sister Ursula informed me, and we got to our feet. "I am needed. Even a hateful nun is sometimes needed."

At the front door, I decided to ask. "One thing," I said. "The fire . . . that destroyed the school?"

Sister Ursula smiled and took my hand. "No," she assured me. "All I did was pray."

She looked off across the years, though, remembering. "Ah, but the flames," she said, her old eyes bright with a young woman's fire. "They reached almost to heaven."

18

DIED AND GONE TO VEGAS

Tim Gautreaux

Raynelle Bullfinch told the young oiler that the only sense of mystery in her life was provided by a deck of cards. As she set up the card table in the engine room of the *Leo B. Canterbury*, a government steam dredge anchored in a pass at the mouth of the Mississippi River, she lectured him. "Nick, you're just a college boy laying out a bit until you get money to go back to school, but for me, this is it." She pulled a coppery braid from under her overalls strap, looked around at the steam chests and piping, and sniffed at the smell of heatproof red enamel. In the glass of a steam gauge she checked her round, bright cheeks for grease and ran a white finger over the blue arcs of her eyebrows. She was the cook on the big boat, which was idle for a couple days because of high winter winds. "My big adventure is cards. One day I'll save up enough to play with the skill boys in Vegas. Set up those folding chairs," she told him. "Seven in all."

"I don't know how to play bourrée, ma'am." Nick Montalbano ran a hand through long hair shiny with dressing. "I only had one semester of college." He looked sideways at the power straining the bronze buckles of the tall woman's bib and avoided her green eyes, which were deep set and full of intense judgment.

"Bullshit. A pet rat can play bourrée. Sit down." She pointed to a metal chair and the oiler, a thin boy wearing an untucked plaid flannel shirt and a baseball cap, obeyed. "Pay attention, here. I deal out five cards to everybody, and I turn up the last card. Whatever suit it is, that's trumps. Then you discard all your nontrumps and draw replacements. Remember, trumps beat all other suits, high trumps beat low trumps. Whatever card is led, you follow suit." She ducked her head under the bill of his cap, looking for his eyes. "That ain't too hard for you, is it? Ain't college stuff more complicated than this?"

"Sure, sure. I understand, but what if you can't follow suit?"

"If nontrumps is led, put a trump on it. If you ain't got no more trumps, just throw your lowest card. Trust me, you'll catch on quick."

"How do you win?" The oiler turned his cap around.

"Every hand has five tricks to take. If you take three tricks, you win the pot. Only on this boat, we got a special rule. If only two decide to play that hand after the draw, then it takes four tricks to win. If you got any questions, ask Sydney, there."

Sydney, the chief engineer, a little fireplug of a man who would wear a white T-shirt in a blizzard, sat down heavily with a whistle. "Oh boy. Fresh meat." He squeezed the oiler's neck.

The steel door next to the starboard triple-expansion engine opened, letting in a wash of frigid air around the day fireman, pilot, deckhand, and welder who came into the big room cursing and clapping the cold out of their clothes. Through the door the angry whitecaps of Southwest Pass raced down the Mississippi, bucking into the tarnished Gulf sky.

"Close that damned pneumonia hole," Raynelle cried, sailing cards precisely before the seven chairs. "Sit down, worms. Usual game, dollar ante, five-dollar rip if you don't take a trick." After the rattle of halves and dollars came discards, more dealing, and then a flurry of cards, ending with diminishing snowstorm of curses as no one took three tricks and the pot rolled over to the next hand. Three players took no tricks and put up the five-dollar rip.

The engineer unrolled a pack of Camels from his T-shirt sleeve and cursed loudest. "I heard of a bourrée game on a offshore rig where the pot didn't clear for eighty-three passes. By the time somebody won that bitch, it had seventeen hundred dollars in it. The next day the genius what took it got a wrench upside the head in a Morgan City bar and woke up with his pockets inside out and the name Conchita tattooed around his left nipple."

Pig, the day fireman, put up his ante and collected the next hand. "That ain't nothin' ." He touched three discards to the top of his bald head and threw them down. "A ol' boy down at the dock told me the other day that he heard about a fellow got hit in the head over in Orange, Texas, and didn't know who he was when he looked at his driver's license. Had amnesia. That sorry-ass seaman's hospital sent him home to his scuzzbag wife, and he didn't know her from Adam's house cat."

"That mighta been a blessing," Raynelle said, turning the last card of the deal to see what trumps was. "Spades." She rolled left on her ample bottom.

"No, it wasn't," the day fireman said, unzipping his heavy green field jacket. "That gal told him she was his sister, gave him a remote control and a color TV, and he was happy as a fly on a pie. She started bringing her boyfriends in at night and that fool waved them into the house. Fixed 'em drinks. Figured any old dude good enough for Sis was good enough for him. The neighbors got to lookin' at her like they was smelling something dead, so she and her old man moved to a better trailer park where nobody knew he'd lost his memory. She started into cocaine and hookin' for fun on the side. Her husband's settlement money he got from the company what dropped a thirty-six-inch Stillson on his hard hat began to shrink up a bit, but that old boy just sat there dizzy on some cheap pills she told him was a prescription. He'd channel surf all day, greet the johns like one of those dried-up coots at Wal-Mart, and was the happiest son of a bitch in Orange, Texas." The day fireman spread wide his arms. "Was he glad to see Sis come home every day. He was proud she had more friends than a postman with a bagful of welfare checks. And then his memory came back."

"Ho, ho, the *merde* hit the blower," the engineer said, slamming a queen down and raking in a trick.

"Nope. That poor bastard remembered every giggle in the rear bedroom and started feeling lower than a snake's nuts. He tried to get his old woman straight, but the dyed-over tramp just laughed in his face and moved out on him. He got so sorry that he went to a shrink, but that just cost him more bucks. Finally, you know what that old dude wound up doin'? He looked for someone would hit him in the head again. You know, so he could get back the way he was. He offered a hundred dollars a pop, and in them Orange bars most people will whack on you for free, so you can imagine what kind of service he bought hisself. After nearly getting killed four or five times, he give up and spent the rest of his settlement money on a hospital stay for a concussion. After that he held up a Pac-a-Bag for enough money to get himself hypnotized back to like he was after he got hit the first time. Wound up in the pen doin' twenty hard ones."

They played three hands of cards while the day fireman finished the story, and then the deckhand in the game, a thick blond man in a black cotton sweater, threw back his head and laughed—*ha-ha*—as if he was only pretending. "If that wadn' so funny, it'd be sad. It reminds me of this dumb-ass peckerwood kid lived next to me in Kentucky, built like a stringbean. He was a few thimbles shy of a quart, but he sort of knew he won't no nuclear-power-plant repairman and he got along with everybody. Then he started hanging with these badass kids—you know, the kind that carry spray paint, wear their hats backward, and pack your mailbox full of live rats. Well, they told the poor bastard he was some kind of Jesse James and got him into stealing hubcaps and electric drills. He started strutting around the neighborhood like he was bad shit, and soon the local deputies had him in the backseat for running off with a lawn mower. Dummy stole it in December."

"What's wrong with that?" the day fireman asked, pitching in a dollar.

"Who's gonna buy a used mower in winter, you moron? Anyway, the judge had pity on him—gave him a pissant fine and sent him to bed with a sugar tit. Said he was a good boy who ought to be satisfied to be simple and honest. But String Bean hung out on the street corner crowing. He was proud now. A real gangster, happy as Al Capone, his head pumped full of swamp gas by those losers he's hanging around with. Finally, one night he breaks into a house of a gun collector. Showing how smart he is, he chooses only one gun to take from the rack, an engraved Purdy double-barrel, mint condition, with gold and ivory inlays all over, a twenty-thousand-dollar gun. String Bean took it home and with a two-dollar hacksaw cut the stock off and then most of the barrel. He went out and held up a taco joint and got sixteen dollars and thirteen cents. Was arrested when he walked out the door. This time, a hard-nut judge sent him up on a multiple bill and he got two-hundred and ninety-seven years in Bisley."

"All right," Raynelle sang. "Better than death."

"He did ten years before the weepy-ass parole board noticed the sentence and pulled him in for review. Asked him did he get rehabilitated and would he go straight if he got out, and he spit on their mahogany table. He told them he won't no dummy and would be the richest bank robber in Kentucky if he got half a chance." The deckhand laughed—*ha-ha*. "That give everybody a icicle up the ass, and the meetin' came to a vote right quick. Even the American Civil Liberties lesbo lawyers on the parole board wanted to weld the door shut on him. It was something'."

The pilot, a tall man wearing a pea jacket and a sock cap, raised a new hand to his sharp blue eyes and winced, keeping one trump and asking for four cards. "Gentlemen, that reminds me of a girl in Kentucky I knew at one time."

"Why? Did she get sent up two hundred and ninety-seven years in Bisley?" the deckhand asked.

"No, she was from Kentucky, like that crazy fellow you just lied to us about. By the way, that king won't walk," he said, laying down an ace of diamonds. "This woman was a nurse at the VA hospital in Louisville and fell in love with one of her patients, a good-looking, mild-mannered fellow with a cyst in his brain that popped and gave him amnesia."

"Now, there's something you don't hear every day," the engineer said, trumping the ace with a bang.

"He didn't know what planet he came from," the pilot said stiffly. "A few months later they got married and he went to work in a local iron plant. After a year he began wandering away from work at lunchtime. So they fired him. He spent a couple of weeks walking up and down his street and all over Louisville, looking into people's yards and checking passing buses for faces in the windows. It was like he was looking for someone, but he couldn't remember who. One day he didn't come home at all. For eighteen months this pretty little nurse was beside herself with worry. Then her nephew was at a rock concert downtown and spotted a shaggy guy in the mosh pit who looked familiar. He was just standing there like he was watching a string quartet. Between songs, he asked him if he had amnesia, which is a rather odd question, considering, and the man almost started crying because he figured he'd been recognized."

"That's a sweet story," the day fireman said, rubbing his eyes with his bear paw-sized hands. "Sydney, could you loan me your handkerchief? I'm all choked up."

"Choke this," the pilot said, trumping the fireman's jack. "Anyway, the little nurse gets attached to the guy again and is glad to have him back. She refreshes his memory about their marriage and all that and starts over with him. Things are better than ever, as far as she is concerned. Well, about a year of marital bliss goes by, and one evening there's a knock at the door. She gets up off the sofa where the amnesia guy is, opens it, and it's her husband, whose memory came back."

"Wait a minute," the deckhand said. "I thought that was her husband on the sofa."

"I never said it was her husband. She just thought it was her husband. It turns out that the guy on the sofa she's been living with for a year is the identical twin to the guy on the doorstep. Got an identical popped cyst, too."

"Aw, bullshit," the day fireman bellowed.

The engineer leaned back and put his hand on a valve handle. "I better pump this place out."

"Hey," the pilot yelled above the bickering. "I knew this girl. Her family lived across the street from my aunt. Anyway, after all the explanations were made, the guy who surfaced at the rock concert agreed it would be best if he moved on, and the wandering twin started back where he left off with his wife. Got his job back at the iron plant. But the wife wasn't happy anymore."

"Why the hell not?" the engineer asked, dealing the next hand. "She had two for the price of one."

"Yeah, well, even though those guys were identical in every way, something was different. We'll never know what it was, but she couldn't get over the second twin. Got so she would wander around herself, driving all over town looking for him."

"What the hell?" The deckhand threw down his cards. "She had her husband back, didn't she?"

"Oh, it was bad," the pilot continued. "She's driving down the street one day and sees the rock-concert twin, gets out of her car, runs into a park yelling and sobbing and throws her arms around him, crying, 'I found you at last. I found you at last.' Only it wasn't him."

"Jeez," the engineer said. "Triplets."

"No." The pilot shook his head. "It was worse than that. It was her husband, who was out on delivery for the iron plant, taking a break in the park after shucking his coveralls. Mild-mannered amnesiac or not, he was pretty put out at the way she was carrying on. But he didn't show it. He pretended to be his twin and asked her why she liked him better than her husband. And she told him. Now, don't ask me what it was. The difference was in her mind, way I heard it. But that guy disappeared again the next morning, and that was five years ago. They say you can go down in east Louisville and see her driving around today in a ratty green Torino, looking for one of those twins, this scared look in her eyes like she'll find one and'll never be sure which one she got hold of."

Raynelle pulled a pecan out of her overalls bib and cracked it between her thumb and forefinger. "That story's sadder'n a armless old man in a room full of skeeters. You sorry sons of bitches tell the depressingest lies I ever heard."

The deckhand lit up an unfiltered cigarette. "Well, sweet thing, why don't you cheer us up with one of your own."

Raynelle looked up at a brass steam gauge bolted to an I beam. "I did know a fellow worked in an iron foundry, come to think of it. His whole family worked the same place, which is a pain in the ass, if you've ever done that, what with your uncle giving you wet willies and your cousin bumming money. This fellow drove a gray Dodge Dart, the kind with the old slant-six engine that'll carry you to hell and back, slow. His relatives made fun of him for it, said he was cheap and wore plastic shoes, and ate Spam, that kind of thing." She turned the last card to show trumps, banging up a king. "Sidney, you better not bourrée again. You in this pot for thirty dollars."

The engineer swept up his hand, pressing it against his T-shirt. "I can count."

"Anyway, this boy thought he'd show his family a thing or two and went out and proposed to the pretty girl who keyed in the invoices in the office.

He bought her a diamond ring on time that would choke an elephant. It was a *nice* ring." Raynelle looked at the six men around the table as if none of them would ever buy such a ring. "He was gonna give it to her on her birthday right before they got married in three weeks, and meantime he showed it around at the iron foundry figuring it'd make 'em shut up, which basically it did."

"They was probably speechless at how dumb he was," the deckhand said out of the side of his mouth.

"But don't you know that before he got to give it to her, that girl hit her head on the edge of her daddy's swimming pool and drowned. The whole foundry went into mourning, as did those kids' families and the little town in general. She had a big funeral and she was laid out in her wedding dress in a white casket surrounded by every carnation in four counties. Everybody was crying and the funeral parlor had this lovely music playing. I guess the boy got caught up in the feeling, because he walked over to the coffin right before they was gonna screw down the lid and he put that engagement ring on that girl's finger."

"Naw," the engineer said breathlessly, laying a card without looking at it.

"Yes, he did. And he felt proud that he done it—at least for a month or two. Then he began to have eyes for a dental hygienist, and that little romance took off hot as a bottle rocket. He courted her for six months and decided to pop the question. But he started thinking about the monthly payments he was making on that ring and how they would go on for four and a half more years, keeping him from affording a decent ring for this living girl."

"Oh, no," the pilot said, as the hand split again and the pot rolled over yet another time.

"That's right. He got some tools and after midnight went down to Heavenly Oaks Mausoleum and unscrewed the marble door on her drawer, slid out the coffin, and opened it up. I don't know how he could stand to rummage around in whatever was left in the box, but damned if he didn't get that ring and put the grave back together slick as a whistle. So the next day, he give it to the hygienist and everything's okay. A bit later they get married and're doin' the lovebird bit in a trailer down by the foundry." Raynelle cracked another pecan against the edge of the table, crushing it with the pressure of her palm in a way that made the welder and the oiler look at each other. "But there's a big blue blowfly in the ointment. She's showing off that ring by the minute and someone recognized the damned thing and told her. Well, she had a thirty-megaton double-PMS hissy fit and told him straight up that she won't wear no dead woman's ring, and throws it in his face. Said the thing gave her the willies. He told her it's that or a King Edward cigar band, because he won't get out from under the payments until the twenty-first century. It went back and forth like that for a month, with the neighbors up and down the road, including my aunt Tammy, calling the police to come get them to shut up. Finally, the hygienist told him she'd wear the ring."

"Well, that's a happy ending," the deckhand said.

Raynelle popped half a pecan into her red mouth. "Shut up, Jack. I ain't finished. This hygienist began to wear cowboy blouses and jean miniskirts just like the girl in the foundry office did. The old boy kind of liked it at first, but when she dyed her hair the same color as the first girl, it gave him the shakes. She said she was dreaming of that dead girl at least twice a week and saw her in her dresser mirror when she woke up. Then she began to talk like the foundry girl did, with a snappy Arkansas twang. And the dead girl was a country-music freak, liked the old stuff, too. Damned if in the middle of the night the guy wasn't waked up by his wife singing in her sleep all eleven verses of 'El Paso,' the Marty Robbins tune.

"He figured it was the ring causing all the trouble, so he got his wife drunk and while she was asleep slipped that sucker off and headed to the graveyard to put it back on that bone where he took it. Soon as he popped the lid, the cops were on him asking him what the living hell he was doing. He told them he was putting a diamond ring back in the coffin, and they said, sure, buddy. Man, he got charged with six or eight nasty things perverts do to dead bodies, and then the dead girl's family filed six or eight civil suits, and believe me, there was mental anguish, pain, and suffering enough to feed the whole county. A local judge who was the dead girl's uncle sent him up for six years, and the hygienist divorced his ass good. Strange thing was that she kept her new hair color and way of dressing, began going to George Jones concerts, and last I heard she'd quit her job at the dentist and was running the computers down at the iron foundry."

"Raynelle, *chère*, I wish you wouldn'ta said that one." Simoneaux, the welder, never spoke much until late in the game. He was a thin Cajun, seldom without a Camel in the corner of his mouth and a high-crowned polka-dotted welder's cap turned backward on his head. He shrugged off a violent chill. "That story gives me *les frissons* up and down my back." A long stick of beef jerky jutted from the pocket of his flannel shirt. He pulled it out, plucked a lint ball from the bottom, and bit off a small knob of meat. "But that diamond shit reminds me of a old boy I knew down in Grand Crapaud who was working on Pancho Oil number six offshore from Point au Fer. The driller was puttin' down the pipe hard one day and my friend the mud engineer was takin' a dump on the engine room toilet. All at once they hit them a gas pocket at five t'ousand feet and drill pipe came back up that hole like drinkin' straws, knockin' out the top of the rig, flyin' up in the sky, and breakin' apart at the joints. Well, my frien', he had a magazine spread out across his lap when a six-inch drill pipe hit the roof like a spear and went through and through the main diesel engine. About a half second later, another one passed between his knees, through the Playmate of the Month and the steel deck both, yeah. He could hear the iron comin' down all over the rig, but he couldn't run because his pants was around his ankles on the other side the drill column between his legs. He figured he was goin' to glory with a unwiped ass, but a worm run in the engine room and cut him loose with a jackknife, and then they both took off over the side and hit the water. My frien' rolled through them breakers holdin' on to a drum of mineral spirits, floppin' around until a badass fish gave him a bite on his giblets, and that was the only injury he had."

"Ouch, man." The deckhand crossed his legs.

"What?" Raynelle looked up while posting her five-dollar bourrée.

The welder threw in yet another ante, riffling the dollar bills in the pot as though figuring how much it weighed. "Well, he was hurt enough to get the company to pay him a lump sum after he got a four-by-four lawyer to sue their two-by-four insurance company. That's for true. My frien', he always said he wanted a fancy car. The first thing he did was to drive to Lafayette and buy a sixty-five-thousand-dollar Mercedes, yeah. He put new mud-grip tires on that and drove it down to the Church Key Lounge in Morgan City, where all his mud-pumpin' buddies hung out, an' it didn't take long to set off about half a dozen of them hard hats, no." Simoneaux shook his narrow head. "He was braggin' bad, yeah."

The engineer opened his cards on his belly and rolled his eyes. "A new Mercedes in Morgan City? Sheee-it."

"*Mais*, you can say that again. About two, tree o'clock in the mornin' my frien', he come out and what he saw woulda made a muskrat cry. Somebody took a number-two ball-peen hammer and dented every place on that car that would take a dent. That t'ing looked like it got caught in a cue-ball tornado storm. Next day he brought it by the insurance people and they told him the policy didn't cover vandalism. Told him he would have to pay to get it fixed or drive it like that.

"But my frien', he had blew all his money on the car to begin with. When he drove it, everybody looked at him like he was some kind of freak. You know, he wanted people to look at him—that's why he bought the car—but they was lookin' at him the wrong way, like 'You mus' be some prime jerk to have someone mess with you car like that.' So after a week of havin' people run off the road turnin' their necks to look at that new

Mercedes, he got drunk, went to the store, and bought about twenty cans of Bondo, tape, and cans of spray paint."

"Don't say it," the deckhand cried.

"No, no," the engineer said to his cards.

"What?" Raynelle asked.

"Yeah, the poor bastard couldn't make a snake out of Play-Doh but he's gonna try and restore a fine European se-dan. He filed and sanded on that poor car for a week, then hit it with that dollar-a-can paint. When he finished up, that Mercedes looked like it was battered for fryin'. He drove it around Grand Crapaud, and people just pointed and doubled over. He kept it outside his trailer at night, and people would drive up and park, just to look at it. Phone calls started comin', the hang-up kind that said things like 'You look like your car,' *click*, or 'What kind of icing did you use?' *click*. My frien' finally took out his insurance policy and saw what it did cover. It was theft.

"So he started leavin' the keys in it parked down by the abandoned lumberyard, but nobody in Grand Crapaud would steal it. He drove to Lafayette, rented a motel room, yeah, and parked it outside that bad housing project, with keys in it." The welder threw in another hand and watched the cards fly. "Next night he left the windows down with the keys in it." He pulled off his polka-dotted cap and ran his fingers through his dark hair. "Third night he left the motor runnin' and the lights on with the car blockin' the driveway of a crack house. Next mornin' he found it twenty feet away, idled out of diesel with a dead battery. It was that ugly."

"What happened next?" The pilot trumped an ace like he was killing a bug.

"My frien', he called me up, you know. Said he wished he had a used standard-shift Ford pickup and the money in the bank. His wife left him, his momma made him take a cab to come see her, and all he could stand to do was drink and stay in his trailer. I didn't know what to tell him. He said he was gonna read his policy some more."

"Split pot again," the deckhand shouted. "I can't get out this game. I feel like my nuts is hung up in a fan belt."

"Shut your trap and deal," Raynelle said, sailing a loose wad of cards in the deckhand's direction. "What happened to the Mercedes guy?"

The welder put his cap back on and pulled up the crown. "Well, his policy said it covered all kinds of accidents, you know, so he parked it back next to a big longleaf pine and cut that sucker down, only it was a windy day and as soon as he got through that tree with the saw, a gust come up and pushed it the other way from where he wanted it to fall."

"What'd it hit?"

"It mashed his trailer like a cockroach, yeah. The propane stove blew up and by the time the Grand Crapaud fire truck come around, all they could do was break out coat hangers and mushmellas. His wife what lef' ain't paid the insurance on the double-wide, no, so now he got to get him a camp stove and a picnic table, so he can shack up in the Mercedes."

"He lived in the car?"

The welder nodded glumly. "Po' bastard wouldn't do nothin' but drink up the few bucks he had lef' and lie in the backseat. One night last fall we had that cold snap, you remember? It got so cold around Grand Crapaud you could hear the sugarcane stalks popping out in the fields like firecrackers. They found my frien' froze to death sittin' up behind the steering wheel. T-nook, the paramedic, said his eyes was open, starin' over the hood like he was goin' for a drive." The welder pushed his down-turned hand out slowly like a big sedan driving toward the horizon. Everybody's eyes followed it for a long moment.

"New deck," the engineer cried, throwing in his last trump and watching it get swallowed by a jack. "Nick, you little dago, give me that blue deck." The oiler, a quiet, olive-skinned boy from New Orleans's west bank, pushed the new box over. "New deck, new luck," the engineer told him. "You know, I used to date this ol' fat gal lived in a double-wide north of Biloxi. God, that woman liked to eat. When I called it off, she asked me why, and I told her I was afraid she was going to get thirteen inches around the ankles. That must have got her attention, because she went on some kind of fat-killer diet and exercise program that about wore out the floor beams in that trailer. But she got real slim, I heard. She had a pretty face, I'll admit that. She started hitting the bars and soon had her a cow farmer ask her to marry him, which she did."

"Is a cow farmer like a rancher?" Raynelle asked, her tongue in her cheek like a jawbreaker.

"It's what I said it was. Who the hell ever heard of a ranch in Biloxi? Anyway, this old gal developed a fancy for steaks, since her man got meat reasonable, being a cow farmer and all. She started putting away the T-bones and swelling like a sow on steroids. After a year, she blowed up to her fighting weight and then some. I heard she'd about eat up half the cows on the farm before he told her he wanted a divorce. She told him she'd sue to get half the farm, and he said go for it. It'd be worth it if someone would just roll her off his half. She hooked up with this greasy little lawyer from Waveland and sure enough he got half the husband's place. After the court dealings, he took this old gal out to supper to celebrate and one thing led to another and they wound up at her apartment for a little slap-and-tickle. I'll be damned if they didn't fall out of bed together with her on top, and he

301

broke three ribs and ruined a knee on a night table. After a year of treatments, he sued her good and got her half of the farm."

The deckhand threw his head back and laughed—*ha-ha*. "That's a double screwin' if ever there was one."

"Hey, it don't stop there. The little lawyer called up the farmer and said, 'Since we gonna be neighbors, why don't you tell me a good spot to build a house?' They got together and hit it off real good, like old drinkin' buddies. After a couple months, the lawyer went into business with the farmer and together they doubled the cattle production, 'specially since they got rid of the critters' worst predator."

Raynelle's eyebrows came together like a small thunderhead. "Well?"

"Well what?" The engineer scratched an armpit.

"What happened to that poor girl?"

All the men looked around uneasily. Raynelle had permanently disabled a boilermaker on the *St. Genevieve* with a cornbread skillet.

"She got back on her diet, I heard. Down to one hundred twenty pounds again."

"That's the scary thing about women," the day fireman volunteered, putting up three fingers to ask for his draw. "Marryin' 'em is just like cuttin' the steel bands on a bale of cotton. First thing you know, you've got a roomful of woman."

Raynelle glowered. "Careful I don't pour salt on you and watch you melt."

The engineer released a sigh. "Okay, Nick, you the only one ain't told a lie yet. Let's have some good bullshit."

The young oiler ducked his head. "Don't know none."

"Haw," Raynelle said. "A man without bullshit. Check his drawers, Simoneaux, see he ain't Nancy instead of Nicky."

Reddening, the oiler frowned at his hand. "Well, the cows remind me of something I heard while I was playing the poker machines over in Port Allen the other day," he said, a long strand of black hair falling in his eyes. "There was this Mexican guy named Gonzales who worked with cows in Matamoros."

"Another cow farmer," the deckhand groaned.

"Shut up," Raynelle said. "Was that his first name or second name?"

"Well, both."

"What?" She pitched a card at him.

"Aw, Miss Raynelle, you know how those Mexicans are with their names. This guy's name was Gonzales Gonzales, with a bunch of names in between." Raynelle cocked her ear whenever she heard the oiler speak. She had a hard time with his New Orleans accent, which she found to be Bronx-like. "He was a pretty smart fella and got into Texas legal, worked a few years and became a naturalized citizen, him and his wife both."

"What was his wife's name?" the pilot asked. "Maria Maria?"

"Come on, now, do you want to hear this or don'tcha?" The oiler pushed the hair out of his eyes. "The cattle industry shrunk up where he was at, and he looked around for another place to try and settle. He started to go to Gonzales, Texas, but there ain't no work there, so he gets out a map and spots Gonzales, Louisiana."

"That that rough place with all the jitterbug joints?"

"Yep. Lots of coon-asses and roughnecks, but they ain't no Mexicans. Must have been settled a million years ago by a family of Gonzaleses, who probably speak French and eat gumbo nowadays. So Gonzales Gonzales gets him a job working for two brothers who are lawyers and who run a horse farm on the side. He gets an apartment on Gonzales Street, down by the train station." The oiler looked at a new hand, fanning the cards out slowly. "You know how badass the Airline Highway cops are through there? Well, this Gonzales was dark, and his car was a beat-up smoker, so they pulled him one day on his way to Baton Rouge. The cop stands outside his window and says, 'Lemme see your license,' to which Gonzales says he forgot it at home on the dresser. The cop pulls out a ticket book and says, 'What's your last name?' to which he says, 'Gonzales.' The cop says, 'What's your first name?' And he tells him. That officer leans in the window and sniffs his breath. 'Okay, Gonzales Gonzales,' he says real nasty, 'where you live?' 'Gonzales,' he says. 'Okay, boy. Get out the car,' the cop says. He throws him against the door hard. 'And who do you work for?' Gonzales looks him in the eye and says, 'Gonzales and Gonzales.' The cop turns him around and slams his head against the roof and says, 'Yeah, and you probably live on Gonzales Street, huh, you slimy son of a bitch.' 'At Twelve twenty-six, apartment E,' Gonzales says."

The deckhand put his cards over his eyes. "The poor bastard."

"Yeah," the oiler said, and sighed. "He got beat up and jailed that time until the Gonzales brothers went up and sprung him. About once a month some cop would pull him over and give him hell. When he applied for a little loan at the bank, they threw his ass in the street. When he tried to get a credit card, the company called the feds, who investigated him for fraud. Nobody would cash his checks, and the first year he filed state and federal taxes, three government cars stayed in his driveway for a week. Nobody believed who he was."

"That musta drove him nuts," the welder said, drawing four cards.

"I don't think so, man. He knew who he was. Gonzales Gonzales knew he was in America and you could control what you was, unlike in Mexico. So when the traffic cops beat him up, he sold his car and got a bike. When the banks wouldn't give him no checks, he used cash. When the tax people refused to admit he existed, he stopped payin' taxes. Man, he worked hard and saved every penny. One day it was real hot, and he was walkin' into Gonzales because his bike had a flat. He stopped in the Rat's Nest Lounge to get a root beer, and they was this drunk fool from west Texas in there making life hard for the barmaid. He come over to Gonzales and asked him would he have a drink. He said sure, and the bartender set up a whiskey and a root beer. The cowboy was full of Early Times and pills, and you coulda lit a blowtorch off his eyeballs. He put his arm around Gonzales and asked him what his name was, you know. When he heard it, he got all serious, like he was bein' made fun of or something. He asked a couple more questions and started struttin' and cussin'. He pulled out from under a cheesy denim jacket an engraved Colt and stuck it in Gonzales's mouth. 'You jerkin' me around, man,' that cowboy told him. 'You tellin' me you're Gonzales Gonzales from Gonzales who lives on Gonzales Street and works for Gonzales and Gonzales?' That Mexican looked at the gun, and I don't know what was goin' through his head, but he nodded, and the cowboy pulled back the hammer."

"Damn," the welder said.

"I don't want to hear this." Raynelle clapped the cards to her ears.

"Hey," the oiler said. "Like I told you, he knew who he was. He pointed to the phone book by the register, and after a minute the bartender had it open and held it out to the cowboy. Sure enough, old Ma Bell had come through for the American way and Gonzales was listed, with the street and all. The cowboy took the gun out Gonzales's mouth and started crying like the crazy snail he was. He told Gonzales that he was sorry and gave him the Colt. Said that his girlfriend left him and his dog died, or maybe it was the other way around. Gonzales went down the street and called the cops. In two months he got a six-thousand-dollar reward for turning in the guy, who, it turns out, had killed his girlfriend and his dog, too, over in Laredo. He got five hundred for the Colt and moved to Baton Rouge, where he started a postage stamp of a used-car lot. Did well, too. Got a dealership now."

The day fireman snapped his fingers. "G. Gonzales Buick-Olds?"

"That's it, man," the oiler said.

"The smilin' rich dude in the commercials?"

"Like I said," the oiler told the table, "he knew who he was."

"Mary and Joseph, everybody is in this hand," the pilot yelled. "Spades is trumps."

"*Laissez les bons temps rouler*," the welder sang, laying an eight of spades on a pile of diamonds and raking in the trick.

"That's your skinny ass," Raynelle said, playing a ten of spades last, taking the second trick.

"Do I smell the ten-millionth rollover pot?" the engineer asked. "There must be six hundred fifty dollars in that pile." He threw down a nine and covered the third trick.

"Coming gitcha." Raynelle raised her hand high, plucked a card, and slammed a jack to win the fourth trick. That was two. She led the king of spades and watched the cards follow.

The pilot put his hands together and prayed. "Please, somebody, have the ace." He played his card and sat up to watch as each man threw his last card in, no one able to beat the king, and then Raynelle leapt like a hooked marlin, nearly upsetting the table, screaming and waving her meaty arms through the steamy engine room air. "I never won so much money in my life," she cried, falling from the waist onto the pile of bills and coins and raking it beneath her.

"Whatcha gonna do with all that money?" the welder asked, turning his hat around in disbelief.

She began stuffing the bib pocket on her overalls with half-dollars. "I'm gonna buy me a silver lamé dress and one of those cheap tickets to Las Vegas, where I can do some high-class gamblin'. No more of this penny-ante stuff with old men and worms."

Five of the men got up to relieve their bladders or get cigarettes or grab something to drink. The pilot stood up and leaned against a column of insulated pipe. "Hell, we all want to go to Las Vegas. Don't you want to take one of us along to the holy land?"

"Man, I'm gonna gamble with gentlemen. Ranchers, not cow farmers, either." She folded a wad of bills into a hip pocket.

Nick, the young oiler, laced his fingers behind his head, leaned back, and closed his eyes. He wondered what Raynelle would do in such a glitzy place as Las Vegas. He imagined her wearing a Sears gown in a casino full of tourists dressed in shorts and sneakers. She would be drinking too much and eating too much, and the gown would look like it was crammed with rising dough. She would get in a fight with a blackjack dealer after she'd lost all her money, and then she would be thrown out on the street. After selling her plane ticket, she would be back at the slot machines until she was completely broke, and then she would be on a neon-infested boulevard, her tiny silver purse hanging from her shoulder on a long spaghetti strap, one heel broken off a silver shoe. He saw her at last walking across the desert through the waves of heat, mountains in front and the angry snarl of cross-country traffic in the rear, until she sobered up and began to hitch, picked up by a carload of Jehovah's Witnesses driving to a convention in Baton Rouge in an un-air-conditioned compact stuck in second gear. Every thirty miles the car would overheat and they would all get out, stand among the cactus, and pray. Raynelle would curse them, and they would pray harder for the big, sunburned woman sweating in the metallic dress. The desert would spread before her as far as the end of the world, a hot and rocky place empty of mirages and dreams. She might not live to get out of it.

19

GOOD FOR
THE SOUL

Tim Gautreaux

Father Ledet took a scorching swallow of brandy and sat in an iron chair on the brick patio behind the rectory, hemmed in by walls of privet stitched through with honeysuckle. His stomach was full from the Ladies' Altar Society supper, where the sweet, sweet women of the parish had fed him pork roast, potato salad, and sweet peas, filling his plate and making over him as if he were an old spayed tomcat who kept the cellar free of rats. He was a big man, white-haired and ruddy, with gray eyes and huge spotted hands that could make a highball glass disappear. It was Thursday evening and nothing much happened on Thursday evenings. The first cool front of the fall was breezing through the pecan trees on the church lot, and nothing is so important in Louisiana as that first release from the sopping, buggy, overheated funk of the atmosphere. Father Ledet breathed deeply in the shadow of a statue of Saint Francis. He took another long swallow, glad that the assistant pastor was on a visit home in Iowa and that the deacon wouldn't be around until the next afternoon. Two pigeons lit on Saint Francis's upturned hands as if they knew who he was. Father Ledet watched the light fade and the privet darken, and then he looked a long time at the pint of brandy before deciding to pour himself another drink.

The phone rang in the rectory, and he got up carefully, moving inside among the dark wood furnishings and dim holy light. It was a parishioner, Mrs. Clyde Arceneaux, whose husband was dying of emphysema.

"We need you for the Anointing of the Sick, Father."

"Um, yes." He tried to say something else, but the words were stuck back in his throat, the way dollar bills sometimes wadded up in the tubular poor box and wouldn't drop down when he opened the bottom.

"Father?"

"Of course. I'll just come right over there."

"I know you did it for him last week. But this time, he might really be going, you know." Mrs. Arceneaux's voice began to sound teary. "He wants you to hear his confession."

"Um." The priest had known Clyde Arceneaux for fifteen years. The old man dressed up on Sunday, came to church, but he stayed out on the steps and smoked with three other men as reverent as himself. As far as he knew, Clyde had never been to confession.

Father Ledet locked the rectory door and went into the garage to start the parish car, a venerable black Lincoln. He backed out onto the street, and when the car stopped, he still floated along in a drifting crescent, and he realized that he'd had maybe an ounce too much of brandy. It occurred to him that he should call the housekeeper to drive him to the hospital. It would take only five minutes for her to come over, but then, the old Baptist woman was always figuring him out, and he would have to endure Mrs. Scott's roundabout questions and sniffs of the air. Father Ledet felt his mossy human side take over, and he began to navigate the streets of the little town on his own, stopping the car too far into the intersection at Jackman Avenue, clipping a curb on a turn at Bourgeois Street. The car had its logical movement, but his head had a motion of its own.

Patrolman Vic Garafola was parked in front of the post office, talking to the dispatcher about a cow eating string beans out of Mrs. LeBlanc's garden, when he heard a crash in the intersection behind him. In his rearview, he saw that a long black sedan had battered the side of a powder-blue Ford. He backed his cruiser fifty feet and turned on his flashers. When he got out and saw his own parish priest sitting wide-eyed behind the steering wheel, he ran to the window.

"You all right, Father?"

The priest had a little red mark on his high forehead, but he smiled dumbly and nodded. Patrolman Garafola looked over to the smashed passenger side door of a faded Crown Victoria. A pretty older woman sat in the middle of the bench seat holding her elbow. He opened the door and saw that Mrs. Mamie Barrilleaux's right arm was obviously broken, and her mouth was twitching with pain. Vic's face reddened because it made him angry to see nice people get hurt when it wasn't their fault.

"Mrs. Mamie, you hurtin' a lot?" Vic asked. Behind him, the priest walked up and put his hand on Vic's shoulder. When the woman saw Father Ledet, her face was transfigured.

"Oh, it's nothing, just a little bump. Father, did I cause the accident?"

The patrolman looked at the priest for the answer.

"Mamie, your arm." He took his hand off the policeman and stepped back. Vic could see that the priest was shocked. He knew that Father Ledet was called out to give last rites to strangers at gory highway wrecks all the time, but this woman was the vice president of the Ladies' Altar Society, the group who polished the old church, put flowers on the altar, knit afghans to put on his lap in the drafty wooden rectory.

"Father, Mrs. Mamie had the right-of-way." Vic pointed to the stop sign behind the priest's steaming car.

"I am dreadfully sorry," Father Ledet said. "I was going to the hospital to administer the Anointing of the Sick, and I guess my mind was on that."

"Oh," Mrs. Barrilleaux cried. "Who's that ill?"

"Mrs. Arceneaux's husband."

Another cruiser pulled up, its lights sparking up the evening. Mrs. Barrilleaux pointed at it. "Vic, can you take him to the hospital and let this other policeman write the report? I know Mrs. Arceneaux's husband, and he needs a priest bad."

Vic looked down at his shoe. He wasn't supposed to do anything like that. "You want to go on to the hospital and then I can bring you back here, Father?"

"Mamie's the one who should go to the hospital."

"Shoo." She waved her good hand at him. "I can hear the ambulance coming now. Go on; I'm not dying."

Vic could see a slight trembling in Mamie's silver-laced curls. He put a hand on the priest's arm. "Okay, Father?"

"Okay."

They got into the cruiser and immediately Vic smelled the priest's breath. He drove under the tunnel of oak trees that was Nadine Avenue and actually bit his tongue to keep from asking the inevitable question. When they were in sight of the hospital, Patrolman Garafola could no longer stop himself. "Father, did you have anything to drink today?"

The priest looked at him and blanched. "Why do you ask?"

"It's on your breath. Whiskey."

"Brandy," the priest corrected. "Yes, I had some brandy after supper."

"How much?"

"Not too much. Well, here we are." Father Ledet got out before the patrol car had completely stopped. Vic radioed his location, parked, and went into the modern lobby to find a soft chair.

The priest knew the way to Clyde Arceneaux's room. When he pushed open the door, he saw the old man in his bed, a few strands of smoky hair swept back, his false teeth out, his tobacco-parched tongue wiggling in his mouth like a parrot's. Up close, Father Ledet could hear the hiss of the oxygen through the nose dispenser strapped to the old man's face. He felt his deepest sorrow for the respiratory patients.

"Clyde?"

Mr. Arceneaux opened one eye and looked at the priest's shirt. "The buzzards is circlin'," he rasped.

"How're you feeling?"

"Ah, Padre, I got a elephant standing on my chest." He spoke slowly, more like an air leak than a voice. "Doris, she stepped out a minute to eat." He motioned with his eyes toward the door, and Father Ledet looked at Clyde's hands, which were bound with dark veins flowing under skin as thin as cigarette paper.

"Is there something you'd like to talk about?" The priest heard the faint sound of a siren and wondered if gentle Mrs. Barrilleaux was being brought in to have her arm set.

"I don't need the holy oil no more. You can't grease me so I can slide into heaven." Clyde ate a bite of air. "I got to go to confession."

The priest nodded, removed a broad ribbonlike vestment from his pocket, kissed it, and hung it around his neck. Mr. Arceneaux couldn't remember the last time he'd been to confession, but he knew that Kennedy had been President then because it was during the Cuban missile crisis, when he thought for sure a nuclear strike was coming. He began telling his sins, starting with missing Mass "damn near seven hundred fifty times." Father Ledet was happy that Clyde Arceneaux was coming to God for forgiveness, and in a very detailed way, which showed, after all, a healthy conscience. At one point, the old man stopped and began to store up air for what the priest thought would be a new push through his errors, but when he began speaking again, it was to ask a question.

"Sure enough, you think there's a hell?"

Father Ledet knew he had to be careful. Sometimes saving a soul was like catching a dragonfly. You couldn't blunder up to it and trap it with a swipe of the hand. "There's a lot of talk of it in the Bible," he said.

"It's for punishment?"

"That's what it's for."

"But what good would the punishment do?"

The priest sat down. The room did a quarter turn to the left and then stopped. "I don't think hell is about rehabilitation. It's about what someone might deserve." He put his hand over his eyes and squeezed them for a moment. "But you shouldn't worry about that, Clyde, because you're getting the forgiveness you need."

Mr. Arceneaux looked at the ceiling, the corners of his flaccid mouth turning down. "I don't know. There's one thing I ain't told you yet."

"Well, it's now or never." The priest was instantly sorry for saying this, and Clyde gave him a questioning look before glancing down at his purple feet.

"I can't hold just one thing back? I'd hate like hell to tell anybody this."

"Clyde, it's God listening, not me."

"Can't I just think it to God? I mean, I told you the other stuff. Even about the midget woman."

"If it's a serious sin, you've got to tell me about it. You can generalize a bit."

"This is some of that punishment we were talkin' about earlier. It's what I deserve."

"Let's have it."

"I stole Nelson Lodrigue's car."

Something clicked in the priest's brain. He remembered this himself. Nelson Lodrigue owned an old Toronado, which he parked next to the ditch in front of his house. The car had a huge eight-cylinder engine and no muffler, and every morning at six sharp Nelson would crank the thing up and race the engine, waking most of his neighbors and all the dogs for blocks around. He did this for over a year, to keep the battery charged, he said. When it disappeared, Nelson put a big ad in the paper offering a fifty-dollar reward for information, but no one came forward. The men in the Knights of Columbus talked of it for weeks.

"That was about ten years ago, wasn't it? And isn't Nelson a friend of yours?" Nelson was another Sunday-morning lingerer on the church steps.

Mr. Arceneaux swallowed hard several times and waited a moment, storing up air. "Father, honest to God, I ain't never stole nothin' before. My daddy told me thievin' is the worst thing a man can do. I hated to take Nelson's hot rod, but I was fixin' to have a nervous breakdown from lack of sleep."

The priest nodded. "It's good to get these things off your chest. Is there anything else?"

Mr. Arceneaux shook his head. "I think we hit the high points. Man, I'm ashamed of that last one."

The priest gave him absolution and a small penance.

Clyde tried to smile, his dark tongue tasting the air. "Ten Hail Marys? That's a bargain, Father."

"If you want to do more, you could call Nelson and tell him what you did."

The old man thought for just a second. "I'll stick with them little prayers for now." Father Ledet got out his missal and read aloud over Mr. Arceneaux until his words were interrupted by a gentle snoring.

Vic sat in the lobby, waiting for the priest to come down. It had been twenty minutes, and he knew the priest's blood-alcohol level was ready to peak. He took off his uniform hat and began twirling it in front of him. He wondered what good it would do to charge the priest with drunken driving. Priests had to drink wine every day, and they liked the taste in the evening, too. A ticket wouldn't change his mind about drinking for long. On the other hand, Father Ledet had ruined Mrs. Barrilleaux's sedan, which for twenty years she had maintained as if it were a child.

A few minutes earlier, Vic had walked down the corridor and peeked into the room where they were treating her. He hadn't let her see him, and he studied her face. Now he sat and twirled his hat, thinking. It would be painful for the priest to have his name in the paper attached to a DWI charge, but it would make him understand the seriousness of what he had done. Patrolman Garafola dealt with too many people who did not understand the seriousness of what they were doing.

The priest came into the lobby and the young policeman stood up. "Father, we'll have to take a ride to the station."

"What?"

"I want to run a Breathalyzer test on you."

Father Ledet straightened up, stepped close, and put an arm around the man's shoulders. "Oh, come on. What good would that do?"

The patrolman started to speak, but then he mentioned for the priest to follow him. "Let me show you something."

"Where are we going?"

"I want you to see this." They walked down the hall and through double doors to a triage area for emergency cases. There was a narrow window in a wall, and the policeman told the priest to look through it. An oxygen bottle and gauges partially blocked the view. Mrs. Barrilleaux sat on an examining table, a blue knot swelling in her upper arm. One doctor was pulling back on her shoulder while another twisted her elbow. On the table was a large, menacing syringe, and Mrs. Barrilleaux was crying, without expression, great patient tears. "Take a long look," Vic said, "and when you get enough, come on with me." The priest turned away from the glass and followed.

"You didn't have to show me that."

"I didn't?"

"That woman is the nicest, the best cook, the best—"

"Come on, Father," Vic said, pushing open the door to the parking lot. "I've got a lot of writing to do."

Father Ledet's blood-alcohol content was well over the legal limit, so the patrolman wrote him a ticket for DWI, to which he added running a stop sign and causing an accident with bodily injury. The traffic court suspended his license, and since he had banged up the Lincoln before, his insurance company dropped his coverage as soon as their computers picked up the offenses. A week after the accident, he came into the rectory hall drinking a glass of tap water, which beaded on his tongue like a nasty oil. The phone rang and the glass jumped in his fingers. It was Mrs. Arceneaux again, who told him she'd been arguing with her husband, who wanted to tell her brother Nelson Lodrigue that he had stolen his car ten years before. "Why'd you tell him to talk to Nelson about the stealing business? It got him all upset."

The priest did not understand. "What would be the harm in him telling Nelson the truth?"

"Aw, no, Father. Clyde's got so little oxygen in his brain, he's not thinking straight. He can't tell Nelson what he did. I don't want him to die with everyone in the neighborhood thinking he's a thief. And Nelson . . . well, I love my brother, but if he found out my husband stole his old bomb, he'd make Clyde's last days hell. He's just like that, you know?"

"I see. Is there something I can do?" He put down the glass of water on the little phone table next to a small white statue of the Blessed Virgin.

"If you would talk to Clyde and let him know it's okay to die without telling Nelson about the car, I'd appreciate it. He already confessed everything anyway, right?

The priest looked down the hall toward the patio, longing for the openness. "I can't discuss specific matters of confession."

"I know. That's why I gave you all the details again."

"All right, I'll call. Is he awake now?"

"He's here at home. We got him a crank-up bed and a oxygen machine, and a nurse sits with him at night. I'll put him on."

Father Ledet leaned against the wall and stared at a crucifix, wondering what Christ had done to deserve his punishment. When he heard the hiss of Clyde Arceneaux's mask come out of the phone, he began to tell him what he should hear, that he was forgiven in God's eyes, that if he wanted to make restitution, he could give something to the poor, or figure out how to leave his brother-in-law something. He hung up and sniffed the waxed smell of the rectory, thinking of the sweet, musky brandy in the kitchen cupboard, and immediately he went to find the young priest upstairs to discuss the new Mass schedule.

On Saturday afternoon, Father Ledet was nodding off in the confessional when a woman entered and began to make her confession. After she'd mentioned one or two venial sins, she addressed him through the screen. "Father, it's Doris Arceneaux, Clyde's wife."

The priest yawned. "How is Clyde?"

"You remember the car business? Well, something new has come up," she whispered. "Clyde always told me he and the Scadlock kid towed the car off with a rope, and when they got it downtown behind the seawall, they pushed it overboard into the bay."

"Yes?"

"There's a new wrinkle."

He put down his missal and removed his glasses to rub his eyes. "What do you mean?"

"Clyde just told me he stored the car. Been paying thirty-five dollars a month to keep it in a little closed bin down at the U-Haul place for the past ten years." She whispered louder: "I don't know how he kept that from me. Makes me wonder about a few other things."

The priest's eyebrows went up. "Now he can give it back or you can give it back when your husband passes away." As soon as he'd said this, he knew it wouldn't work. It was too logical. If nothing else, his years in the confessional had taught him that people did not run their lives by reason much of the time, but by some little inferior motion of the spirit, some pride, some desire that defied the simple beauty of doing the sensible thing.

Mrs. Arceneaux protested that the secret had to be kept. "There's only one way to get Nelson his car back like Clyde wants."

The priest sighed. "How is that?"

Mrs. Arceneaux began to fidget in the dark box. "Well, you the only one besides me who knows what happened. Clyde says the car will still run. He cranks it up once every three weeks so it keeps its battery hot."

The priest put his head down. "And?"

"And you could get up early and drive it back to Nelson's and park it where it was the night Clyde stole it."

"Not no," the priest said, "but hell no!"

"Father!"

"What if I were caught driving that thing? The secret would get out then."

"Father, this is a part of a confession. You can't tell."

The priest now sensed a plot. "I'm sorry, but I can't help you, Mrs. Arceneaux. Now I'm going to give you a penance of twenty Our Fathers."

"For telling one fib to my daughter-in-law?"

"You want a cut rate for dishonesty?"

"All right," she said in an unrepentant voice. "And I'll pray for you while I'm at it."

After five o'clock Saturday Mass, Father Ledet felt his soul bang around inside him like a golf ball in a shoe box, something hard and compacted. He yearned for a hot, inflating swallow of spirits, longed for the afterburn of brandy in his nostrils. He went back into the empty church, a high-ceilinged Gothic building over a hundred years old, sat in a pew, and steeped himself in the odors of furniture oil, incense, and hot candle wax. He let the insubstantial colors of the windows flow over him, and after a while, these shades and smells began to fill the emptiness in him. He closed his eyes and imagined the housekeeper's supper, pushing out of mind his need for a drink, replacing the unnecessary with the good. At five to six, he walked to the rectory to have his thoughts made into food.

The next evening, after visiting a sick parishioner, he was reading the newspaper upstairs in his room when the housekeeper knocked on his door. Mrs. Mamie Barrilleaux was downstairs and would like to speak with him, the housekeeper said.

The first thing Father Ledet noticed when he walked into the downstairs study was the white cast on the woman's arm.

"Mamie," he said, sitting next to her on the sofa. "I have to tell you again how sorry I am about your arm."

The woman's face brightened, as though to be apologized to was a privilege. "Oh, don't worry about it, Father. Accidents happen." She was a graying brunette with fair skin, a woman whose cheerfulness made her pretty. One of the best cooks in a town of good cooks, she volunteered for every charity work connected with a stove or oven, and her time belonged to anyone who needed it, from her well-fed smirk of a husband to the drug addicts who showed up at the parish shelter. While they talked, the priest's eyes wandered repeatedly to the ugly cast, which ran up nearly to her shoulder. For five minutes, he wondered why she had dropped in unannounced. And then she told him.

"Father, I don't know if you understand what good friends Clyde Arcenaux's wife and I are. We went to school together for twelve years."

"Yes. It's a shame her husband's so sick."

Mrs. Barrilleaux fidgeted into the corner of the sofa, put her cast on the armrest, where it glowed under a lamp. "That's sort of why I'm here. Doris told me she asked you to do something for her and Clyde, and you told her no. I'm not being specific because I know it was a confession thing."

"How much did she tell you?" The priest hoped she wouldn't ask what she was going to ask, because he knew he could not refuse her.

"I don't know even one detail, Father. But I wanted to tell you that if Doris wants it done, then it needs doing. She's a good person, and I'm asking you to help her."

"But you don't know what she wants me to do."

Mrs. Barrileaux put her good hand on her cast. "I know it's not something bad."

"No, no. It's just . . ." He was going to mention that his driver's license was suspended but realized that he couldn't even tell her that.

Mamie lowered her head and turned her face toward the priest. "Father?"

"Oh, all right."

He visited Mrs. Arceneaux on a Wednesday, got the keys, and late that night he sat outside on the dark rectory patio for a long time, filling up on the smells of honeysuckle. The young priest walked up to him and insisted that he come in out of the mosquitoes and dampness. Upstairs, he changed into street clothes and lay on the bed like a man waiting for a firing squad. Around midnight, his legs began to ache terribly, and the next thing he knew, they were carrying him downstairs to the kitchen, where the aspirin was kept, and as his hand floated toward the cabinet door to his right, it remembered its accustomed movement to the door on the left, where a quart of brandy waited like an airy medicinal promise. The mind and spirit pulled his hand to the right, while the earthly body drew it to the left. He heard the drone of an airplane somewhere in the sky above, and he suddenly thought of an old homily that told how people were like twin-engine planes, one engine the logical spirit, the other the sensual body, and that when they were not running in concert, the craft ran off course to disaster. The priest supposed he could rev his spirit in some way, but when he thought of driving the stolen car, he opted to throttle up the body. One jigger, he thought, would calm him down and give him the courage to do this important and good deed. As he took a drink, he tried to picture how glad Nelson Lodrigue would be to have his old car back. As he took another, he thought of how Mr. Arceneaux could gasp off into the next world with a clear conscience. After several minutes, the starboard engine sputtered and locked up as Father Ledet lurched sideways through the dark house looking for his car keys.

At one o'clock, he got into the church's sedan and drove to the edge of town to a row of storage buildings. He woke up the manager, a shabby old man living in a trailer next to the gate. Inside the perimeter fence, Father Ledet walked along the numbered roll-up doors of the storage areas until he found the right one. He had trouble fitting the key into the lock but finally managed to open the door and turn on the light. The Oldsmobile showed a hard shell of rust and dust and resembled a million-year-old museum egg. The door squawked when he pulled on it, and the interior smelled like the closed-in mausoleum at the parish graveyard. He put in the key, and the motor groaned and then stuttered alive, rumbling and complaining. Shaking his head, the priest thought he'd never be able to drive this car undetected into the quiet neighborhood where Nelson Lodrigue lived. But after he let it idle and warm up, the engine slowed to a breathy subsonic bass, and he put it in reverse for its first trip in ten years.

The plan was to park the car on a patch of grass next to the street in front of Nelson's house, the very spot where it had been stolen. The priest would walk into the next block to Mrs. Arceneaux's house, and she would return him to his car. He pulled out of the rental place and drove a back road, past tin-roofed shotgun houses and abandoned cars better in appearance than the leprous one that now moved among them. He entered the battered railroad underpass and emerged in the better part of town, which was moon-washed and asleep. He found that if he kept his foot off the accelerator and just let the car idle along at ten miles an hour, it didn't make much noise, but when he gave the car just a little gas at stop signs, the exhaust sounded like a lion warming up for a mating. The priest was thankful at least for a certain buoyancy of the blood provided by the glasses of brandy, a numbness of spirit that helped him endure what he was doing. He was still nervous, though, and had trouble managing the touchy accelerator, feeling that the car was trying to bound away in spite of his best efforts to control it. Eventually, he turned onto the main street of Nelson's little subdivision and burbled slowly down until he could see the apron of grass next to the asphalt where he could park. He turned off the car's lights.

One of the town's six policemen had an inflamed gallbladder, and Patrolman Vic Garafola was working his friend's shift, parked in an alley next to the Elks Club, sitting stone-faced with boredom, when a shuddering and filthy Toronado crawled past in front of him. He would have thought it was just some rough character from the section down by the fish plant, but he got a look at the license plate and saw that it bore a design that hadn't been on any car in at least five years. Vic put his cruiser in gear, left his lights off, and rolled out into the town's empty streets, following the Toronado at a block's distance past the furniture store, across the highway, and into little Shade Tree Subdivision. He radioed a parish officer he'd seen a few minutes earlier and asked him to park across the entrance, the only way in or out of the neighborhood.

Even in the dark, Vic could see that the car's tires were bagged out and that it was dirty in an unnatural way, pale with dust—the ghost of a car. He closed in as it swayed down Cypress Street, and when he saw the driver douse his lights, he thought, Bingo, someone's up to no good, and at once he hit his headlights, flashers, and yowling siren. The Toronado suddenly exploded forward in a flatulent rush, red dust and sparks raining backward from underneath the car as it left the patrolman in twin swirls of tire smoke. Whoever was driving was supremely startled, and Vic began the chase, following but not gaining on the sooty taillights. Shade Tree Subdivision was composed of only one street that ran in an oval like a racetrack. At the first curve, the roaring car fishtailed to the right, and Vic followed as best he could, watching ahead as the vehicle pulled away and then turned right again in the distance, heading for the subdivision exit. When Vic chased around the curve, he saw a white cruiser blocking the speeding car's escape. The fleeing vehicle then slowed and moved again down Cypress Street toward the middle of the subdivision. Vic raised a questioning eyelid as he watched the grumbling car drive off the road and finally stop in front of Nelson Lodrigue's brick rancher. The patrolman pulled up, opened his door, and pointed his revolver toward the other vehicle.

"Driver, get out," he barked. Slowly, a graying, soft-looking man wearing a dark shirt buttoned at the top button slid out of the vehicle, his shaking hands raised high.

"Can you please not yell?" The old man looked around at the drowsing houses.

Vic stared at him, walked close, and looked at his eyes. He holstered his revolver. "Why'd you speed away like that, Father?"

The priest was out of breath. "When you turned on those flashers, it frightened me and, well, I guess I pressed the accelerator too hard, and this thing took off like a rocket."

Vic looked at the car and back to the priest. "The tag is expired on your vehicle, and it doesn't have an inspection sticker." He went to his patrol car and reached in for his ticket book.

"Could you please turn off those flashers?"

"Have to leave 'em on. Rules, you know," Vic said in a nasty voice. "You want to show me your proof of insurance, driver's license, and pink slip?" He held out a mocking hand.

"You know I don't have any of those."

"Father, what are you doing in this wreck?"

The priest put his hands in front of him, pleading. "I can't say anything. It's related to a confession."

"Oh, is this a good deed or somethin'?"

The priest's face brightened with hope, as though the patrolman understood what this was all about. "Yes, yes."

Vic leaned in and sniffed. "You think it's a good deed to get drunk as a boiled owl and speed around town at night?" he hollered.

"Oh, please, hush," Father Ledet pleaded.

Vic reached to his gun belt. "Turn around so I can cuff you."

"Have some mercy."

"Them that deserves it get mercy," Vic told him.

"God would give me mercy," the priest said, turning around and offering his hands at his back.

"Then he's a better man than I am. Spread your legs."

"This won't do anyone any good."

"It'll do me some good." Just then, a porch light came on and a shirtless Nelson Lodrigue padded out to the walk in his bare feet, his moon-shaped belly hanging over the elastic of his pajamas.

"Hey. What's goin' on?"

Other porch lights began to fire up across the street and next door, people coming out to the edge of their driveways and looking.

"It's Father Ledet," Vic called out. "He's getting a ticket or two."

Nelson was standing next to the car before his eyes opened fully and his head swung from side to side at the dusty apparatus. "What the hell? This here's my old car that got stole."

Vic gave the priest a hard look. "Collections been a little slow, Father?"

"Don't be absurd. I was returning Nelson's car."

"You know who stole my car?" Nelson lumbered around the hood. "You better tell me right now. I didn't sleep for a year after this thing got taken. I always had a feeling it was somebody I knew."

"I can't say anything."

"It came out in a confession," Vic explained.

Nelson ran his hand over the chalky paint of the roof. "Well, charge him with auto theft and I'll bet he'll tell us."

Two ladies in curlers and a tall middle-aged man wearing a robe and slippers approached from across the street. "What's going on, Vic?" the man asked. "Hello, Father."

The priest nodded, hiding the handcuffs behind him. "Good evening, Mayor. This isn't what it appears to be."

"I hope not," one of the women said.

Other neighbors began walking into the circle of crackling light cast by the police car's flashers. Then the parish deputy pulled up, his own lights blazing. Vic looked on as the priest tried to explain to everyone that he was doing a good thing, that they couldn't know all the details. The patrolman felt sorry for him, he really did, felt bad as he filled out the tickets, as he pushed the old head under the roofline of the patrol car, and, later, as he fingerprinted the soft hands and put the holy body into the cell, taking his belt, his shoelaces, and his rosary.

Father Ledet had to journey to Baton Rouge to endure the frowns and lecturing of the bishop. His parish was taken away for two months, and he was put into an AA program in his own community, where he sat many times in rusty folding chairs along with fundamentalist garage mechanics, striptease artists, and spoiled, depressed subdivision wives to listen to testimonials, admonitions, confessions without end. He rode in cabs to these meetings, and in the evenings no one invited him to the Ladies' Altar Society dinners or to anyplace else. Mrs. Arceneaux never called to sympathize, and pretty Mrs. Barrilleaux would not look at him when he waved as she drove by the rectory in her new secondhand car. The first day he was again allowed to put on vestments was a Sunday, and he went in to say the eleven o'clock Mass. The church was full, and the sun was bleeding gold streamers of light down through the sacristy windows behind the altar. After the Gloria was sung by the birdlike voices of a visiting children's choir, the priest stood in the pulpit and read the Gospel, drawing scant solace from the story of Jesus turning water into wine. The congregation then sat down in a rumble of settling pews and kicked-up kneelers. Father Ledet began to talk about Christ's first miracle, an old sermon, one he'd given dozens of times. The elder parishioners in the front pews seemed to regard him as a stranger, the children were uninterested, and he felt disconnected and sad as he spoke, wondering if he would ever be punished enough for what he had done. He scanned the faces in the congregation as he preached, looking for forgiveness of any sort, and fifteen minutes into the sermon, he saw in the fifth pew, against the wall, something that was better than forgiveness, better than what he deserved, something that gave sudden light to his dull voice and turned bored heads up to the freshened preaching. It was Clyde Arceneaux, a plastic tube creeping down from his nose and taped to his puckered neck. He was asleep, pale, two steps from death, his head resting against the wall, but at least he had finally come inside.

20

A FATHER'S STORY

Andre Dubus

My name is Luke Ripley, and here is what I call my life: I own a stable of thirty horses, and I have young people who teach riding, and we board some horses too. This is in northeastern Massachusetts. I have a barn with an indoor ring, and outside I've got two fenced-in rings and a pasture that ends at a woods with trails. I call it my life because it looks like it is, and people I know call it that, but it's a life I can get away from when I hunt and fish, and some nights after dinner when I sit in the dark in the front room and listen to opera. The room faces the lawn and the road, a two-lane country road. When cars come around the curve northwest of the house, they light up the lawn for an instant, the leaves of the maple out by the road and the hemlock closer to the window. Then I'm alone again, or I'd appear to be if someone crept up to the house and looked through a window: a big-gutted gray-haired guy, drinking tea and smoking cigarettes, staring out at the dark woods across the road, listening to a grieving soprano.

My real life is the one nobody talks about anymore, except Father Paul LeBoeuf, another old buck. He has a decade on me: he's sixty-four, a big man, bald on top with gray at the sides; when he had hair, it was black. His face is ruddy, and he jokes about being a whiskey priest, though he's not. He gets outdoors as much as he can, goes for a long walk every morning, and hunts and fishes with me. But I can't get him on a horse anymore. Ten years ago I could badger him into a trail ride; I had to give him a western saddle, and he'd hold the pommel and bounce through the woods with me, and be sore for days. He's looking at seventy with eyes that are younger than many I've seen in people in their twenties. I do not remember ever feeling the way

321

they seem to; but I was lucky, because even as a child I knew that life would try me, and I must be strong to endure, though in those days I expected to be tortured and killed for my faith, like the saints I learned about in school.

Father Paul's family came down from Canada, and he grew up speaking more French than English, so he is different from the Irish priests who abound up here. I do not like to make general statements, or even to hold general beliefs, about people's blood, but the Irish do seem happiest when they're dealing with misfortune or guilt, either their own or somebody else's, and if you think you're not a victim of either one, you can count on certain Irish priests to try to change your mind. On Wednesday nights Father Paul comes to dinner. Often he comes on other nights too and once, in the old days when we couldn't eat meat on Fridays, we bagged our first ducks of the season on a Friday, and as we drove home from the marsh, he said: For the purposes of Holy Mother Church, I believe a duck is more a creature of water than land, and is not rightly meat. Sometimes he teases me about never putting anything in his Sunday collection, which he would not know about if I hadn't told him years ago. I would like to believe I told him so we could have a philosophical talk at dinner, but probably the truth is I suspected he knew, and I did not want him to think I so loved money that I would not even give his church a coin on Sunday. Certainly the ushers who pass the baskets know me as a miser.

I don't feel right about giving money for buildings, places. This starts with the Pope, and I cannot respect one of them till he sells his house and everything in it, and that church too, and uses the money to feed the poor. I have rarely, and maybe never, come across saintliness, but I feel certain it cannot exist in such a place. But I admit, also, that I know very little, and maybe the popes live on a different plane and are tried in ways I don't know about. Father Paul says his own church, St. John's, is hardly the Vatican. I like his church: it is made of wood, and has a simple altar and crucifix, and no padding on the kneelers. He does not have to lock its doors at night. Still it is a place. He could say Mass in my barn. I know this is stubborn, but I can find no mention by Christ of maintaining buildings, much less erecting them of stone or brick, and decorating them with pieces of metal and mineral and elements that people still fight over like barbarians. We had a Maltese woman taking riding lessons, she came over on the boat when she was ten, and once she told me how the nuns in Malta used to tell the little girls that if they wore jewelry, rings and bracelets and necklaces, in purgatory snakes would coil around their fingers and wrists and throats. I do not believe in frightening children or telling them lies, but if those nuns saved a few girls from devotion to things, maybe they were right. That Maltese woman laughed about it, but I noticed she wore only a watch, and that with a leather strap.

The money I give to the church goes in people's stomachs, and on their backs, down in New York City. I have no delusions about the worth of what I do, but I feel it's better to feed somebody than not. There's a priest in Times Square giving shelter to runaway kids, and some Franciscans who run a bread line; actually it's a morning line for coffee and a roll, and Father Paul calls it the continental breakfast for winos and bag ladies. He is curious about how much I am sending and I know why: he guesses I send a lot, he has said probably more than tithing, and he is right; he wants to know how much because he believes that I'm generous and good, and he is wrong about that; he has never had much money and does not know how easy it is to write a check when you have everything you will ever need, and the figures are mere numbers, and represent no sacrifice at all. Being a real Catholic is too hard; if I were one, I would do with my house and barn what I want the Pope to do with his. So I do not want to impress Father Paul, and when he asks me how much, I say I can't let my left hand know what my right is doing.

He came on Wednesday nights when Gloria and I were married, and the kids were young; Gloria was a very good cook (I assume she still is, but it is difficult to think of her in the present), and I liked sitting at the table with a friend who was also a priest. I was proud of my handsome and healthy children. This was long ago, and they were all very young and cheerful and often funny, and the three boys took care of their baby sister, and did not bully or tease her. Of course they did sometimes, with that excited cruelty children are prone to, but not enough so that it was part of her days. On the Wednesday after Gloria left with the kids and a U-Haul trailer, I was sitting on the front steps, it was summer, and I was watching the cars go by on the road, when Father Paul drove around the curve and into the driveway. I was ashamed to see him because he is a priest and my family was gone, but I was relieved too. I went to the car to greet him. He got out smiling, with a bottle of wine, and shook my hand, then pulled me to him, gave me a quick hug, and said: "It's Wednesday, isn't it? Let's open some cans."

With arms about each other we walked to the house, and it was good to know he was doing his work but coming as a friend too, and I thought what good work he had. I have no calling. It is for me to keep horses.

In that other life, anyway. In my real one I go to bed early and sleep well and wake at four forty-five, for an hour of silence. I never want to get out of bed then, and every morning I know I can sleep for another four hours, and still not fail at any of my duties. But I get up, so have come to believe my life can be seen in miniature in that struggle in the dark of morning. While making the bed and boiling water for coffee, I talk to God: I offer Him my day, every act of my body and spirit, my thoughts and moods, as a prayer of thanksgiving, and for Gloria and my children and my friends and two women I made love with after Gloria left. This morning offertory is a habit from my boyhood in a Catholic school; or then it was a habit, but as I kept it and grew older it became a ritual. Then I say the Lord's Prayer, trying not to recite it, and one morning it occurred to me that a prayer, whether recited or said with concentration, is always an act of faith.

I sit in the kitchen at the rear of the house and drink coffee and smoke and watch the sky growing light before sunrise, the trees of the woods near the barn taking shape, becoming single pines and elms and oaks and maples. Sometimes a rabbit comes out of the treeline, or is already sitting there, invisible till the light finds him. The birds are awake in the trees and feeding on the ground and the little ones, the purple finches and titmice and chickadees, are at the feeder I rigged outside the kitchen window; it is too small for pigeons to get a purchase. I sit and give myself to coffee and tobacco, that get me brisk again, and I watch and I listen. In the first year or so after I lost my family, I played the radio in the mornings. But I overcame that, and now I rarely play it at all. Once in the mail I received a questionnaire asking me to write down everything I watched on television during the week they had chosen. At the end of those seven days I wrote in *The Wizard of Oz* and returned it. That was in winter and was actually a busy week for my television, which normally sits out the cold months without once warming up. Had they sent me a questionnaire during baseball season, they would have found me at my set. People at the stables talk about shows and performers I have never heard of, but I cannot get interested; when I am in the mood to watch television, I go to a movie or read a detective novel. There are always good detective novels to be found, and I like remembering them next morning with my coffee.

I also think of baseball and hunting and fishing, and of my children. It is not painful to think about them anymore, because even if we had lived together, they would be gone now, grown into their own lives, except Jennifer. I think of death too, not sadly, or with fear, though something like excitement does run through me, something more quickening than the coffee and tobacco. I suppose it is an intense interest, and an outright distrust: I never feel certain that I'll be here watching birds eating at tomorrow's daylight. Sometimes I try to think of other things, like the rabbit that is warm and breathing but not there till twilight. I feel on the brink of something about the life of the senses, but either am not equipped to go further or am not interested enough to concentrate. I have called all of this thinking, but it is not, because it is unintentional; what I'm really doing is feeling the day, in silence, and that is what Father Paul is doing too on his five- to ten-mile walks.

When the hour ends I take an apple or carrot and I go to the stable and tack up a horse. We take good care of these horses, and no one rides them but students, instructors, and me, and nobody rides the horses we board unless an owner asks me to. The barn is dark and I turn on lights and take some deep breaths, smelling the hay and horses and their manure, both fresh and dried, a combined odor that you either like or you don't. I walk down the wide space of dirt between stalls, greeting horses, joking with them about their quirks, and choose one for no reason at all other than the way it looks at me that morning. I get my old English saddle that has smoothed and darkened through the years, and go into the stall, talking to this beautiful creature who'll swerve out of a canter if a piece of paper blows in front of him, and if the barn catches fire and you manage to get him out he will, if he can get away from you, run back into the fire, to his stall. Like the smells that surround them, you either like them or you don't. I love them, so am spared having to try to explain why. I feed one the carrot or apple and tack up and lead him outside, where I mount, and we go down the driveway to the road and cross it and turn northwest and walk then trot then canter to St. John's.

A few cars are on the road, their drivers looking serious about going to work. It is always strange for me to see a woman dressed for work so early in the morning. You know how long it takes them, with the makeup and hair and clothes, and I think of them waking in the dark of winter or early light of other seasons, and dressing as they might for an evening's entertainment. Probably this strikes me because I grew up seeing my father put on those suits he never wore on weekends or his two weeks off, and so am accustomed to the men, but when I see these women I think something went wrong, to send all those dressed-up people out on the road when the dew hasn't dried yet. Maybe it's because I so dislike getting up early, but am also doing what I choose to do, while they have no choice. At heart I am lazy, yet I find such peace and delight in it that I believe it is a natural state, and in what looks like my laziest periods I am closest to my center. The ride to St. John's is fifteen minutes. The horses and I do it in all weather; the road is well plowed in winter, and there are only a few days a year when ice makes me drive the pickup. People always look at someone on horseback, and for a moment their faces change and many drivers and I wave to each other. Then at St. John's, Father Paul and five or six regulars and I celebrate the Mass.

Do not think of me as a spiritual man whose every thought during those twenty-five minutes is at one with the words of the Mass. Each morning I try, each morning I fail, and know that always I will be a creature who, looking at Father Paul and the altar, and uttering prayers, will be distracted by scrambled eggs, horses, the weather, and memories and daydreams that have nothing to do with the sacrament I am about to receive. I can receive, though: the Eucharist, and also, at Mass and at other times, moments and even minutes of contemplation. But I cannot achieve contemplation, as some can; and so, having to face and forgive my own failures, I have learned from them both the necessity and the wonder of ritual. For ritual allows those who cannot will themselves out of the secular to perform the spiritual, as dancing allows the tongue-tied man a ceremony of love. And, while my mind dwells on breakfast, or Major or Duchess tethered under the church eave, there is, as I take the Host from Father Paul and place it on my tongue and return to the pew, a feeling that I am thankful I have not lost in the forty-eight years since my first Communion. At its center is excitement; spreading out from it is the peace of certainty. Or the certainty of peace. One night Father Paul and I talked about faith. It was long ago, and all I remember is him saying: Belief is believing in God; faith is believing that God believes in you. That is the excitement, and the peace; then the Mass is over, and I go into the sacristy and we have a cigarette and chat, the mystery ends, we are two men talking like any two men on a morning in America, about baseball, plane crashes, presidents, governors, murders, the sun, the clouds. Then I go to the horse and ride back to the life people see, the one in which I move and talk, and most days I enjoy it.

It is late summer now, the time between fishing and hunting, but a good time for baseball. It has been two weeks since Jennifer left, to drive home to Gloria's after her summer visit. She is the only one who still visits; the boys are married and have children, and sometimes fly up for a holiday, or I fly down or west to visit one of them. Jennifer is twenty, and I worry about her the way fathers worry about daughters but not sons. I want to know what she's up to, and at the same time I don't. She looks athletic, and she is: she swims and runs and of course rides. All my children do. When she comes home for six weeks in summer, the house is loud with girls, friends of hers since childhood, and new ones. I am glad she kept the girlfriends. They have been young company for me and, being with them, I have been able to gauge her growth between summers. On their riding days, I'd take them back to the house when their lessons were over and they had walked the horses and put them back in the stalls, and we'd have lemonade or Coke, and cookies if I had some, and talk until their parents came to drive them home. One year their breasts grew, so I wasn't startled when I saw Jennifer in July. Then they were driving cars to the stable, and beginning to look like young women, and I was passing out beer and ashtrays and they were talking about college.

When Jennifer was here in summer, they were at the house most days. I would say generally that as they got older they became quieter, and though I enjoyed both, I sometimes missed the giggles and shouts. The quiet voices, just low enough for me not to hear from wherever I was, rising and falling in proportion to my distance from them, frightened me. Not that I believed they were planning or recounting anything really wicked, but there was a female seriousness about them, and it was secretive, and of course I thought: love, sex. But it was more than that: it was womanhood they were entering, the deep forest of it, and no matter how many women and men too are saying these days there is little difference between us, the truth is that men find their way into that forest only on clearly marked trails while women move about in it like birds. So hearing Jennifer and her friends talking so quietly, yet intensely, I wanted very much to have a wife.

But not as much as in the old days, when Gloria had left but her presence was still in the house as strongly as if she had only gone to visit her folks for a week. There were no clothes or cosmetics, but potted plants endured my neglectful care as long as they could, and slowly died; I did not kill them on purpose, to exorcise the house of her, but I could not remember to water them. For weeks, because I did not use it much, the house was as neat as she had kept it, though dust layered the order she had made. The kitchen went first: I got the dishes in and out of the dishwasher and wiped the top of the stove, but did not return cooking spoons and pot holders to their hooks on the wall, and soon the burners and oven were caked with spillings, the refrigerator had more space and was spotted with juices. The living room and my bedroom went next; I did not go into the children's rooms except on bad nights when I went from room to room and looked and touched and smelled, so they did not lose their order until a year later when the kids came for six weeks. It was three months before I ate the last of the food Gloria had cooked and frozen: I remember it was a beef stew, and very good. By then I had four cookbooks, and was boasting a bit, and talking about recipes with women at the stables, and looking forward to cooking for Father Paul. But I never looked forward to cooking at night only for myself, though I made myself do it; on some nights I gave in to my daily temptation, and took a newspaper or detective novel to a restaurant. By the end of the second year, though, I had stopped turning on the radio as soon as I woke in the morning, and was able to be silent and alone in the evening too, and then I enjoyed my dinners.

It is not hard to live through a day, if you can live through a moment. What creates despair is the imagination, which pretends there is a future, and insists on predicting millions of moments, thousands of days, and so drains you that you cannot live the moment at hand. That is what Father

Paul told me in those first two years, on some of the bad nights when I believed I could not bear what I had to: the most painful loss was my children, then the loss of Gloria, whom I still loved despite or maybe because of our long periods of sadness that rendered us helpless, so neither of us could break out of it to give a hand to the other. Twelve years later I believe ritual would have healed us more quickly than the repetitious talks we had, perhaps even kept us healed. Marriages have lost that, and I wish I had known then what I know now, and we had performed certain acts together every day, no matter how we felt, and perhaps then we could have subordinated feeling to action, for surely that is the essence of love. I know this from my distractions during Mass, and during everything else I do, so that my actions and feelings are seldom one. It does happen every day, but in proportion to everything else in a day, it is rare, like joy. The third most painful loss, which became second and sometimes first as months passed, was the knowledge that I could never marry again, and so dared not even keep company with a woman.

On some of the bad nights I was bitter about this with Father Paul, and I so pitied myself that I cried, or nearly did, speaking with damp eyes and breaking voice. I believe that celibacy is for him the same trial it is for me, not of the flesh, but the spirit: the heart longing to love. But the difference is he chose it, and did not wake one day to a life with thirty horses. In my anger I said I had done my service to love and chastity, and I told him of the actual physical and spiritual pain of practicing rhythm: nights of striking the mattress with a fist, two young animals lying side by side in heat, leaving the bed to pace, to smoke, to curse, and too passionate to question, for we were so angered and oppressed by our passion that we could see no further than our loins. So now I understand how people can be enslaved for generations before they throw down their tools or use them as weapons, the form of their slavery—the cotton fields, the shacks and puny cupboards and untended illnesses—absorbing their emotions and thoughts until finally they have little or none at all to direct with clarity and energy at the owners and legislators. And I told him of the trick of passion and its slaking: how during what we had to believe were safe periods, though all four children were conceived at those times, we were able with some coherence to question the tradition and reason and justice of the law against birth control, but not with enough conviction to soberly act against it, as though regular satisfaction in bed tempered our revolutionary as well as our erotic desires. Only when abstinence drove us hotly away from each other did we receive an urge so strong it lasted all the way to the drugstore and back; but always, after release, we threw away the remaining condoms; and after going through this a few times, we knew what would happen, and from then on we submitted to the calendar she so precisely marked on the bedroom wall. I told him that living two lives each month, one as celibates, one as lovers, made us tense and short-tempered, so we snapped at each other like dogs.

To have endured that, to have reached a time when we burned slowly and could gain from bed the comfort of lying down at night with one who loves you and whom you love, could for weeks on end go to bed tired, and peacefully sleep after a kiss, a touch of the hands, and then to be thrown out of the marriage like a bundle from a moving freight car, was unjust, was intolerable, and I could not or would not muster the strength to endure it. But I did, a moment at a time, a day, a night, except twice, each time with a different woman and more than a year apart, and this was so long ago that I clearly see their faces in my memory, can hear the pitch of their voices, and the way they pronounced words, one with a Massachusetts accent, one Midwestern, but I feel as though I only heard about them from someone else. Each rode at the stables and was with me for part of an evening; one was badly married, one divorced, so none of us was free. They did not understand this Catholic view, but they were understanding about my having it, and I remained friends with both of them until the married one left her husband and went to Boston, and the divorced one moved to Maine. After both those evenings, those good women, I went to Mass early while Father Paul was still in the confessional, and received his absolution. I did not tell him who I was, but of course he knew, though I never saw it in his eyes. Now my longing for a wife comes only once in a while, like a cold: on some late afternoons when I am alone in the barn, then I lock up and walk to the house, daydreaming, then suddenly look at it and see it empty, as though for the first time, and all at once I'm weary and feel I do not have the energy to broil meat, and I think of driving to a restaurant, then shake my head and go on to the house, the refrigerator, the oven; and some mornings when I wake in the dark and listen to the silence and run my hand over the cold sheet beside me; and some days in summer when Jennifer is here.

Gloria left first me, then the Church, and that was the end of religion for the children, though on visits they went to Sunday Mass with me, and still do, out of a respect for my life that they manage to keep free of patronage. Jennifer is an agnostic, though I doubt she would call herself that, any more than she would call herself any other name that implied she had made a decision, a choice, about existence, death, and God. In truth she tends to pantheism, a good sign, I think; but not wanting to be a father who tells his children what they ought to believe, I do not say to her that Catholicism includes pantheism, like onions in a stew. Besides, I have no missionary instincts and do not believe everyone should or even could live with the Catholic faith. It is Jennifer's womanhood that renders me awkward. And womanhood now is frank, not like when Gloria was twenty and there were symbols: high heels and cosmetics and dresses, a cigarette, a cocktail. I am glad that women are free now of false modesty and all its attention paid the flesh; but, still, it is difficult to see so much of your daughter, to hear her talk as only men and bawdy women used to and most of all to see in her face the deep and unabashed sensuality of women, with no tricks of the eyes and mouth to hide the pleasure she feels at having a strong young body. I am certain, with the way things are now, that she has very happily not been a virgin for years. That does not bother me. What bothers me is my certainty about it, just from watching her walk across a room or light a cigarette or pour milk on cereal.

She told me all of it, waking me that night when I had gone to sleep listening to the wind in the trees against the house, a wind so strong that I had to shut all but the lee windows, and still the house cooled; told it to me in such detail and so clearly that now, when she has driven the car to Florida, I remember it all as though I had been a passenger in the front seat, or even at the wheel. It started with a movie, then beer and driving to the sea to look at the waves in the night and the wind, Jennifer and Betsy and Liz. They drank a beer on the beach and wanted to go in naked but were afraid they would drown in the high surf. They bought another six-pack at a grocery store in New Hampshire, and drove home. I can see it now, feel it: the three girls and the beer and the ride on country roads where pines curved in the wind and the big deciduous trees swayed and shook as if they might leap from the earth. They would have some windows partly open so they could feel the wind; Jennifer would be playing a cassette, the music stirring them, as it does the young, to memories of another time, other people and places in what is for them the past.

She took Betsy home, then Liz, and sang with her cassette as she left the town west of us and started home, a twenty-minute drive on the road that passes my house. They had each had four beers, but now there were twelve empty bottles in the bag on the floor at the passenger seat, and I keep focusing on their sound against each other when the car shifted speeds or changed directions. For I want to understand that one moment out of all her heart's time on earth, and whether her history had any bearing on it, or whether her heart was then isolated from all it had known, and the sound of those bottles urged it. She was just leaving town, accelerating past a night club on the right, gaining speed to climb a long gradual hill, then she went up it, singing, patting the beat on the steering wheel, the wind loud through her few inches of open window, blowing her hair as it did the high branches alongside the road, and she looked up at them and watched the top of the hill for someone drunk or heedless coming over it in part of her lane. She crested to an open black road, and there he was: a bulk, a blur, a thing running across her headlights, and she swerved left and her foot went for the brake and was stomping air above its pedal when she hit him, saw his legs and body in the air, flying out of her light, into the dark. Her brakes were screaming into the wind, bottles clinking in the fallen bag, and with the music and wind inside the car was his sound, already a memory but as real as an echo, that car-shuddering thump as though she had struck a tree. Her foot was back on the accelerator. Then she shifted gears and pushed it. She ejected the cassette and closed the window. She did not start to cry until she knocked on my bedroom door, then called: "Dad?"

Her voice, her tears, broke through my dream and the wind I heard in my sleep, and I stepped into jeans and hurried to the door, thinking harm, rape, death. All were in her face, and I hugged her and pressed her cheek to my chest and smoothed her blown hair, then led her weeping to the kitchen and sat her at the table where still she could not speak, nor look at me; when she raised her face it fell forward again, as of its own weight, into her palms. I offered tea and she shook her head, so I offered beer twice, then she shook her head, so I offered whiskey and she nodded. I had some rye that Father Paul and I had not finished last hunting season, and I poured some over ice and set it in front of her and was putting away the ice but stopped and got another glass and poured one for myself too, and brought the ice and bottle to the table where she was trying to get one of her long menthols out of the pack, but her fingers jerked like severed snakes, and I took the pack and lit one for her and took one for myself. I watched her shudder with her first swallow of rye, and push hair back from her face, it is auburn and gleamed in the overhead light, and I remembered how beautiful she looked riding a sorrel; she was smoking fast, then the sobs in her throat stopped, and she looked at me and said it, the words coming out with smoke: "I hit somebody. With the *car*."

Then she was crying and I was on my feet, moving back and forth, looking down at her asking *Who? Where? Where?* She was pointing at the wall over the stove, jabbing her fingers and cigarette at it, her other hand at her eyes, and twice in horror I actually looked at the wall. She finished the whiskey in a swallow and I stopped pacing and asking and poured another, and either the drink or the exhaustion of tears quieted her, even the dry sobs, and she told me; not as I tell it now, for that was later as again and again we relived it in the kitchen or living room, and if in daylight, fled it on horseback out on the trails through the woods and, if at night, walked quietly around in the moonlit pasture, walked around and around it, sweating through our clothes. She told it in bursts, like she was a child again, running to me, injured from play. I put on boots and a shirt and left her with the bottle and her streaked face and a cigarette twitching between her fingers, pushed the door open against the wind, and eased it shut. The wind squinted and watered my eyes as I leaned into it and went to the pickup.

When I passed St. John's I looked at it, and Father Paul's little white rectory in the rear, and wanted to stop, wished I could as I could if he were simply a friend who sold hardware or something. I had forgotten my watch but I always know the time within minutes, even when a sound or dream or my bladder wakes me in the night. It was nearly two; we had been in the kitchen about twenty minutes; she had hit him around one-fifteen. Or her. The road was empty and I drove between blowing trees; caught for an instant in my lights, they seemed to be in panic. I smoked and let hope play her tricks on me: it was neither man nor woman but an animal, a goat or calf or deer on the road; it was a man who had jumped away in time, the collision of metal and body glancing not direct, and he had limped home to nurse bruises and cuts. Then I threw the cigarette and hope both out the window and prayed that he was alive, while beneath that prayer, a reserve deeper in my heart, another one stirred: that if he were dead, they would not get Jennifer.

From our direction, east and a bit south, the road to that hill and the night club beyond it and finally the town is, for its last four or five miles, straight through farming country. When I reached that stretch I slowed the truck and opened my window for the fierce air; on both sides were scattered farmhouses and barns and sometimes a silo, looking not like shelters but like unsheltered things the wind would flatten. Corn bent toward the road from a field on my right, and always something blew in front of me: paper, leaves, dried weeds, branches. I slowed approaching the hill, and went up it in second, staring through my open window at the ditch on the left side of the road, its weeds alive, whipping, a mad dance with the trees above them. I went over the hill and down and, opposite the club, turned right onto a side street of houses, and parked there, in the leaping shadows of trees. I walked back across the road to the club's parking lot, the wind behind me, lifting me as I strode, and I could not hear my boots on pavement. I walked up the hill, on the shoulder, watching the branches above me, hearing their leaves and the creaking trunks and the wind. Then I was at the top, looking down the road and at the farms and fields; the night was clear, and I could see a long way; clouds scudded past the half-moon and stars, blown out to sea.

I started down, watching the tall grass under the trees to my right, glancing into the dark of the ditch, listening for cars behind me; but as soon as I cleared one tree, its sound was gone, its flapping leaves and rattling branches far behind me, as though the greatest distance I had at my back was a matter of feet, while ahead of me I could see a barn two miles off. Then I saw her skid marks: short, and going left and downhill, into the other lane. I stood at the ditch, its weeds blowing; across it were trees and their moving shadows, like the clouds. I stepped onto its slope, and it took me sliding on my feet, then rump, to the bottom where I sat still, my body gathered to itself, lest a part of me should touch him. But there was only tall grass, and I stood, my shoulders reaching the sides of the ditch, and I walked uphill, wishing for the flashlight in the pickup, walking slowly, and down in the ditch I could hear my feet in the grass and on the earth, and kicking cans and bottles. At the top of the hill I turned and went down, watching the ground above the ditch on my right, praying my prayer from the truck again, the first one, the one I would admit, that he was not dead, was in fact home, and began to hope again, memory telling me of lost pheasants and grouse I had shot, but they were small and the colors of their home, while a man was either there or not; and from that memory I left where I was and while walking the ditch under the wind was in the deceit of imagination with Jennifer in the kitchen, telling her she had hit no one, or at least had not badly hurt anyone, when I realized he could be in the hospital now and I would have to think of a way to check there, something to say on the phone. I see now that, once hope returned, I should have been certain what it prepared me for: ahead of me, in high grass and the shadows of trees, I saw his shirt. Or that is all my mind would allow itself: a shirt, and I stood looking at it for the moments it took my mind to admit the arm and head and the dark length covered by pants. He lay face down, the arm I could see near his side, his head turned from me, on its cheek.

"Fella?" I said. I had meant to call, but it came out quiet and high, lost inches from my face in the wind. Then I said, "Oh God," and felt Him in the wind and the sky moving past the stars and moon and the fields around me, but only watching me as He might have watched Cain or Job, I did not know which, and I said it again, and wanted to sink to the earth and weep until I slept there in the weeds. I climbed, scrambling up the side of the ditch, pulling at clutched grass, gained the top on hands and knees, and went to him like that, panting, moving through the grass as high and higher than my face, crawling under that sky, making sounds too, like some animal, there being no words to let him know I was here with him now. He was long; that is the word that came to me, not tall. I knelt beside him, my hands on my legs. His right arm was by his side, his left arm straight out from the shoulder, but turned, so his palm was open to the tree above us. His left cheek was clean-shaven, his eye closed, and there was no blood. I leaned forward to look at his open mouth and saw the blood on it, going down into the grass. I straightened and looked ahead at the wind blowing past me through grass and trees to a distant light, and I stared at the light, imagining someone awake out there, wanting someone to be, a gathering of old friends, or someone alone listening to music or painting a picture, then I figured it was a night light at a farmyard whose house I couldn't see. *Going*, I thought. *Still going*. I leaned over again and looked at dripping blood.

So I had to touch his wrist, a thick one with a watch and expansion band that I pushed up his arm, thinking *he's left-handed*, my three fingers pressing his wrist, and all I felt was my tough fingertips on that smooth underside flesh and small bones, then relief, then certainty. But against my will, or only because of it, I still don't know, I touched his neck, ran my fingers down it as if petting, then pressed and my hand sprang back as from fire. I lowered it again, held it there until it felt that faint beating that I could not believe. There was too much wind. Nothing could make a sound in it. A pulse could not be felt in it, nor could mere fingers in that wind feel the absolute silence of a dead man's artery. I was making sounds again; I grabbed his left arm and his waist, and pulled him toward me, and that side of him rose, turned, and I lowered him to his back, his face tilted up toward the tree that was groaning, the tree and I the only sounds in the wind. Turning my face from his, looking down the length of him at his sneakers, I placed my ear on his heart, and heard not that but something else, and I clamped a hand over my exposed ear, heard something liquid and alive, like when you pump a well and after a few strokes you hear air and water moving in the pipe, and I knew I must raise his legs and cover him and run to a phone, while still I listened to his chest, thinking *raise with what? cover with what?* and amid the liquid sound I heard the heart then lost it, and pressed my ear against bone, but his chest was quiet, and I did not know when the liquid had stopped, and do not know when I heard air, a faint rush of it, and whether under my ear or at his mouth or whether I heard it at all. I straightened and looked at the light, dim and yellow. Then I touched his throat, looking him full in the face. He was blond and young. He could have been sleeping in the shade of a tree, but for the smear of blood from his mouth to his hair, and the night sky, and the weeds blowing against his head, and the leaves shaking in the dark above us.

I stood. Then I kneeled again and prayed for his soul to join in peace and joy all the dead and living; and, doing so, confronted my first sin against him, not stopping for Father Paul, who could have given him the last rites, and immediately then my second one, or, I saw then, my first, not calling an ambulance to meet me there, and I stood and turned into the wind, slid down the ditch and crawled out of it, and went up the hill and down it, across the road to the street of houses whose people I had left behind forever, so that I moved with stealth in the shadows to my truck.

When I came around the bend near my house, I saw the kitchen light at the rear. She sat as I had left her, the ashtray filled, and I looked at the bottle, felt her eyes on me, felt what she was seeing too: the dirt from my crawling. She had not drunk much of the rye. I poured some in my glass, with the water from melted ice, and sat down and swallowed some and looked at her and swallowed some more, and said: "He's dead."

She rubbed her eyes with the heels of her hands, rubbed the cheeks under them, but she was dry now.

"He was probably dead when he hit the ground. I mean, that's probably what killed—"

"Where was he?"

"Across the ditch, under a tree."

"Was he—did you see his face?"

"No. Not really. I just felt. For life, pulse. I'm going out to the car."

"What for? Oh."

I finished the rye, and pushed back the chair, then she was standing too.

"I'll go with you."

"There's no need."

"I'll go."

I took a flashlight from a drawer and pushed open the door and held it while she went out. We turned our faces from the wind. It was like on the hill, when I was walking, and the wind closed the distance behind me: after three or four steps I felt there was no house back there. She took my hand, as I was reaching for hers. In the garage we let go, and squeezed between the pickup and her little car, to the front of it, where we had more room, and we stepped back from the grill and I shone the light on the fender, the smashed headlight turned into it, the concave chrome staring to the right, at the garage wall.

"We ought to get the bottles," I said.

She moved between the garage and the car, on the passenger side, and had room to open the door and lift the bag. I reached out, and she gave me the bag and backed up and shut the door and came around the car. We sidled to the doorway, and she put her arm around my waist and I hugged her shoulders.

"I thought you'd call the police," she said.

We crossed the yard, faces bowed from the wind, her hair blowing away from her neck, and in the kitchen I put the bag of bottles in the garbage basket. She was working at the table: capping the rye and putting it away, filling the ice tray, washing the glasses, emptying the ashtray, sponging the table.

"Try to sleep now," I said.

She nodded at the sponge circling under her hand, gathering ashes. Then she dropped it in the sink and, looking me full in the face, as I had never seen her look, and perhaps she never had, being for so long a daughter on visits (or so it seemed to me and still does: that until then our eyes had never seriously met), she crossed to me from the sink, and kissed my lips, then held me so tightly I lost balance, and would have stumbled forward had she not held me so hard.

I sat in the living room, the house darkened, and watched the maple and the hemlock. When I believed she was asleep I put on *La Bohème*, and kept it at the same volume as the wind so it would not wake her. Then I listened to *Madame Butterfly*, and in the third act had to rise quickly to lower the sound: the wind was gone. I looked at the still maple near the window, and thought of the wind leaving farms and towns and the coast, going out over the sea to die on the waves. I smoked and gazed out the window. The sky was darker, and at daybreak the rain came. I listened to *Tosca*, and at six-fifteen went to the kitchen where Jennifer's purse lay on the table, a leather shoulder purse crammed with the things of an adult woman, things she had begun accumulating only a few years back, and I nearly wept, thinking of what sandy foundations they were: driver's license, credit card, disposable lighter, cigarettes, checkbook, ballpoint pen, cash, cosmetics, comb, brush, Kleenex, these the rite of passage from childhood, and I took one of them—her keys—and went out, remembering a jacket and hat when the rain struck me, but I kept going to the car, and squeezed and lowered myself into it, pulled the seat belt over my shoulder and fastened it and backed out, turning in the drive, going forward into the road, toward St. John's and Father Paul.

Cars were on the road, the workers, and I did not worry about any of them noticing the fender and light. Only a horse distracted them from what they drove to. In front of St. John's is a parking lot; at its far side, past the church and at the edge of the lawn, is an old pine, taller than the steeple now. I shifted to third, left the road, and, aiming the right headlight at the tree, accelerated past the white blur of church, into the black trunk growing bigger till it was all I could see, then I rocked in that resonant thump she had heard, had felt, and when I turned off the ignition it was still in my ears, my blood, and I saw the boy flying in the wind. I lowered my forehead to the wheel. Father Paul opened the door, his face white in the rain.

"I'm all right."

"What happened?"

"I don't know. I fainted."

I got out and went around to the front of the car, looked at the smashed light, the crumpled and torn fender.

"Come to the house and lie down."

"I'm all right."

"When was your last physical?"

"I'm due for one. Let's get out of this rain."

"You'd better lie down."

"No. I want to receive."

That was the time to say I want to confess, but I have not and will not. Though I could now, for Jennifer is in Florida, and weeks have passed, and perhaps now Father Paul would not feel that he must tell me to go to the police. And, for that very reason, to confess now would be unfair. It is a world of secrets, and now I have one from my best, in truth my only, friend. I have one from Jennifer too, but that is the nature of fatherhood.

Most of that day it rained, so it was only in early evening, when the sky cleared, with a setting sun, that two little boys, leaving their confinement for some play before dinner, found him. Jennifer and I got that on the local news, which we listened to every hour, meeting at the radio, standing with cigarettes, until the one at eight o'clock; when she stopped crying, we went out and walked on the wet grass, around the pasture, the last of the sunlight still in the air and trees. His name was Patrick Mitchell, he was nineteen years old, was employed by CETA, lived at home with his parents and brother and sister. The paper next day said he had been at a friend's house and was walking home, and I thought of that light I had seen, then knew it was not for him; he lived on one of the streets behind the club. The paper did not say then, or in the next few days, anything to make Jennifer think he was alive while she was with me in the kitchen. Nor do I know if we—I—could have saved him.

In keeping her secret from her friends, Jennifer had to perform so often, as I did with Father Paul and at the stables, that I believe the acting, which took more of her than our daylight trail rides and our night walks in the pasture, was her healing. Her friends teased me about wrecking her car. When I carried her luggage out to the car on that last morning, we spoke only of the weather for her trip—the day was clear, with a dry cool breeze—and hugged and kissed, and I stood watching as she started the car and turned it around. But then she shifted to neutral and put on the parking brake and unclasped the belt, looking at me all the while, then she was coming to me, as she had that night in the kitchen, and I opened my arms.

I have said I talk with God in the mornings, as I start my day, and sometimes as I sit with coffee, looking at the birds, and the woods. Of course He has never spoken to me, but that is not something I require. Nor does He need to. I know Him, as I know the part of myself that knows Him, that felt Him watching from the wind and the night as I kneeled over the dying boy. Lately I have taken to arguing with Him, as I can't with Father Paul who, when he hears my monthly confession, has not and will not hear anything of failure to do all that one can to save an anonymous life, of injustice to a family in their grief, of deepening their pain at the chance and mystery of death by giving them nothing—no one—to hate. With Father Paul I feel lonely about this, but not with God. When I received the Eucharist while Jennifer's car sat twice-damaged, so redeemed, in the rain, I felt neither loneliness nor shame, but as though He were watching me, even from my tongue, intestines, blood, as I have watched my sons at times in their young lives when I was able to judge but without anger, and so keep silent while they, in agony of their youth, decided how they must act; or found reasons, after their actions, for what they had done. Their reasons were never as good or as bad as their actions, but they needed to find them, to believe they were living by them, instead of the awful solitude of the heart.

I do not feel the peace I once did: not with God, nor the earth, or anyone on it. I have begun to prefer this state, to remember with fondness the other one as a period of peace I neither earned nor deserved. Now in the mornings while I watch purple finches driving larger titmice from the feeder, I say to Him: I would do it again. For when she knocked on my door, then called me, she woke what had flowed dormant in my blood since her birth, so that what rose from the bed was not a stable owner or a Catholic or any other Luke Ripley I had lived with for a long time, but the father of a girl.

And He says: I am a Father too.

Yes, I say, as You are a Son Whom this morning I will receive; unless You kill me on the way to church, then I trust You will receive me. And as a Son You made Your plea.

Yes, He says, but I would not lift the cup.

True, and I don't want You to lift it from me either. And if one of my sons had come to me that night, I would have phoned the police and told them to come meet us with an ambulance at the top of the hill.

Why? Do you love them less?

I tell Him no, it is not that I love them less, but that I could bear the pain of watching and knowing my sons' pain, could bear it with pride as they took the whip and nails. But You never had a daughter, and, if You had, You could not have borne her passion.

So, He says, you love her more than you love Me.

I love her more than I love truth.

Then you love in weakness, He says.

As You love me, I say, and I go with an apple or carrot out to the barn.

IN THE BEGINNING

In the beginning was the Word.

Peacocks preen
on the ruddy soil of a Georgia farm,
and elsewhere Old Red,
mysterious as a Latin *sanctus*,
evaporates in the forest.
From such familiar landscapes
rise voices like vapors
mingling in yarns
and postmodern parables.
So on newly minted pages
two brothers replay an old biblical tale
and the ancient question reverberates
off trees beside a darkened country road.

The Word dwells among us.

Wearing the stigmata of a promise,
a husband tries to climb Jacob's ladder
while in the Bible Belt
poison oak blesses equally with honeysuckle
as grace gnaws through violence
and grief.
Elsewhere, an allegory rolls like sagebrush
across the southwestern desert
as a family drives

to the needed cemetery.
And, though Roman-collared men swat temptations
or wrestle angels,
a whiskey priest is transfigured
into a chalice of redemption.
Still, even into this millennium,
The Prince of Darkness, barely masked,
peddles his works and pomps
in upscale suburbs.

Human words reveal the Word.

Somewhere a father justifies his ways to God,
and bruised memories of a gothic nun
bleed onto pages
like Christ's wounds on a Spanish crucifix.
In both city and commune
baby boomers seek the Holy Grail
but simmer in their discontent,
lives burning down like Easter candles.
And still sunlit blossoms
on the peach trees
glow like incandescent flecks of grace.
Though sin abounds,
fresh absolutions fall with every shower,
and each near creek is filled
with unseen bream.

And the Word enfolds all.

PATRICIA SCHNAPP, R.S.M.

SELECTED BIBLIOGRAPHY

Boyle, T. Coraghessan. *Drop City*. New York: Viking Books, 2003.

———. *Riven Rock*. New York: Penguin USA, 1998.

———. *The Road to Wellville*. New York: Penguin Books / Granta, 1993.

———. *T. C. Boyle Stories: The Collected Stories of T. Coraghessan Boyle*. New York: Penguin USA, 1998.

———. *The Tortilla Curtain*. New York: Viking Books, 1995.

Deaver, Philip. *Silent Retreats*. Athens: University of Georgia Press, 1988.

———. *How Men Pray*. Tallahassee, FL: Anhinga Press, 2005.

Dubus, Andre. *Adultery and Other Choices*. Boston: David R. Godine, 1999.

———. *Broken Vessels*. Boston: David R. Godine, 1992.

———. *Dancing after Hours*. New York: Vintage Books, 1996.

———. *Meditations from a Movable Chair*. New York: Alfred A. Knopf, 1998.

———. *The Times Are Never So Bad: A Novella & Eight Short Stories*. Boston: David R. Godine, 1983.

Gautreaux, Tim. *The Clearing*. New York: Alfred A. Knopf, 2003.

———. *The Next Step in the Dance*. New York: Picador USA, 1998.

———. *Same Place, Same Things*. New York: Picador USA, 1996.

———. *Welding With Children*. New York: Picador USA, 1999.

Gordon, Caroline. *Aleck Maury, Sportsman*. Athens: University of Georgia Press, 1996.

———. *The Collected Stories*. Nashville, TN: J. S. Sanders & Co., 1999.

———. *The House of Fiction: An Anthology of the Short Story, with Commentary*. With Allen Tate. New York: Scribner, 1960.

Gordon, Mary. *The Company of Women*. New York: Random House, 1980.

———. *Final Payments*. New York: Random House, 1978.

———. *Men and Angels*. New York: Random House, 1985.

———. *Spending: A Utopian Divertimento*. New York: Scribner, 1998.

———. *Pearl*. New York: Random House, 2005.

———. *Temporary Shelter*. New York: Random House, 1987.

Greeley, Andrew. *The Catholic Imagination*. Berkeley: University of California Press, 2000.

Hansen, Ron. *Atticus*. New York: HarperCollins, 1996.

———. *Mariette in Ecstasy*. New York: HarperCollins, 1991.

———. *Nebraska: Stories*. New York: The Atlantic Monthly Press, 1989.

———. *A Stay against Confusion: Essays on Faith and Fiction*. New York: HarperCollins, 2001.

Hassler, Jon. *Keepsakes & Other Stories*. Afton, MN: Afton Historical Society Press, 1999.

———. *North of Hope*. New York: Ballantine, 1990.

———. *Rookery Blues*. New York: Ballantine, 1995.

———. *Rufus at the Door & Other Stories*. Afton, MN: Afton Historical Society Press, 2000.

———. *Staggerford*. New York: Simon & Schuster, 1977.

Horgan, Paul. *A Distant Trumpet*. Boston: David R. Godine, 1991.

———. *Great River: The Rio Grande in North American History*. 2 vols. Austin: Texas Monthly Press, 1984.

———. *Lamy of Santa Fe*. Middletown, CT: Wesleyan University Press, 2003.

———. *The Peach Stone: Stories from Four Decades*. New York: Farrar, Straus, and Giroux, 1967.

———. *The Thin Mountain Air*. New York: Farrar, Straus, and Giroux, 1977.

———. *Things as They Are*. Chicago: Loyola Classics, 2006.

———. *Whitewater*. New York: New York: Farrar, Straus, and Giroux, 1970.

Labrie, Ross. *The Catholic Imagination in American Literature*. Columbia: The University of Missouri Press, 1997.

O'Connor, Flannery. *The Complete Stories*. New York: The Noonday Press, 1996.

———. *The Habit of Being*. Ed. Sally Fitzgerald. New York: Farrar, Straus, and Giroux, 1979.

———. *The Violent Bear It Away*. New York: Farrar, Straus, and Giroux, 1960.

———. *Wise Blood*. New York: Farrar, Straus, and Giroux, 1952.

Powers, J. F. *Morte D'Urban*. Garden City, NY: Doubleday, 1962.

———. *The Stories of J. F. Powers*. New York: New York Review Books, 2000.

———. *Wheat that Springeth Green*. New York: Alfred A. Knopf, 1988.

Russo, Richard. *Empire Falls*. New York: Alfred A. Knopf, 2001

———. *Nobody's Fool*. New York: Random House, 1993.

———. *Straight Man*. New York: Random House, 1998.

———. *The Whore's Child and Other Stories*. New York: Vintage Books, 2002.

Wolff, Tobias. *Back in the World: Stories*. New York: Houghton Mifflin, 1985.

———. *The Barracks Thief*. New York: HarperCollins, 1984.

———. *In the Garden of North American Martyrs: A Collection of Short Stories*. New York: HarperCollins / Ecco Press, 1981.

———. *Night in Question*. New York: Random House Value Publications, 1999.

ABOUT THE
CONTRIBUTORS
AND EDITORS

T. Coraghessan Boyle is a prolific author of both short stories and novels, including *The Road to Wellville* (1994), *The Tortilla Curtain* (1996), and *Riven Rock* (1999). Sixty-eight of his short stories are collected in *T. C. Boyle Stories* (1998). The winner of numerous literary honors, Boyle has received the O. Henry Award several times and the PEN/Faulkner Award for best novel of the year in 1988 with *World's End*. In 2003, his *Drop City* was a National Book Award Finalist. Boyle has been a member of the English Department at the University of Southern California since 1978.

Philip Deaver, winner of the Flannery O'Connor Award for Short Fiction with his first collection of stories, *Silent Retreats* (1988), writes of Midwestern baby boomers suffering post-modern blues. Deaver grew up in the fifties, "with Latin, incense, roman collars and Dominican habits, sermons from a tough Irishman every Sunday. The texture of it is in me." His first book of poetry, titled *How Men Pray,* was published recently. Born in Chicago, he teaches at Rollins College in Florida.

Andre Dubus was the son of Cajun and Irish Catholic parents who lived in the bayous of southern Louisiana. Born in 1936, he served as a captain in the Marine Corps and received a masters in writing from the University of Iowa in 1964. In 1986 he lost the use of both legs when hit by a car; reflections on his life afterward are in the essay collections *Broken Vessels* (1991) and *Meditations from a Movable Chair* (1998). Among his twelve books of fiction are *Adultery and Other Choices* (1977), *The Times Are Never So Bad* (1983), and *Dancing After Hours* (1996). After decades of life in northeastern Massachusetts, he died in Haverhill in 1999.

Tim Gautreaux lives in Hammon, Louisiana, with his family, and recently retired from a long term position as Writer in Residence at Southeastern Louisiana University. *The Next Step in the Dance* won the 1999 Southeastern Booksellers award, and his second novel, *The Clearing*, appeared in 2003. He has published two collections of short fiction, *Same Place, Same Things* (1996) and *Welding With Children* (1999).

Caroline Gordon's most important mentor was Ford Madox Ford, as she was Flannery O'Connor's. She was born in Kentucky in 1895. During her troubled marriage to critic and intellectual Allan Tate (they were married in 1925, but divorced once in 1945 and again for good in 1959), she was host and friend to many important writers. She published ten novels, twenty-nine short stories, and several books of criticism, including (with Tate) *The House of Fiction* (1950). A convert to Catholicism in 1947 and later a protester against some Vatican II changes, she died in 1981.

Mary Gordon teaches at Barnard College. Her first three novels, *Final Payments* (1978), *The Company of Women* (1986), and *Men and Angels* (1985), present women inhibited by their gender and struggling with guilt and a sense of duty, all fostered by their Catholic consciences. But her more recent novels move in other directions. *Spending* (1998) features a woman enjoying a hedonistic romp through mid-life, while *Pearl* (2006) centers on a young woman who stages a hunger strike in Dublin. Gordon has also produced many works of nonfiction.

Ron Hansen, currently Gerard Manley Hopkins, S.J., Professor of the Arts and Humanities at Santa Clara University, was born in 1947, in Omaha, Nebraska. Experimental in terms of style and perspective, meticulous in historical research, he is best known for the novels *Mariette in Ecstasy* (1991) and *Atticus* (1996), a collection of short stories, *Nebraska* (1989), and the non-fiction *A Stay Against Confusion: Essays on Faith and Fiction* (2001).

Jon Hassler, retired after many years at St. John's University in Collegeville, Minnesota, has published, among other works, nine novels, including *Staggerford* (1977), *North of Hope* (1990), and *Rookery Blues* (1995), and two recent collections of short stories, *Keepsakes & Other Stories* (1999) and *Rufus at the Door & Other Stories* (2000). One of his themes is the descent of contemporary American culture into what one of his characters, Agatha McGee, calls "the new Dark Ages." Born in Minnesota in 1933, he was diagnosed with Parkinson's in 1993 and has struggled with the disease ever since.

Paul Horgan, though sometimes called "the Dean of southwestern writers," was born in Buffalo, New York, in 1903, and lived much of his life in Connecticut. Much honored and prolific in many genres, his best known novels are *Whitewater* (1969) and the the semi-autobiographical "Richard trilogy," *Things as They Are*. Many of his short stories were collected in *The Peach Stone: Stories from Four Decades* (1967). Also well known are his history of the Rio Grande and biography of Bishop Juan Bautista Lamy of Santa Fe. He died in 1995.

Daniel McVeigh is a Professor of English at Siena Heights University. He lives in Adrian, Michigan.

Flannery O'Connor spent most of her brief life in Milledgeville, Georgia, where she observed and satirized the Bible Belt's "good country people." In her stories, shafts of grace are often delivered by grotesque characters in bizarre ways. In the personal correspondence published in *The Habit of Being* (1988) readers can trace the roots of her tales to a profound Catholic faith and concern with sin and redemption. Perhaps her most familiar story is "A Good Man Is Hard to Find," the title story of one of her collections. O'Connor also wrote two novellas, *Wise Blood* (1952) and *The Violent Bear It Away* (1960). Born in 1925, she died of lupus in 1964.

J. F. Powers was born in Jacksonville, Illinois, in 1917 and died in 1999. Jailed as a conscientious objector during World War II, he was Professor of English and writer in residence at St. John's University and the College of St. Benedict in Minnesota from 1975-1993. Famous for his droll humor, among his best-known works are the short stories in *Lions, Harts, Leaping Does* (1944) and the novels *Morte D'Urban* (1963) and *Wheat that Springeth Green* (1988).

Richard Russo's *Nobody's Fool* (1993), made into a film starring Paul Newman, and his Pulitzer-Prize-winning *Empire Falls* (2001) portray the struggles of blue-collar people living in towns whose chief industry has declined. His *Straight Man* (1998) satirizes a dysfunctional college English Department. Russo believes that "having turned God out of the picture," people have only themselves to look to "for wisdom and purpose," and that makes for human misery in abundance. Raised in Johnstown, New York, Russo lives in coastal Maine with his family.

Patricia Schnapp is a member of the Sisters of Mercy, of Cincinnati, Ohio, and associate professor of English at Siena Heights University. She lives in Adrian, Michigan.

Tobias Wolff, currently teaching at Stanford University, is primarily a short story writer but has also written a novel and two memoirs. *The Barracks Thief* received the PEN/Faulkner Award for Best Work of Fiction in 1984, and his short stories have won the O. Henry Prize. Wolff draws heavily on his own experiences, often reflected in tales of "the strange, nomadic, puzzling life." The conclusions in many of his stories are unexpected. Wolff and his family live in northern California.